Other books by Rod Flint

The Year 1070 – Survival

The Year 1071 – Resistance and Revenge

The Year 1072 – Retribution

The Year 1092 – Cumbria Invaded

What others say

"Rod Flint has pulled off the difficult task of blending historical accuracy with a pacey, action-packed plot. The background detail is convincing, the dialogue consistent and linguistically plausible and the characterisation empathetic. I am looking forward to the sequels."

"Well researched and evocative of the period and place. Well recommended. I am looking forward to the next one."

"It provides a story of humanity in the midst of violent upheaval and a glimpse of how average people, who are so often my own heroes, might have coped and sought to claim back their own future."

"A grand romp through a part of our country too little appreciated in the company of likeable characters. Accessible by all ages. An easy and relaxing read. Another good read from this talented author."

"I just wanted to say thank you so much for writing The Harrying of The North series...they are absolutely wonderful."

"I bought the first a year ago...I couldn't put it down and got the rest of the series for Christmas."

"I can't remember enjoying books as much since Bernard Cornwell's 'Last Kingdom' series, and so you are up there with him in my eyes."

ROD FLINT

The Year 1102
~Jaws of Borrowdale~

The Harrying of the North
Book Five

Hindrelag Books
www.hindrelag.uk

The Year 1102
~Jaws of Borrowdale~

This is a work of fiction. Names, characters, organisations, places, events and incidents are either a product of the author's imagination or are used fictitiously.

Text Copyright © Rod Flint 2023.

The right of Rod Flint to be identified as the author of this work has been asserted by him in accordance with the Copyright, Designs and Patents Act 1988.

All Rights reserved.

No part of this book may be reproduced or stored in a retrieval system or transmitted in any form, or by any means, electronic, mechanical, photocopying, recording or otherwise without express permission of the author.

Cover photo by Paul Flint
Art work by Woofdog: www.woofdog.co.uk

For the young people in my family. May the series and the characters inspire them to discover more about their distant family history.

Contents

Author's Note

My motivation for writing the tale of Hravn and Ealdgith and their experience of the Harrying of the North, was a desire to leave something for my family's future generations that brings to life an early and easily forgotten period in our past. My parents' families, the Flints, Martins, Wilsons, Mattinsons, Pattinsons, Curwens et al can trace their lineage through 1000 years of life in Cumbria and the Borders, as far back as the nobility of the pre-Norman north, and through Gospatric to Earl Uhtred of Northumberland, King Ethelred II of England and King Malcolm II of Scotland.

Modern Western societies are increasingly equal and diverse in their social attitudes. The Anglo-Saxon and Norse societies of pre-Norman England had evolved from pre-Roman Germanic cultures and followed an Orthodox English Christianity. They were more equal in their attitude to women and their legal status than the strongly Catholic, constraining and more misogynistic society that developed under the Normans. I wanted my characters to reflect all that is good about today's society whilst remaining true to their own time.

Whilst writing, I have tried to use words that are authentic and made a deliberate effort to avoid those that have a French or post-invasion origin. That is why 'stake-wall' is used instead of the French word palisade.

I now live in Richmondshire, but spent many childhood holidays in the Eden Valley and on the fells of the Lake District, where I chose to use the traumatic time of the Harrying of the North as a vehicle for this tale. The geography speaks for itself. These are places I have known and loved all my life.

I would like to thank all those who have supported and encouraged me, not least in the laborious task of proof reading and for helping to ensure that the story is understandable to all. In particular, my wife Judith for her support and encouragement; my mother Clarissa, herself a true Cumbrian and incredible font of family history; my daughter Lara, always full of enthusiasm for the tale and in some little way a role-model for Ealdgith; my son Ian, for his calm interest; my granddaughter Serena for her views on female characters, and my brother Paul for suggesting ideas, proof-reading and the cover photograph of Castle Crag.

My thanks are also due to Glenn Bailey from Woofdog for his graphic design and art work, and to Kathleen Herbert whose book 'Spellcraft – Old English Heroic Legends,' recounts the tale of Hildegyd and Waldere, from which I drew in Book 1, and helped inspire the characters of Ealdgith and Hravn. Finally, I must acknowledge two excellent sources for information about life in Cumbria in the early 12th century: Richard Sharpe's 'Norman Rule in Cumbria 1092-1136' and William E Kapelle's 'The Norman Conquest of The North – 1000 to 1135'.

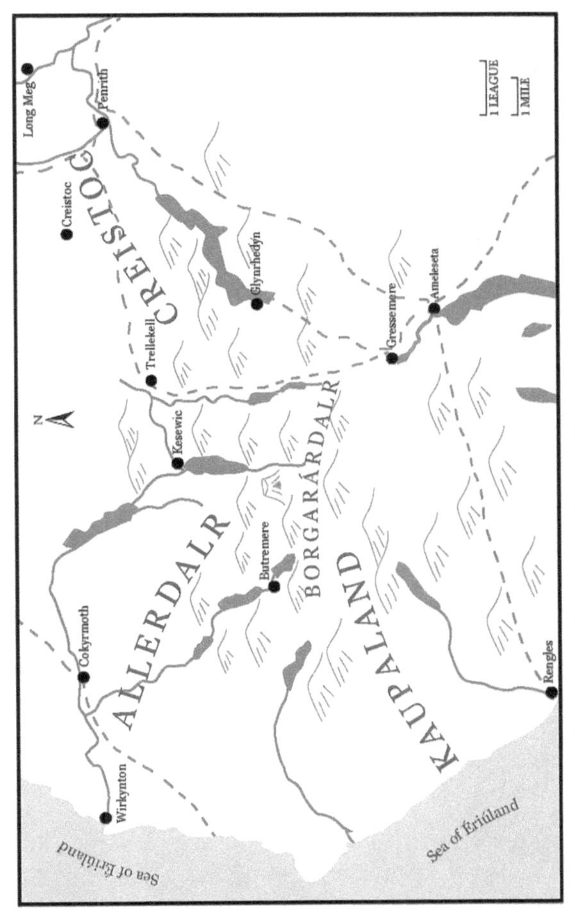

Cumbraland Dales
N
Long Meg
Penrith
Creistoc
CREISTOG
Trellekell
Glynrhedyn
Gressemere
Ameleseta
Kesewic
Cokyrmoth
ALLERDALR
BORGARÁRDALR
Butremere
KAUPALAND
Wirkynton
Rengles
Sea of Eridland
Sea of Eridland
1 LEAGUE
1 MILE
Named Place
The Crag
Old Road
River
Lake

BORGARÁRDALR

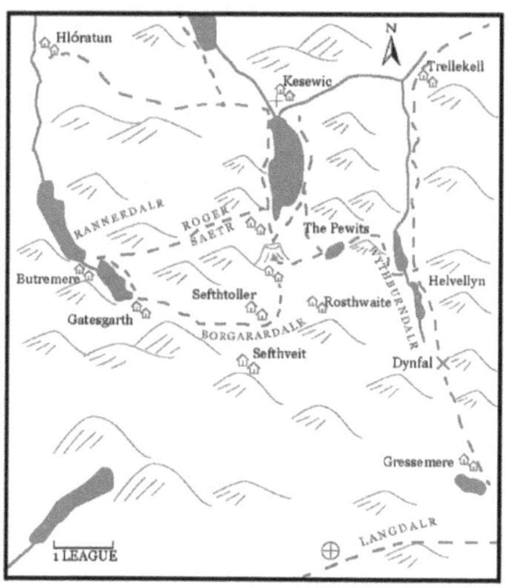

Place Names

Place names are those shown in the Oxford Dictionary of English Place-Names. I have used the name for the date nearest to 1100. Where a similar name has several spellings, I have chosen a common one in order to avoid confusion. Places that existed in 1100 but aren't listed retain their present name.

Aldeneby. Alston. Farmstead or village of a man named Halfdan.

Allerdalr. Allerdale.

Ameleseta. Ambleside. Shieling or summer pasture by the river sandbank.

Aplebi. Appleby in Westmoreland. Village where apple trees grow.

Askum. Askham. Place at the Ash trees.

Bartun. Bartun. Barley farm.

Bebbanburge. Bamburgh. Stronghold of a Queen called Bebbe.

Bogas. Bowes. The river bends.

Borgarárdalr. Borrowdale. Valley of the stream by a fort.

Brethstrett. High Street. The ancient British and Roman way over the fells linking the Eden Valley to the Windermere Valley at Ambleside.

Butremere. Buttermere. Buthar's mere.

Burc. Brough. Stronghold or fortification. OE. Burh.

Caluethweyt. Calthwaite. Clearing where calves are kept.

Carleol. Carlisle. Celtic; fortified town at a place belonging to Luguvalos.

Cat's Bield. Cat Bells. Lakeland fell. 451M summit. Possibly shelter of the wild cats.

Cletergh. Cleator Moor. Hill pasture where burdock grows.

Cokyrmoth. Cockermouth. Mouth of the river Cocker. Celtic, meaning crooked, plus 'mütha'.

Creistoc. Greystoke. Probaly secondary settlement by a river once called *Cray*. Lost Celtic river-name (meaning fresh, clean) + OE stoc.

Cumbraland. Cumberland. Region of the Cumbrian Britons.

Dacor. Dacre. Named for Dacre Beck, a Celtic river name meaning 'the trickling one'.

Defena. Derwent, or River Derwent. From the Brythonic Derventio, meaning valley thick with oaks.

Doolish. Douglas, on the Isle of Man.

Dunholm. Durham. Island with a hill.

Dyflin. Dublin. Norse, derived from Gaelic 'Dubh Linn', meaning 'black pool'.

Eithr's Lake. Hayeswater. The lake by the enclosure.

Ériúland. Eire / Ireland.

Ermitethwait. Armathwaite. Clearing of the hermit.

Gatesheued. Gateshead. Goats headland or hill.

Ghellinges. Gilling West. Capital of the Wapentake of Ghelliges-scir.

Ghellinges-scir. Approximates to Richmondshire. North Yorkshire local government district embracing Swaledale, Arkengarthdale and Wensleydale.

Glynrhedyn. Glenridding. The valley overgrown with bracken. Cumbric / Welsh. Glyn meaning valley. Rhedyn meaning ferns.

Gressemere. Grassmere. Grass lake.

Gríssmór. Grasmoor. OScand. Lakeland fell. 852M summit. Home of wild boar.

Gríssdalr. Grizedale. OScand. Valley where young pigs are kept.

Haugr-Gils. Howgills. Hills and narrow valleys.

Heltewatra. Elterwater. Lake frequented by swans.

Hep. Shap. Heap of stones.

Hestrskeith. Hesket, High and Low. Probably boundary land where horses graze.

Hindrelag. Richmond. English name before 1070. Origin not known.

Hlóratun. Lorton. Probably farmstead on a stream called Hlóra. OScand river name meaning 'roaring one' + OE tūn.

Hoton. Hutton (in the Forest). Farmstead on or near a ridge or spur.

Kaupaland. Copeland. ON. Bought land.

Kesewic. Keswick. Farm where cheese is made.

Karcoswald. Kirkoswald. Church of St. Oswald, a seventh century king of Northumbria.

Kircabi Kendala. Kendal. Village with a church in the valley of the River Kent (1095).

Kircabi Stephan. Kirkby Stephen. Village with the church of St. Stephen.

Kircabi Thore. Kirkby Thore. Village with a church in the manor of Thore.

Konungrtūn. Coniston. The king's manor. OScand Konungr + OE tūn.

Lauder. Lowther, River. Possibly an OScand river name meaning 'foamy river', or Celtic in origin.

Leisingebi. Lazenby. Farmstead of the freedmen, or a man called Leysingr. OScand.

Lincolia-scir. Lincolnshire.

Loncastre. Lancaster. Fort on the River Lune.

Lousewater. Loweswater. Leafy lake.

Lune. The River Lune derives its name from the Old English word Lon which has its origins in an Irish Celtic word meaning health giving.

Patrichesdale. Patterdale. Valley of a man named Patrick.

Penrith. Penrith. Chief ford.

Pulhoue. Pooley Bridge. Hill or mound by a pool. The 'Bridge' was added in 1800.

Rengles. Ravenglass. Either derived from words equivalent to Welsh *yr afon glas*, meaning "the greenish or blueish river", or the name may be of Norse-Irish origin containing the Irish personal name *Glas* and meaning "Glas's part or share".

Richemund. Richmond. Norman name after 1070; meaning strong hill.

Roger Saetr. Now known as Newlands Valley. OScand. The summer pasture belonging to Roger.

Salchild. Salkeld. Sallow-tree wood.

Sefthveit. Seathwaite. Sedge clearing.

Sefthtoller. Seatoller.

Sheltone. Skelton. Farmstead on a shelf or a ledge.

Sourebi. Temple Sowerby. Farmstead on sour ground. Temple affixed in 1292 due to its early possession by the Knights Templars.

Stanmoir. Stainmore. Rocky or stony moor.

Swale. River Swale. Old English 'Sualuae', meaning rapid and liable to deluge.

Thouthweyt. Southwaite. Clay clearing.

Tibeia. Tebay. Island of a man named Tiba.

Tinan. River Tyne. Celtic or pre-Celtic, meaning river.

Trellekell. Threlkeld. Spring of the thralls or serfs.

Ulueswater. Ullswater. Lake of a man called Ulfr.

Vatndalr. Wasdale. Old Scandinavian. Valley of the water.

Westmoringaland. Westmorland. District of the people living west of the moors (Pennines).

Winandermere. Windermere. Lake of a man called Vinandr. OScand pers. name + OE mere.

Wirkynton. Workington. Estate associated with a man named Weorc.

Wra. Wreay. A crooked piece of land.

Yuegill. Ivegill. Deep narrow valley of the River Ive.

Principal Characters

*Historical character

Lady Ealdgith. Held the lands around Ullswater as a gift from *Earl Gospatric of Cumberland.
Her children (in age order):
> **Aesc**, known as **Bear**. Married to Eir.
> **Aebbe**. Married to William of Kendala. Lord Ketel's son.
> **Gytha**. Married to Leofric.
> **Freja**. Married to Gille from Buttermere.

Ulf. Lady Ealdgith's master-at-arms and life-long friend.
His children, (natural and adopted):
> **Adelind** (adopted). Married to Agnaar.
> **Agnaar** (adopted). Married to Adelind.
> **Aelfswip**, known as **Eir**. Married to Bear.
> **Leofric**. Married to Gytha.
> **Osberht** (adopted).

Neven. Gytha's housecarl.
Dai. Gytha's master-at-arms.
Wealmaer. Bear's master-at-arms.
Jarl Buthar of Buttermere. A Cumbrian-Norse leader.
Frytha. An orphan. Jarl Buthar's adopted daughter. Known as **Rauði**.
Bjorn. An orphan at Buttermere.
***Lord Walthoef**. Lord of Allerdale. A son of Earl Gospatric.
***Ranulf Le Meschin**. King Henry I's enforcer in Cumbria.
***Forne Sigulfson**. Lord of Greystoke.
***'Black' William**. Ranulf Le Meschin's brother.

The Harrying of the North

The Year 1102
Jaws of Borrowdale

Sumor 1101

Chapter 1

"Run her onto the strand, Leif, then moor a stone's throw off and wait for us." Gytha called to her boatmaster as she stood up in the sleek svanmeyja and braced herself against the tall graceful S-shaped stem of the bow, judging the moment to jump.

Pebbles scrunched briefly under the weight of the boat, then it floated free as Gytha sprang ashore. She landed simultaneously with Loki, her wolfhound. The grey dog bounded ahead, glancing left and right as if searching for a foe, then looped back to his mistress. Gytha paused, waiting whilst Leif steadied the boat with the oars and watched as Neven and Dai made their way along the svanmeyja, stepping over the thwarts and swinging around the mast before jumping onto the beach.

Neven, Gytha's female housecarl, was dressed unconventionally like her mistress, wearing a green tunic and leather breaches above cloth bound legs and mid-calf boots. It was the hallmark of those who fought for Gytha and her brother, Bear. Dai, her deputy and leader of her war band when her duties took her elsewhere, followed. He too, wore a green tunic.

Gytha's eyes scanned the far lakeshore. Its beauty always thrilled her, and never more than on this still midsummer morning, with the perfect calm of the lake disturbed only by the dying ripples from the svanmeyja's wake. The unbroken line of fells ran from the forbidding craggy slopes of Scawdell Fell on the left, from where it dominated her home in the long Borgarárdalr valley, then along the long sloping ridges of Maiden Moor and Cat's Bield before descending steeply to the lake. The higher summits of Causey Pike and the great massif of Gríssmór lay behind, concealing Jarl Buthar's secret valley, her sister's new home, and the families with whom her own people were allied in their resistance against Norman attempts to control the vast mountain fastness of the Cumbric fells.

"Come on." Gytha glanced at the sun and urged her two companions. "The meeting with Aric is at noon, and having to row the length of the lake has set us back." She laughed, "Why's there never any wind when you want it?"

Dai set the pace across the fields towards a wood. Beyond the trees, smoke from domestic fires rose in the still air. He was squat and powerful, and his short legs appeared to move at twice the speed of the long-legged women alongside him. They paused momentarily at the far side of the wood, their attention drawn to a swirling mass of people, animals and bright colours.

"Good, Kesewic's market is in full swing. That'll provide all the distraction we need." Gytha glanced at Neven. "Whilst Dai and I meet Aric, go and buy us some mutton pies. You know, the ones that Vivi bakes. Oh, and something for Brynhildr. I've been neglectful of her of late. I'm to meet Aric by the old oak on the bank of the Greta, yon side of the vill. Meet us there."

"Aye, Lady." Neven nodded, happy to have some brief time to herself in the market.

"Let's cut around the edge of the market, Dai." Gytha tossed her head to clear her long fair hair from her eyes, and as she turned it glinted gold in the sun.

Dai smiled to himself; he could never quite reconcile Gytha's beauty with her ability to fight. Ten years her senior, he had sworn to serve Gytha when she was just fifteen and had been forced to lead their war band in the defence of their lands along Ulueswater when the Normans first invaded Cumbraland. They had come a long way since then, and Gytha, along with her husband

Leofric, was now responsible in her own right for her family's new lands in Borgarárdalr. Gytha led instinctively, and Dai was happy to follow.

"Surely you'll receive news this time, my Lady?" Dai's question was well founded.

Gytha met her contact on every fourth market day, but on the last two occasions he had nothing to report, and was increasingly worried for the wellbeing of their spy in the court of Ranulf le Meschin, the King's agent in Cumbraland. The spy was Ligulf, the very elderly Sherriff of Bebbanburge, and last of her family with a connection to the great Northumbrian fortress. Bebbanburge had been the stronghold of her mother's cousin, Earl Gospatric, and in the period immediately after the brutal harrying of Yorkshire and Dunholm thirty years earlier, Ligulf, a relative of Gospatric, had served the Bishop of Dunholm and been at the centre of a network of spies within the Norman Church. Gospatric had been the Earl of Northumberland and Cumbraland. Following his involvement in two failed rebellions he had been banished by the new Norman king, William. Gytha's parents had worked for Gospatric, raiding Norman estates across the North East before making a new life on land granted to them by him in the Eden Valley and along the shores of Ulueswater. The Norman invasion of the Cumbric shires of Cumbraland and Westmoringaland in ten ninety-two had been a disaster for Gytha's family. Her father, Hravn, had been killed and they had lost their lands in the Eden Valley. Gospatric's surviving family had suffered too. His eldest son, Dolfin, had been forced from Carleol and now only the younger son, Walthoef, retained some power and influence as an under lord, holding the lands of Allerdalr. Ligulf, meanwhile, had continued to work against Norman hegemony and through Lady Ealdgith, Gytha's mother, had kept the surviving family informed about Norman plans and politics in the North. His responsibility as Sherriff of Bebbanburge included Carleol, which had no Sherriff of its own. It was from there that he managed to glean information,

"I hope so, Dai. Le Meschin was brutal enough when Red William was king. But from what I hear he's always been Henry's man, and the new king seems to have a desire to seize all the Cumbric lands once and for all. One reason Walthoef is happy for me to hold Borgarárdalr in Moder's name, and exploit the lead there, is that she keeps him informed about Ligulf's news."

"Well, at least Aric seems to be waiting. That looks like him lounging with his back to the tree where the rivers meet." A man wearing drab non-descript clothes was resting against a solitary ancient oak that cast its shade over several knee-high boulders. The place served as a local meeting point. A couple of goats roamed free, cropping the grass and standing on the boulders to nibble the lower foliage. They scampered, bleating, at Loki's approach.

"Aye, happen." Gytha acknowledged Dai's observation whilst thinking that her contact wasn't lounging, but rather had chosen the best place from which to watch all that passed by without exposing his own back to attack.

A roan horse grazed by the river bank. Dai nodded towards it. "Aric must've had an early start to get here from Cokyrmoth. His horse is certainly enjoying the grass."

"Aye, but it's those two I'm more interested in." Gytha gestured casually towards two men standing on the bank a hundred paces up river from the oak.

"Mmm...I've seen them." Dai's eyes narrowed as he spoke. "I'll take a walk up there and ask about the fishing. That'll distract them if Aric passes you anything." He set off, loosening the thong that secured his sword in its scabbard.

Gytha sensed that Aric had guessed what Dai was doing. Giving the slightest nod of recognition, he turned and walked across to his horse, patted its nose then bent to lift its foreleg as if to examine the shoe. Gytha bade Loki to stay, then followed on cue, enquiring in a loud clear voice, "Is anything amiss?"

Aric continued to hold the hoof and replied clearly, "Aye, Lady. Mayhap a thorn."

She came close, and bent to look. With his free hand, Aric deftly pulled a sealed scroll from within his cloak and passed it to Gytha. As she tucked it into the front of her tunic he stood up, speaking softly, "My master said not to wait for a reply. The matter is grave and will need consideration before we next meet."

Gytha nodded, whispering, "Thank you, Aric. Meet by the church next time," then added loudly, "I'm glad all is well with your horse, sir. Sometimes a lady's nimble fingers are all that are needed. God speed." As Aric mounted and turned the horse towards the track she called Loki to heel, walked back to the tree and sat on a boulder to wait for Neven and Dai.

Dai returned having walked further along the river bank with the two men. He spoke dismissively, "They were harmless enough, but it was best to check. Look, there's Neven."

Gytha glanced over her shoulder. Neven always looked imposing. Tall and lithe, with her almond-shaped face and deep brown eyes framed by long black hair that fell in a braid down to the small of her back. A long dagger was sheathed on her belt, and she had a sack over her shoulder which she placed on the ground. "Vivi says they're the freshest she has," she said breathlessly, handing out the mutton pies.

Gytha ate hers quickly, savouring the warm meat and glutinous gravy, worried that once she read Ligulf's message that she would lose all appetite. She was right. She threw the crust to Loki then slit the scroll's seal with her finger nail and began to read, thankful that her mother had insisted that her children learned to read and write both English and Norman French, and aware of a nagging guilt that she must soon start to teach her daughter. Use of written English had been banned by the Normans two generations earlier, which was why Ealdgith and Ligulf persisted in using it for their secret communications, confident that few, if any, could now read them.

Neven sensed the impact of the message as she watched Gytha's jaw tense and her complexion pale. Gytha's eyes stopped scanning the text and she sat frozen-faced, staring. Loki's whine broke her trance, and she stuffed the scroll back inside her tunic.

"You both need to know, but keep it to yourselves until I've spoken to Moder and Bear." Gytha spoke hesitantly. Neven could see that she was struggling not to cry. "It's happening again. Our lands are to be taken from us and there is nothing we can do, not this time."

Dai and Neven stared at her, aghast. Dai spoke. "What? Borgarárdalr?"

Gytha replied, shaking her head. "No, Ulueswater. That...that treacherous bastard, Forne Sigulfson. He has succeeded at last, and taken by stealth that which he couldn't take by force. The King has granted him the mining rights around the lakeshore, which means he has the right to the source of our wealth. The vills of Glynrhedyn and Patrichesdalr will become his in all but name. I wonder just how much gold he paid?" She paused, then added with a sarcastic laugh, "Or mayhap that's why he was so willing to let his daughter go as one of the King's mistresses."

Dai blew out a long breath and his head dropped as he shared Gytha's despair. "The clever, conniving little skíta. This way your moder loses the right to the lead, although it's on her land."   "But surely she keeps control of the land?" Neven interrupted.

Gytha shook her head slowly. "She and Fader were granted the land by Earl Gospatric in the name of the Scots' king. When Red William seized Cumbraland from the Scots, he chose which English lords to leave in place, and dispossessed the others. That's why Moder insisted that all our Eden lands were gifted to Aebbe and written into a charter. Her husband is Anglo-Norman."

"...And it worked." Neven interrupted again. "Mayhap she could do so once more?"

Dai gave a scathing laugh. "I think not. Lady Edie has bloodied too many noses, Norman and Cumbric. Forne Sigulfson is a traitor to all true Cumbric and Norse men...and women," he added with a wry smile at his two companions. "The bastard's wheedled his way into the King's favour, and his daughter into Henry's bed. I doubt he'll have paid as hefty a sum for those rights as others would. He knows we can't move against him, he'll work the mines hard and the law will be on his side. Gytha's right, there's nothing we can do."

"Agreed!" Gytha stood up quickly. Her face was dry-eyed and determined. "We'll solve nothing sitting here, and the sooner I speak to Moder and Bear the quicker we can get ahead of Sigulfson's plans. The three of us must get to Moder's hall in Glynrhedyn by dusk."

*****

Gytha rolled her shoulders to relax them after their brisk one and a half league row along the length of Defenawater, back to the mouth of the Borgarárdalr valley. She untethered her fell pony, mounted swiftly and urged it forward. Dai and Neven followed. As they cantered across the water meadow at the lake's edge Gytha looked above the trees ahead, towards the steep tooth-like crag that dominated the middle of the valley. The sides of the high rock and tree-clad fells surrounding the valley rose steeply about her. The solitary tall crag, dominating the entrance to Borgarárdalr, reminded her of a rocky fang in an ancient jaw. Her people called the place the Jaws of Borgarárdalr. The houses of her household and her men-at-arms were clustered out of sight beyond the foot of the crag, whilst the main vill was on the crag's lower left slopes, just above a broad shallow river. Her hall overlooked all from the level summit. A man and a girl stood at the edge, watching. As the man waved in recognition the girl turned and ran out of sight. Gytha knew that her daughter would be leaping down the rock-cut steps to meet her at the bottom of the crag.

"Leave everything to me, my Lady. I'll ready us for the journey whilst you and Dai speak to Leofric," Neven called across to Gytha as they rode into the settlement. Dai waved his agreement.

"Moder! I missed you." Gytha swung off her pony and bent to embrace the seven-year-old girl as she ran into her arms.

"And I missed you, Brynhildr." The girl, the image of her mother in both looks and dress, clung tightly. "Before I talk to your fader, shut your eyes and hold out your hands." Gytha dipped her hand into her saddle bag, retrieved a polished wooden spinning top and a stick bound with a long cord, then placed them gently between her daughter's expectant fingers. "Now open them."

"Oh Moder! Thank you." Brynhildr beamed as she reached up on her toes to kiss her mother.

With her hand resting on Brynhildr's shoulder, Gytha looked up towards the steep track that wound its way around the crag. A stocky bearded man with tousled yellow hair trotted down towards her. "Leo, is Agnaar around? We four need to speak urgently." She gestured with her head towards Dai. "Aric's news was grave."

Leofric nodded. "Aye, he's just back from the mines. Dai, you'll find him at the forge. We'll talk here." He kissed his wife quickly then, with a tenderness that belied his strength, he held Gytha's face between his hands. "You're tense my love. Is the news that bad?"

Gytha nodded as Leofric let his hands drop. "I must ride to Glynrhedyn now, with Dai and Neven. Whilst we are gone there is work that you and Agnaar must start." She turned to her daughter. "Brynhildr, go and find Duwe and stay with her. I'll come and find you shortly."

Gytha talked quickly whilst watching Brynhildr skip past the line of grey slate and wooden houses that butted against the edge of the crag. Leofric listened, his jaw dropping. She paused when Dai returned. He was accompanied by a squat man with long jet-black hair and piercing blue eyes. Agnaar, limping as a consequence of an old wound, walked towards her across the wide dusty clearing. His forced smile told Gytha that Dai had forewarned him.

"Agnaar, it's best that Leo fills in the details for you later. We have to ride for Glynrhedyn now if we are to get there before dark. We'll be back as soon as we can, but it could be a couple of days. Moder will make the final decision, but we have to assume that she will want many of her people to retreat here before Sigulfson claims his mining rights around the lake. Stop the men mining for now, and have them gather as many building materials here as they can: boulders for foundation stones, slate blocks for walls, trunks for house frames; you know better than me what will be needed. I'm sure Ulf will have a say when he gets here." She threw a quick smile at her husband. "This is just the sort of challenge that your fader thrives on, Leo, so let's surprise him."

"Aye, he does that. But Agnaar and I can handle what's needed." He glanced at his foster brother, seeking agreement, "Tell Fader to concentrate on moving people here. Edie will need all the help he can give her."

"I will." Gytha nodded agreement whilst giving Agnaar a faint smile, "Thank you, Agnaar." She knew that he had more reasons than most of them to feel anger at what was happening. Normans had slain his father and then, only months later, his mother had died bereft leaving him to be adopted by Ulf.

Leofric took his wife's hand. "I think we should speak to Brynhildr together. Mayhap she should spend the next few days with Duwe and Owst. I'll not have time to care for her properly, and I'm sure she could help Duwe in the spinning shed."

*****

Gytha called to Loki as he reached the crest of the ridge and bade him wait whilst she caught up. She wheeled her pony and looked back as Dai and Neven rode alongside. "The sun's not yet down to the fell tops. We've time to give the ponies a quick breather."

"Aye." Dai agreed, panting from the exertion of goading his fell pony up the steep track. "I could do with one myself."

Neven shielded her eyes with her hand, screening them from the glare of the sinking sun. "No matter the weather or the season, I can never tire of this view." Gytha knew that she was recalling the winter's morning nearly ten years ago, when they had both first crossed the high fells above Glynrhedyn and made the long journey to Jarl Buthar's hall at Butremere.

"Ah, but can you name the fells?" Dai teased her, knowing that he could not do so.

"Some. That's Wythburndalr below, with its little lakes and the old road along their shores, linking Kesewic in the north with Ameleseta to our south. It crosses the pass known as Dynfal Raise, where the old king of Cumbraland, Dynfal ab Owain, was slain by the English King Edmund. There's a cairn where surviving Cumbric prisoners piled rocks on his body. It's said that some of his men fled with his crown and threw it into Gríssdalr Tarn to be safe until some future time when Dynfal will return to lead them. Every year the warriors go to the tarn, recover the crown and carry it down to the cairn. There they strike the cairn with their spears and a voice is heard from deep inside the stones, saying 'Not yet, not yet; wait awhile, my warriors.'" Neven paused, then laughed, trying to supress a smile of satisfaction at Dai's surprise.

"You should listen, Dai, when Lady Edie talks about the history of Cumbraland. Anyway, the high moor beyond is where Watendlath is, with the little tarn and the small farm. Borgarárdalr is further yet. We can't see it, but we can see Scawdell Fell, with Cat's Bield to its right and the big top of Gríssmór rising behind them. Butremere is beyond those tops, but to the left a bit."

Gytha laughed too, and squeezed her huscarle's arm. "Neven. You really have been listening, to me as well as Moder. I couldn't name them any better myself. Now, if you look along the length of my arm I'll show you somewhere else too." Gytha pulled Neven close, extended her left arm and opened her fingers. "Line up Gríssmór with the tip of my thumb, and look carefully. Great Gable is just above my little finger. See how it slopes down to the left?"

"Mmm...yes, just. The valley's in shadow."

"That's it. That's Styhead, with the little tarn at the top of the pass we use when we jagger the lead from

Borgarárdalr through Sefthveit, then over the pass, down to Vatndalr and past the lake to the sea at Rengles."

Dai gave a low whistle. "I'm impressed, my Lady. You too, Neven. I'll hang my head in shame for evermore. But, if we stay up here much longer we'll be in the dark before we get to Glynrhedyn."

Gytha nodded her agreement. "Lead on then Dai. See if you can get there ahead of us and make sure Moder doesn't send the cook to bed."

Chapter 2

Leofric sat on the northern edge of the ancient turf-covered rampart enclosing the level area at the top of the crag. With his elbow on his knee, and his palm supporting his chin, he stared vacantly towards the lake and the sunlit peak of Skiddaw beyond. For once the beauty of the early morning light failed to impress him; his mind was elsewhere, as it had been since Gytha's departure the previous afternoon. He turned, sensing movement behind him. A woman was making her way past his Norse-style hall. The moss-covered shingles of its steeply sloped roof glowed green in the light of the rising sun and Leofric smiled slowly as his sister stepped up onto the higher of the three levelled areas within the enclosure.

"Adelind!"

"I saw you when I went to fetch water from the spring. Have you slept?" Adelind's voice was concerned, her frown questioning. His senior by six years, she had always had a rather motherly relationship with her younger brother.

Leofric gave a heavy sigh. "A little, though not since first light. Agnaar's told you?"

Adelind nodded, smoothing her grey woollen dress and blue linen apron as she sat next to him. She had the fair hair, broad face and almond eyes of their late mother. "Aye, it awakens too may bad memories. Are they on your mind too?"

Leofric shrugged, and put his arm around Adelind, rubbing her shoulder. "Don't get cold. You're right, partly, but I was thinking more about how the valley was when we came here, and about what to do next."

Adelind sighed deeply. "Aye...well. We've achieved a lot since we were granted the lands in the dale, but it was your vision, and Agnaar's, that has driven everything. The desolation left after the floods a generation ago: fields stripped of their soil, long tracts of boulders scattered across them and all piled over with decaying timber; settlements wiped away and bleached bones still lying where animals left them; I sometimes still shudder at the memory." Leofric felt Adelind give an involuntary shiver knowing that it had nothing to do with the cool air. "The few people who had survived were near to starving; it was as if God had wrought vengeance for a terrible crime. And yet, now, those who survived have gathered at Rosthwaite. It's a good vill, and we have new vills for the mines at Sefthveit and Sefthtoller, and here too of course."

"I know, but if Edie is forced to bring many of those at Patrichesdalr and Glynrhedyn here, then we will have to build a new vill for them. We can't expand any of those that are here, and there is Edie herself, and Bear and our fader too."

Adelind placed her hand on Leofric's knee. "They aren't part of the problem. Edie should come here, to the hall, with you and Gytha. These are all her people, after all, and the hall is the only fitting place for her."

Leofric nodded, "You're right, and we can expand it. There's room within the bounds of this rampart and the ruins of the old fort that was here, but not for Bear and Eir and their family. I ..."

Adelind interrupted. "They should be wherever you decide to build the new vill. That will help bind together all the people from Ulueswater, and give the new community a focus."

"Of course, and Fader?" Leofric's frown faded as he spoke.

"He should be with Agnaar and me. That way he is on hand to counsel Edie when he thinks she needs it, but he won't be in her way." Adelind suppressed a giggle. "You know what he's like for giving counsel."

Leofric squeezed his sister's arm and turned to face her. "I should listen to you more often. Sometimes it seems that you know what I think before I do myself."

"No, I don't. All I've done is make you put your thoughts into words."

He smiled. "Mayhap, but I've decided about where to place the new vill. I'll speak to Agnaar first, but I think it should be near the lake shore, high enough up to avoid flooding, but close enough to work on boats. I think, too, that we must persuade Edie that her boat builders need to move here. We could do with exploiting the lead in the fells on yon side of the lake and will need more boats to move it. Let's go down and I'll see what Agnaar thinks." Leofric stood, but Adelind's hand urged him to sit.

"There is something else. It's one reason I came up. I needed to talk to you alone." Adelind took Leofric's hand between hers. "Remember, I'm your sister, and we can sometimes share things that it might be difficult to share with others, even those we love." Adelind squeezed Leofric's fingers and smiled reassuringly, holding his worried gaze with her eyes. "Don't worry, Leo. Just listen. Gytha thinks she should have another child. She's talked to me about it several times of late."

Leofric gasped. "But she can't! She mustn't. Not after Brynhildr. You were there. She bled so much and we nearly lost her. That's why Duwe had to wet-nurse little Bryny."

"I know." Adelind spoke with a soft reassurance, sounding calmer and more at ease than she felt. "I know how hard it has been for you both ... and I know that you have found other ways to pleasure one another, and that when you do make love Gytha uses the herbs that Edie has taught all our women to use. So far they have stopped her from being with child again."

Leofric nodded slowly, unsure and surprised that his sister knew and understood the most intimate secrets of his life.

"Gytha is sure that you want a son, and she feels that she is failing you by not providing you with one. She's been trying to summon the courage to tell that she wants to try again. But I fear that what is happening now will prevent that. Gytha can't carry a child and lead the green men to battle alongside Bear."

Leofric gasped. "I...I didn't know. She's been a bit withdrawn of late, but I thought she was worrying about her moder. Edie seemed unwell when Gytha last saw her.

A son though! Of course, I would like a son. What man wouldn't? But not at the risk of losing Gytha. She is not failing me by not having one. Never! And we can't risk Brynhildr losing her moder."

Adelind stood slowly. "That's what I knew you would say. Talk to Gytha once she's back, but don't tell her we've spoken. Put her mind at rest, please."

Leofric nodded, sat a moment longer, and then followed Adelind down the steps and along the steep track to the settlement below. Acrid blue smoke from cooking fires and burning mutton fat wafted up through the trees towards them.

"I'll take those." Leofric picked up two wooden buckets that Adelind had filled earlier from the pool at the bottom of a small waterfall issuing from a gulley higher up the crag face; fed by a spring, it served those living in the hall as well as the houses clustered together at its southern base. They walked side by side down the rest of the track and across the dry-earth clearing at the centre of the settlement, towards the larger of the buildings below the crag. He could see Agnaar, crouched by the entrance showing a small boy how to carve using a short stubby knife. A girl of Brynhildr's age swept dry, crushed rushes out of the door. Agnaar stood at Leofric's approach.

Leofric ruffled the boys head. "That's a fine boat you're carving there, young Ole. Though mind your fingers on that blade." He winked at the girl, "I hope your big brother's not still abed, mistress Frida?"

She giggled as a slightly older boy, red-faced with embarrassment, appeared behind her clasping a bundle of fresh rushes.

Leofric put the buckets down, stepped forward laughing, and clasped the boy on the shoulder. "Good work, Orme. A true man should never be ashamed at sharing in women's tasks. Your moder always made sure I did my share, but that is big sisters for you, always bossing you around. Now, your fader and I must talk." He flashed a smile at his sister, then turned to Agnaar. "Let's take a walk down to the river bank."

The two men chatted inconsequentially as they moved downhill to skirt the edge of the larger settlement until they reached the river on the eastern edge of the crag and were out of earshot. Leofric turned to business, "Assuming Gytha is correct, and I'm sure she is, then more people will move from Ulueswater than we can fit into any of our vills. We'll need to build afresh. Do you agree?"

Agnaar slowed his pace, kicked absentmindedly at a protruding tree root, then smiled at his friend. "I do, and I think you are going to tell me where."

"Wherever it is, Bear needs to live there as the focus for the community. At the moment, all our family is here, along with the sections of green men, clustered around the crag from where we can defend ourselves. We guard the entrance to the dale, the vills are behind us, and Jarl Buthar is at Butremere. He guards our rear and the hawse at Honister. When we lose our lands at Ulueswater, and I'm sure we will, the crag and Edie should be at the centre of all we control, not on the edge. I think the new vill should be towards the lakeshore, mayhap near where the tracks around both sides of the lake come together at the ford over the river. What do you think?" Leofric asked with a questioning look.

"Sss..." Agnaar paused, sucking his lips whilst his eyes narrowed in thought. "Yes, it could work, and it ties in with something that's been on my mind. We're getting lots of that soft black stuff out of the ground above Sefthveit, but very little proper lead. In order to get much more lead from there we will have to go under the ground. Some of the men think they know how we can dig down, but I'm not so sure. The veins at Sefthtoller are still good though. As you know, I've already started taking some lead from Yewthwaite, just on yon side of Cat's Bield. If we settle the new vill by the river crossing, it would make it much easier to mine on the hill above...and there's more."

"Go on." Leofric encouraged.

Agnaar continued. "We need to exploit the land beyond Cat's Bield, westward into the dales of Roger

Saetr. I'm sure there is a lot more lead to go at there, and mayhap other metals. I've seen traces in the rocks. It's just hard and bloody work to haul it from there, especially if we take it up over the ridges and across to the high passes. But if we start to open up the tracks on the west side of the lake, and mayhap build more boats, it would provide an easier way out and could work for us."

"Good, but what about Sefthveit? If there is no decent lead to be got from there, what's the future of the vill?"

Agnaar raised his hand to reassure Leofric. "I didn't mean that the soft stuff is no good. Aidan is looking for a market for it. He says that it might be good for making moulds for casting iron, for polishing and protecting ironware, and for glazing earthenware pots. It has plenty of uses, we just need him to find the market for those uses."

"Ah, yes." Leofric nodded reflectively. "I've seen the shepherds marking their sheep with it. Those soft flakes rub into the fleece and leave an individual sign. Gytha says it's good for writing on parchment too. When sharpened to a point it's as good as ink, and easier to make."

*****

At about the same time as Leofric and Agnaar were agreeing where to site the new vill, Gytha sat outside the Glynrhedyn hall with her mother and brother, waiting for Ulf to join them. Loki slept in a shaft of early morning sunlight, whilst his brother Sköll and mother Hati lounged alongside him.

The hall was built upon a low bluff overlooking the vill's lake-side shingle beach. Gytha, as tired as her hound after her rushed journey and late arrival, sat back letting her family talk whilst she studied them through half-closed eyes.

Although her mother was into her mid-forties, and greying, Gytha always thought how alike her she looked; only this time she noticed worrying bruise-coloured shadows under her mother's eyes. Her brother Æsc, known by all as Bear on account of his height and powerful build, was gently teasing his mother when Eir, his wife and Leofric's second sister, pushed the hall's stout door open and came to join them. She placed a flagon of cold spring water on the table as she spoke, "Ulf's just coming, look, he's on the track below."

Gytha turned towards the track. Ulf, her father-in-law, was walking purposely up the hill. She was impressed that whilst Ulf was into late middle age, he was still an imposing figure. In his youth, Ulf had been taller than Bear, but his left arm, withered after a sword blow twenty years ago, was now permanently bound across his chest forcing him to adopt a slight stoop.

Ulf was beginning to breath heavily as he walked up the steps. Gytha stood and welcomed him with a kiss. "It's good to see you again, Fader."

The power of Ulf's right arm lifted Gytha clear of the ground as he embraced her. "And you too, my Valkyrie. I hear trouble is again following in your wake."

Gytha laughed. "I think not. Rather, it is I that follow in its wake."

Ealdgith's mood lightened as she joined in the laughter. "Join us Ulf, and take a seat whilst we bring refreshment."

Bear turned to Wealmaer, his master-at-arms. "Send for watered ale, then join us with Dai and Osberht."

Osberht appeared moments later bearing two full cups. He passed the first to Bear and the second to Ulf. "There you are, Fader." The closeness between the two men epitomised Ealdgith's extended family. Osberht was Agnaar's younger brother. His parents had been Ealdgith's closest friends. Orphaned as a baby, he had been fostered at first by Ealdgith's housecarls, Godric and Ada, then after their deaths at the hand of Forne Sigulfson, Ulf had taken him in as part of his own very extended family. Though not related, Bear and Osberht had the same jet-black hair. The differences were that Osberht lacked Bear's stature and had inherited his mother's piercing blue eyes, whereas Bear had the raven eyes of his late father, Hravn.

Ealdgith called them to order when Dai and Wealmaer finally joined the meeting. Heavy wooden chairs grated on the grey slate floor slabs as the men sat down. "I had two letters yesterday, both with equally worrying news. The first from my daughter's husband, Lord William, and the second, that Gytha delivered, was from Ligulf. Both gave warning that the new King's intentions will have very grave consequences for all of us."

Ulf's eyes flicked quickly around the table. It was obvious from their expressions that the others had some inkling of one or other of the messages.

"As you are all too well aware, our fortunes changed when Ranulf le Meschin acceded to the lordship of Carleol and became the King's man in Cumbraland and Westmoringaland. Until then we had some guarantee of security through William; his mother, Christiana, being Norman and the daughter of the previous king's agent, Ivo de Taillebois and his first wife. Ranulf, through his marriage to Ivo's second wife and young widow, Lucy, has secured the lordship of lands along the length of the Eden, from Carleol southwards, and then beyond into Amounderness. He has also swept up the Cumbric seaboard in Furness and Kaupaland."

Gytha glanced at her brother and Ulf as Ealdgith spoke. Although these facts were well known to them, both nodded sombrely.

"This means that the only lands around the central fells that are not under direct Norman control are those of William, his brother Orm, and their father Ketel at Kendala; Forne Sigulfson's to our north around Creistoc and towards Kesewic; and Lord Walthoef's to the north west in Allerdalr."

Ulf interrupted, "Aye, Edie, but this isn't new. What's changed?"

Ealdgith smiled at her long-time friend and former master-at-arms. "Patience, Ulf, I'm simply making sure everyone understands, there are some that lack your knowledge. What's changed is that Ranulf's younger brother, William, has returned from the crusade and has been granted Kaupaland by his brother. I'll call him Black William just to avoid confusion with our own William."

Ealdgith glanced around the table looking for confirmation, finding it in nods and smiles.

"Good. We have to assume that Black William is a proven soldier and, between the two of them, the Le Meschin brothers now have the strength and ability to carry out King Henry's desire to take control of all of Cumbraland. Ameleseta lies within Orm's lands and Ranulf has ordered him to make it a base for expanding northward towards Kesewic, westward through Langdalr and around the lake at Konungrtūn. William says that it will be the Le Meschins' men, not theirs, that will be responsible for confronting any resistance. That way, the Le Meschin brothers take control of the main dales and separate the eastern fells from those in the west."

Bear groaned. "That's going to block our jagger route for the lead. We have to take the ponies over Kirkstein pass, down to Ameleseta and through Langdalr. Surely Orm will permit us access through Amelseta?"

Ealdgith gave a slight shake of the head. "I wouldn't bet any of our lead on it. William says that the King is testing the loyalty of his Anglo-Norman lords. Ketel and his sons can't risk being dispossessed for disloyalty. I am confident that whist they will be blind to anything we do on their lands, we can't place them in jeopardy, particularly when Le Meschin's men are likely to be present. Remember, Orm is married to Walthoef's sister. I'm sure that Borgarárdalr will still be secure, as will Butremere. Orm and Walthoef would never betray their kith and kin. It is the lands around these hidden dales of ours that will be at risk."

"What about shipping the lead from Rengles?" Gytha asked, suddenly very alarmed by the implications.

"If Black William asserts control over Kaupaland, then that will be difficult." Ealdgith took a deep breath and sighed, "Ye gods! Bear, you need to speak with Aidan. I doubt there're other harbours with secure warehousing that he can use. If there is one, it would have to be on the Allerdalr coast."

"Sheesh!" Bear rubbed his hand across his mouth, then ran his fingers through his short black beard in agitation. "Any move like that would need to be agreed first with Walthoef."

Ealdgith placed her palms on the table and, taking a deep breath, said. "There's more. Gytha's brought word from Ligulf. The King has sold Forne Sigulfson the mineral rights on all the lands around Ulueswater." She sat back, watching as those around the table exploded with indignation.

"I'll kill the bastard first!" Osberht smote the table with   his   fist.

"No Osberht! You won't." Ealdgith's icy tone was mirrored in the cold green of her eyes. It was sufficient to still the dissent. "Listen, all of you. We've been out-played, and we'll be played for fools if we don't act decisively now. We couldn't hold our lands in the Eden Valley when Count Alan of Richemund invaded ten years ago, though he was given a very bloody nose." She paused, "...and I live with that cost every day. Yes, we stopped that fool De Kiberen when he tried to seize the lake, but he acted for himself. We weren't the Norman's target then. That traitor Sigulfson is a different matter. He nearly succeeded in seizing our lands a year later, and his defeat came at a very great cost. I can tell you Osberht, that I want revenge for the death of your foster parents every bit as much as you do, but an open fight with Sigulfson is not the way to do it."

Osberht stared sulkily. Gytha felt for him. She knew how the naturally gregarious and impish boy had been changed by the incident, becoming moody and prone to violent outbursts. It was why her sister, Freja, had found it impossible to stay close to her childhood companion.

Ulf spoke again. "I know what you will say, Edie, but I will ask the question all the same, just so that everyone understands. Sigulfson may have bought the mineral rights, but that doesn't give him the land rights, does it. Those are still yours, are they not?"

Ealdgith's tension eased, she smiled at Ulf. "You're right of course, Ulf. But who gave me the right to the land?"

"Your uncle, the old earl, acting in the name of the King of the Scots, and...Hel's teeth!" Ulf realised that his argument was flawed. His violent exclamation shook them all.

Ealdgith arched her eyebrows and looked around the table, studying each face in turn. "And there you have it. The Scots lost Cumbraland nigh on ten years ago. My right to these lands ceased then and would probably not stand up in an English court, and certainly not in a Norman one. The only thing in my favour is that I doubt Sigulfson realises that; not yet."

Bear looked confused. "So, no-one owns these lands, or are they the King's? What do we do now?"

"With regard to the land rights, that's surprisingly straightforward. Remember that your fader and I gifted our Eden Valley lands to Aebbe so that she could hold them with William. That charter was dated before Red William seized Cumbraland and Westmoringaland, and her ownership has been accepted. I'm going to propose to William that we add an addendum to the charter. It will be back-dated and say that I gave Aebbe all the lakeside lands on the proviso that I have their use free of tithes for so long as I desire. That way I hope that we might keep the lands in the family and protect the livelihoods of those in the vills around the lakeshore. They will be William's responsibility, not Sigulfson's." Ealdgith spoke with a sanguine tone.

"But..." Bear chose his words slowly as he took stock of the implications, "That would mean that we could no longer mine, and would no longer be able to afford to stay here. As a family, and with men-at-arms to maintain, we are nothing without the income from mining." He took a deep breath, "And, given that we do not have the King's permission to employ men-at-arms, we are outside the law and can be hunted down by Sigulfson or any other of the King's agents."

Ealdgith pursed her lips, then said sombrely. "That's a fair summary, Bear."

Gytha leant forward to catch her mother's eye. She spoke with a stern authority that surprised her and all at the table. "Moder, I realised as soon as I read Ligulf's letter that the family couldn't stay here. Before I left Borgarárdalr I asked Leo and Agnaar to start amassing building materials and to decide whereabouts in the dale we could resettle all those whom you decide should move there. I hope you won't chide me for acting without your say so, but I think we have to move quickly, before Sigulfson claims his mining rights."

Ealdgith's expression froze, then relaxed into a smile. She reached across the table and squeezed her daughter's hand briefly. "That is exactly what I was about to propose, and by your quick action we are in a much better place than I could have hoped. Thank you."

Gytha watched the eyes around the table flick towards her brother. She knew that the decision was for her family alone to make, and that her mother was already in agreement. Bear's jaw muscles tensed visibly as he ground his teeth.

"So be it. We have no other choice."

Ulf spoke next. His bald head and face looked redder than usual above his thick white beard. "Well said, Bear." He paused briefly. "Edie, this is the fourth time that Norman greed and our own peoples' treachery have forced both of us from our homes. There are some battles that can never be won and this is one of them. Our green men are good, but they cannot stand against armoured men-at-arms or war horses. The battles that we can fight and win are those of mobility, stealth and ambush with bow and crossbow. Don't you agree Bear?"

"Of course, but..."

Ulf interrupted with a wave of a finger and a conspiratorial smile. "It's for you and Bear to decide, Edie, but my advice is that we need to distract Sigulfson's attention whilst we prepare to move; God knows, there will a lot to do. And, I know just the man to provide that distraction…what do you say, Osberht?”

Osberht's sulkiness had dissipated whilst listening to Ulf. The hint of a smile played around his lips. “Aye, Fader. Let me talk to Bear, but a wee raid or two north of Creistoc might just be in order.”   Ealdgith nodded approval towards Bear then looked pointedly at Osberht, holding his eyes with hers. “That is exactly what Hravn would have done, but his planning would have been meticulous. Make sure yours is.”

“And take fire-arrows, plenty of them, with the shaft ends wrapped in fleece and soaked in pine tar; just a tip from an old hand.” Gytha sounded almost apologetic as she gave her mother a cheeky smile.

Ealdgith rapped the table with her knuckles. “Right! Thank you Gytha. Let's get on, there is a lot to discuss and then to plan. Gytha, as soon as we finish and you understand what I have in mind, you must return to Borgarárdalr. Whilst you are waiting for Bear to join you, go and warn Jarl Buthar. I will hold a folk moot here in two days' time and I will have Mungo the Reeve call all the vill headmen to attend, including those from Haugr-tun and Pulhoue. My advice will be that they should stay under William's lordship. I will however urge the miners and boat builders, and all who support our households, to move with us. After that I'm going to see William and Aebbe. I'll need you with me, Wealmaer.”

Ealdgith turned towards her son. “Bear, agree plans for the raids with Osberht. If you can annoy Sigulfson for a month it will probably tie him up for another month after that trying to make sure his lands are pacified. Once I have held the folk moot, join Gytha in Borgarárdalr. I want both of you to see Lord Walthoef, warn him about the Le Meschins and Sigulfson's intentions, and agree the change in our status at Borgarárdalr. We are going to need his support more than ever now. After that, go to Rengles and see Aidan. Ulf, we'll organise everything here. I think we should jagger the last of our lead over to Rengles as soon as we can.”

She paused, glancing quickly around the table. "Is there anything else we need to discuss now? If not, I suggest we meet again when we eat this evening."

Slowly nodded heads confirmed understanding, though most were simply stunned by the sudden change in their lives and the speed of Ealdgith's decision making. "Good, now Bear and Gytha, I want a word. Ulf, please stay and listen."

Ealdgith pushed her chair back and, speaking softly, looked her children in the eye whilst Ulf stood behind her. "Ulf will, I am sure, agree with what I say. Moving from here and forging a new life for our people will be the biggest challenge we've faced these past ten years, and it will be for both of you to lead our people through it. Ulf and I are getting old..." Ealdgith stayed Gytha's interruption with a wave of her forefinger. "No, Gytha, listen. I lack the energy I once had, Ulf too. There is much we can still do, and the big decisions will still be mine to take, but the hard work will be yours." Taking Gytha's hand in hers she added, "It will be hardest for you, my love. I know you're recognised as a natural leader by the green men, but as I step back many may expect Leo, as your husband, to lead along with Bear. But Leo isn't a leader, he is a loyal deputy and a good organiser, but not the strong leader that you are." Squeezing her daughter's fingers, she said, "It's time to step out of my shadow. Our people will follow you, as they followed me, of that I'm sure."

"Thank you, Moder." Gytha nodded then tensed, as she felt Ulf's hand gently squeeze her shoulder. She relaxed as he spoke. "Your moder's right, and I know it is what Leo will expect. Now, before you go I need a word too."

"And Gytha," Ealdgith spoke firmly, "when you leave, take Queen Aethelflaed's mail and sword with you. Keep them safe. When the time comes, they will be the symbol of your authority, and will serve you as they have served me."

Surprise caught Gytha's breath. She knew what the sword and mail meant to her mother, and could feel the weight of responsibility that they symbolised pressing upon her shoulders as if she was already wearing the mail suit. She stood up, then bent to kiss her mother with a grave formality. "I shan't fail you, Moder. Thank you."

Then, as they all stood to take their leave, Ulf took Gytha to one side and asked what she had in mind for Borgarárdalr.

She answered quickly, confident in what needed to be done. "The crag is like a fang in the dale's narrow jaws. If we hold it, and I'm sure we can, then we will block all entry into the dale beyond. That way we secure our lands and the rear Of Jarl Buthar's too. Likewise, by holding Butremere secure he protects the depth of our lands." As she spoke, she read agreement in the old man's eyes.

His next question surprised and pleased Gytha. "If a mangonel was on the top of the crag, could it cover the whole valley?"

She gasped and clasped her hand over her mouth to suppress a laugh. "Ye gods! Fader, it might." She cast her mind back to the only time she had seen the mangonel used, remembering the carnage it had wrought amongst the Norman boats that tried to seize the head of Ulueswater. "It's over two furlongs to the river, mayhap three to the crags on yon side. But from the heights of the crag I'm sure it would be able to fling rocks wherever we need them. You'd have to dismantle it to get it up there."

Ulf grinned conspiratorially, "You've no worry on that account, the old one is well rotted by now. I would have to build anew. But..." he tapped his forehead and gave Gytha a knowing wink, "the know how is all up here."

Gytha pulled herself against Ulf's broad chest. His arm wrapped her in a close hug, before he stepped back with a smile and a wink. "Stay safe, Valkyrie. Just keep that mean beast in mind whilst making your plans."

Chapter 3

"Those wispy clouds have been getting denser all day, I'd say we're in for a change." Gytha sat next to Leofric on the rocky ledge he had shared with Adelind earlier in the day. The sun, having moved from the right side of the valley to its left, was now a dusky red ball sinking behind the long crest of Maiden Moor, its low rays reflecting off the high clouds. "Bear will join us in a few days, we can tell him about the new vill then, and ask him to site his new hall. I'm sure he will approve of your plan."

"Agnaar and I have already marked out possible places for house platforms. We've been using all the men from the sections, and the miners too, to cart material down there. We should be ready to begin building by then. It would be good to get Bear's approval before we start."

"Guess what your fader's intending to do?" Gytha glanced sideways.

Leofric shook his head, pretending to show despair. "I've no idea, but I'm sure it's something out of the ordinary."

"He wants to build a new mangonel on this very platform. I thought he might have been teasing me at first, but it really would work. We may well have to fight for this place one day, horrible though that thought is, and it could make all the difference. From up here we could drop rocks onto just about all the flat ground across the valley."

Leofric pulled Gytha close. "The thought of having to fight has been on my mind too, and Agnaar's. I fear nothing will be quite the same again."

Resting her head on Leofric's shoulder, Gytha took a deep breath. She was about to speak when her husband beat her to it.

"I wish it could always be just the three of us up here, just you, me and Bryny. Plus, Neven and the house staff of course." He sighed wistfully. "Let's make the most of the few quiet moments we have left. Y...You..." Leofric stuttered, nervous emotion catching in his throat. "You and Bryny are all I want. I couldn't live if I lost either of you...and why would I want a son if my daughter grows up to be anything like her moder?" He spoke softly, gently squeezing Gytha's shoulder.

She gasped, then stifled a low sob. "How do you know? Has someone spoken?"

Leofric caressed Gytha's cheeks with his free hand, his fingers smearing her tears as he did so. "No one. I just sensed what was on your mind, and now I know that I was right. I am, aren't I?"

Gytha gave a slight nod, then spoke quietly. "Thank you. I feared that I was failing you."

Leofric turned Gytha's face towards his. "You could never fail me, my darling. Come, whilst Brynhildr is still with Duwe, let us enjoy our privacy. Tomorrow you have to ride to Butremere."

*****

Dark wind-whipped clouds swirled around the tops of the steep craggy slopes either side of the long pass joining the valley heads of Borgarárdalr and Butremere. Gytha pulled her cloak closer around her shoulders as she urged her bay fell pony up the steepening ground. The cloak's mottled green colour darkened slightly as a few large drops struck with surprising force. "I hope this holds off until we are on yon side of the pass." She shouted across to Neven, riding alongside on a plain brown pony.

"I think it might." Neven cast her eyes upwards. "The wind's moving the clouds pretty swiftly. This is just Borgarárdalr weather."

"Well, at least this is one place where the weather is our only threat." Gytha referred to their freedom to ride through the high passes without the need to take a section as their escort. Ealdgith had long ago devolved responsibility for her men-at-arms to her son and middle daughter, after both had proven their ability to command them in combat. The men-at-arms were deployed in groups, or sections, of four. The logic for the grouping was that the men should work in pairs, with two pairs supporting each other. A section of four men was

28

sufficient for an effective ambush and small enough to be able to move quickly and unobtrusively across the rough fellsides. It was a proven tactic, and experience had shown that the protection they provided was essential for movement outside the family's lands.

"Aye." Neven agreed. "I fear the sections are going to get little rest in the next few months. If they're not building the new vill, they'll be assisting with the move."

"That, and patrolling." Gytha added. "I'm sure that once Sigulfson has taken our lands around Ulueswater, he'll start to push into Wythburndalr, and towards Kesewic, and see how far he can encroach into Lord Walthoef's lands. There're no agreed boundaries within these central fells."

The two women continued to discuss the dangers of the new reality whilst they crossed the top of the pass and began their descent into a long narrow valley, its sides randomly strewn with house-sized boulders. Neven had never seen one of the giant boulders move, but she often wondered how they had got there and what would happen if one started to roll. Their ponies' hooves skittered on the muddy cobbles as they rode through the small vill of Gatesgarth, with its herds of half-wild goats grazing on the craggy slopes, then the track descended to the shore of a small lake.

"Butremere, at last. There's Jarl Buthar's hall, on the neck of land between this lake and the next." Gytha gestured towards a cluster of wooden buildings on a low slope leading to a large turf-roofed wooden hall with dragon heads decorating its high gable ends.

"Look!" Neven exclaimed suddenly, distracted by two small boats in the middle of the lake. "They're still using dugouts to fish!"

Gytha laughed, "And why not? They may be as old as the Jarl's grandfather but, if they are sound, why not use them? Especially on a small lake like this. I know that there are at least a couple of svanmeyjas on the next lake. They are the ones that we sent Alv to build after we first came to terms with the Jarl. Remember?"

Neven nodded, then pointed ahead. "Riders. Two at least."

Gytha called Loki to heel as she spurred her pony into a canter. "They're wearing the brown cloaks of Buthar's men. Let's join them."

A decade ago Bear and Gytha had, at the Jarl's invitation, trained his chosen men to patrol and fight like their own green men. But in order to retain a sense of identity, and to keep control when working together, the Jarl had chosen to dress his men-at-arms in brown cloaks and tunics. The brown was almost as effective as the mottled green in providing concealment.

"Gille!" Gytha shouted to one of the men as he closed with her, then reined her pony into a walk. "It's good to see you. How is Freja?"

"Freja's well. She is with Moder. And you, sister? What brings you here?" Gille, stocky, yellow haired and blue eyed, sat awkwardly on his fell pony.

"I need to speak with your fader, and his elders." Gytha gave a teasing laugh, "Which means you too Gille. Is the Jarl at home?" Gytha always found Gille a little too serious and couldn't resist the urge to tease him. He was so different to Osberht that Gytha supposed Freja had felt driven to choose a partner that wouldn't remind her of her childhood love.

"He is, as are Ari Knudson, Aikin, and Hákon." Gille turned to his young companion. "Bjorn. Ride quickly and warn Fader and the others. I'll stay with Lady Gytha and Neven."

*****

Gytha grimaced and blinked on entering Jarl Buthar's great hall. Its size always impressed, but the constant wood smoke and odour of stale sweat always irritated her. The Jarl rose from his seat at the end of the hall's long table. Gytha noticed how his thick yellow hair and beard were now streaked with a grey that matched his eyes. "Hah! My Lady of the Lake. Welcome, and where is that bear-like brother of yours?" Gytha smiled at the Jarl's

30

teasing greeting. The epithet was one he had given her upon their first meeting, after she had told him about her role in using a fleet of small boats to harass the Norman incursions around Ulueswater. It pleased her; she knew that praise from a Norse Jarl was praise indeed.

"He sends his greetings, Jarl, as does Lady Edie. As you will soon hear, this is a grave time for us all."

Buthar's eyes held Gytha's, and then slowly narrowed into a frown. He gestured to the bench next to him. "Sit by me, you too Neven. Bring food and ale!" He clapped his hands to attract the attention of a serving girl and gestured to his elders to shift along the bench.

As Gytha stepped over the bench and sat down she glanced at the four men on the benches either side of the table, and noticed a dozen more eyes upon her from within the shadows of the hall. Taking a deep breath, Gytha related all that had happened in the past two days. She paused only to eat the bread and hard sheep's milk cheese brought to her.

The Jarl listened without interrupting, at times tugging his beard irritably. He spoke at last. "What would you have me do?"

"Bear and I will ride to Cokyrmoth in the next few days and tell Lord Walthoef what I have just told you. He may know more, and advise us further, but in the meantime mayhap you should look to the safety of your lands to the southwest?"

"Aye." The Jarl spoke slowly, his words delayed by thought. "I doubt Black William, as you call him, has little knowledge about our whereabouts here. I deliberately stop my people from moving onto the far slopes of those fells. Most of our business is in Allerdalr, to the north."

Ari Knudson grunted, then interrupted, "Aye, Lord, but word spreads and we can be sure that he will have an inkling that there are free men in these more secret dales. If the Le Meschin brothers are bent on enforcing the King's will there is little to stop Black William investigating the dales that border with Allerdalr, and we have many who farm in Ennerdalr. We should set men to patrolling the high ground south of that lake, and mayhap send a spy into Cletergh to see if men-at-arms are there." He spoke with a deep, grating, voice; his dark brown eyes alive with energy. Gytha always felt awed by the intensity of the lithe, tautly-muscled, veteran. She spoke in agreement.

"I agree Lord. Bear says we can no longer risk jaggering our lead to the harbour at Rengles. All the lead we mine in Borgarárdalr goes over the hawse at Styhead and down into Vatndalr, then through Kaupaland Forest to the coast. That route will also be lost to us. We're going to ask Lord Walthoef if we can use a harbour within his lands. If there is one we will have to come over Honister and through here to reach the flat lands and the way to the coast somewhere north of Cletergh. It would be good to know that Cletergh is clear of men-at-arms."

Ari Knudson's bright-eyed wink was all the confirmation Gytha needed that he would ensure Cletergh was closely watched.

"Is there a way or track from here that would be suitable for laden ponies?" She asked.

Buthar looked around at his deputies with a questioning shrug.

Hákon spoke first. "Aye Lord Jarl, from the vill here, then over the hawse into Mosedalr, along the shore of Lousewater. There's a low hawse beyond the lake that drops into a river valley leading into the Defena. There is a harbour at Wirkynton, where the Defena joins the sea. Lady Gytha, tell Lord Walthoef that is where you should ship your lead from."

"That's much as I'd have said." Buthar acknowledged his younger chieftain, then laughed openly. "You'll tell me next, young Gytha, that I should be prepared to fight to protect Crummock Water." He referred to the crooked shaped lake immediately to their north.

Gytha shrugged, giving a coy smile. "Not I, Lord Jarl. Is that not the reason why you had me train your men to sail those svanmeyjas that you had my men build for you all those years ago?"

Buthar gave another chuckle, then his face froze as he came to a decision and peered sternly around the table. "Ari, recruit and train more men. Aikin, Hákon, have the men start watching the dale entrances. Gytha, before you leave, tell me once again how you and Bear held that lake of yours against the Normans."

Gytha nodded, then glanced up, her attention caught by the stare of girl in her mid-teens. She had long, braided red hair and was wearing a blue woollen dress. It wasn't so much the girl's pale beauty that drew Gytha's eye, as the serious intensity of her expression. Switching her attention quickly back to the Jarl, she said, "With pleasure, Jarl. We'll do so now, if you have time. It's as well that your men fight like ours, in sections; that gave us the flexibility to attack the Norman men-at-arms with small, quick-moving groups, using the cover of the dense lakeside woodland." She placed her hand gently upon the Jarl's broad wrist, deliberately flattering him. "Do you recall, Lord Jarl, Bear telling you about the road we disguised in order to lead the Normans into our ambush. I have an idea something like that could help in your defence."

Buthar smiled, enjoying the young woman's attention. "It'll be a sad day for all when I'm finally beguiled and led away by a Valkyrie like you, but go on, Gytha, tell me more."

Later, after more food had been brought to the table and Jarl Buthar had become preoccupied in deep conversation with Ari Knudson, Gytha felt a gentle tap on her shoulder. She turned, coming face to face with the red-haired girl as she bent down to talk confidentially.

"My Lady, I am Frytha. I've listened to all that you have said. I am a fosterling here; my family were slain by the Normans when I was little. If there is to be a war with the Normans I want to fight and avenge my family, but the Jarl does not let his women folk ride with his men. I have spoken with your sister. I know it is different with your people. Can I ride and fight with you?"

Gytha's jaw dropped with surprise, then she quickly recovered her composure and smiled in interest. "Can you ride?" She asked with a questioning frown.

"Yes, my Lady, and use the bow. Bjorn taught me."

Gytha remembered Gille's young companion. "And who is Bjorn?"

"He's another fostri. Lord Gille has just taken him to ride with him. His fostri-fader is Haethcyn, the harpist. Bjorn's a harpist too."

"So, he is a fosterling, a warrior and a harpist? What else can he do?" Gytha couldn't resist a gentle tease. "Did you flee together?"

The girl shook her head. "No, Bjorn was here when I arrived. He was little too, and we both lived in the women's hall until he was old enough to join the men."

Gytha peered intently into the girl's grey eyes, studying her face. There was a sadness in her expression; she sensed honesty, and could see determination too. "If you work for me you won't have a woman's normal life. I will train you hard and you will have to stand and face danger at times, though I will make sure you can defend yourself properly, which means you will be taught to kill. I had to at your age, and it's not easy. Are you sure that is what you want?"

Frytha answered without hesitation. "It is. As soon as Freja told me about you, I've been waiting for you to visit so that I could ask you. Though I was mayhap only five at the time, I still remember the screams of my family and their servants when I was carried to safety. It was my fader's shepherd who got me away and brought me here. My fader held lands near Carleol, so I'm told." She paused to emphasise her answer. "I have a lot to avenge."

Gytha smiled reassuringly. "I understand. Is the shepherd your fostri now? I will need his permission."

Frytha laughed. "No, my Lady. The night he brought me here, I was passed to the Jarl and sat upon his knee. The Jarl is my fostri."

"What?!" Gytha mouthed silently. Then, nudging Loki with her foot to make him move away from the bench, she said. "Come, sit with Neven and me. She'll tell you more about how we live whilst I try and get a word in edgeways with your fostri-fader."

Gytha edged closer to the Jarl, biding her time whilst she judged when to interrupt. She gave a low gasp of surprise as Buthar turned towards her suddenly. "Did you hear that? Ari makes a good point. We need to keep each other informed. I don't want a Norman force marching over Honister and through my back door, and nor do you. What do you suggest?"

Gytha laughed. "That is just what I've been waiting to tell you. I've been talking to Frytha. Your fostri is a true Valkyrie. She wants to ride with me and I am very happy to have her. That's if you can spare her, and trust me to care for her? She can be my messenger back to you, and mayhap Bjorn, who I am told is one of Gille's new men, could join her for a while, get to know my lands, and be your messenger back to me? I'll make sure they are both well trained."

Buthar frowned momentarily as his eyes flicked towards his foster daughter. Then his face relaxed into a broad grin and he laughed loudly, drawing the attention of all in the hall. "By the gods! She may be Saxon but she has Norse blood in her somewhere. As do you, Lady Gytha." He gestured towards Frytha, "Don't let me down, lass. Go and pack a saddle bag, and tell young Bjorn to do likewise." He looked pointedly at his son, before turning his attention back to his foster daughter. "Gille will release him. You'll both accompany Lady Gytha when she leaves later today."

Frytha jumped up, a broad smile breaking out on her serious face. "Thank you, Fader, and you too my Lady. I'll get Bjorn now, and ready our ponies."

Buthar interrupted Gytha's thanks. "They'll both serve you well. Bjorn is barely old enough to ride with my men, but he is as fired with the desire to avenge his family as Frytha. That's why I allowed him to serve Gille. Keep him with you and I'll train two other lads as my messengers. Frytha has a good spirit, but I don't want her completely alone on the fells."

Gytha clasped the back of the Jarl's broad hand. "Thank you. I agree. Now, if you will excuse me, Jarl, I will go and have a word with Freja before we leave."

As Gytha walked around to the women's hall she caught sight of Frytha saddling two fell ponies, and walked up to her. "There is no need to rush, Frytha. Your fader has agreed that Bjorn can join me permanently too. Can you make sure he knows, and that he should bring his harp?" She hesitated, then took the girl's hands in hers. "I was thinking, our names are so alike that there is bound to be confusion. Do you have a byname?"

The girl gave a slow nod, followed by a shy smile. "Bjorn calls me Rauði, after my red hair."

"That's pretty, and I'm sure it describes your character perfectly. Rauði it is." Gytha said, with a gentle squeeze of the girl's arm. "You'll need a cloak, Rauði, just for the journey. When we get to my hall I'm sure that Neven and I can find you enough clothes to dress you as one of my green men, and I'll have more clothes made for both of you."

Gytha let go of Rauði's arm and swung round as Neven laughed behind her. "I think we should be called the green women now that there will be five of us."

Gytha laughed too. "I agree." Then added, "Rauði, whilst I see my sister, why don't you take Neven to the women's hall. She can help you decide what to bring with you. Then, Neven, can you ride ahead as quick as you can, warn Leo that we will have two more living at the hall, and tell Dai to get all the sections together for me to talk to in the morning."

*****

Bjorn and Rauði sat on a ledge at the foot of the crag, dangling their legs whilst watching the little vill's early-morning routine. Rauði felt very self-aware. She delighted in the freedom that her new clothes gave her. Free from the confines of the long woollen dress, the tunic and breaches allowed her to move easily and she longed to explore the crag's many crevices and ledges. But instead, she watched patiently, sure that the men of the vill must be questioning why she was dressed as she was; not that she was attracting any questioning glances.

Bjorn nudged her. "Stop looking so self-conscious. The folk here are different. Everything is different, even the way they build their houses."

Rauði stopped fretting and took stock of her surroundings. "You're right. There is so much stone hereabouts that they use it for the walls, or the lower walls anyway. Look, over there." She pointed across the clearing. "There's space for the animals under the main house. They are so different to our wooden houses, and I love how the turf and thatch roofs blend into the moss and ferns on the crag behind. You hardly notice some of the houses."

"The way the houses are standing amongst the trees, and on all different levels, it's so different to where we live." Bjorn agreed, rather awed by the little vill.

"Hah! Don't you mean, where we lived?" Rauði teased her friend.

"And the forge." Bjorn added, ignoring her. "With stone walls, then open sides and a slate roof raised above, there's much less risk of it catching fire."

They turned suddenly, as a commotion of shouting, barking and bleating erupted from around the corner. A flock of herdwick sheep being driven towards them passed under the ledge a hand-span below their feet. The thick-fleeced grey sheep, with white faces and legs, were turning this way and that, frantically calling to their much darker coloured lambs, and very wary of the small brown shaggy-coated herding dogs running around the outer sides of the flock.

"They must be bringing them down from the fells for shearing," observed Bjorn. There's a wattle stockade over there, by the track on the way out of the vill." They watched, amused at the antics below. As the last of the sheep passed, and the cacophony died down, Bjorn pushed himself forward and jumped down from the ledge. Rauði followed, shouting, "I can see Neven, coming down the track."

"Gather in!" Neven called, with a wave. She waited as the pair ran towards her, then added. "Gytha's on her way. Dai has gathered the men in the clearing at the edge of the wood. She'll speak to them there, and introduce you."

"Neven?" Bjorn asked urgently. "What do we call her? Gytha, I mean. We don't want to embarrass her, or ourselves."

Neven's normally serious expression relaxed. "Gytha normally, but my Lady when you're with the men or somewhere formal. She's very relaxed, as is her mother Lady Ealdgith, and her brother. You'll meet them too, soon enough. Their family is related to the old Lords of the North and they have more cause to curse the Normans than any of us."

Loki ran up, heralding Gytha's arrival. He nuzzled the three of them in turn, then ran back to his mistress. Bjorn and Rauði fell into step behind Gytha and Neven, and followed them through the open woodland to the clearing.

Bjorn gave a low whistle, and turned to Rauði with a look of surprise. He was impressed by the formality of the gathering, having expected to see just a group of men clustered together. Four groups of four green-clad men stood in a line across the clearing. Each held the reins of a pony in his left hand. Within each group, three stood side by side whilst a fourth stood in front. A seventeenth man stood in front of the four groups. Each wore a steel helmet with nasal guard. Rauði's mouth gaped. She was less surprised by the display of order and discipline than by the sight of two women in the fourth section. One taller than her, the other squat and obviously powerful. Instead of a steel helmet the women wore what appeared to be a helmet of hard boiled leather. As Gytha approached the foremost man stepped forward and raised the knuckles of his right hand to the side of his head. Neven stopped, letting Gytha move ahead.

"It's a salute. It's the men's way of showing their respect to their captain." Neven spoke quietly, without turning her head. The men treat Bear and Lady Ealdgith the same too. Gytha insists on it, it helps remind some of the men that they serve a woman."

Gytha stopped two paces away from Dai. He spoke as she did so. "The men await your inspection, my Lady." Dai stepped alongside Gytha whilst she addressed her men-at-arms.

Gytha stood with her legs apart and her arms relaxed by her sides. She moved her hands from time to time to emphasis a point as she spoke. "Relax, there will be no inspection for I am sure that your dress and equipment are to their usual high standard. Instead, I want to tell you of changes to how we will work. You are all well aware of the new threats that we face?" It was a statement and a question. Gytha looked intently at the men's faces, seeking confirmation of understanding.

"Good. For the foreseeable future one section is to be on constant patrol, either on the high ground between here and Wythburndalr, and down into the Vale of Saint John, or over Dynfal's Raise towards Ameleseta. By doing so we will be forewarned if either Sigulfson or Le Meschin himself show an interest in our lands. We are not ready for a fight, and I don't expect one, not yet. But if we are forced to fight, we will. We will soon be reinforced when Lady Ealdgith and my brother join us with their men and families. We also have the support of Jarl Buthar. I spoke with him yesterday and the two people behind me are to act as my messengers to keep him informed. They have joined the ranks of the green men and women, so welcome them as your own. Dai and Neven will see to it they are properly trained."

Gytha gestured behind her. "I'll introduce them in a moment. The sections that aren't on patrol will work with Leofric and the miners to build the new vill. It will be something of a race, for I think we can expect the first families from Ulueswater to arrive in a month or so, and the last within two months. During which time, there will also be sheep to shear and a harvest to gather in." She paused, letting the implications sink in.

"My brother's deputy, Osberht, is going to try and buy some time by raiding Sigulfson's lands. If he can distract Sigulfson into late haerfest, we may be secure until after winter. Time will tell. I want to fill that time by making sure we have the strength to hold the jaws of this dale against any threat. Dai is to recruit another section to ride alongside you, and two more to crew the svanmeyjas and hold the lake's shores. I want all of you to get the word out into the vills. You know what it takes to be a good green man. I'll take younger people though, and women too, for the svanmeyja crews. Once we get them together I will then use one section to train the riders, whilst Neven trains the boat crews."

As Gytha paused, Neven urged Bjorn and Rauði forward.

"Meet Bjorn and Rauði. The will serve me and Jarl Buthar. Rauði is the Jarl's daughter, so treat her as you would your sister." The inference behind Gytha's humour was clear.

Pointing towards the section on her left, Gytha began to introduce the section commanders. "My commanders are Godfrid, Cerdik, Gufa and Kai. They are the most experienced of men, having served my fader and moder before me. I'll leave you now to get to know them, and their men...and women." She added, after a pause. "Gwenn and Tanuw will have much to tell you, I am sure. Then be back at the hall for noon, when you will start to train in earnest." Gytha turned to her master-at-arms and her housecarl. "Now, as to that training. Let's agree exactly what needs to be done for Bjorn and Rauði. My thoughts are that Neven should concentrate on teaching them both how to fight unarmed and to use the bow properly, whilst Dai covers the spear with them both, the short-sword with Rauði and the crossbow with Bjorn."

Dai nodded, adding with a chuckle, "Aye Gytha, and strength training too."

Chapter 4

Try as she might, Ealdgith could not sleep. She blamed the lumpiness of her mattress, the humid air following a day of rain, the repetitive call of two owls in the trees outside and the unexplained nagging pain in her chest; but she could not escape the truth that the real reason was worry about the folk moot in the morning. She was confident that her decision to flee from her lands around Ulueswater was right, she had no option, but what should she advise her people? Although many families had farmed around the lake for generations, others had followed her from her lost lands in the upper Eden valley. Whilst she hoped that William would be fair in his treatment of those who chose to remain, she couldn't guarantee that he would be able prevent Sigulfson claiming the land as well as the mineral rights. What should she advise them to do? Then there was Hravn. Memories of the day she had cremated his body and scattered his ashes on the lake still haunted her. Her reassurance in the dark days that followed his death had been the conviction that his body lived on within the fish of the lake and that his spirit flew free, embodied in the large black ravens that roosted in the high crags and daily soared over the lake. That link would now be severed. As her worries and memories merged into a tangled web of ever-changing images Ealdgith drifted into a fitful sleep until the dawn chorus roused her.

*****

Ealdgith stopped speaking and stood for a moment at the top of the bank above the shingle beach, looking out across the rows of faces in front of her. She knew each of the many men and few women that crowded the broad beach. Their grave expressions told her that the many implications of her message had been understood. "Don't give me your answer today. Go home, speak to your families, then those who want to follow me to

Borgarárdalr should speak to Mungo the Reeve by the week's end." She held her arms wide, as if to embrace all gathered at the folk moot. "And be reassured that I will speak to you all again, after I have spoken to Lord William."

Ulf had been standing behind Ealdgith. He stepped forward and placed his hand gently on her shoulder. "That was well said, Edie. You can't do any more, they wouldn't expect you too."

Ealdgith replied whilst watching the meeting slowly disperse. "Thank you, Ulf. Mungo has already told me that we can expect many of those who came with us to Glynrhedyn, to follow us to Borgarárdalr. Asta and Alv too."

"That's as I heard, and Bjarni thinks those at Haugr-tun, Sandrwic and Pulhoue will stay. Those vills are closer to Lord William's lands, and are less likely to be of interest to Sigulfson." Ulf turned away from the lake. "Shall we walk back to the hall?"

"Aye, Ulf." Ealdgith's voice sounded quietly reflective. "You and I are the only ones now alive from our days in Ghellinges-scir, and only Tófi remains from Bebbanburge. Do you think he will come?"

Ulf's gruff chuckle cheered Ealdgith. "Of course. He, like me, gave you his oath. Albeit he was a lad then, and is a farmer now. He'll always serve you. It'll be a bit of a challenge for that young wife and family of his though, but..."

Ealdgith interrupted, taking Ulf's hand in hers. "We'll make it work, Ulf. We always have, though it's much harder without Hravn."

Ulf released Ealdgith's hand and placed his arm around her shoulder as they walked. "Aye, lass, and harder since I lost Cyneburg too." They fell into step, each thinking of the past and how the Norns had intertwined their lives within Wyrd's web.

Ulf spoke first. "Will you take an escort to Kendala?" He was reluctant to say that she must.

"Wealmaer will come. The sections will all be committed: two with Osberht and the other two preparing for the move and to escort the jaggers to Rengles. I'm sure you can manage here single-handed." Ealdgith teased, knowing that Ulf would appreciate her black humour.

Ulf laughed gruffly, "Aye, you'll be safe enough with a master-at-arms at your side and a wolf hound at your heels."

*****

Ealdgith and Wealmaer rode out just as the early sun was lighting the eastern slopes of the fells. It would be a half day's ride and she planned to return the following morning. The journey took them along the old stone road over the high pass of Kirkstein, then down towards the long waters of Winandermere. They kept clear of Ameleseta and followed the old tracks and stretches of stone road, skirting around the southern feet of the fells to Ketel's great hall at Kendala, where it stood alongside the smaller halls of his two sons, Orm and William. Ealdgith stopped at the back of the great hall, swung down from her black mare, threw the reins to a stable lad and stretched her stiffening back before walking briskly around to the front of the long Norse-style building with its steep shingle roof. The carved head of a mythic monster, protruding from the gable, glared at her.

"Edie!" A man of medium height and with the stature of middle age turned towards her in surprise, breaking off conversation with a younger man of similar build.

"Ketel, Orm, we need to talk, urgently." Ealdgith spoke loudly as she approached them, still slightly breathless from her ride. She embraced each quickly then asked, "Is William around too. This concerns us all, but him and Aebbe in particular."

Ketel quickly overcame his surprise. "Aye, Edie, he is. It's best you find him Orm." He said, turning to his son.

"And Aebbe too, if you can." Ealdgith added, then asked as Wealmaer joined them, "Shall we sit inside?"

43

Ketel opened the hall door, clapped his hands and ordered refreshment, before ushering Ealdgith and Wealmaer to seats at the main table. He sat with a look of grave concern. Ealdgith watched Hati sniff out the hounds' water trough in the corner, then sat opposite Ketel.

"I have news from Carleol, but tell me, has anything further happened since William's letter to me?" Ealdgith asked as William and Orm burst through the door.

William embraced his mother-in-law, then stood back whilst still holding her shoulders, gazing at her questioningly. "Aebbe's on her way, she was feeding the baby." William referred to Ealdgith's fourth grandchild.

"Good." Ealdgith gave him a quick smile then sat and turned back to Ketel. "Any further news?"

The older man shook his head. "No, though it's been made very clear that King Henry has the support of younger knights, some whose fathers took English brides and lands, and others from Brittany and Maine. All see that it is in their interest to help him gain new northern lands, and any of the old Cumbric lords who don't support him will forfeit their lands to these new knights."

William interrupted. "I'm sorry, Moder. There's nothing we can do."

Ketel raised his hand from the table, regaining control of the conversation. "There is a lot we can do, William, but Edie, there are also some things we can't do." He paused momentarily, tapping his fingers on the table. "We can care for those who are on our lands, even those who might be displaced. We can also stop intrusion by other lords, though we can't resist any direct orders from Ranulf le Meschin. He is the King's man." He hesitated, seeing the cold impatience in Ealdgith's expression. "There's more, isn't there?"

The three men listened with growing agitation whilst Ealdgith explained Ligulf's message and how she was going to respond to the threat from Forne Sigulfson. Aebbe entered whilst she spoke, then sat quietly, awed by her mother's stoic courage.

"Why don't you come and live here, Moder?" Aebbe asked when Ealdgith finished.

Ealdgith answered her daughter with a slow, kind smile. "If only it was that simple, my love. This household is part Norman, which is why it is tolerated. Your fader and I always fought the Normans. We lived outside the law after the harrying, and have lived on the edge of their laws since they seized the Cumbric lands. If I, or your brother or sister joined you here, Le Meschin's wrath would surely follow."

"Edie's right, my love. Ranulf is too powerful to cross. I may be half Norman, but my mother's blood won't save us from his wrath." William spoke gently to his wife, then turned to Ealdgith. "Edie, you said Osberht will buy you time by harrying Sigulfson's lands. Where will he base himself?"

Wealmaer interrupted. "My Lady, if I may. I talked of this with Bear and Osberht last night. We think the wilds of Mosedalr will serve them well. There's a steep pass north of Kesewic that leads up and around the back of Blencathra and down into Mosedalr. The valley opens into the Creistoc forest, so we should be well hidden." He looked around with a confident beam that faded as he caught Ketel's eye.

"That would be a fine plan if all things were equal, but tell young Bear to think again." Ketel spoke sharply then continued quickly, seeing Ealdgith's sudden consternation. "Not only is Mosedalr too close to you, if Sigulfson finds that he is being harried from the west he will immediately suspect Walthoef and call for Le Meschin's intervention, with all that implies for your future in Borgarárdalr."

Wealmaer sighed heavily. "I agree Lord, but if we move further east we will have the Eden at our back, no way over it, and nowhere to flee if Sigulfson closes in."

"Mayhap you would." Orm glanced at his father. "When grandfader settled the east fellside with people from his estates in Lincolia-scir he had a bridge built at Karcoswald."

Ketel grunted gruffly. "Aye lad, he did, and as far as I know it still stands."

Wealmaer looked from Orm to Ketel then, his eyes alight with enthusiasm, turned to Ealdgith. "My Lady, when Lord Hravn and I harried the Normans when they first seized these lands we used a back road behind the hill at Penrith, it was overgrown and little used and crossed the Eamont at Sourebi. That gives us one line of escape and another would be over the Eden at the bridge at Karcoswald, and then over the ford at Aplebi, to get us back onto the west bank. It would be a clear ride from there to Hep." He paused, looking at William for the authority to escape via his lands.

Ketel spoke for him, "Of course, though mind they know to keep well clear of Burc. There is a well manned castle there now, and there are still men-at-arms in the old stone fort at Brougham."

Wealmaer nodded his understanding then looked questioningly at Ealdgith.

Ealdgith pushed her chair back, and was about to stand as she said. "Yes Wealmaer, I know. We need to return to Glynrhedyn at once. Osberht is due to leave in the morning."

Ketel caught the sudden disappointment in his daughter-in-law's expression. "Edie, bide a bit longer. Aebbe will take you to see her children whilst I call for food. There is time enough, and you'll be over the top of Kirkstein before nightfall. I'll have two men go with you as well. They can return tomorrow."

*****

Ealdgith forced the pace on their ride back. She wasn't driven by the urgency of her mission so much as her worry that the men would see her tears. It was all they could do to guide their ponies as they followed her over rough tracks in the failing light. An inner sense told Ealdgith that she would never see her daughter and her grandchildren again. She knew that the nagging pain in her chest was a sign that her health was failing. She knew

46

too that despite her skill in the medicinal use of herbs the problem was not one she could cure. Whatever the future of her people was to be, she feared that she would not be part of it.

*****

Bear pushed his trencher aside, drained the last mouthful of watered ale from his cup, and then leant across the broad table in his Glynrhedyn hall. "Ketel was right to question our plans, I should have realised the threat it posed for Walthoef. Wealmaer, you're the only one here who knows the land around Penrith and on yon side of the Eden. Where do you suggest we should make a base?"

Wealmaer rubbed his forefinger across his lips, as he always did when thinking, "Well, Lord, Agnaar spent more time raiding around there than I did, he stayed on after your fader was killed, but he did speak about a hill above a place at Salchild where people fear to go. There's a circle of giant stones, overgrown with trees and scrub, that are said to be where a witch called Meg, and her coven, were turned to stone by the old gods. I'm up for it, but it will depend on what you think about the power of the old gods. Agnaar used it for a while and came to no harm, it was later that his foot got crushed. I'm sure Meg had nothing to do with that."

Bear laughed. "Fader certainly had faith in the old gods, it's just the sort of place he'd have chosen. Osberht, what about you?"

The younger man grinned, "Fine by me. I'm sure my men will be too. Mayhap God-fearing Normans will think twice about venturing near there."

"I hope you're right." Bear turned from Osberht to Wealmaer. "Because you're the only one with knowledge of the area I want you to go with Osberht. Ulf can cover for you here. It's a shorter journey across the vale of Eden than the one we'd planned through Kesewic, so sort yourselves out today and leave tomorrow."

"Aye Lord." Wealmaer agreed, then asked, "What about remounts? You'll need as many ponies as possible for the move to Borgarárdalr, but we'll need some to carry supplies. I suggest four, that's two per section."

"Agreed." Bear confirmed, whilst Osberht nodded. Bear pushed his stool back, stood up and looked directly at Osberht. "I'm leaving for Borgarárdalr now. Don't let Moder down. Draw Sigulfson's attention well away from here but don't risk getting caught. If he connects you with Moder we will have the ire of Le Meschin and the King to answer to."

Chapter 5

Bear rode to Borgarárdalr alone, leaving the remaining sections to work under Ulf. His liver chestnut coloured stallion moved quickly and methodically, needing little guidance to find its way across the rough fellsides and through the birch and rowan thickets covering many of the lower slopes. Rider and pony blended perfectly with the abounding hues of brown and green. Sköll ran ahead, looping back and forth, distracted by myriad tantalising scents.

The sun was just at its zenith, and man and pony were perspiring, as Bear directed their way cautiously down the side of a steep gill flowing from Watendlath tarn. Where the ground levelled, he urged the pony into a trot and headed across a ford before turning north onto the southern slope of the crag. Moments later they entered the clearing amidst the settlement.

Bear wiped his brow, then grimaced, realising that he had probably achieved nothing more than the transfer of dust from his hands to his face. He glanced around, surprised but impressed at the turmoil around him. A line of fell ponies, laden with panniers of square-hewn blocks of slate and labouring under a cloud of dust, were being led slowly down a track skirting the cluster of buildings. Sheep, disturbed by the ponies and penned onto the fellside beyond the track, bleated frantically, whilst the smith at the forge strove to make shoes for a further group of ponies waiting to be reshod. He turned towards the forge, then stopped, distracted by a woman's shrill laugh. It came from a clearing beyond the settlement. A brief flash of red hair caught his attention and he rode on, intrigued.

A group of three green-clad figures were at one end of the clearing, taking it in turns to loose arrows at a wicker target. Recognising Neven, Bear called out, "Ho! Neven! You've been recruiting again I see."

"Relax, Bjorn. Sling the bow over your shoulder. Now, both of you, meet Lord Æsc." Neven turned as she spoke and waived a greeting to Bear. He rode over and, as he dismounted, Neven said, "These aren't our ordinary recruits, Bear. Meet Rauði, Jarl Buthar's fostri, and Bjorn. He too is the Jarl's man. They joined us yesterday and will ride with Gytha whilst I set to recruiting and training more sections."

Bear's eyes widened slightly in surprise, then narrowed in thought. "The Jarl's fostri you say? I remember a girl sat on his knee once when Gytha and I first visited his hall. Could that be..."

Rauði interrupted, her pale cheeks blushing, "Yes, Lord, though I don't remember much from that time. It would have been when I had been taken to safety there, after the Normans slew my family near Carleol. When Lady Gytha called on my fostri-fader I asked to serve her in the fight to come and help avenge my family. Bjorn did likewise."

Rauði relaxed at Bear's warm smile, his casual confidence and the offer of his hand. "Welcome, Rauði, and you too Bjorn. Know me as Bear, everyone does. You've the best of teachers in Neven, though I may lend a hand too. Gytha and I will ride to Lord Walthoef tomorrow and you should ride with us." He turned to Neven, "And where is my sister? She's usually around if there is a chance to show off with a bow."

Neven gave a low laugh. "Aye, happen you're right, but she has more on her mind now that her men are building you a new hall. She's there with Leo. I'll take you and let these two carry on here. It seems that the Jarl's men trained Bjorn well and that Rauði has a natural eye. We just need to get more strength into her arms. I'll fetch my pony from the stables and ride down with you."

*****

Bjorn stifled a yawn. Still recovering from rising at daybreak, he watched fascinated whilst Gytha's two section commanders deftly instructed their men and sorted their weapons and ponies in preparation for the ride to Cokyrmoth. Godfrid moved off first, taking one

50

man with him.   "They'll make sure the track is always clear two furlongs ahead." Bear spoke quietly to Bjorn. "His other two men will ride with us, whilst Kai's section will follow a furlong behind." Bear glimpsed Bjorn's concerned surprise and added, "Not that I expect any trouble in the heart of Lord Walthoef's lands. I always insist that our men ride as if there is a threat, even if there isn't. It's good practice and prevents complacency. Now, I want you to ride alongside me and talk as we go. Gytha will want to talk in confidence with Rauði. Life as a woman surrounded by men is not easy when living under the stars, and there is a lot Rauði needs to know. We'll leave them to it."

Bjorn nodded, thankful that Bear had anticipated one of his worries about Rauði. He looked quizzically at Bear's pony. Although the stallion was one of the largest in the team of horses it looked too small to carry Bear's tall powerful frame. Bjorn glimpsed the pony's eye peering at him from under its long thick mane; it was black, rimmed with white and laced around with thin red blood vessels. He looked away, intimidated.

Bear sensed Bjorn's concern, and laughed reassuringly, "I call him Óðr, after one of the old gods. He has the eagerness and anger of his namesake. He's likely to try and give you a swift nip until he gets to know you."

The ponies moved confidently and briskly along the firm well-trodden track that followed the contours above the western side of the lake. Sköll and Loki trotted dutifully at the heels of their masters' mounts. "Tell me about yourself," Bear asked. "With brown hair and eyes, you look Cumbric, but your name is certainly Norse. Rauði said you were a fostri too."

"I wish I could tell you." Bjorn spoke wistfully. "My fostri-fader says he took me from my moder's arms just as she died. She'd fled from the south and was starved to death by the time she reached Butremere. Bjorn was the name I was given then. I was brought up in the women's hall, played with Rauði when she was brought there, and then joined my fostri-fader when I was too old

51

for the hall. He's Haethcyn, the Jarl's harpist, and he taught me to play." Bear gave an appreciative smile, but said nothing, letting the youth talk. "Although I was barely old enough to ride with the Jarl's men I urged him to let me train, and Gille took me on last year. When Rauði asked to serve Lady Gytha she wanted me to come too."

Bear glanced sideways, studying the young man whilst he rode. "We always have room for a harpist," he said lightly, "and even more so for one who can ride and wield a sword."

Bjorn relaxed momentarily, before being shaken by Bear's next question. "How close are you to Rauði? If she is to serve Gytha she will have to give all her attention to her. You do know that?"

"I...I," Bjorn stuttered, then spoke with a confidence that he didn't feel, "I've always hoped that we will be hand-fasted one day. But that could never be. Not when she is the Jarl's daughter. Mayhap if we both serve Lady Gytha then we might find some time together?"

Bear nodded, then winked. "Aye, mayhap indeed. Thank you for being honest. Serve my sister well and she will look after you. That's all I can promise." He changed the subject. "As we ride, why don't you show me some more of your skills. See yon willow overhanging the lake? Tell me when we are within a hundred paces of it."

Their route skirted to the west of Kesewic, then over a high pass that Bear said was called Whinlatter. They descended into a wide lush valley where they shattered the peace of a small farmstead, scattering a flock of hens, sending them fluttering and squawking in protest. "This is Hlóratūn," Bear shouted over the noise, "it is named after the river that flows in swift twists and turns down the valley." He turned and pointed up the valley to their left, "Look, those are the fells beyond Butremere, the river flows from the two lakes in the middle of the Jarl's lands."

Bjorn gave a breathless whistle of surprise. "I recognise the fells, but I've never ventured this far from Crummock Water." He grinned, more to himself than to

Bear. "I begin to see it now, how the fells and valleys link together."

Bjorn found that the journey passed quickly. Bear's testing questions about judging distance and identifying the position of prominent objects became increasingly challenging; it was a challenge he enjoyed. Then, when Bear seemed satisfied with Bjorn's ability, he started to relate his family's story. Bjorn listened agog whilst Bear explained how his parents had escaped the Normans harrying their lands on the other side of the Pennine fells, and how they had formed a resistance and created the green men when they were much the same age as Bjorn. He began to understand not only the very real threat that they all faced, but also why the family that now embraced him so warmly was driven to fight so strongly to preserve the freedom they had won. After a while he summoned the confidence to interrupt.

"What I don't understand is why your men-at-arms, the green men, are so different to the Jarl's. Most of his are older, his leaders certainly are. And your women too? They have freedoms that the women at Butremere will never have."

Bear gave an amused smile. "That's a fair question, and one many ask. The Jarl's way is the normal way. I spoke to my fader about it once. When he and Moder, that's Lady Ealdgith, fled the Normans and formed the green men he insisted that the two of them fought together and led the men together. It was hard for Moder at first. She had to earn their respect, sometimes engaging dissenters in single combat to prove her worth. She had been taught a way of fighting unarmed that few men can overcome. That was her secret strength. Gytha and Neven practice it too. You'll be taught soon enough, as will Rauði; I'm sure she will have to prove her worth one day." Bear edged his pony closer to Bjorn's and glanced back towards Gytha before speaking quietly.

"Moder has the blood of a long-dead English queen in her veins. She is descended from Aethelflaed of the Mercians through her uncle. We are too." He nodded back towards Gytha. "If the Normans knew, it would doubtless place us even more at risk. Moder has a suit of mail and a sword that were once the Queen's, though she has just given it to Gytha. She is a sight to behold when she wears it; men rally to her, or fear her." Bear laughed at Bjorn's expression, "Close your mouth lad, lest you catch a fly."

He continued, amused by Bjorn's reddening face, "Moder and Fader also agreed that to succeed in the fast-moving ambushes that give us the strength to keep the Normans at bay they needed men who were not just fit, but also motivated and quick thinking. That's why many of our men are young, even the section leaders. The best, like Dai, are retained as masters-at-arms. That keeps the experience we need. Others are given land to farm when they age and slow, or marry and feel the need to settle."

Bear flicked another backward glance, then continued. "As to women. Most of our people have fled Norman oppression. They want to live a free life, and have accepted that if they are to do so, they must serve a woman. Moder won't interfere in how people live, but she does make sure that women have freedom to choose. Gytha proved herself a capable fighter and leader when she was Rauði's age, and since then she's taken to letting women serve as green men, I have too. They may lack strength when wielding a sword, but they are canny with the bow or slingshot in an ambush. I've long recognised that a well-motivated woman is an asset to the sections."

"But don't you get problems? Surely some of the men will want something more from them?" Bjorn asked urgently, concerned about Rauði.

Bear's expression darkened. "One did, and he paid with his life. He was hanged from a tree for all to see. Since then we haven't had a problem. We insist the women work as pairs, never alone. If they are with child, then they must leave. It is simple, well understood, and seems to work." Bear laughed suddenly, "And before you ask. Yes, Gytha has a daughter. But she also has a very good husband, and we all know that the only person who can break the rules is the one who makes them. Now, let's quicken the pace and close upon Godfrid. We're within a league of Cokyrmoth."

*****

Bear took over the lead when the track led them past a granary adjacent to a mill, and then into a maze of narrow dusty alleyways winding around shabby wattle and daub cottages. Dogs barked at them then slunk away growling upon sight of the wolf hounds, suspicious eyes peered from darkened doorways, and once a bucket of slops was slung out onto the road ahead of Dai. His loud "Oi!" resulting in the slamming of a door. The acrid stench of close living and wood smoke cloyed at their throats. Bear cleared his throat and spat sideways, grimaced, then laughed across to Bjorn. "If you think this is bad, wait 'til you smell Carleol. All towns seem to be the same." The rutted earthen track suddenly opened onto a broad sloping tract upon which a few pigs rooted in the bare soil. The low hill was topped by a fence of stakes with a wide gate standing open.

"It looks like we're expected." Bjorn sounded surprised.

"And so we should be," Bear called over his shoulder as he urged Óðr up the slope. "Gytha sent a messenger to warn of our coming."

From the top of the slope Bjorn saw that the fast-flowing river joined a much wider and slower one flowing from the east. The hill dominated the junction of the two.

Halting in a courtyard in front of a large, aged, Norse-style hall flanked by more recent outbuildings, Bear waited for his party to close up, then dismounted and handed his reins to one of many staff who ran forward to receive them. Gytha turned to her commanders, "Have the ponies fed and watered first, then our Lord Walthoef will provide food for all. You know where the kitchen is. I intend to start our return not long after midday."

"Bear! Gytha! Welcome. Come inside and eat." A balding stocky man whose body was going to fat called from the hall porch, then he waited for his guests to join him. He was hard to age but Bjorn guessed at mid-thirties.

Bear led the way into the hall, then gestured for Rauði and Bjorn to come forward. "Lord Walthoef, these are Rauði and Bjorn, they have joined Gytha's household from Jarl Buthar's. Rauði is the Jarl's fostri."

*****

Walthoef's food was welcome. Anticipating their early start, he had brought forward the hall's main meal of the day. He then listened silently whilst Gytha reported the news from Ligulf and Ketel, her mother's intention to leave her Ulueswater lands, and the necessity of distracting Forne Sigulfson's attention by harrying Creistoc from east of the River Eden. His complexion reddened gradually as she spoke.

His voice, when he finally spoke, was cold and measured. "The conniving bastard! I'd call Sigulfson a traitor." He laughed sarcastically, "Only he's the King's man and we would be named as traitors instead. I'm all too aware of how the new King views those of his Cumbric nobles who've so far kept their lands...and their heads. Everything you're doing makes sense, and it helps me." With a deliberate glance at Rauði, he added, "Holding Borgarárdalr for me helps keep an eye on that cunning Jarl."

Rauði sensed their eyes upon her, and blushed. Gytha, sitting next to her, felt her tension and gently placed a restraining hand on her thigh. Rauði listened without saying anything as Walthoef continued. "I mean him no insult, lass, but he has a habit of rustling sheep and cattle out of Kaupaland and Allerdalr. That said, at least he now pays me homage for the lands that he, ... er, acquired when my family was thrown into turmoil after Red William seized Cumbraland from the Scots."

Gytha interrupted quickly. "You'll have no worry there, cousin. I know Jarl Buthar well and he's not the half-rogue that he once was. I was in his hall only days ago. He ordered his men not to venture into Kaupaland or

56

to risk drawing Black William's attention. We've sworn to work together to keep the central falls free from Norman incursion. I'd vouch that he is very much your man these days, wouldn't you agree Rauði?"

"Yes, of course, but I..." Rauði faltered, intimidated by Walthoef's expression.

"What?" Gytha looked from Rauði to Walthoef. She too paused, sensing that her cousin's face was almost trance-like. When he spoke, his voice was soft and slow.

"Your face, it's hers. Grey eyes, red hair, skin as pale as carved walrus bone...you are the image of Octreda, my cousin Maldred's wife."

Rauði gasped and sat back sharply, her hand to her mouth. She lowered it as she spoke, breathless with emotion. "You know my family? We're kin?"

Walthoef nodded slowly. "Yes, I think we must be. Distant kin, but kin all the same. As are Bear and Gytha your kin too, that is if what I suspect is true." He continued, with a wistful expression. "Octreda was feisty. When first I met her, she was serving in her father's hall. It was a great feast, I forget why, but his men were all there and the women of his family served them. Octreda was pouring ale when one grabbed her bottom. You know it happens," Walthoef said with a wry smile in reaction to the look of distaste on the women's faces. "More to the point, is that Octreda didn't flinch. She spun around, up-ended the flagon on the man's head, and went to fetch another. Her father, having seen everything, thumped the table to still the room, then said calmly that the next man who touched one of the women would be for ever known as 'claw-hand'. The point was made. That was when Octreda came to Maldred's attention." He sighed, "Aye, she was a beauty, and canny too. She had Maldred thinking he was doing all the running, but he was hers as soon as they met."

With a shake of his head, as if to clear it of memories, Walthoef said, "Enough, there is more I will tell you, but later. Bear, there is much to discuss."

Rauði, her heart racing, only half-listened whilst her new-found kin planned their response to the Le

Meschin and Sigulfson threats. Bjorn didn't listen, but looked at the tears welling in Rauði's glazed eyes, wanting to hold her. He felt too, a nagging void in his stomach. He was alone now in having no family. Would he be accepted by Rauði's kinfolk?

Walthoef stressed the need to avoid giving Sigulfson's men an excuse to enter his lands, albeit if they did any incursion was to be resisted firmly. He welcomed Gytha's suggestion that they should ship their lead from Wirkynton, and surprised Bear by refusing any share of income from its sale for the foreseeable future, saying, "Any profit will soon be eaten by feeding and arming the men you need to recruit. I just need to be sure that no word of the lead reaches the King. Ship it from Wirkynton, then sell it through your Manx agent. We should be safe so long as when the lead is sold back to the Normans it is seen as coming from Doolish."

Later, their plans resolved, Walthoef called to a servant standing in the shadows, "Ask my good-wife to join us, then fetch food and mead for a toast." Turning to Rauði, he said, "Sit by me lass whilst I tell you more about your family. Your moder came from yon side of Carleol, but I forget from where exactly. Her dowry was her beauty and her great love for Maldred. His lands were around Hestrskeith. It's fertile ground for raising horses, and those herds were his wealth."

"...And the envy of Sigulfson, no doubt? Hestrskeith's on his border." Gytha interrupted, incurring an annoyed glance from Walthoef.

"That was the rub." Walthoef continued. "My brother fled to Dunbar just before the Normans seized Carleol. Everywhere was in chaos after that. It was all I could do to secure Allerdalr. The King made that bastard, De Taillebois, his man in Cumbraland and that turn-coat, Sigulfson, wheedled his way into his service. Then, acting in De Taillebois's name, he claimed all the grazing around Hestrskeith."

Walthoef watched as tears glistened on Rauði's cheeks. "I remember you as a child. That is why I know you now, you were as beautiful as your moder, even then. But your name wasn't Rauði, it was…"

"Frytha," Rauði interrupted, her eyes, bright with tears, were fixed upon Walthoef. "Rauði's my byname, and Frytha is so like Gytha that we thought it best to change."

Walthoef gave her a sad smile. "Frytha…yes, it is. I'm sorry, Frytha, but Maldred and his family vanished the night his manor was burned." His hand reached out and took hers, "Though I didn't know it then I have a lot to thank Jarl Buthar for. You're very welcome to join my family here, and I know my wife would embrace you, but I rather think that the path you are following is the one your moder would have chosen for you."

As Walthoef released Rauði's hand Gytha leant over and embraced her warmly, whispering into her ear, "Welcome home, cousin."

As she did so, Bear winked at Bjorn and mouthed, "You too."

Chapter 6

"Kai, take the lead with Gunnar and follow the track to Kesewic. Send Gwenn and Tanuw to ride with Rauði. Bjorn, you're with Gytha and me." Bear gave a quick order and waved a casual salute towards Walthoef as he urged Óðr into a trot. Sköll followed alongside.

Brother and sister talked loudly as they rode. Bjorn strove to listen and heard most of what was said, thankful that Gytha rode on Bear's other flank as her higher pitched voice carried more clearly as she asked, "Do you think we should train the men to fight wearing mail? You all wore it when we stood against the Normans at Ulueswater, and we didn't take any casualties, not serious ones anyway. But Godric wasn't wearing it when Sigulfson's men ambushed him a year later. Mail would probably have saved him."

"I agree, it would. But Godric made a decision to stand and face Sigulfson's men. I've since trained ours to use the advantage of speed and mobility that they gain by not wearing mail. We should be the ones setting the ambushes, striking quickly and moving away." Bear was loath to amend his chosen way of fighting. "A green man can outrun a mail-clad man on a fellside. Just as our ponies can move more quickly if their riders aren't weighed down by coats of metal."

Gytha fell silent for a moment, a doubt nagging at her mind. "You're right, of course, but we've trained the men to take the fight to our enemy, whoever he is; just as Osberht is doing now. But it might be different if he brings the fight to us. I remember Ulf once telling us how Osberht's father fell with many of the original green men in a shield wall in Northumberland. But they were all wearing mail and carried shields, and in the end, most of them did survive. Without mail and shields, all would have fallen."

It was Bear's turn to take stock of her argument. "It would take time to train them. I could do it, along with

Ulf, Dai and Wealmaer. The more experienced men will still have the skills, though they be rusty. I suppose..."

Gytha interrupted, laughing, "At least the mail won't be rusty. Thank the gods that we kept our armourers busy polishing it."

Bear gave a defeated smile. "Have you been scheming with Ulf? He's always insisted we keep the mail and the shields in good order."

"Not I," Gytha laughed lightly. "but I have been thinking about it. If we are to stop an incursion, as Walthoef thinks we might, then we may need mailed men to block a track whilst we spring an ambush from a flank. I've already started recruiting more men, and women. I want my best men to train to fight in mail. The new ones, and Gwenn, Tanuw and any more women we recruit, can concentrate on ambushes. What do you think?"

Bear's loud chortle startled Óðr, and he spent moments calming the stallion before he replied. "What I think, sister, is that I should have taken heed all those years ago when Ulf first told me to listen to you when it comes to tactics."

Gytha smiled disarmingly. "I recall that day too...and we all know that Ulf is rarely wrong."

"Mayhap." Bear pulled a face and turned to Bjorn. "Take heed young Bjorn," he said, nodding his head towards the three women riding behind, "I rather think that one day soon you too may well be taking advice from that young lass of yours. She's canny, and once my sister gets to work on her, well..." He stopped, with a flinch, as he felt Gytha's boot kick his leg.

*****

"Wooah!" Bear reined Óðr to a sudden halt, signalling for those around him to do likewise and be silent. They understood immediately, watching entranced as the two hounds, a hundred paces ahead, scented a deer. Loki ran swiftly along the track before looping to his right whilst Sköll sunk onto his haunches and crept into the undergrowth. Bear knew that the hounds had

61

instinctively realised that they were downwind of their prey, and that one of them could drive the deer onto the other. All was quiet for a few moments, with the hounds and deer out of sight. A sudden squeal and crashing in the undergrowth, followed by a brief rhythmic thumping, told them that the deer was down. Bear dismounted quickly and dashed down the track and into the undergrowth, following the route Sköll had taken. He found the hounds lying down, staring fixedly at the deer as it twitched weakly in its final death throws.

"Good boys! Away now!" The hounds backed off as Bear took hold deftly of the deer's hind legs and swung it over his shoulder. As he turned around he could just see Bjorn and Gytha's heads over the top of the scrub, and waved.

"Bjorn, lead Óðr down to the river. I'll meet you there." He shouted loudly and walked on without waiting for Bjorn's acknowledgement. The hounds followed close upon Bear's heels, anticipating the reward that they knew was to come. The deer, a young female roe, was heavy upon Bear's shoulders and his feet slipped slightly as he descended the earthy river bank. He chose a large boulder by the water's edge and draped the warm carcass across it, head down. With a swift slash of his knife he cut the deer's throat and stood back whilst dark blood gushed into the river.

Bear ignored the hounds as first Loki, and then Sköll, started to bark excitedly. Working quickly, he slit the stomach, pulled out the intestines and internal organs, separated them, divided the offal into equal portions and threw it to the slavering hounds.

Bjorn tethered Óðr at the top of the bank and jumped down to assist. "I'm impressed. That was the quickest kill I've ever seen." Bear looked up, grinning at the compliment.

"Credit these boys, not me. Now, grab the front legs and we'll wash it quickly in the river and clear away most of the blood. Then, take handfuls of long grass, twist it into strands and knot the ends to make a rough cord.

We'll bind the stomach closed before tying the deer across Óðr's back."

Bjorn helped Bear to carry the carcass up the river bank and, having secured it behind Bear's saddle, they mounted and trotted to join the waiting women.

"I have my uses, sister," Bear teased. Ignoring Gytha's poked tongue, he urged Óðr forward to close up upon Kai and Gunnar.

Bear shouted a greeting to an old man chopping wood as they retraced their way through Hlóratún and then, with the track narrowing, he bade Bjorn drop behind. Moments later Bjorn was surprised when Gwenn moved alongside.

"We can only ride two abreast, so I'll join you." Gwenn spoke with a softer accent than Bjorn was used to. "What do you think of us? Is it different to serving the Jarl?" By the tone of her questions Bjorn thought that Gwenn already knew his answer.

He laughed. "What do you think? I'm sure Rauði has told you that the Jarl won't have women working with his men-at-arms, other than to do all their chores. They even live in a separate hall. His men-at-arms are older too. Some grow old and grey serving him."

Gwenn gave Bjorn a quizzical look. It accentuated the elfin features of her face, and her pale blue eyes narrowed as she studied him. He marvelled at how Gwenn managed to control her pony without watching where she was riding. Her height gave her a natural elegance and an aura of being in control. She spoke at last, "Is Rauði right when she says that she came here because she wants to avenge her family? That you both do?"

Bjorn paused before looking quickly at Gwenn and replied, "She is, all we know is that our families were slain by Normans. Rauði heard today what happened to hers. I doubt I ever will hear about mine, but it is something that binds us together."

Gwenn glanced forward and squeezed with a thigh to guide her pony along the track. Bjorn thought she must be a few years older than him. With her fair hair braided into a think plait that hung below her tan coloured helmet, and her skin darkened by wind and sun, she looked to Bjorn just like a Valkyrie from one of the sagas that were regaled around the Jarl's hearth on a winter's night. As she spoke, he recognised her accent as that of the people of the Eden valley.

"My family were forced to flee too, but at least we all lived. I was mayhap ten when the Normans came over the pass at Stanmoir and there was a big battle above Burc. That's where we lived. Bear rode in and told us to flee and follow him, and we did. Lady Ealdgith gave my fader land at Glynrhedyn after we got there. Then, there were more battles as the Normans tried to seize the lake. Lady Ealdgith led us well, and we sank their boats and killed many. That's when I first saw women fight alongside men."

"When did you join Gytha?" Bjorn asked, slightly awed by the woman beside him.

"Oh, two summers back," Gwenn answered casually. "It was when my parents wanted to marry me to one of the lads in Glynrhedyn, the cobbler's son." She laughed dismissively. "He stank of the hides the family cured. I wanted more, so I spoke to Gytha when I had a chance. That's when I came to Borgarárdalr. It's when Tanuw joined too, and we've worked together ever since."

Bjorn found Gwenn easy to talk to and he relaxed as she told him more about her life and the ways of the green men. It was only when he realised that Bear and Gytha had joined up with Kai, and stopped within sight of a cluster of buildings, that he became aware of his surroundings.

"That's the edge of Kesewic," Gwenn said, pointing as she spoke, "the vill is set back a bit from the edge of the lake. I wonder why we are here?"

Her question was answered by Bear's orders to Kai. "Wait for Godfrid, then take both sections down to the boat landings and wait for us there. Gytha wants to show me the places where she meets her agent. Then we'll go to the market and see what we can get everyone to eat."

"A sack of Vivi's pies wouldn't go amiss, Lord." Kai saluted, with a cheeky wink at Gytha.

She laughed, "Aye Kai, mayhap."

*****

"That's the third of the meeting places, under the old oak by Saint Kentigern's Church. There's a hollow in the trunk where messages can be left." Gytha spoke casually without drawing attention to the tree as the foursome rode past without stopping. "The market's yonder, at the foot of the hill." She pointed to a throng of people on a patch of bare earth at the edge of the vill.

"Whoa! That's strange." Gytha surprised Bear by reining to a sudden halt. "There's half a dozen horses tethered at the edge of the wood, on the slope yon side of the market."

"Aye, and some sort of commotion." Bear added as the sound of a woman's angry shout resounded above the hubbub of the market. "There're men-at-arms down there. Look! There's the glint from mail."

"Ye gods! They're not Walthoef's men, though they're on his land." Gytha's curse, and the command that followed, surprised the girl beside her. "Rauði, ride like the wind. Go around the back of the market then head straight to the lake shore. Get the men back here as quick as you can. Bjorn, by the look of it there isn't a guard on those horses. Make your way to them without drawing attention. Wait until you hear my horn, then cut their tethers and drive them off." Bjorn's eyes flicked briefly to the ornate white ivory and silver horn that hung at the small of Gytha's back.

Bear gave a slow smile. "Then it's up to you and me, sister. That's just what I was about to suggest." Gytha accepted Bear's compliment, knowing that he had the sense not to take charge of her men without her permission. "I suggest we stay mounted," he added, loosening the cord that secured his sword in its scabbard.

Gytha felt her stomach tighten. It was a long time since she had confronted an armed man, but her nervousness passed quickly, calmed by the surge of adrenalin that came when she was threatened. Urging their ponies to trot down to the crowd, they slowed and made their way through the throng. Sensing the animals behind them, most stepped out of the way. Controlling her pony with her knees, Gytha unslung her bow from her shoulder and notched an arrow to the string. She could see over the top of the heads that the men-at-arms were at Vivi's stall. They had their backs to the crowd. One appeared to be controlling the stall-holder with the point of his sword whilst the others crammed Vivi's food into their mouths, mocking her whilst they ate.

They spoke in heavily accented English. Bear recognised the dialect as that of fen-country men who Ivo de Taillebois had forced from his southern lands into the Eden valley a few years earlier. They undoubtedly now served Forne Sigulfson and would have little empathy with the local Cumbric-speaking people. The crowd fell silent slowly as Bear eased his spear from its sheath behind his saddle and pointed it ever closer to the back of the neck of the man with the sword.

Gytha clicked her fingers to control the hounds, turned sideways to have a clear shot at any of the men-at-arms, and braced her bow.

Bear lowered his spear tip and with a deliberate jab, drew blood from the man's neck.

Bellowing with pain and rage the man swung his sword around and turned to face his assailant, allowing Vivi a chance to drop to the ground and roll away under the table.

As the other men turned they froze. Two snarling wolfhounds threatened their genitals whilst Gytha's green eyes stared into theirs. The tip of her arrow threatened to pierce the face of any who resisted. The swordsman's weapon never made contact with Bear's spear. The spear's tip was so close to the man's nose that he stood still in fear and anger.

"Drop it!" Bear nodded towards the sword. "You, the man next to him, unsheath your sword and drop it, that dagger too. The rest of you follow on, one at a time."

As the last weapon fell with a metallic thud Gytha released the tension in her bowstring and, still holding the bow with her left hand she reached with her right for her horn and raised it to her lips to blow one long solitary note.

The men-at-arms stood still, their anger turning to dismay, at the whinnying of startled horses.

"Who is in charge?" Gytha's icy voice carried clearly. After a silent pause she added, "I won't ask again," and retensioned her bow string, pointing the arrow directly at the man in front of her. "Although you wear mail, this arrow will pierce your innards at this range. Speak!"

"I am." A swarthy man, slightly older than the rest, spoke up.

"Good, so now you understand me. I believe I know whom you serve, but I want to hear it from your mouth. Tell me." She spoke tersely.

"Lord Sigulfson, and he will want revenge for..."

"Revenge be dammed! Your name is?" Gytha's tone caused Loki to expose his fangs whilst he gave a low growl.

"Cola." The man almost spat as he spoke.

"You'll call me 'my Lady' when next you speak, Cola. I hold this land for Lord Walthoef, as does my brother. Sigulfson has no say here, and you have no right here." Gytha paused, partly for effect, but also to listen to the sound of hooves galloping over turf. She knew without looking that her men had arrived and now stood behind her. The consternation in the eyes of the men in front of her confirmed it.

"We could have you hanged for what you have done. I know your lord, and that is what he would do, is it not, Cola?"

Cola nodded slowly, his eyes holding Gytha's.

"Well, Cola, when you return to your lord tell him that the lady whose fells these are is merciful and wants no trouble on her borders."

Cola was silent for a moment; he scowled, seeming to have difficulty accepting a woman's authority. He spoke when Bear's spear tip flicked towards him. "Thank you, my Lady...and our swords?"

"Are forfeit, as are your horses. Godfrid!" Gytha called to the section commander that she knew would be in place behind her. "See these men off our land. Bind their hands until you release them at Trellekell. We will wait for you here. Kai, round up their horses. Bjorn is still up at yon wood where they were tethered, he should be able to show you where they ran to." She pointed as she spoke.

Gytha eased her pony backwards and dismounted as Godfrid's men moved forward to take charge of the prisoners. She turned as Rauði came next to her and smiled at the look of pure admiration on the girl's face, and then glanced around as she heard Bear.

"Well done, sister. You're every bit the Valkyrie that Fader always said you were. He would have been proud of you."

Gytha blushed, embarrassed at the praise from her brother and her newly found cousin, and laughed, "Come on. I want to see that Vivi is alright, and then buy food for the men. We all deserve a meal after this."

"Not so fast," Bear hugged Gytha quickly, "I was proud of you just now. And you were right. We do need to train the men to fight in mail and use shields. Sigulfson is going to keep pushing us, I know it. With those horses, we can at least match his men with one section. After you've seen to Vivi I want us to search out the head of the vill and see if Sigulfson's men have done this before."

Chapter 7

"Ye gods! My shoulders are so stiff." Rauði clasped her hands behind her head and braced her shoulders. "Just how many days is it that we've been training like this?"

Bjorn puffed his cheeks and blew out slowly. "Seven, eight, I forget. Forever, mayhap. It certainly feels like it." He lowered the sack of dry pine needles that they had gathered in the wood, and started to scatter them on the pony-cropped turf. The patch of ground, ten paces by ten, was worn and torn by their feet after days of training unarmed or with wooden weapons. "At least these might help soften the falls."

Rauði laughed. "I've stopped feeling the falls. Thanks." She took the water flask that Bjorn offered her, un-stoppered it, and drank a long swig. "You finish it," she said, handing it back. "We've time for one more bout before we meet Neven at the butts."

"She's a hard mistress for certain." Bjorn wiped sweat from his brow. "I'm sure she pushes us more than Dai does."

"She does, and do you know why?" Rauði replied, and then answered her own question. "She's a woman in a man's world. She can't be seen to be lenient. I'll be the same." She added firmly.

"Mmm, I'd never thought of it like that, but I see what you mean." Bjorn agreed, picking up his wooden training sword. "Now, show me what Neven's spent all this time teaching you. Are you going to be lenient on me?" He teased Rauði with a cheeky glint in his eye.

"Not if I can help it. I beat you in the end last time." Rauði was suddenly serious and her expression darkened as she took up a stance squarely in front of Bjorn, just beyond the reach of his sword. "Come on, take me if you dare," she challenged, drawing her wooden dagger from her belt and circling to her left.

"You don't always fight with your sword in your left hand? Last time it was in your right. Why?" Rauði asked sharply, partly to try and control Bjorn's attention, but she was also genuinely interested. She felt that it might give him an advantage against a right-handed swordsman; it certainly unsettled her as she faced him.

Bjorn grinned, tossing the sword from one hand to the other. "Gille insisted that I use my right hand but Dai says to play to my strengths. I'm far more relaxed with it in my left. Now, did Neven tell you how she learned to fight like this?"

Rauði knew that Bjorn was trying to distract her, but she played along, talking whilst she worked out how to get past the wooden blade without it touching her. "She said Ealdgith learnt the skill when she was our age, and that she insists that all the women who serve her learn it too. When she and her husband, Hravn, fled from the harrying in Ghellinges-scir they tried to reach Westmoringaland through the Mallerstang forest. They struggled in the depths of winter and were befriended by a hermit-monk who lived in a cave. He had once served in the Eastern Emperors' Varangian guard. This monk, Oswin he was called, though disillusioned with the violence of the world, knew all too well the dangers that a lone woman would face, and he taught them both the eastern arts of fighting only with a knife. Apparently, it has saved Ealdgith's life several times, Gytha's too...oof!"

Bjorn waited until Rauði finished talking and then lunged at her midriff. Caught almost unaware, Rauði twisted quickly to her right, span around, and brushed alongside Bjorn's left shoulder. She realised in an instant that this was her chance; she was inside the circle of the sword. As she touched Bjorn's shoulder she hooked her left calf in front of his left leg, twisted, and threw her weight against his back.

Bjorn, already on the edge of his balance, stumbled forward and fell heavily. As he tried to retain a grip on his sword and roll away he felt Rauði's weight land on his side and the tip of her wooden dagger press against his throat.

"Sorry," she laughed, "that was too easy." As she rolled off him, they turned in surprise at the sound of clapping.

Leofric stood at the edge of the marked turf. "Neatly done, Rauði. I'm impressed, though mayhap it was too easy. I sparred with Gytha when she learned to fight like that and we found that we soon learned each other's tricks and weren't as aggressive as perhaps we should be. It's a while since I wielded a sword, but let's see how you are when you really vent your aggression on someone you're not attached to."

"What? You're my..."

Leofric interrupted her, laughing. "No, I'm not your lord. I'm your cousin, so there'll be no need to feel embarrassed when you topple me. That is if you think you can, but I'm not so sure." He paused, goading her. "I challenge you to a holmganga."

"A what?" She gasped.

"A holmganga. A contest within marked boundaries, just like you have here. In days of old it was to the death, but perhaps not today. Shall we?" Without waiting for Rauði's reply Leofric held out his hand to Bjorn. "Toss me your sword, Bjorn."

Rauði's initial nerves dissipated quickly when Leofric stepped across the threshold of the square. She tightened the strap holding her borrowed helmet in place and watched him intently, assessing the challenge that he posed. Only marginally taller than her, Leofric had a sturdy frame and short legs. She knew instantly that his low centre of gravity would make him harder to topple and that it would be difficult for her to dive between his legs, which was one of the moves that Neven had shown her. She banished all other thoughts from her mind and focused on the ten square paces of trampled ground. Keeping clear of the edge so that she had room to move, she began to circle to her right, away from the sword in Leofric's right hand. Neven's words came back to her: keep your helmet strap tight, it will protect your head from a sword blow; use his weight and movement against him; rile him so that he loses concentration; make his anger distract him; watch his eyes, if you know where he's looking you can anticipate his next move; above all keep moving and make him waste his strength thrusting at thin air.

Leofric spoke first, he knew that if he could annoy Rauði, her anger would drive her to fight with aggression, and really show her ability. "Come on lass, I could flick that dagger out of your hand and give you a good thrashing. Just what do they teach the women of Butremere? Is patting butter and carding wool the best you can do?"

Leofric's words stung. Rauði was sure he didn't mean them, but what if he did? Did he secretly resent their presence and her new-found status? She looked directly into his eyes, trying to discern his emotions and read his intentions. They were bright blue, expressionless. She continued to hold Leofric's eyes as she circled, keeping his sword hand in the periphery of her vision, and hoping that she could anticipate Leofric's move before he made it.

His grip tightened, and she stepped swiftly to her right just before Leofric's sword stabbed past her left shoulder. Leofric gave a mocking smile and shrugged tension from his shoulders before regaining his stance.

Rauði forced a laugh. "You must be getting old, or were you always that slow?" Her voice sounded strangely detached, as if someone else had spoken, but its sound boosted her confidence. "If Butremere women need teaching, come on, teach me," she goaded him again and, as she saw his weight shift onto his left leg, rolled forward in a swift somersault before standing quickly, turned and stepped back briskly.

Leofric's sword slashed through empty air and his feet skidded slightly on the turf as he wheeled around to his left, momentarily unsure where Rauði was.

As Rauði's confidence grew she began to take the initiative by enticing Leofric forward with her fingers, and dancing through the circle of his sword tip before he could bring it to connect with her body. She was beginning to enjoy herself and was oblivious to Bjorn's gasps of anguish. All the time holding Leofric's eyes with hers, she danced to the left, then to the right. 'At last', she thought, as beads of sweat tricked down Leofric's brow and into his eyes, 'the salt will sting and blur his vision'.

Rauði ducked down into a low crouch as she anticipated another slash across her shoulder line, and then stood and skipped lightly backwards to the edge of the square.

Leofric reacted quickly, barged forward intent on thrusting Rauði across the line and out of the contest. As he did so, Rauði knew that she had him. Certain that Leofric would expect her to move sideways, Rauði turned, dropped to her knees in a ball and rolled sideways into Leofric's legs. He collapsed over her, falling spread-eagled onto the grass outside the square. Rauði winced from the impact of Leofric's knees on the side of her body, stood up and kicked the sword out of Leofric's reach. He surprised them both by rolling onto his back, before sitting and laughing.

"Well fought, Rauði. You remind me of Gytha. Many is the time she's had me rolling in the dirt. You move like her too, with a graceful fluidity, just like water swirling between the rocks of a beck."

Rauði stepped forward, offering Leofric her hand as he raised himself up off the grass. With a beguiling smile she said, "Thank you...cousin." Then, after a slight pause whilst she held his eyes, "What you said about Butremere women...you didn't mean it?"

Leofric roared with laughter, "I know nothing about Butremere women. What I do know is that you have the makings of a half-decent green woman. Come on, I'll walk you both to the butts."

*****

Bjorn staggered up the slope to the edge of their training ground. His lungs screamed for air and his left shoulder ached from Rauði's weight.

"We're there. Put me down! I can't take any more of your shoulder jabbing into my stomach." Rauði hissed through clenched teeth. She breathed in deeply as Bjorn bent forward and lowered her to the ground.

"Phew!" He blew out harshly, and stood panting, before taking a long deep breath.

"Well done, both of you." Neven was fulsome in her praise. "I'm not sure who had it hardest? Rauði carrying your weight down to the beck, or you coming back up the hill. It's a good way to build your strength up, but it's enough for today. Take some time to yourselves before you go and see Bran the armourer to get your helmets fitted properly." She turned, leaving the couple to recover, and headed towards the houses in the woods by the crag.

"I don't know about you, but I'm so hot and sticky that I could do with bathing in that pool Adelind told me about. It's deep and private and we can lay out on the rocks to dry off. Come on." Rauði urged Bjorn, pulling his hand with hers as she set off down the hill. He hesitated briefly, and then ran after her, not quite sure what to think.

The pool was a short walk up the river, beyond a stand of birch and oak. The slope of the hill ended above a low crag, at the base of which flat grey water-worn slabs of rock framed a shallow gravel-floored pool of clear water.

Rauði sensed Bjorn's uncertainty, and was about to suggest that they both just strip off and jump in, when Bjorn said, "I don't think we should bathe together, just in case anyone comes. You go first, I'll keep watch up here," He sat down on the edge of the crag, trying to hide the rising urge to take her in his arms.

Giving a light laugh, Rauði teased him, "Don't be embarrassed, we've nothing to hide from each other." She turned and walked down to the water's edge. Bjorn watched whilst she turned away from him, removed her boots and stripped off her tunic, laying it over the rocks so that the heat of the sun would dry her perspiration. Although he had seen Rauði naked before, she had been much younger, when they weren't confined by the strictures of their adult life at the Jarl's hall. The slender curve of Rauði's pale body enthralled him; he watched transfixed as she waded into the clear thigh-deep water, crouched and finally sat to let the water flow over her shoulders. Suddenly, she dipped her head momentarily, scrubbed at her face with her hands, and stood quickly, as she called to Bjorn. "By Freja! That's cold! But it's good, I feel so much fresher, though I can't stay in much longer" She took a few steps towards the edge of the rocks and beckoned, "Come on down, it's your turn."

"No, it's better that I wait until you've dried off." Bjorn spoke with so much regret in his voice that Rauði glanced up briefly in puzzlement. He cursed the game that Wyrd was playing: their new-found freedom to be together was surely a trap. If they enjoyed that freedom as a man and women naturally would, he risked Rauði being with child and the wrath of not only her foster father but also her new-found family. Fear of what might befall them clouded his thoughts: would Gytha still want Rauði to serve her if she was carrying a child and of no use as a green woman? Though Rauði was acknowledged as a woman of status, he was just a minstrel's fosterling. If she fell with child, his child, would she be disgraced. Mayhap Rauði was happy for them to just lie together naked in the sun, but could they restrain themselves; could he? Bjorn clenched his fists, feeling his nails dig into his palms. Surely frustration was better than disgrace.

Bjorn waited until Rauði reached for her clothes. He could tell by the swift, jerky manner of her dressing that she was annoyed, so he decided to strip off where he was, bound swiftly past her and dived headlong into the glittering water.

Rauði's disappointment dissipated into an amused giggle, and then a raucous laugh, as Bjorn staggered to his feet, gasping for breath.

"Ye gods! There's cold, and then there is this! It's freezing!" He turned towards Rauði and froze as she gasped. "S...sorry," he stammered, sitting down with a sudden splash, trying to hide his manhood and his embarrassment.

Rauði laughed again and spoke seriously whilst patting the rock next to her. "Come, sit by me and dry off. That water has cooled any ardour that either of us may have felt." She lay back, "Let's just soak up the sun and listen to the birdsong. It'll be all you can do to stop me falling asleep."

Bjorn lay back too, relaxing at last, the heat from the rock soothing his muscles. He listened to Rauði's breathing and as it became deep and regular he waited for a while, letting her sleep, before he wakened her with a gentle brush of his lips against hers.

*****

"Rauði! Over here." Rauði spun around, startled, and then waived when she saw Adelind gesturing to her. They met on the dusty earth outside Adelind's house. Adelind looked somewhat embarrassed and Rauði frowned, puzzled.

Adelind's gentle smile reassured her. "Don't be worried, it's just that I've a difficult question to ask you. I er..." Adelind hesitated, "...I saw you both by the pool yesterday. I was about to bathe myself, but stopped. I hope you don't mind, but I couldn't help but notice how Bjorn was. It's very obvious that he loves you deeply, but that he is hesitant to..."

Adelind stopped as Rauði gasped, her complexion reddening. "I'm sorry, I..."

"No, don't be." Rauði interrupted. "You're right." She glanced around and bent close to Adelind. "We want each other so much. We could never be together before. Now that we can, it scares Bjorn," she sighed, "me too a bit, if I'm honest. But it's a risk I would take."

"But Bjorn won't. Is that it?" Adelind looked directly into Rauði's eyes, reading her expression, gaining understanding without asking. Rauði nodded imperceptibly.

Adelind took Rauði's arm and walked her slowly away from the houses. "Edie was once our people's wise-woman, it is a skill that she passed on to me and my sister,

76

Eir. The secrets of heeling, and more besides, were passed to her by her ealdmoder. It's how we women look after each other, our families and our menfolk. There are herbs I can show you that will stop you falling with child." She heard Rauði's sharp intake of breath, but carried on talking, "Sometimes they can make you feel sick, but if you use them as I tell you to, and follow the practices that I will explain, then you will have some control over when it is safe for you to be together."

Rauði stopped, and turned to face Adelind. Her eyes were wide with surprise, and hope. "Thank you, oh thank you." She gasped, pulling Adelind to her in a tight hug. "There is so much I want to ask that I never been able to ask anyone before."

Adelind held Rauði close, sure that she could feel the taller younger woman's tears fall onto her cheek.

*****

Gytha sat on the rocks above her hall. Her arms were braced behind her as she looked up at the brightening sky, trying to discern any sign that the hot dry weather might at last turn to rain. She was unsure what would be for the best. The unusual drought in this, the wettest of valleys, had enabled Leofric to call the hay harvest early, but the dry conditions meant that the crops that would be harvested next were already at risk of perishing due to lack of water. As she scanned the clear blue above she searched in vain for the thin high clouds that would herald change. She sat up and took in the scene before her: a cart laden with quarried stone raised a trail of dust as it made its way slowly down the valley towards the men who, even at this early hour, were labouring over the foundations of the new vill. Some buildings were roofed with heather or reeds, others were still just bare walls of wattle and fresh daub. In the fields closer to the crag, men and women moved in a line scything the long yellow grass, whilst teams of children followed behind, bundling it into stooks to dry further. Voices close behind broke her reverie. She stood, ready for the meeting.

"We'll sit here, with this breeze its cooler than the hall." Gytha waited until everyone was seated, and gestured to Rauði and Bjorn who were hesitating, "You too, of course. I want you both involved in all our plans. It's as well you know what we are doing, and why."

She sat, and spoke as faces turned towards her. "I'll be brief, for there is a lot to be done. I need to know what we have achieved and what is outstanding. Leo, I'm sorry I can't spare you the green men that I promised. How is the harvest?"

Leofric shrugged non-committedly. "We're getting there. Each vill is looking to itself, though having the miners do the building at the lake shore is hampering us at Sefthveit and Sefthtoller. But there is an urgency that is good to see. The fact that Neven is training more men hasn't gone unnoticed."

With a grateful smile at her husband, Gytha continued. "Agnaar?"

"The new vill is coming on quickly. The roofs we're putting on will see them through the winter. They will need attending to again next year, but we'll have a house or shelter for everyone that Bear brings with him." He glanced at Leofric. "Leo's agreed to help with the Sethveit harvest once Rosthwaite's is in, and then with Sefthtoller's. That's reassured the men that their families won't lose out."

Gytha nodded appreciatively. "And Neven. Recruiting and training?"

Neven cleared her throat to speak. "Good. We've the extra three sections you wanted and have more willing should you need them." Her eyes flicked towards Rauði. "Once word got around that you have another green woman at your side several more younger women came forward. I've accepted two and told the others to wait until we've spoken. They're all fit, unattached and very keen."

"Hah!" Gytha gave a low laugh and turned to Leofric and Agnaar, stern-faced. "Keep an eye on the men in the vills. I don't want any chuntering about women doing men's jobs. I fear that we will need every man and woman we can get for the struggle ahead. Neven, Dai, take as many women as you can. I want them to form the force we will use to guard the lakeshore. The men will do the patrolling. Dai, I want you to lend Kai's section to Neven to train the women. Neven, the women will be yours to command. They are to concentrate on crewing the svanmeyjas and setting ambushes along the lake shore using bows, slings and traps, just as we did at Ulueswater. Mayhap appoint Gwenn and Tanuw as section leaders. They are both good enough. Dai, take charge of all the new men. Once they are trained, restructure the sections and appoint new leaders from the more experienced men. Talk to me first about who you choose, then spread the new men amongst the sections. They will learn more quickly that way. I know we've talked about dressing a section in mail, but I'll wait 'til Bear is here before we do that." Gytha paused, waiting for her spate of orders to register.

"I've asked Tyr to join us because I'm worried that we won't have enough boats and don't have time to build more. Tyr, tell them what we discussed." Gytha gave the normally reticent boat builder an encouraging smile.

Tyr spoke methodically. "My Lady's right. We have two svanmeyjas and a kára." Tyr referred to the larger tub-like boat they used to transport cargo and livestock. "We lack the time to build from scratch, and the kára isn't really suitable for use in the shallows. But we do have three old dugouts that are sound enough. I can clean them up and add an out-rigger to each. They'll take two people with ease, mayhap three with the out-rigger to balance the extra weight. Oh, and several coracles too. They could be handy if you want someone to bob around observing the shore."

Gytha slapped her hand against her thigh enthusiastically. "Thanks Tyr. That'll work. From what Neven says we'll have enough women for three, mayhap four, sections of women, or women and men if needs be, to cover the lakeshore, and at least six sections of men to patrol. What do you think?"

Leofric spoke first. His hint of a smile belied the meaningful look in his eyes as he looked deliberately at his wife. "Recruiting more men is all well and good, but they need to be properly equipped. I know for certain that we don't have enough green cloaks. Duwe is hard pushed as it is and Asta will certainly need more than an extra pair of hands to dye the fabric, even if she does have enough woad and dyers' greenweed." He added, sounding uncertain.

Gytha's expression froze momentarily and then she sighed. "You're right as always, my love. Speak with them and see just what they can do, and what they need. I'll get word to moder and see what we can get from Glynrhedyn. There's Kesewic too. The merchants there will be all too happy for our business."

Dai spoke next. "I think it will work, my Lady. In truth, I know it will. But have we enough weapons?"

Gytha laughed scornfully, her confidence returning. "Surely a good master-at-arms knows just how many weapons he has at his disposal? I trust that was a jest? Of course we have enough swords. Have a word with Bran, he may need to refurbish some of the spares we brought from Glynrhedyn. Rhun and Tyr are going to make more bows, arrow and spear shafts, and heads for both.

Dai raised his eyes and shook his head. "That wasn't a jest, just a daft question, I apologise. But what of your own plans, my Lady?"

"I have to meet Aric in Kesewic tomorrow. I'll see what we can source from there and I'll warn off the cobbler whilst I'm about it. We'll take a look at the lakeshore track on the way there. Rauði and Bjorn, I want you to accompany me. I'm confident that you're well enough trained now, so in future you will ride with me, freeing Neven and Dai to command the sections. I can't call you my huscarles, not yet, and not without more experience," Gytha paused deliberately, letting Neven appreciate that her role wasn't being usurped. "But you will provide all the protection I need. Then, depending upon Aric's news, we will go to Butremere and bring the Jarl up to date about our meeting with Lord Walthoef." She turned to Rauði and Bjorn, "And once the men in the

Jarl's hall hear what Lord Walthoef told you about your past, you may well find that they see you both in a very different light."

Chapter 8

"There, that's the first one. Do you see it?" Wealmaer spoke with a hushed urgency, though there was really no need to be so quiet. From his vantage point on top of the old Roman fort overlooking the River Petteril he knew that the only men in the vicinity were Osgar, next to him, and the section of men in the fort below.

"No...yes, aye I can. Just down from the skyline." Osgar turned and glanced over his shoulder at the moon. Its full, pock-marked, face was still screened by thin high clouds covering the eastern sky, only a dull glimmer marked its rise in the east. "Not a moment too soon. We're in for another bright night once it swings over to the west. It's already looking brighter over there."

"Aye, if Osberht's timing is right they should be back here before it is. We could do with the light to help us find our way back to Meg's stones, but not yet." Wealmaer kept staring intently towards the higher ground to their south west. "That must have been the granary at Sheltone, the mill at Hoton will be next, then..."

Osgar's tap on his shoulder stopped Wealmaer. "Listen...was that a horn?"

Wealmaer turned his head towards the stiffening south westerly breeze and cupped the back of his ear with his hand. The faint sound of a horn came again. "Yes. That'll be from Creistoc. Sigulfson must have a watch posted on the tower there."

Osgar chuckled. "Well, his men are certainly getting practiced at crashing out and chasing shadows."

Wealmaer didn't share Osgar's humour. He answered gruffly. "They're not fools. They weren't expecting last week's raids over at Yuegill and down the Caldew from Sabergham. But you saw how many men he sent north into the Caldew valley to try and find us." Wealmaer referred to the series of mills and granaries they had torched in the long night of their first raid. "They'll be recalled after this and the lands west of the

Petteril will be closed to us. It's only a matter of time before they come looking across the Eden."

Osgar was still upbeat. "No doubt, but Osberht will have us all back at Glynrhedyn by then. He's a canny knack for this way of fighting."

"He has that, so long as success doesn't get to him. He's driven by a lust for revenge, and that doesn't bode well for the rest of us. It's best to remember that." Wealmaer's sombre warning stilled their conversation until a distant ball of flame flared suddenly. It was followed moments later by a muffled bang.

"Phew!" The two men glanced at each other, wide-eyed, and Osgar gave a low laugh. "That must have been quite a blast. I hope they were well clear."

"It must have been grain dust exploding. My guess is that they set a fire inside the mill and then the upper floor collapsed and the sacks burst. It'll be a beacon to attract Sigulfson's men, that's for certain." Wealmaer grinned at last. "It's just the distraction that Osberht needs. Go and get the men mounted and down to the ford. I'll watch from here until I see them coming, and then I'll join you. Hoton's barely a league away. They'll be here in a matter of minutes."

Wealmaer gradually discerned the outline of the five fast-moving ponies as they galloped across the open pasture on the far side of the Petteril. He was proud of his men, and pleased with their training. The ponies and the riders were simple grey shadows, nothing glinted and no pale flesh glimmered in the star light. With all metal and skin blackened by soot, and all equipment securely fastened to their bodies or their saddles, the men and animals moved as one. Only the sound of the ponies' panting and their hooves upon the turf marked their passage.

Osberht arrived first, with Ranald close behind. Their ponies skittered to a halt and raised their heads, gulping for air. Osberht's eyes were wide with excitement, his body pumped full with adrenalin and his face glistened where trails of sweat now trickled down the soot-marked cheeks. He spoke quickly, almost gabbling. "That was closer than I would have liked. Sigulfson has patrols out now. We almost bumped into the bastards this side of Skeltone, but we saw them sky-lined ahead of us and let them move on. Ranald's sure that they gave chase after he torched the granary but they were a good half league behind. They'd have been near the mill when the roof blew off. There's been no sign of them since."

Wealmaer hoped Osberht was right. It would be hard to move without being seen by anyone within half a league once the full moon escaped the cover of the clouds. He gave his young commander an encouraging grin: "Good work. Get across the bridge as fast as you can and wait for us there. We'll follow more slowly and guard our rear."

Osberht nodded, wheeled his pony around, splashed through the ford, and urged it back to a gallop. Wealmaer winced as the still night was shattered by the sound of hooves striking water and the rocky river bed. He turned to Osgar. "Follow them to the bridge, but quietly. I'll keep Gorm with me and we'll watch from the top of Leisingebi fell to make sure they're not being tailed."

Wealmaer and Gorm observed the dark landscape long enough to be sure that Osberht hadn't been followed. The distant fires were dying as they cantered down the back of the hill to the bridge at Karcoswald. Wealmaer led his pony cautiously across the rickety wooden planks and then flicked an upraised thumb towards the men on the far bank. Osberht nodded in appreciation, wheeled his pony and led the troop away to their sanctuary amidst the standing stones.

*****

Wealmaer lay half upright with his back against the cool smooth side of a standing stone. He was half asleep, thinking of his wife, Revna, and his small son. He knew she wanted him to stay closer to her, but soldiering was his life and his status as master-at-arms gave them a lifestyle that nothing could match. With quarters in Bear's

84

hall, and Revna working alongside Eir as a wise-woman, he felt no desire to change. He opened his eyes and watched the sun starting to light up the northern edge of Cross Fell, wondering idly if the witchcraft of the stones was linked to Fiends Fell, which was what the broad flat summit of Cross Fell had been called in the old times; he felt sure they must have been. Although it had been a very short warm night, Wealmaer's back was stiff from the hard ground and cold rock. He flexed his shoulders to get his blood circulating whilst watching the early activity as the camp came to life.

He was secretly pleased with how the men had created a private space within the bounds of the extensive patch of scrub and briars surrounding the circle of old stones. They had spent their first day hacking a way through to the stones and then cleared an area within their perimeter. The stones formed a circle one hundred paces across, whilst the scrub extended for up to another twenty paces outside. The tallest of the stones, the one that Wealmaer assumed was referred to as Long Meg, was outside the circle and on the edge of the scrub. It was its association with the spell-craft of the old gods that Wealmaer presumed had prevented any grazing or cultivation of the place.

He had insisted that the men cut three ways through the scrub and then bundle the cuttings so that they formed movable barriers to conceal the entrances. The rest of the brash was used to thicken the outer perimeter. He was confident that movement within the circle would be screened from the outside and that it would be difficult for any attackers to force their way through. The ponies were corralled at one side of the circle, where they were free to graze on the scrub and the lower branches of the few trees.

Smoke from the one permitted cooking fire began to curl slowly upwards. It was the only sign that they were there, and Wealmaer insisted that it was only lit whilst a man stood guard on a low hill two hundred paces to the west, from where he could observe the slopes down to the River Eden. He stood up, walked across to a small spring bubbling from the centre of the circle, filled his flask, returned to collect a bowl from his saddlebag, and went to get his breakfast and to speak to Osberht.

"You look as rough as I feel," Wealmaer joked as he walked up to Osberht and laughed at the finger gesture he received in reply. "Come, let's step away from the lads and go over what needs doing next."

"Don't worry, that's what stopped me from getting any sleep." Osberht gave a long yawn and took another spoonful of broth. "It's good, this," he added, wiping his mouth with the back of the hand that held the spoon. "Now, this is what I think."

"Go on." Wealmaer replied, without showing his concern that Osberht's confidence after the night's success might lead to his taking unnecessary risks.

"The next raids should be our last. If we keeping moving further east, as we must if we are to avoid those searching for us, then we'll soon run out of space."

Wealmaer nodded slowly in agreement with the younger man's logic.

"I think we make more of an impact torching mills. The granaries are empty because the harvest is still being cut. By destroying the mills, we destroy Sigulfson's ability to process the grain. That's really going to play on his mind until he can get them rebuilt. We'll split the lads into pairs, with you and me going with those without a section commander. We'll torch four mills at once if we can, on the Petteril and the Eden, then instead of returning here we'll make a break for it, straight down the old road behind Rhudd Hill so that we avoid Penrith and the men in the old fort at Brougham. We'll cross the Eamont at the ford, hide up in the woods on Whin Fell, rest during daylight, and on the next night get back to Pulhoue and along the lakeshore to home. What do you think?"

Wealmaer smiled, relieved and not a little surprised at Osberht's sound appreciation and plan. "It's good, very good. It's just what we need to do. Though we'll need to get a careful look at the ground first."

"I've thought of that too. Wulf and I will leave tonight, after we've had some shut eye. I'm sure we can find a wood on the high ground south of Hestrskeith. The next night we'll find two suitable mills on the Petteril, and the night after we'll find two on the Eden. We'll get back here the night after that."

Wealmaer shook the last drips of broth out of his bowl, licked his spoon clean, tucked it into a pocket, and clasped Osberht on his shoulder. "That's a plan that Hravn himself would have been pleased with. I'm assuming that we will leave here the night after you return and that we'll take the remounts with us. Each pair can lead one?"

Osberht nodded, relief at Wealmaer's praise showing as he relaxed. "I'll brief all the men the morning I return, we can get on our way as dusk gathers.

"And I'll have everything cleared, packed and ready before that. I'll set a watch on the bridge too. Go on, get your head down. I'll warn off Wulf and sort out a sack of rations for you both." Wealmaer was impressed.

*****

Wealmaer called in the guard and then kept watch across the flanks below the wood in which they were concealed, whilst Osberht briefed the men. Having already discussed their plans in detail, and made some significant changes, he was very familiar with the coming night's attacks. He listened whilst those responsible for leading the four pairs responded to Osberht's request for questions.

"That's a fair point, Ranald. I thought someone would question that." Osberht replied to the more experienced of his commanders. "I want the three mills on the Petteril to be torched at the same time. Barely two leagues separates yours at Thouthweyt to the north and Osgar's at Caluethweyt to the south. Wulf's is in the middle, and if the alarm goes up too soon he could get caught out. The time to strike is the moment the sun drops below the horizon. Make sure you escape to the south of this fell before cutting east to yon side of Leisingebi fell, once the fells are behind you head south down the track by the Eden. I don't want you getting caught up with the little diversion that Wealmaer and I have in mind for Hestrskeith. Is that clear?"

Osberht continued as Ranald nodded. "Good. Now, just to reconfirm, Gorm, you won't be able to see the other mills, and you'll be so deep in the valley that for you the sun will be down well before it is for the others. Take your lead from me, and fire the mill at Ermitethwait as soon as we set light to the stables on the top of the ridge. The flames should draw attention like a candle draws moths, so head straight down the Eden track once the mill is ablaze. Wealmaer and I will be close behind you. The chances are, if you hear someone on your heels, it'll be us catching up with you. All of you, remember it's a good five leagues or more south to Whin Fell. Don't stop until you enter the wood on the fell top. You'll cross the main stone road a couple of furlongs after you ford the Eamont, and should see the outline of Whin Fell in front of you. At that point, there is a track up to the wood on the top. Shelter just inside the wood and guard the entrance. We'll make camp once we are all together."

Osberht glanced reassuringly at each of his men and said confidently, "Good, if there are no more questions make your final preparations and move off in your own time. Get into a hide close to the target, keep your tinder dry and to hand. Then strike as soon as the sun drops below the hills." He turned to Wealmaer. "Let's check those fire-arrows again. This is the one thing that mustn't fail."

*****

Wealmaer checked that their ponies were tethered securely. He was confident that from the shallow gulley on the wooded fellside the ponies would not be able to see the flames from the blazing stables and would not be scared. He turned and ran to catch up with Osberht, who was following the contour of the slope to a point at

88

the edge of the wood overlooking the Hestrskeith plateau and a sprawling complex of stables.

"This must be where Sigulfson breeds his herd." Osberht observed, as he screened his eyes from the lowering sun, and peered intently at the maze of fenced fields and crudely thatched shelters at the bottom of the slope.

"Not just his own herd. What I heard is that years ago he stole the land and the herd from a Cumbric lord called Maldred. He then bred horses for Count Ivo, and now for Ranulf le Meschin. They've a lot of men to provide mounts for." Wealmaer spoke more quietly than he needed to.

Osberht was silent for a few moments, biting his lower lip in concentration. He spoke slowly. "I might be wrong, but those don't look like proper fences. They're simply trestles with a single fence-rail laid between them. I think they must move them around as grazing demands. They won't hold panicked horses, that's for sure."

Wealmaer nodded in agreement and spoke softly, "Aye, happen you're right," and then with greater urgency added. "Yes, it's what I thought when I saw these yesterday, from the top of the hill. There's a double row of big stables this side of the vill, then smaller ones dotted around in the fields. The big ones will be for winter stabling, the smaller ones for the summer, that's why the horses are out in the fields at the moment."

"Ah ha!" Wealmaer saw sudden understanding in Osberht's eyes. "We could give ourselves a clear way in and out to those big stables, by simply lifting the rails off the trestles to find cover from view in one of the smaller shelters close to the stables."

"Look." Wealmaer nudged close to Osberht and pointed. "The second stable in from the left. To its right, and this way fifty paces, there's a shelter with side walls."

"Hmm, and it looks to be within bow range of that first row of stables, do..."

"Never doubt me." Wealmaer interrupted Osberht's question with a gruff chuckle. "If you feed me the fire-arrows, I could drop two on to each of that first row of stables within a minute. The roofs look to be that dry that they would catch straight away. What worries me, is dogs."

"There's no sign of any, not in the fields, nor have I heard any." Osberht spoke confidently.

"Aye, that's as may be, but there will be dogs somewhere. Though I agree, if the stables are empty they won't be guarded. Mayhap they're complacent. Any road, that's why I brought what's left of that hare we caught yesterday. Some fresh meat might just buy us time."

The sun was continuing to fall. With the barns beginning to cast long shadows over the fields, Wealmaer decided it was time to move. He thumped Osberht on the shoulder enthusiastically. "Come on, another hundred feet down the slope and we'll be in dead ground. We won't be seen from the vill, and shadows from the shelters will hide us from pretty much anyone. If we're methodical we can drop the fence-rails without startling any horses."

As they ran down the slope Wealmaer realised, with a sickening jolt in his stomach, that they had mistimed their move. He called to Osberht as they reached the bottom. "We're nearly out of time. As we've come lower, see how much closer to the horizon the sun is. The lads down in the valley must be about to strike. From where they are the sun will have almost set."

Osberht understood instantly. "Just run in and topple the fence-rails as we go. We won't be seen, the light's almost gone."

As they reached the shelter they heard a shout from the far side of the barns, it was followed by a cacophony of barking, more shouts and neighing of horses. "There go the mills. This might work in our favour if the men from the vill rush down to help fight the fires. Take your time, Osberht. I'll clear away anything that might catch and spread the fire when you light the kindling." Wealmaer worked quickly, sweeping dry straw clear of the place where Osberht was taking flint, steel and fine dry kindling from a leather pouch and preparing to start a small fire with which to light the torch he would use to ignite the fire-arrows.

Wealmaer licked a finger and held it up to check the wind direction. He then pulled an arrow from the quiver on his shoulder, braced his legs, drew his bow and as he said, "Ready," Osberht held the torch to the tip of the arrow. Wealmaer waited for the shortest of moments and loosed the arrow into the darkening sky. It soared high, dipped quickly and fell in a steep trajectory, weighed down by the cumbersome mass of blazing wadding.

The men tracked the dart of light towards the barn furthest to their right. It fell just to the far side of the thatch and disappeared from sight.

"Skita!" Wealmaer muttered through pressed lips, aware that he had underestimated the speed of the wind over the high roofs. "Again." He warned Osberht as he drew his second arrow, "Now."

"Yes!" Osberht hissed expectantly, moments before the arrow sliced into the top of the far barn's roof beam. "Look! It's taken." They watched, relieved, as smoke began to rise from the thatch.

"I'll drop the next lower and to the left. The thatch will burn better from the eaves up, and it will hide the flames from those on yon side a while longer."

They worked quickly. Wealmaer moved his point of aim progressively to his left, lessening the tension in the bow as the distance to the barn roofs reduced, and placed two arrows into each roof.

"What about your last three?" Osberht asked, as the flames from the ninth arrow streaked into the last barn.

"I'll send them over the top and hope that they hit the barns beyond. Even if they strike the side they should still set the place alight." Wealmaer spoke calmly as he adjusted the aim and power of the bow to increase the arrow's range.

"Ye gods! Listen!" As the last arrow disappeared over the roof top, Osberht turned in surprise at the sound of horses squealing in panic. "They are either in the far barn or corralled outside it. Let's go."

"Torch this place first." Wealmaer gestured roofward with his eyes.

It was only as they turned to run that they noticed the commotion behind them. Horses ran in frantic circles within the fenced enclosures until one and then another, toppled the rails and trestles and bolted into the dark, whinnying in fright. Wealmaer placed a hand on Osberht's arm. "Walk, don't run. Give them time to clear. There'll be no reasoning with a spooked stallion. I'll scatter the meat behind us as we go. It could buy some time if dogs are sent out."

*****

With the waning moon now in its final quarter, Osberht decided to wait until its shining crescent rose early in the hours after midnight. Combined with the cold light of the stars it would give them enough to see by on their journey across the folds of the land, and back to the sanctuary of Ulueswater. They gave the garrison in the old stone fort at Brougham a wide berth, forded the River Lauder at Askum, headed north of the high ground of Heughscar and then, just as they reached the final crest before the descent to the lake shore at Pulhoue, the sun broke over the summit of Cross Fell. It lifted their spirits as well as warming their backs.

Osberht raised his hand to halt the column of men and ponies, turned in his saddle, and called back, "Take a break lads, if you've anything left in your saddle bags eat it now. There's no point in getting back to our Lady's hall in Glynrhedyn until the hearth fires have been lit. He swung down from the saddle, led his pony to drink from the lake, and then did likewise, scooping water with the palm of his hand.

Wealmaer joined him, and as the younger man stood up with water dripping from his chin, he held out his hand and said, "Speaking as your master-at-arms, and your friend, I have to say, well done. I know Lady Edie had some doubts, but you've proved to be in every way as good a commander as Bear, and Hravn before him. Your fostri-folk would have been rightly proud of you." Wealmaer referred to Godric and Ada, Ealdgith's house carls, both of whom had died at Sigulfson's hand.

Osberht grasped Wealmaer's hand, clenching it tightly as he strove to stop the water in his eyes becoming a tear. "Thanks, Wealmaer. That means a lot. I feel that at last they are in some way avenged."

Wealmaer turned and clasped Osberht's shoulder, "Come, whilst the men rest let us walk and talk about your fostri-folk. They were two of the bravest people I've known. This is a fitting time and place to remember them."

*****

"Osberht, Wealmaer! Where have you sprung from? I thought you were away singeing Sigulfson's beard"

Gytha's call surprised Osberht as he rounded the corner to the front of the hall, having finished helping his men tend to the ponies. "Hah! We're back from doing just that. Why, what have you heard?" He asked, wondering if news of their raids had somehow got back to Ealdgith.

"Good news travels fast, or mayhap bad news does too, depending on whose news it is." Gytha replied with a laugh. "That's why I'm here. I had a messenger yesterday. It was Aric's man, and he only uses him if it is a matter of the greatest urgency. He brought warning that Le Meschin is out for blood. Someone's been burning Sigulfson's mills and granaries, and he has sort Le Meschin's support in hunting them down. I wonder who that might be?" Gytha teased coyly, before adding seriously, "I came to warn Moder that there is a price on the head of anyone caught. Le Meschin has demanded that they be taken to him at Carleol. We all know what would happen there." She paused, and then asked with a note of uncertainty, "I'm glad your back. All safe, I hope?"

Osberht beamed proudly, thinking that was all the answer Gytha needed, whilst Wealmaer reassured her. "Aye, my Lady. There's none of us has even a scratch. But who is this with you?"

Gytha turned, and gestured for Rauði and Bjorn to step forward. "Sorry, I should have introduced you. Osberht and Wealmaer, Bear's captain and master-at-arms, meet Rauði and Bjorn. They are my new green men and companions, whilst Neven and Dai look to train new sections for me. Both are from Butremere, where Rauði is the Jarl's fostri."

Gytha continued gaily, noticing Osberht's jaw slowly drop in surprise. "She is my cousin too. It was only when we met Lord Walthoef that we discovered she is the daughter of our cousin Maldred. The rest of her family were slain, and their lands at Hestrskeith seized by Sigulfson some ten years ago."

"What?" Osberht exclaimed, as he stepped forward to take Rauði's hand in his. "Welcome Rauði! You're amongst friends here." Then, as he looked into her eyes, added softly, "Sigulfson killed my fostri-folk too. And now at last, after too many years, I've gone some way to avenging their loss, and mayhap yours too. Wealmaer and I torched the stables at Hestrskeith and scattered the bastard's breeding herd, just the night before last."

Gytha gave a whoop of glee as Rauði's stony-faced expression of uncertainty gave way slowly to a broad smile. "Come tell us all. Let's find food and ale for you both."

Haerfest 1101

Chapter 9

Ealdgith stood with Bear and Ulf, and turned to question a short wiry middle-aged man, whilst watching scenes of labour in the fields around Patrichesdalr. "Mungo, How long 'til the harvest's in here? Glynrhedyn's finished yesterday."

Her reeve answered in the slow, deep voice of one who always considers every aspect of a reply, "By t' week's end, m'Lady. Fields up at Hartsop will be t' last. They're more in t' shadow of t' fells, and t' barley ripens slower there."

"How much longer?" Bear asked, sounding frustrated.

"Mayhap ten days, Lord." Mungo replied. "It might be best to leave it t' those who are staying put t' harvest." He added, anticipating the next question.

"I agree." Ulf tapped the foot of his staff on the ground. His impatience was obvious. "We need the grain threshed, bagged and ready to go by the time Bear's back from Rengles. That'll be a week from today.

Ealdgith came to a decision. "Ulf, Mungo, put everyone we've got onto harvesting what's here and getting it threshed and under cover by sun-fall tomorrow." She cast her eyes upward. "By the look of yon clouds, we'll have rain the day after. There's no point in lugging damp grain to Borgarárdalr. Once Bear's sold the last of our lead, we'll depart with what grain we've got. Anyway, those who are staying deserve their fair share of the harvest too."

Bear pulled a face and grumbled, whilst nodding in agreement. "Aye, it looks like a wet end to Æfteraliða, and a wet trip to Rengles. Anyhow, I'll be off at first light tomorrow, and will just take Osberht and the one section. The others are yours, Ulf, to help with the harvest." He took his leave and walked back up the hill to the hall and stables. It would be a long journey. Twenty-five leagues over three high mountain passes would take its toll on the laden pack ponies; not to mention the toll the weather could take on all of them.

*****

The sun's early rays had yet to penetrate the gloom of the valley-head south of Patrichesdalr. Bear was already mounted at the head of the column and signalled for the lead jagger to move on. The score of pack ponies, with a jagger riding alongside every fourth animal, began its slow grind up the semi-paved road from Patrichesdalr, over the pass called Kirkstein, and then the steep descent to the old town of Ameleseta.

Bear sent Osberht ahead. Later, having rested the ponies at the summit and begun the steep slow descent, he saw Osberht urging his pony up the track towards him. He gestured for the leading jagger to stop and told Ranald to wait with the long line of lead-laden ponies, before galloping down to join Osberht. The younger man saw him coming and waited, glad of the brief rest.

"Grimr's given the all clear, for tonight anyway." Osberht called to Bear as he rode up alongside. Bear could tell from Osberht's expression that he had more to tell.

"And?"

"Men-at-arms were there two days ago. They ordered him to ready space for six of them to live at the ale house. He expects them back within the week."

"Ye gods!" Bear cursed. "It's what I feared, but at least we are good for now. Did he say whose men they were? ...No matter." He added, seeing Osberht shake his head. He turned, gestured to Ranald and waved the column of ponies forward.

The sun was dipping towards the western fells as they reached the clustered cottages of Ameleseta and threaded their way through the narrow streets and alleys towards the old fort by the lakeshore. To their right, as they crossed the water meadows on their final leg, were the old quarries from which stone for the fort had been hewn.

Leaving Ranald's section and the jaggers to water, feed and pen the ponies, Bear took Osberht to the ale house. It was in an old, stone-walled Roman building on the edge of the vill, its tiled roof long since replaced with thick slabs of turf. Bear coughed and blinked as the acrid smoke of a blazing fire in the hearth stung his eyes. It always did, but at least the flames lit the large, otherwise windowless, room. They chose to sit at an aged ale-stained table as far from the fire as possible, and were quickly joined by a pot-bellied man with an unkempt beard and long, greasy, greying hair. Before he sat, he clasped Bear on the shoulder by way of greeting. Moments later a thin, wispy-haired, serving girl set two cups of ale in front of them. Osberht drank his quickly whilst Bear spoke.

"Thanks for the warning, Grimr. I fear this will be the last time I jagger lead through Ameleseta."

"Aye, Lord, it's come about much the way you warned it would." Grimr spoke in a thick Gallo-Norse accent. "You'll still need my services though?"

"Of course, even more so. I'll have a man stop by every month. He'll see you right." Bear referred to Grimr's role as an informant. "So, whose men are you going to be putting up?"

Grimr frowned. "I'm not sure. They weren't forthcoming, but I'd say they were Lord Orm's. Their accents were local, so they weren't Norman or mercenaries."

"I think you're right." Bear agreed." Ketel and his sons, William and Orm, are in a difficult position, torn between loyalty to their people, our family and having to prove loyalty to Le Meschin and the King. You should be alright with them, but beware of any of Le Meschin's men who might be with them."

"Or Sigulfson's." Osberht chipped in. "Although we hope that William and Ketel can keep hold of the

Ulueswater lands, Sigulfson's men are going to be in there overseeing mining sooner than later."

Bear downed his ale in a long swig and placed more coins than needed on the table as he stood to take his leave. "Thanks again Grimr," he said, holding out his hand, "until next we meet."

*****

Their second day was a long, slow grind over one high pass and then another, with the night spent in the shelter of a dilapidated fort on a high plateau just beyond the summit of the second pass. The next morning's descent to the coast was easy and uneventful, with the rocky moorland giving way to woods and then strips of fields, some of which were being harvested frantically in a bid to gather the crops ahead of rain that threatened to fall at any time. They kept a close eye on the land to the south, across the valley of the Esk, but saw nothing. Bear was cautious. These lands, which had long been something of a Norman backwater, were now under the control of Black William. He hoped that the younger Le Meschin brother had yet to stamp his authority upon the little harbour of Rengles. It was the only option open to them until he could speak to Aidan, his shipping agent, and arrange for their lead to be sold through Wirkynton.

Bear paused on the approach to Rengles, straining to see more of what was happening in the port. It was tucked close by the shore of a wide enclosed bay from which the sea drained completely at low water. The harbour was natural, not man-made, and it was always busy. Two large tub-like boats that Bear recognised as knörrs were getting under way to catch the ebb tide, as a third nosed its way in with wind in its sail. The place looked dark and uninviting in the gloomy sunless morning light. A series of low jetties stretched into the water and were connected above the high-water line by a hard-packed earth track, bordered on the landward side by a series of large stone buildings. These were warehouses that Bear surmised had been built by the long-gone Romans.

Bear and Osberht left Ranald to command the column of ponies and rode briskly to the waterfront. Bear showed a confidence that he certainly didn't feel, as he scanned the way ahead for any sign of men-at-arms. The smell of the Rengles waterfront always intrigued him. Salt water, seaweed, rotting fish and wet sand combined into an exotic aroma that excited his nose; it was so unlike the cloying, throat-gagging smell of which the city port of Carleol reeked.

Approaching the warehouses, he spotted a plump, black-bearded, balding man in a dark green tunic who was in heavy conversation with two more plainly dressed figures. He and Osberht hung back and waited for Aidan to finish. The agent spotted them, dismissed the men quickly and, raising his hand in welcome, strode across to Bear and embraced him warmly, before giving Sköll a welcoming scratch behind his ears.

"Where are your ponies?" Aidan enquired, surprised that Bear wasn't with his jagger train.

"Waiting out of sight, just yon side of the vill. I wanted to be sure that Le Meschin's men weren't here." Bear replied, now feeling more confident that their way was clear.

Aidan's dark brows narrowed in a frown. "You were as well to. It's safe at the moment, but the young Le Meschin is tightening his grip all along this coast. His men are here at least weekly, checking what we're shipping. He's upping his taxes too, which I'm trying to get around," he added, with a knowing look at both men.

"Is it still safe for you to handle our lead?" Bear asked urgently.

"Of course, of course." Aidan reassured him quickly, with a flap of his hands. "If you can get it down here now, I can get it aboard that knörr." He pointed to a vessel dropping its sail as it swung alongside a jetty. "She's back to Mann on the next tide. As soon as she's empty I'll get the lead aboard and into the bottom of her hold."

Bear grinned with relief, and turned to see that Osberht was already remounting his pony. "I'll have them down here within the hour," he called over his shoulder.

"We've urgent business, cousin. Do you have time to talk?" Bear used the term 'cousin' warmly, referring to the link between Aidan's father-in-law and his own family.

"Yes, I thought we might. Let's go inside, away from any unwelcome eyes. I'm afraid that nowhere is quite the same these days."

Aidan listened with growing concern whilst Bear explained how Ealdgith had been outplayed and the family forced from their lands. He waited without interrupting until Bear had finished.

"Yes, yes, Wirkynton will be excellent," he said at last, "I have an agent there. But given what you say, I may well have to move there myself, we'll see. Now you mention it, Walthoef must be kin to my wife too, and I would rather pay tax to him than an upstart Norman bastard too full of his own skita." Bear laughed; Aidan's language normally wasn't at all coarse.

They both looked up at a sudden noise outside. The ponies were arriving just as the first heavy drops of rain fell, bouncing off the hard earth, quickly turning the dust to mud.

"Get your men to unload at the foot of the knörr's jetty. The sooner the lead is out of sight, the better. Tell me how many pigs of it there are, I'll sort out payment and you can be on your way. It's not a day I'd want to be up on the fells, so good luck to you." He held out his beringed hand, "Send word through my man in Wirkynton. I'll meet you there, next time. Oh, and be sure to give my regards to your moder and sister."

*****

Bear ducked under the low edge of one of the shelters in the old fort and breathed deeply, glad to be

100

clear of the cloying wood smoke inside. Fires weren't needed for warmth in the heavy humid air, but heat to dry their rain sodden clothes was. The view wasn't what he had expected. Instead of the broad expanse of the Manx Sea and the distant fells of the Isle of Mann he was faced with a dull grey wall of mist and the shapeless forms of barely visible crags. He breathed in again, stretched and ducked back inside to rouse Osberht and send him to gather the men. They could stop and breakfast once they were over the top of the pass and down out of the damp clouds; but at least the rain had passed.

The ponies' iron shod hooves slipped and skidded on the wet moss covered rock of the old stone road as they wound their way down from Hard Knott and across the flat land of Wrynose Bottom. "At least they're not laden," Osberht quipped as he rode alongside Bear, "We'll need to take care that we don't lose any when we make the move to Borgarárdalr. That's going to be hard going in places, and they'll have a lot to carry."

"Aye, I was thinking the same. I'd rather make more trips and carry less. We can't risk more than a couple going lame."

They fell silent as the ground steepened again and the long line of beasts wound its way up the next pass through a countless series of zig-zag bends around towering buttresses of rock. The clouds lifted slowly, staying just above their heads until they finally reached the summit.

"Phew! I'm glad that's done." Osberht sighed with relief, surprised that he felt almost as exhausted as his pony. "But what a view!"

"Aye," Bear agreed. He was always impressed, not least because the descent was to be their last. It was then largely flat all the way to Ameleseta.

"Do you plan to stop in the town?" Osberht was conscious that Bear had not suggested otherwise in view of Grimr's warning.

Bear gave him a secretive smile. "Mayhap. It would be easier for us. The alternative route over to Gressemere, up Dynfal's Raise and over the pass to

Gríssdalr and its tarn is even more of a grind than Kirkstein. I asked Grimr to send warning if the men-at-arms are back. Even if they are Orm's men, I can't take the risk, I don't want to compromise his loyalty."

Their pace picked up on the long straight descent into Langdalr. Less than a league later Bear called across to Osberht and pointed to a terraced mound off to their left. "That is the Ting Moot where our Norse forebears met whenever they had a problem to share. They'd call a meeting the same as we'd call a Folkmoot. I'm minded that we will need to use it again before long. Once Moder's secure at Borgarárdalr, I want her to call the people of these southern dales together and warm them of what is to come."

Osberht understood Bear's intention immediately. "I'm not sure that we could help them much, but they could certainly forewarn us if Le Meschin masses men to make a move north."

Bear gave Osberht and appraising look before replying, "You read my mind, young captain, and we could train them to hold these passes for themselves."

Osberht glanced around at the lay of the fells. "Aye, and I can see why that Ting Moot is here. It's a natural meeting of the valleys and the ways through them. But who's that?" he exclaimed, pointing to a nondescript looking man sitting on a boulder beside the road ahead.

"Hel! I fear that Wyrd is against us. I think that might be Grimr's man, and that his news won't be good." Bear replied with a sigh, urging Óðr into a brisk canter.

Bear's suspicions proved to be correct and, after a quick estimate of how much daylight remained, he turned northward over a low pass to Heltewatra, and then over a second to the southern shore of Gressemere in search of a rudimentary campsite.

*****

Leaden clouds still hung low over the fells, hiding their tops and confining the world below into a grey two-dimensional gloom. After a final push over the steep hause above Gríssdalr the weary ponies, and equally weary men, descended for their final haul down the long valley to reach Patrichesdalr just as the light began to fade.

Approaching the hall, Bear rode up alongside Osberht and, forcing a tired grin, said, "Well, I suppose that could have been worse. Take charge of the lads in getting the ponies fed and watered. I'll ask Eir to get the cooks on the go. We can report to Moder in the morning." He dismounted stiffly, passed the reins to a stable lad, and gave a long stretch before walking around to the front of the building. Skoll followed at his heels, keen to find food, water, and a place by the hearth.

"Bear!" Gytha exclaimed in surprise. "We thought that mayhap you'd been delayed and would be back on the morrow." After a brief embrace, she stepped back and give him a quizzical look. "You look done in. Is anything up?"

"No, just the weather, Normans and too many passes." He slumped onto a bench. "Ye gods! That saddle kills my back at times."

Gytha clapped her hands to attract the attention of a group of their men squatting by the hearth. "Fetch your lord a cup of ale and ask Eir to join us. She turned back to Bear with a quizzical look and sat beside him. "Normans? Does that bode ill?"

Bear breathed out deeply and shook his head. "No, it's much as we expected. Orm now has men at Ameleseta, and Black William is tightening his grip on Rengles. It's as well we went when we did."

"What about the lead?" Gytha was thinking about future shipments.

"We got it straight onto a knörr bound for Mann and cleared out just as the heavens opened...oh, sorry, yes I see what you mean," Bear saw that he had misunderstood, "Yes, Wirkynton works well for Aidan. I have the name of his man, and Aidan himself will meet our first shipment through there. He sends you his greeting too, by the way."

"Oh, thanks." Gytha's lips twitched in a faint smile, she sensed Aidan had a fondness for her.

"Anyway, what has brought you across here? Er, thanks." Bear asked Gytha, just as one of the men offered him a cup of ale.

Gytha beamed proudly. "To tell you that your new vill is ready for families to start moving in as soon as you can move them from here."

"What? Well done little sister, and well done Leo and Agnaar." Bear patted Gytha's knee appreciatively with his free hand. "That's quicker than I had hoped. I left Ulf readying everything. We'll see him in the morn, but I'd say within days."

"Good, they need to know that it will be a long, hard journey. On foot and with ponies to lead, it will take most of the day light we have. It must be eight leagues, and there's Sticks Pass and The Pewits to go over." Gytha cautioned him with a series look.

"Don't I know it," Bear sighed, "but it has to be done, and I agree that it has to be done in a day."

"Once we know the day you plan for the first group, Leo will arrange for welcoming fires and food at the new vill on the evening they arrive. After that we'll provide the food and those at the vill can prepare it. And...." Gytha forestalled Bear's thanks, "I've restructured and expanded my sections. The first two that are fully trained will be keeping Wythburndalr secure. You won't see them when you come through as I'll have them guarding Dynfal's Raise and the narrows in the Vale of Saint John. The beck that runs from there to Trellekell is close to our border with Sigulfson. Hopefully he's still away chasing Osberht's shadow, but I won't take the risk of any more intrusions like the one at Kesewic."

Bear chortled, attracting attention from around the hall, but it was the look of pride in his eyes that was all Gytha needed to see. "It'll be a swift fly that can land on you, little sister."

Gytha shared Bear's joke, warmed by his praise, and stood to leave. "Here's Eir with food. I'll go back to Moder's hall and tell her you're home safe. See you in the morning."

Chapter 10

Ealdgith rose early. The constant pressing pain in her chest, combined with the heavy muggy night air, hampered her sleep. Hers was a world in limbo: neither awake nor asleep, her thoughts racked by dark worries. When light filtered in from the open shutters of her window, she dressed, wrapped her cloak around her shoulders, pulled back the thick drapes screening her room from the hall and slipped quietly out of the back entrance with Hati at her side. She walked purposefully up onto the little knoll overlooking the two halls and sat on a mossy boulder, feeling worryingly out of breath as she looked down onto the still-quiet buildings and the lake beyond. The low clouds looming just above the fell tops brought an early gloom to the day, matching her mood. Ealdgith hugged the cloak around her more for comfort than warmth, and wondered what to do. She had to talk to someone, but who? It couldn't be Gytha, not yet, she wasn't ready for the questions that she knew her daughter would ask; that was why she had left the hall early, before Gytha rose. She knew too that Gytha and Bear would soon be looking for her, expecting her to take a lead in decision-making. But as she had already tried to tell them, those decisions were now theirs to take. It was better that they accepted her absence and told her later what they had decided.

The buildings below came slowly to life. She watched Bear walk onto the paving in front of his porch, pause briefly to enjoy the fresh air and lake view, as she knew he would, and then walk briskly around to her hall. Her decision made, Ealdgith stood and walked with a lighter heart to the door at the back of Bear's hall, and called "Eir. Are you about?"

Eir had been increasingly worried that her mother-in-law was ill. Ealdgith's pallid face and dark rimmed eyes confirmed her suspicions, but she knew that Ealdgith wouldn't welcome too much sympathy. She pulled aside a drape and ushered Ealdgith into her private space, saying, "Come, Bear is away to your hall to talk to you, so I know he won't disturb us here."

Ealdgith sat on a large oak clothes chest. Eir sat next to her and took her mother-in-law's hands in hers. She waited for Ealdgith to speak, before breaking the silence: "We'll be quite private here, but if you'd prefer to walk down to the lake we..."

Ealdgith interrupted. "No, here is fine. I...I need to talk. There's no one else who can understand."

Eir replied softly, "You know I'm here Edie. I know too you've been hiding that you aren't well. I've seen it for a while. But it was you who trained me to be a wise-woman. You'll know better than me what ails you."

Ealdgith wheezed slightly as she took a deep breath to speak. Eir knew before the words were spoken that Ealdgith feared she was dying. "I have no name for it, but I have seen it before: Ingra at the dairy at Crosebi, then Gorm the miner, you might remember him." Eir could see that Ealdgith was searching for the right words. "It was just the same. They felt pressure in the chest, a shortness of breath and wheezing when speaking. Just as I have. Then came coughing, blood in their spittle, lethargy, getting thinner..."

"I know Edie, I remember. I remember too how you tried, and what came next." Eir squeezed Ealdgith's fingers and sat in silence, their eyes locked together, until Eir spoke. "But there are things we can do to ease the pain when it comes, and it could be a long time yet. It's because you know the signs that you know what is to happen. Others don't, and live in ignorance."

Ealdgith nodded, accepting Eir's advice, "You're right, of course, and there is much that I can't do for myself that you can do for me."

"Yes, I can start by testing the colour and taste of your urine to check the balance of the humours. Mayhap a little bloodletting too, but only a little of course, we don't want to weaken you. Use of hot cups might be best." Eir spoke encouragingly, hoping she sounded more optimistic than she felt.

"It would certainly help if you could bind a hot poultice to my tummy, to draw out bad humours. Mayhap infusions of mint and nettle, and chamomile too?" Ealdgith paused, suddenly concerned, "Our herb garden! We must take it with us. There will be no one remaining here that can use it, and we will need all we have."

Eir's soft smile in reply reassured Ealdgith. "Worry not. I have taken all the seeds I can, and as we speak Revna is carefully packing the plants into sacks. She will be with you when you leave in a few days' time. And tell Adelind what you've told me. She'll understand and help you until I come with Bear." She squeezed Ealdgith's hand again. "Now, Edie, it is important that you aren't stressed. You do know that? It's more important than ever that you leave matters to Bear and Gytha, Ulf and me too."

Ealdgith sighed in agreement. "Yes but...but, I can't tell them, not yet. I can't answer the questions I know they will ask."

"But I can." Eir's voice was firm. "Let me speak for you. Then they can come to you in their own time. I'll do it now. Stay here whilst I go to your hall."

*****

Eir stood with Gytha, Bear and Ulf to one side of the flagstones outside Ealdgith's hall, and away from the bustle of morning routine. She put her arm around her husband's waist. His shock was obvious. Gytha looked from Eir to Ulf, and as if speaking to herself said, "I knew Moder wasn't right, but I didn't dare ask."

"Nor me," Ulf said, striving to stop his voice breaking whilst putting his good arm around Gytha. "Nor me."

"Gytha!" Bjorn's urgent shout carried from the lakeshore. They turned in surprise. Bjorn was running towards the hall, whilst Rauði was with a small group of people and ponies on the shore-side track.

Gytha looked quickly at her brother. "Go and see Moder, I'll see what's up."

"Go on," Eir agreed. "I want to talk to Fader by himself." As she turned to Ulf, Gytha ran down to join Bjorn.

He waited for her and then spoke so swiftly that Gytha held her hand up to stop him gabbling. "Three men and a woman, they just rode in from Haugr-tun, but they've come from Richemund, or so they say. The men were men-at-arms serving the Normans, until they fled."

Gytha glanced quickly at the group around Rauði. "Fetch Ulf," she ordered brusquely, and strode purposefully towards the track. Her mind was still on the news of her mother and the last thing she wanted was strangers in their midst.

The three men had an unkempt but soldierly appearance. One, in his mid-twenties and of average height, had the bearing of someone used to taking charge. The other two, though obviously healthy, seemed somewhat younger and more reserved. The fourth person, a very petite young woman with sharp features, was in animated conversation with Rauði.

Gytha was about to speak loudly to attract attention when the man pulled himself to attention, touched the knuckles of his right hand to the side of his head, and stilled the group in an authoritative voice, "Lady Gytha, we're here to join your service...if you will have us, that is?"

Gytha, although slightly taken aback, was impressed by his respectful self-confidence. She said with a smile, "I see that Rauði has made my introductions for me. Now, who are you and why are you here. And more importantly, how do you know we are here?"

The man relaxed, but still stood respectfully. "I'm known as Eadulf Cudel, or more usually, just Cudel."

Rauði burst into a giggle, and in so doing earned a sharp glance from Gytha, who couldn't help but smile herself.

"And just why are you called cuttlefish?" Gytha asked, amused.

Cudel gave a self-deprecating look. "Now that's a long tale, and one that does me few favours." With a sheepish grin, he added, "A surfeit of cudel might have had something to do with it."

"Ah," Gytha replied, surmising the reason, "and these others?"

"My Lady, the ugly one is Wulfric, the love-struck one is Eadwig, and the object of his love is Aelf. Aelf is, well, Aelf." Cudel pointed to each in turn.

Gytha understood at once Cudel's comment about Aelf. Her pixie-like face, hazel eyes and braided brown hair spoke for themselves. Gytha thought that the young woman would have no difficulty standing up for herself.

"But why we're here will take longer to tell." Gytha inferred from Cudel's tone that perhaps he could tell her in the comfort of her hall.

She glanced up at the sun, smiled, and said, "The sun's still low, we have all day. The sooner you start..." Gytha left the rest unsaid.

Cudel gave a shrug, "The three of us are, or were, lowly sergeants serving Count Stephen of Richemund. He's started to employ English as well as Bretton foot soldiers. I was in charge of these two and we manned a perrièr, a sort of catapult, on the walls. Our boss was Lagu, a senior sergeant and a Bretton. Back in Lencten we were testing the range of different stone balls, using the perrièr to fling them across the Swale onto the tilting field. When we had finished, we took a pony apiece and rode down to collect them, packing them into panniers. We'd seen a couple of women washing clothes on the rocks by the falls, but hadn't thought anything of it. Then we noticed Lagu wasn't around. We were about to ride back without him when we heard a short, choked off scream."

Gytha noticed Cudel glance apologetically towards Aelf. She was looking at her feet, red-faced, whilst Eadwig grasped her hand in his. Gytha feared she knew what Cudel would say next, but let him continue.

"Sorry Aelf, but Lady Gytha needs to know. The women had gone from the falls, when we saw Lagu lying on the ground. Someone seemed to be struggling under him. We ran through the river, Eadwig was in the lead and he had one of the small round stones we'd been flinging in his hand..." Cudel's account was interrupted by Eadwig's soft slow voice. It was the first Gytha had heard him speak.

"I didn't know who Lagu was on top of, but I knew what he was doing. He was like that. He was scum. I paused when I got to the top of the river bank and hurled the stone at his back. It...it cracked the back of his skull."

Aelf looked up sharply. Her jaw was firm and her face now flushed with anger as she relived the moment. "But you didn't kill him. I already had. I've learned to keep a knife tucked down the side of my boot, under my skirts. That bastard wasn't the first to think he could...well, anyway, as he came for me and forced me down I grabbed the knife and stuck his guts with it." She looked at Gytha is if she was afraid she would still be judged. "I had to. I was trying to get from under him when Eadwig's rock hit him."

"And you were right to defend yourself, Aelf. It's what I teach all my women to do." Gytha looked into Aelf's eyes as she spoke. Her soft tone surprised and reassured Aelf.

Gytha realised what the dark faded patches on Aelf's skirts were, but she didn't want to be side-tracked. "Then what? And what of the woman with you?" Although the question was about Aelf, Gytha addressed it to Cudel.

"Eneda, as we called her, was hiding. We fled together, hoping that we had been too close to the bottom of the castle walls to have been seen. Aelf's skirts were soaked in blood. What justice would we have had from a Norman court? Killing a senior sergens would have seen us all hanged. We emptied the panniers and rode the ponies straight up the river track to Rie; Aelf and Edena sharing Lagu's mount."

"Were you followed?" Rauði couldn't help interrupting.

"Mayhap, but we didn't stop. That dale is a good dozen leagues long. Each vill we passed through was smaller and poorer than the last, until finally we came to Kelda, just as the light faded and with the ponies in a state of collapse. We had never heard about the upper dale, and we hoped the castle's garrison hadn't either, so we asked for help. They warned us that men-at-arms did come, but infrequently."

"And did you get any help?" Ulf's gruff demand surprised them all. Gytha hadn't realised that he was behind her. "Sorry Gytha, I didn't want to interrupt their tale, but if they can tell me about Kelda I'll know they are genuine. Richemund's too close to our troubles of the past for us to take this at face value." Catching the shock and disappointment on the four faces he added. "I'm our Lady Ealdgith's master-at-arms, and Richemund, as you call it, was once her family's manor. If you know Normans, you will be able to guess why we are here and not there. Now, did you stay long at Kelda?"

"We stayed and helped with their harvest, by way of payment, but a couple of weeks ago the castle's reeve came with men-at-arms. Not for us, but to collect his tax. We weren't recognised, but we couldn't stay." Cudel sounded deflated, his confidence shaken by Ulf's challenge.

"So, you would know the headman?"

"Áki, yes."

Ulf frowned, and then remembering his own age, asked instead: "Did Áki mention his father?

Cudel shook his head, beginning to worry. "No, his father died some while past. His mother's still alive, just. Eneda became close to her. Agata was her name, though she was as old as the fells."

Ulf guffawed loudly. "Old! She's my age! He stepped forward with his good hand outstretched. "That's good enough for me. Welcome, all of you. I'm glad the folk of Kelda showed you the hospitality they once showed Lady Ealdgith's family. Before your time, Gytha lass." He added as an aside.

Ulf took charge of the questions. "Before we go up to the hall, tell me how you come to be here?"

"It was Agata. She told us of people who had fled from the Normans in the past, settled around Mallerstang, then been forced to flee again into the safety of the fells west of Hep. We were warned that there is a castle at Mallerstang, and that somehow we would have to get past it."

Ulf grunted. "Is there a castle now? That's no surprise, but it would be a problem I've no doubt. Go on."

"It was a problem," Cudel glanced at the others, "that's where we lost Eneda. We were in a wood at the bottom of some cliffs, trying to skirt around the vill, when we saw the castle through the trees. It's a wooden one, on a low mound, and was on our side of a river. We knew we would be seen if we went further, so we back tracked to a cave we had passed. Edena and Aelf hid there, whilst we rode back aways to try and find a way over the river further up from the vill."

"I told her not to leave the cave," Aelf interrupted, "but she insisted. Edena went to fill our water sacks from a spring. She said we would need them when the men returned. It was moments later that I heard her scream, and men's voices outside. I scrambled into the dark at the back of the cave just as one of them looked in, but he couldn't see me. I could hear Edena sobbing, then a loud slap. She went quiet after that and the men rode off. I waited and waited, before crawling out. The water sacks were on the ground, but Edena had gone. They must have taken her to the castle."

"That's when we came back." Cudel continued. "We rode like the hounds of Hel itself were behind us, perhaps they were. It was a couple of leagues before we crossed the river into the fells. The next day we rode to the top of one and worked out a way to go, crossing the old stone road then following around the bottom of the fells to the lake. Our first food for days was at Haugr-tun yesterday. The people there told us how to get here."

Cudel fell silent. Gytha, momentarily lost for words, felt overwhelming empathy for the foursome, and then she spoke. "Welcome to my service. I'm glad you came, we have an urgent need for men-at-arms, don't we Ulf. Aelf, please join my household. But...," Gytha held up her hands to stop the cries of thanks, "the Normans are pressing us everywhere. My hall is well beyond the fells behind us and my moder and brother are soon to leave here to join me there. Come, I'll introduce you to them, and find you food in my moder's hall."

Gytha was about to turn towards the hall when Rauði interrupted, "Gytha, it looks like you're needed there anyway. Something's up."

As she spoke, Neven came running towards them down the slope from the hall. "Neven's my huscarle," she explained quickly, "but she should be ten leagues away in Borgarárdalr." As she spoke she noticed the expressions on Cudel and Aelf's faces. Both seemed fascinated by the woman running towards them: Cudel, perhaps by the woman herself, whereas Aelf by the woman's clothes, sword and the authority they inferred in a man's world.

Neven slowed to regain her composure whilst pulling a parchment scroll from inside her tunic. "Gytha," she panted, "Aric arrived last night, with this from Ligulf. I'd just got back from seeing the Jarl. He'd summoned me to warn that Black William's men have imposed his will in Ennerdalr. They rounded up the people from the farms there, many of whom were the Jarl's men albeit they didn't farm on his land, and only freed them after they handed over half their newly gathered harvest in lieu of tax. They didn't encroach onto Lord Walthoef's land. Aric said his master insisted this letter must reach you immediately. Mayhap it's related to Black William's actions."

Gytha 's expression froze as she listened to Neven. Slitting the seal with her thumb nail she read the message quickly, oblivious to the look of awe on the faces of the people around her. Of those there, only Neven and Ulf had ever seen anyone read.

"Ye gods! It's worse." Gytha exclaimed, her face flushing with sudden anger. "Le Meschin is summoning all the Cumbric lords to Carleol. They are to be ordered to impose the King's will and taxes across all their lands."

"It seems that his brother has already started. But it means there's an urgency to get the folk from here across the Wythburndalr valley before Sigulfson interferes." Ulf understood the immediate implications of the order.

"Indeed." Gytha said curtly. "You and I need to find Bear and Moder immediately. Rauði, take everyone up to the hall for food, then take them to the stables. Their ponies will need attending to. Cudel, you'll all leave with me at first light tomorrow. Be ready."

Neven stayed with Rauði and deliberately walked close alongside Cudel as they went up to the hall.

*****

Ulf stood in front of the hearth fire in Ealdgith's hall, enjoying a cup of ale with the new men-at-arms, whilst Aelf listened with wide-eyed enthusiasm to Rauði's tales of the green women.

Neven hovered close by, standing so that she could catch Cudel's eye. Giving his excuses to Ulf, he followed Neven to the door. Ulf, watching, saw Neven turn and smile over her shoulder, locking eyes with Cudel and ensuring that he was following. Neven waited in the shadows outside the hall, then leaning forward, quickly took Cudel's hand in hers and led him into the night.

Ulf was at the stables early the next morning. As the men-at-arms arrived he pointed to Cudel and said quietly, "A word, lad." He led Cudel to one side and warned him in a firm, but brotherly way: "You strike me as a good soldier, Cudel, but remember that you serve Lady Gytha, as does Neven. I've never seen her take to a man before, not like she did to you last night."

Cudel's jaw dropped.

"Aye lad, I saw, but I doubt others did. Keep it that way, be discrete. Neven's a tough lass, but I won't see her hurt. If you want her as much as she seems to want you, then you must commit to her. And remember, her first loyalty is to her mistress, as is yours now. Understood?" Ulf raised an eyebrow.

"Aye sir...and thank you." Cudel replied respectfully, grateful for Ulf's understanding.

Ulf clapped Cudel on his shoulder. "Good lad, I want us to work together. I'll join you in Borgarárdalr in a couple of days and I'll need your advice on catapults."

115

Chapter 11

"Kraa! Kraa!" Ealdgith flinched as a giant night-black raven swooshed over her. She felt the movement of air around her head and the fleeting touch of its feet on her hair. It then hovered just in front of her, moving forward slowly, keeping pace with the laboured plod of her pony as it climbed the steep track up Stybarrow Dodd towards the pass that would lead her down to Wythburndalr. Suddenly, it flexed its primary feathers and, with a twitch of its tail, soared and turned, dived down once more and then flew on ahead, rising effortlessly above the fellside and west towards Borgarárdalr. Ealdgith smiled, recognising the black-eyed bird as a symbol of Hravn's presence and his approval of her journey. It helped ease the sorrow of her departure. With one last backward glance at the fast disappearing lake she urged her pony to the summit and beyond.

Gytha sat astride her pony on top of High Seat, the peak that dominated the high ground between Borgarárdalr and Wythburndalr. By screwing up her eyes and screening them with her hands she could just discern a long blur of movement on Helvellyn's distant flank over a league away. She knew it heralded the arrival of the families from Glynrhedyn and she waited until the first ponies came into view on the fellside below, then rode down to join her mother as she crossed The Pewits' pass and made the steep descent to Watendlath. They spoke little. Gytha could see that her mother was finding the journey emotionally and physically hard. After a while she sidled her pony close to Ealdgith and said, "Moder, I have to leave you with Rauði and go back to check on those walking. You understand, don't you?"

Ealdgith forced a tired smile. "Of course, you've spent too long with me already. Go, lead them home, as I would once have done."

*****

It was late in the month of Weodmonath before the last of the three migrations was complete. Gytha daily thanked The One God, and all the old gods, for their intervention in keeping the weather neither wet nor too hot, and for a lack of Norman interest in the Wythburndalr valley.

Ealdgith settled quickly into the hall on the crag and took the upheaval in her life as the opportunity to step back from daily decision making. The hall, and the crag-top solitude that it offered, became her sanctuary. With Adelind's help she established a daily routine of treatment, and found that it helped ease the pain and her breathing. Although, upon reflection in quiet moments at night, she realised that more than anything it was her new role as tutor to Brynhildr that gave her most peace of mind.

Ulf, too, found a renewed purpose in life. But rather than stepping back from active involvement in affairs he threw himself into planning the crag's defence. Gytha welcomed his enthusiasm. She had yet to agree defined responsibilities with Bear and for the present was happy for her brother to focus on his new hall and vill. He was thankful for this, and appreciative when she paired Bear's sections with her own so that his men could quickly come to terms with the more challenging geography and patrol routes of the central fells.

Early one morning, as the month drew to a close and the days were beginning to become noticeably shorter, Ulf went to choose a site for the catapult that he was sure was the key to defending the crag and the communities clustered around it. He found Gytha seated on the crag's ledge, lost in thought. "Now then, Gytha lass, shall I tell you what I think we should do up here?"

She turned and smiled, not having heard him approach. "You could, Fader. I've seen you in deep conversation with Cudel so many times that I'm sure you have a plan; or were you simply warning him off about Neven again?" She added, knowingly.

Ulf chuckled, and Gytha could tell from the glint in his eyes that the couple's affair amused him. "Good luck to them both. It's high time Neven found a man. She can't be bound to you forever, you do know that?" Ulf was suddenly serious.

Gytha surprised Ulf by agreeing. "I was thinking the same. I'm glad for her. There's a rough-edged cheekiness about Cudel that seems to appeal to her. They're well matched and he's not awed, as many men are, by her skill at arms. Actually, I think that is what attracts her to him. I'm fine with Rauði. She's capable enough, and now that she is kin and a friend, I want to keep her close. She's good to have around, and Bjorn is too."

"Aye, and you know he's scared stiff of upsetting you and losing her." Ulf was still looking amused. "... to be young again." He said wistfully.

"It's as well he is wary," Gytha said lightly. "We can do without amorous accidents for the time being. Anyway, Ulf, tell me what you have in mind up here. It's where I escape to think, you know. I must keep the solitude it gives me."

"Um." Ulf put on such a show of looking crestfallen that Gytha couldn't help but laugh.

"You're good to tease, Ulf. There are plenty of other quiet spots I use, but this is the best of them. No matter, tell me."

Ulf was enthusiastic. "Young Cudel has a bright head on him. That perrièr that he was in charge of at Richemund was set up in a spot similar to this, high up on top of crags from where it commanded the land below. Do you remember the mangonel, and how it was a bugger to set up, and how it kicked like a mule when the brake was released?"

Gytha nodded. She had watched Bear and Agnaar practicing with it. "Yes...and that great skein of rope wound round and round to create the tension. I remember once when it broke..." She could see from Ulf's expression that he had something much better in mind. "Go on."

"The mangonel is a bugger to make, and hard to move once it's in position. It has a lot of power though, and is just the thing to use to smash through a stone wall or to lob a boulder into a boat. Cudel says the perrièr is different. Instead of a skein of rope, it uses the weight of a team of hefty men, each holding a rope. They jump down and pull at the same time. That swings the arm holding the rock upward, and away it goes. It might not have the power of the mangonel, but we don't need that. We just need to get rocks up into the air, their weight and height above the ground will do the rest."

Gytha's eyes gleamed with enthusiasm. "I'm guessing that without the need for the skein it's easier to make and lighter to move?"

"Cudel assures me it is."

"Where would you place it? There's a wide arc to cover and from what I recall about the mangonel, it's hard to move."

Gytha could see Ulf's wide grin through his thick beard. "That's the beauty of the perrièr. The beam sits atop a rotating post held in place by the frame. It could turn it a full circle if needs be. But you're right about the wide arc that we have. Look, I'll show you." He walked Gytha to the eastern edge of the crag.

She understood immediately. "I can see it. This is the closest point to the river and it's the narrowest part of the gorge. If attackers got past here and moved up river we couldn't see them due to that spur, and we certainly couldn't stop them."

"Yes, they would be around and into the vill in moments. But, what else do you see?" Ulf placed his hand on Gytha's shoulder and turned her to look to her left.

"Ah! Not a lot. We can't see the track up the west side from here. We'll need another one over there, won't we?"

"Right in one, lass. I've talked it through with Cudel, and Rhun and Tyr are sure they can build what we want. We'll make the one for yon side of the crag first and see just how much range it gives us. The lessons we learn will then help with one for here. It might have to be bigger to give us the range to reach beyond the river. I'll show you the spot for the first one." Ulf led the way across the plateau.

As they walked Gytha asked, "How many men will you need? You'll need two teams for two catapults."

"Cudel reckons teams of six to give us the power and weight we'll need. He suggests that Wulfric and Eadwig take charge of them. He'll be in command and coordinate them. I'll be up here too, to oversee everything."

Gytha stopped and took his arm. "I agree. I'm glad you're here Ulf. It takes a load off my mind. Can I talk through what I'm thinking about for down below? Once we know how far the catapults can reach I want to channel the approach routes so that attackers are forced into killing areas, just like we did at the hause behind Haugr-tun, do you remember?"

Ulf laughed, remembering the first battle that Gytha had led. "I do that lass. You and Leo together, as I recall. You laid fields of rocks that were just big enough to prevent horses moving or men running. They had to pick their way so carefully that your archers and slingers knocked them down one by one."

"That's it Ulf. I'm sure it would work again here." Ulf could see that although Gytha was confident of her plan, she wanted his approval.

"Of course, lass, I've always said you have a master's eye for tactics." Ulf squeezed Gytha's shoulder fondly as he stood next to her. "What was it that was on your mind when I came up here? Is there anything I can do for you whilst Bear is preoccupied?"

"There is, as it happens." Gytha smiled up at him, pleased that he had anticipated her. "I need to get out with Osberht and Wealmaer, show them the land, check the men and see that they are patrolling where I want. My and Bear's men have rarely worked together 'til now and I want Osberht, in particular, to understand what I expect. I know Wealmaer was impressed with how he led the raids against Sigulfson, but I still have my worries." She gave Ulf a knowing look. "Dai is still training new recruits and if Cudel and his lads are building catapults, can you keep an eye on Neven's training of the new green women? If she focuses on the boat work you could concentrate on field craft, use of bow and sling, and setting ambushes. There are some really good killing zones along that lake path."

"Of course!" He chuckled. "I couldn't have put it better myself."

*****

"We've chosen spots all along the high ground this side of Wythburndalr from which we can see the old road through the dale and around the two lakes." Gytha sat on her pony alongside Osberht and Wealmaer on a shoulder of fellside overlooking the dale, whilst enjoying the cool mid-morning sunshine on the first day of Hāligmonath. "Across to our right is the track you followed when you moved from Glynrhedyn, and to our left is Raven Crag. The sections use it as a base when patrolling to the north. That's where we should find Kai and Ranald."

"Where's the edge of Walthoef's lands, or our lands I suppose I should say? Is there a proper border?" Osberht enquired, staring down into the valley.

"Now there's a question," Gytha sighed, "not as such. The edge of the lands Moder was gifted by her uncle all those years ago is the top of the fells either side of Helvellyn, yonder." She traced the ridge line with her finger tip. "But Walthoef says his land ends at the Wythburn beck and at yon side of the two lakes. If you look carefully you can see the line of the old stone road, most of it is grassed over now, but it's good to ride on. See how it runs along yon side of the beck and the far side of the lakes."

"Which probably means it's in no-man's land. That's not good." Osberht grimaced.

"No, it's not," agreed Gytha, "I work on the assumption that the road is ours to control, but Sigulfson could claim the right to use it, and of course Le Meschin wants the eastern fells separated from the central ones, so

121

I suppose that would give Sigulfson the right. That's why we need to keep a close eye on it. There are a couple of ways over into Borgarárdalr as well as the one you followed. They're not good ones, but the wrong people in Wythburndalr would certainly pose a threat."

Gytha led off, Osberht and Wealmaer were close behind, whilst Rauði and Bjorn followed.

They heard Kai's call for help just before they rode into a camp in a clearing amongst mature birch and rowan trees.

"What's happened Kai?" Gytha shouted as she dismounted and ran to where Kai was bent over a body. Ranald sprinted over. "It's Gorm, one of mine. He just rode in, slid off his pony and collapsed. He was paired with Gunnar and sent to patrol the old road."

Gorm slowly pushed himself up onto his elbows. "I'm sorry. I...I think Gunnar is dead." He spoke quietly, panting for breath. Dark blood was oozing from a gash in his thigh.

Kai was about to speak when Gytha knelt by Gorm and shouted over her shoulder. "Rauði! There's clean cloth in my saddle bag. Fetch it." Placing her hand on his heaving chest she said, "Relax Gorm. We'll bind that wound in a moment. Tell me quickly, what happened?"

Gorm looked momentarily puzzled. It was the first time that he had met Gytha; but he realised at once why her men were so loyal. Reassuringly calm and gentle, yet decisive and firm in this sudden crisis; he knew he could trust and follow her. He spoke between deep breaths and relaxed slowly. "There were three of them...on horses on the track this side of the lake...heading towards Armboth. We tried to shadow them...riding through the trees on the fellside...then we lost them. The next we knew was when Gunnar was hit in the chest by a quarrel and thrown off his pony. I...I heard his neck break when he hit the ground. Then I got hit in the leg. I clung to the reins and managed to get clear, and came straight here. I didn't see the men at all."

"I can see them! Back on the track and still riding south. They're moving slowly and there're definitely three." One of Kai's men was looking down into the valley from the edge of the crag.

Gytha made her decision instantly. "We need to get down there and ambush them. If they are heading towards Armboth I think they will be looking to find the farms that can be taxed, but they might also see the track up to The Pewits and across to Watendlath. They mustn't find it. Get all your weapons, get mounted and follow me. Rauði, Bjorn. Stay with Gorm and dress and bind his wound. Keep him warm. Light a fire if needs be." As she swung across into her saddle, Gytha called to Wealmaer. "I have a place in mind. When we get there, I want Kai and his remaining man to get further north up the track and worn us of those men's arrival. That'll give us six for the ambush." Digging her heels into her pony's flanks she led off at a canter.

They re-traced the route Gytha had taken only ten minutes earlier. The track split after half a league and she followed it down to her left, angling across the fellside towards the head of the northern lake and the junction with the track up to The Pewits. She slowed her pony to a walk, and then halted, careful that it didn't slip on the steep ground. "Tether them here," she called to the men dismounting behind her, "and then follow me."

Trees snagged at her tunic as Gytha ran through the wild woodland, skirting around the denser thickets, and looping back towards the lakeside track. She stopped on a low steep headland that jutted into the lake. The track wound around its point about twenty feet below. "Wealmaer, I want the men in a row here, on the south side of the point. It's completely hidden from the rest of the track. Those with crossbows in the middle, bows at either end. Normal drill, hit the horses first, then the men... Kai's section, follow me." As she ran she kept checking that she could still see the ambush site. She stopped after two hundred paces. "This will do, Kai. I want a man here that can see me and you at all times. I want you a bit further on, where you can get a clear view down the track. Warn me as soon as you see the riders."

Gytha waited until she saw Kai take up his position. She was about to turn away when he turned to face her, held up his right thumb and then showed five fingers. She waived her thanks and ran back to the headland. "Five minutes." She cautioned breathlessly.

The immediate track wasn't visible from the headland but Gytha could see the foot of the small lake about half a league away. A brief glint of reflected light caught her eye. "Osberht," she hissed, "here, quickly. Can you see movement, near where the beck leaves the lake?"

Osberht stood and joined her. He saw movement at once. "Yes. Where the track fords the river just beyond the foot of the lake. I think there're another three."

"That's what I thought," Gytha agreed, "and they are riding more quickly. They could be here in ten minutes."

With a tight smile at Osberht's questioning look, Gytha said in a voice that would carry fifty feet, but no further, "Men! There're another three. The first group must be just two minutes away now. Once we've hit them, and there's no one left alive to give warning, move to the other side of the headland. We'll have to hope that that second lot don't get wind of the first attack." She watched Kai's man as she spoke, saw him wave, and hissed, "Ready!"

Gytha pulled an arrow from her quiver, notched it to her bow string and drew. She stood to the right of her men, behind one of the ancient trees dominating the headland, and tracked the first horse to come around the point. The men were riding slowly, presumably scanning the ground for signs of activity or another track. She controlled her breath, keeping her arrow tip aligned with the front of the horse's neck and waited until the third horse was in sight within the corner of her eye. As the first rider drew level with her, she loosed her arrow and shouted, "Now!"

Every arrow and quarrel found its mark. At such short range, they couldn't miss. Gytha felt no immediate guilt at killing. The thrill of the fight and the challenge of directing its course always carried her along. But she knew the emotions that would come to her in the next few nights.

For Gytha, time seemed to freeze for a moment. Two men were thrown as their horses reared up. One appeared to break his back as he fell, the other was pitched into the shallows of the lake and writhed, choking, unable to keep his head above water. The third urged his failing horse forward until it collapsed and rolled onto him. The two wounded horses staggered further down the track. One collapsed and fell, sobbing for breath. The other kept whinnying in terror.

"Move to the north side!" Gytha shouted urgently. "Keep low...and well done! Osberht, take charge whilst I warn Kai."

Gytha ran quickly towards Kai's position. He appeared out of the wood just as she reached his first man. "Three more are coming at a gallop." He shouted, "I think they heard that horse scream."

"We're ready for them." Gytha called back. "Keep low as you cross the headland, then cover the right-hand side in case any get around the point."

Osberht held up two fingers to Gytha as she ran back, and gestured with the palm of his hand for her to stay low as she approached. She crouched beside him and notched an arrow to her bow. "Kai will take any that get past us and around the point," she whispered.

Gytha raised her head; she knew at once that the ambush would go badly. With their horses at a gallop, the men were closing upon them too quickly. She shouted, "Now," and loosed her arrow at the second horse whilst it was galloping square on towards her. The horse collapsed as the arrow pierced its heart, rolling forward and pitching its rider headfirst into the craggy side of the headland. The first horse meanwhile escaped past the headland with its rider wounded by a quarrel. The third horse had lagged slightly behind and Gytha cursed as its rider reined it into a sharp U-turn into the lake and away from them, leaving a frothy wake as a reminder of its escape.

"Got him! But the horse got away." Gytha span around, hearing a shout behind her, and saw Kai waiving his crossbow enthusiastically.

Gytha responded with a raised thumb and turned to Wealmaer. "I want the bodies stripped of mail and weapons. We'll need to take them with us. It's messy work but has to be done. But before you do that Osberht and I will check if there is anything that identifies whose men they are. Have the bodies buried under a cairn by the lake shore and see if we can capture that stray horse. It can carry the weapons and mail."

"Aye Lady, it's a while since any of us have been in a fight like this, some of the lads never have. It'll be a good lesson for them." Gytha detected a note of concern in Wealmaer's voice.

She reassured him quickly, "The lads did well, very well. Even the new ones. Gather them together when we've finished and I'll have a word."

He brightened. "Thanks, they'll appreciate that. Oh, and don't fret about the one that got away. He'll spread the word that we aren't to be tangled with."

"My Lady, can you come down here." Kai's urgent shout from the bottom of the headland drew Gytha's attention away.

Osberht followed Gytha as she scrambled down to the site of the first ambush. She saw at once what Kai had found. "Well, we now know who sent them. That's Cola, the cocky skita that we took at Kesewic. It's a pity he didn't heed my warning. This will either make Sigulfson think twice, or redouble his efforts to discover where we are." Gytha surprised herself with her choice of words, but neither man seemed fazed.

What Osberht said next surprised and pleased her. "I'd like to stay on here, with Kai and Ranald. Finish the patrol and get to know the valley better. We'll need to watch this stretch for a week or so in case there is a follow up."

Gytha smiled her thanks. She was beginning to agree with Wealmaer that Osberht had changed. "Agreed. We need to recover Gunnar's body first. I'll take it back with me, along with Gorm and that horse when we've caught it. I'll send supplies to you at Raven Crag tomorrow."

Chapter 12

Five ponies walked steadily through the thick forest, the winding undulating track, and patches of wetland in the dips, hindered any thought of a trot. Bear and Gytha led, Raudi and Bjorn followed leading the fifth pony. Instead of a saddle it carried Gunnar's body bound across its back; his torso was wrapped in his green cloak, his bootless legs were in rough sacking. The weather added to the gloom of the spectacle: an early autumnal mist filled the valley, dulling the yellow and russet colours of the lakeshore woods. Fine droplets coalesced into heavy drips that dropped intermittently from the moss and lichen encrusted branches of the ancient oaks. Even the two hounds sensed the mood, following head-down at the heels of the leading ponies.

"This dale has to be the wettest of places. Patrichesdalr could be damp, but this is a different world entirely." Bear grimaced as another drop dripped from the brow of his helmet onto his cheek.

"You'll get used to it, big brother. I did, after a year or two. But I suppose that the bigger you are, the wetter you'll get." Gytha teased in reply. "But thank you for coming with me. You didn't really know Gunnar."

"No, but he was a green man, and they all have my respect. Besides, from what you say, he was a strong believer and had no family, so we have to see him properly buried, and Saint Kentigern's is the only church in the dale."

"Aye, yes he was, and no he hasn't," Gytha agreed, "he joined me here not long after Leo and I arrived. He'd fled from somewhere near Trellekell rather than knuckle under to Sigulfson."

"Do you normally take your dead to Kesewic? I've never considered what you did here. As you know, Moder always had Father Cedd take care of the dead. No one's died since he passed away just after Ēostre, so it wasn't a problem. How will we cope without a priest?" Bear's concern surprised Gytha, he wasn't deeply religious. She shrugged.

"I let the families choose. Many are happy for me to speak over the body. We bury them in the softer ground north of the crag. Even then, the graves are shallow and we set a low cairn over them to keep animals at bay. Others, those who had a stronger faith or whose family do, take the body to Kesewic in the kára, and then hire a pony or carry the body up to the church themselves."

"Ah ha." Bear sounded relieved. "I was worried that we would need to find a priest, and that's the last thing I have time for at the moment." He paused a moment. "I think we need to agree how to split responsibilities, don't you?"

Gytha noted the hesitancy in Bear's voice and worried that he might be intending to take over control of the green men. She spoke quickly, wanting to get her thoughts out before Bear. "That's been on my mind too. I left it because you're so busy with the new vill. I'm happy for you to lead. It's your right now that you're here and Moder is so unwell." She tried to give Bear a confident smile. "I think you should be in charge of everything, just as Moder was at Ulueswater, and that I should lead the green men, with Osberht as deputy, just as you did under Moder. He's a good deputy, I don't have Moder's reservations about him."

Bear gave Gytha an appraising look and flicked his head to shake water off his helmet. "You're right about Osberht, but there're a lot of men to command now that you've recruited so many more. Don't you..."

Gytha's frown stopped Bear from saying more. "No, in fact it'll be easier for me than when I just had Dai. I'll have Osberht in charge of the day to day patrols, Dai and Wealmaer as masters-at-arms, and Neven in charge of all the women. I've spoken to Ulf and he will look after the defence of the crag and the jaws of Borgarárdalr as he calls them. That way I can take a step back, control all our defences and go out on patrol as needed. It'll free you to oversee everything else, build relations with Walthoef and Jarl Buthar, control the mines with Agnaar, oversee Leo and the estates, and look after our relations with Aidan. That's what I call a plateful."

Bear continued to look at Gytha fixedly, trusting his pony to make its own way, and smiled. "You're ahead of me once again, little sister. That would work. There's just one thing; I'll need a good man at my back."

Gytha laughed, relieved. "Of course. You know the men you brought with you better than I. But choose from all of them. Good huscarles are more than just good men-at-arms." She glanced over her shoulder towards the pony trailing behind, "Gunnar would have been a good choice."

Bear nodded, understanding the sadness in Gytha's voice.

They fell silent for a while, each imagining what the future held for their families and how they would cope with the challenges of their newly shared responsibilities. Their route took them through Kesewic, up a low raise and through a gate in a dry-stone wall to Saint Kentigern's ancient wooden church. Its lichen stained walls were almost as green as the surrounding fields and fells, and the sun-bleached shingles cladding its roof were as grey as the mist above. Gytha wondered if it really was the gateway between man's Earth and God's heaven. Suddenly humbled and fretful of breaking the still peace by calling to Bjorn, she gestured to him to join her. "Go and find a couple of spades, they're probably in the shack by the churchyard wall." Turning then to Bear, she said, "We'll leave Rauði to care for Gunnar and go and search out Father Oswin. You'll need to deal with him yourself in future."

Gytha led Bear towards a small extension to one side of the church. "We may find him here. He lives within, much as a monk does in his cell." The door opened before Gytha could knock.

"Ah, Lady Gytha. I thought the voice was yours." Father Oswin's tone was noticeably cold.

Bear studied Father Oswin whilst Gytha made their introductions. The priest wasn't as he had expected. Young, slightly built, with his long black hair tonsured at his crown; he immediately struck Bear as being one of the new breed of celibate priests demanded by the Norman church. His sudden worry that Oswin's loyalty might be misplaced was soon quelled by Gytha.

"My cousin, Lord Walthoef, sends his greetings Father. Lord Æsc and I spoke to him a few months back and he said to pass on his best wishes when we next met. Gytha gave the priest a warm smile, which she knew would disconcert him, and continued sombrely, "Sadly one of my men left this world yesterday. He was a good man, and one of strong faith. I will miss him greatly but will be reassured in the knowledge that his soul is in your hands. Could you attend to him please? We will of course prepare his grave."

Gytha deliberately refrained from explaining the circumstances of Gunnar's death, and Oswin didn't ask. Whilst respectful of Gytha's role in keeping the Allerdalr fells secure for his Lord, he was sufficiently aware of Norman politics to know that she could be considered to be outside the King's law. The less he knew the safer it was for him, Gytha, and the people she led.

"Of course, my Lady. Please dig his grave alongside the others, you'll see one that is newly dug. What was his name?"

"Gunnar, Father. I have a marked stone to place above his head. Shall we get on whilst you return to your prayers. I'll let you know when his grave is ready."

"Yes, of course." Oswin nodded agreement and disappeared quickly into his cell.

"A strange one." Bear muttered under his breath as they walked to where Bjorn was standing with two spades.

"Yes, not at all like Father Cedd, and not, I think, a man who appreciates women taking a lead. But he is Cumbric, is loyal to Walthoef, and above all is discrete. Doubtless he will take to you better than he does me." Gytha sounded as if this was one responsibility that she would be glad to pass to her brother.

Bear and Bjorn worked quickly, carefully slicing the turf from the earth and placing it to one side before digging down to the bedrock below. Gytha knew that the grave would be too shallow to ensure that animals wouldn't scent Gunnar's remains and took Rauði to collect a layer of smaller rocks that they could lay between the body and the surface.

Already damp from the mist, Bear's head was now soaked with sweat. He wiped it as best he could with the bottom of his cloak and, pulling a face, told Gytha he would collect the priest, adding, "It always helps to befriend a priest if you want to know what's afoot. I rather sense Oswin is shrewd enough to realise that he can get word to Walthoef through me if he needs to, which could serve our interests as well as his."

Oswin's words of committal were curt, but well considered, and certainly gave no cause for emotion. After the priest bid them a courteous farewell, Bear broke their temporary inertia by calling them to action, "The sooner we get poor Gunnar properly covered over the sooner we can head back. Shovel soil onto his feet Bjorn whilst I cover his head. We can cover him with Gytha's rocks, spread more soil, and top off with the turfs."

Gytha appreciated Bear's business-like tone, and as they worked she retrieved the headstone from her saddle bag. When the men finished, she set it into the ground above Gunnar's head: a small block of greenish grey slate engraved to the best of her ability with a '✝' set above 'Ꮸᴜɴɴᴀʀ'. In response to Rauði's look of puzzlement she said, "That's how his name is written. Mayhap one day someone will be able to read it, and know who he was. Now come, let's be on our way."

As they mounted their ponies Rauði sidled hers next to Gytha's and, with a gesture to Bjorn to ride next to Bear, asked quietly, "Can you tell me about Osberht's fostri-folk? They are much referred to, but what happened to them is never mentioned, though it must have had great effect on Osberht? Their deaths, and those of my parents, are all due to Sigulfson, or so it seems."

Gytha gave Rauði a measured look and agreed with her. "It did, it did on everyone, and yes, Sigulfson is the cause of much grief. It's best you know because it changed Osberht, it certainly affected Freja, and the impact on Moder was profound. But I'm not the one to really tell you. Speak to Ulf, and tell him I told you to ask. All I'll say is that they were Moder's huscarles. Moder rescued Ada from abuse by a Norman when she was very young and Ada became bound to her through love and service. Godric served her uncle, but swore his allegiance to Moder the day they met. His respect for her was immense, almost love. Godric was slain trying to defend Glynrhedyn from Sigulfson, and Ada died trying to avenge his death. She got into their camp the night after Godric died and almost killed Sigulfson; the scar on his cheek is from her blade. Ulf found that out later, all that he found at the time was her mutilated body. The scars from their deaths are still very raw, so say nothing to Osberht until you've spoken to Ulf. Heed his counsel first." Gytha's stern look reinforced the gravity of her words. She then lightened, seeing that they had had the desired effect upon Rauði. "Come on, let's catch the men up. I want to see how Neven is getting on before we head home."

*****

A stiffening breeze cleared the mist, and by noon the fell tops were free of cloud. "Ah, At last!" Bear gave a relieved sigh as he felt his clothes' sticky dampness begin to dry.

"Take the track that's coming up on your right." Gytha shouted ahead to him. "It might be easier to walk. The branches will have your head off."

Bear saw what she meant, dismounted, and with Bjorn waited for her to catch up.

The track led through a long stand of pines on a low rocky promontory, from the end of which they could see along the length of the lake to the crag itself. "Impressive, isn't it?" As Gytha spoke, a svanmeyja accompanied by a dugout with an outrigger sailed around the corner of a large island barely three hundred paces from them. A thin column of wood smoke rose from somewhere in the middle of the island.

"Is that Neven?" Bear asked hesitantly.

"Either her, or one of her sections leaders." Gytha replied, raising the silver mouth piece of her horn to her lips and blowing a long, steady note.

The crew of the svanmeyja acknowledged by dropping its sail and turning towards them, followed by the dugout. "They'll have to row to cut across that westerly wind." Gytha said quietly, assuming rightly that neither Rauði nor Bjorn had much experience of sailing.

"The two lasses in the dugout are doing well to keep up," Bear observed, watching the women in it paddle with long brisk strokes.

"Aye, Tyr was right to suggest using them. They've such a shallow draft that they almost skim along," Gytha agreed, "and with that outrigger they're stable enough for one of the crew to kneel and use a bow."

As the craft neared they could count five bodies in the svanmeyja. "Neven's there, there's only one with black hair blowing from under her helmet."

"Well spotted, you've sharper eyes than me." Bear praised Bjorn and then voiced his instructions: "Whilst we wait, the two of you can take the ponies down to the shore to water them, and then join us back here whilst we discuss plans with Neven."

Just as the svanmeyja grounded on the narrow gravel beach the woman in the bows leapt over the gunwale and pulled the boat further up the beach. Neven, sitting in the stern, waited until the section was ashore before following. Meanwhile Gytha stepped deftly down the rocky slope and jumped onto the beach. "That was as good a display of boatmanship as I've seen in a fair while," she said by way of greeting. "You've trained them well, Gwenn." Gytha gave her new section leader an encouraging smile. "Carry on with what you had planned. I need to catch up with Neven for a while. I'll sound the horn when I need you."

Gytha and Neven clambered up the side of the promontory and sat on the top with the others. "How many women have you now?" Gytha asked, uncertain as to how successful Neven's recruiting had been.

"Twelve including Aelf, which is all I need. I've split them into two sections of six, under Gwenn and Tanuw, as you suggested. Each has a svanmeyja and a dugout, which leaves room for me in either svanmeyja, or I can take the third dugout myself if needs be."

"I see that you're using Crow Island as a base. That makes sense."

"Yes, we moor the boats on the west side. They're completely hidden there and we can move up and down the lake as I choose." Neven appreciated Gytha's praise. "The lake shore opposite the eastern side of the island is very marshy and hard to cross, but it's clear of trees, which gives us good sight of the track. Unfortunately, there aren't as many good ambush positions as I had hoped. The track switches between being too close to the lake to being too far away from it. I'd say there are four good spots, and several that would work if we had a section on ponies."

Bear interrupted. "That's what I thought when we rode along it this morning, but how would you know when an attack is coming?"

Neven looked tight-lipped. "That's the problem. We can't keep a permanent watch from within Kesewic bay itself, and the land is so flat that we can't set a decent look out on the shore. The best place is on that cone shaped fell over yonder. It dominates the track between here and Kesewic, but is close on half a league away." Neven pointed behind them.

"Mmm, it's a good spot for an ambush. I thought that as we rode back just now." Gytha glanced from Neven to Bear. "We can't keep sections on guard permanently, waiting for Sigulfson or Black William to impose their will in the central dales, but we could keep a small presence on Neven's island and arrange for the headman in Kesewic to send warning."

"Aye, that could work. I could keep three girls here and swap them over by half-sections every other day. That would give us plenty of time to train and prepare ambush sites. We could certainly build a decent shelter to see us through the winter."

"And build a beacon." Bear was enthusiastic. "Just as we did for the defence of Ulueswater. A beacon here, or on the island, is in line of sight with the crag; look!" He pointed directly down the lake."

Gytha nodded agreement. "Yes, of course, I should have thought of that already. It needs to be on the south edge of the island so that nothing obstructs our view of the flames and smoke. Even if the clouds are low it'll still be seen. That's the problem with beacons on the fell tops. They're useless when the mist comes down." Gytha came to a decision. "Neven, you just need two girls here, with a dugout. That way you can move everyone here in the svanmeyjas as soon as you get warning. The girls can watch the track from the island and react to any messenger from Kesewic. Bear and I will warn our contacts there and we'll pay a boatman a retainer so that he's always on hand." She looked at Bear, "You could have a word with Oswin too."

"What about those places where the track is too far from the lake?" Neven raised a questioning eyebrow.

"Talk to Dai and tell him where you have in mind. I'll have him commit the men you need, but I would guess at two sections, with one of them being on the fell that Neven pointed out, let's just call it Cone Fell for simplicity. What do you think, brother?"

Bear chuckled. "I think it's your game, and you're playing it very well."

"How many sections are there now?" Neven asked, concerned. "Can you afford two for here?"

"We certainly can." Gytha said with confidence, and a note of pride. "Thanks to you and Dai, and those that Bear brought, we have ten plus your women, and they equate to three normal sized sections. That's over fifty green men and women." She paused for a moment, frowning, and turned to Bear. "We should return to Kesewic now and speak to Bran He's the headman there. After what's just happened in Wythburndale we have to plan on Sigulfson trying an approach this way at any time."

"Aye, you're right," Bear agreed. "We've got to keep ahead of his game."

Gytha turned back to Neven. "Start the watches tomorrow and work your training around them." Then she added, with a teasing smile, "At least Cudel will be pleased to see you back for a cuddle tonight.

Neven gave a short gasp, blushed, and laughed.

*****

Gytha was in high spirits when she finally returned to the crag. Bran had agreed to do all they had asked and she felt a new confidence that they would be forewarned and could forestall a threat along the lakeshore. The defence of the crag, its settlements and the new vill were her next priority. Dismounting at the stable, she was about to attend to her pony when a cry of "Moder!" caused her to stop and turn. Brynhildr was feet away, running straight to her.

"Come, Moder. Let me show you what Ealdmoder has taught me. She's up at the hall. Ulf is there with Osberht too." Her daughter gabbled excitedly and held her arms up for a kiss.

"You go on, Gytha, we'll look after the ponies." Rauði gave Gytha an amused smile as she spoke. "I'll go and see Adelind after we've finished."

Brynhildr held Gytha's hand tightly as she led her enthusiastically up the steps to the hall. She listened attentively as Brynhildr described how she could now write her name; and praised her daughter whilst wondering what Osberht had to report.

Gytha relaxed once she saw Leofric drinking a cup of ale with Ulf and Osberht, and went with Brynhildr to find Ealdgith and see the letters Brynhildr had diligently written on a length of parchment. She smiled indulgently as she watched her daughter slowly write the letter **B**. The cost of the parchment was considerable, and it was difficult to obtain, being acquired through Aidan. But the power and influence that the ability to read and write brought was worth far more than the cost of the

137

parchment. Gytha gently kissed the top of her daughter's head and turned to Ealdgith, "Thank you, Moder. You're giving Bryny a gift that is worth more than any gold could buy." She bent to kiss her too and quietly left the two together.

"I'm glad you're here, Osberht. How was the rest of your patrol?" Gytha asked as Leofric passed his ale cup to her. She took a long mouthful and returned it.

"Very quiet. We took a close look at Saint John's in the Vale. Keeping to the high ground, of course." He added quickly, noticing the fleeting concern in Gytha's eyes. "But there was no follow-on activity at all. Mayhap Sigulfson got the message."

"We can but hope. Did you go get a look down Dynfal's Raise too?"

"Aye we did, all the way into Gressemere. The folk there have seen nowt of Orm's men."

"Good, and what does that tell you?" Gytha's test of Osberht's awareness sounded like a tease.

"That only his men are at Ameleseta. If Le Meschin's were there, they would doubtless have thrown their weight around in the nearby vills."

"You're right there, lad." Ulf was fulsome in his praise. "I reckon you deserve another of these." He raised his empty cup.

"Aye, thanks Fader. But first I want to suggest something to Gytha." Osberht passed his cup across to Ulf. "We lose a lot of patrolling time coming back here. I spoke to the folk at Watendlath and they would be happy for us to base some men there. In fact, they would welcome it."

Gytha laughed, giving Osberht a bright smile. "Now there's a thought. I've just had Neven set a permanent watch with a beacon on Crow's Island, and was thinking we need something up on the tops too. What do you have in mind?"

Osberht looked momentarily surprised, he hadn't been sure that Gytha would agree. "At least a couple of sections. And a beacon is a good idea. That craggy fell, yon side of the valley would be best for it. It's this side of the tarn and would save us a lot of time in raising the alarm."

"You mean Brund Fell? Yes, that would be ideal for a beacon. As to sections, mayhap three would be better. One on patrol at any one time and two training and ready to block our back door if Sigulfson does come calling. You could prepare an ambush site where the track from the tops drops down through the wood on yon side of the tarn. Could the folk there put that many men up?" Osberht's request had confirmed an idea that Gytha had been toying with during her ride back.

"They could that. There's an empty barn they're happy to give us."

Gytha held out her hand for Osberht to shake. "Well done. I'm glad I have you as my deputy. Bear and I have agreed that all the green men and women will come under me whilst he takes charge across the board. I'd like you and Wealmaer to share the duties up there. I've committed two sections to help Neven on the lake track, so that leaves us the five newest ones back here for Dai to keep training, and mayhap add to."

Osberht grasped her hand firmly and smiled appreciatively. He knew that Gytha was someone he could work under, and he felt that their handshake bonded that relationship.

Gytha turned her attention to Ulf. "Now, Fader, when are you going to show me these catapults?"

"How about in the morn. I've stood the lads down for now. We've the first one in place, and it can fling a mean load of fist-size rocks, but not quite as far as I would like. The next one's going to be bigger."

Leofric bent forward laughing. "You do love your toys, Fader! The crag will be half its height by the time you stop chipping it to bits and flinging it away...and when are you going to stop poaching my men?" he added, sounding more serious.

"Ah! You must mean those that want to fling rocks for me. Rest assured that they can go back to their normal work once I've trained them. After that I'll just need them a couple of hours a week to keep their eye in. Don't worry,

Leo." Ulf gave Leofric a broad grin, hoping to reassure him. He was well aware of the disruption he was causing.

"I hope so Fader, because all the extra grain I'm having to buy in from Kesewic is starting to drain the coffers. The kára's been making a trip a day for the past week, and with Agnaar's miners having to help build the new vill we're short of lead to sell as well." Leofric's concern was obvious.

"Fret not, Leo. Bear is going to oversee everything. We spoke this morning and he's going to work closely with you and Agnaar. The coffers won't be drained, don't forget they've been topped up with everything Moder brought with her. Now come on, it's good for us all to raise a cup together." Gytha squeezed her husband's arm, took the ale cup from his hand, and took another swig.

As she spoke Bjorn walked in with his harp-sack over his shoulder. "I heard that a barrel of ale had been broached. It seems the perfect time for some music. Rauði's on her way, just wait 'til you hear her sing."

Winter 1101

Chapter 13

Gytha led the way over the saddle between Cat's Bield and Maiden Moor, towards what were to her the largely unknown lands of Roger Seatr. She was the only one of the four who had ridden there, and then only once, but she understood that it was a shorter, albeit less obvious route to Butremere than over Honister pass. Bear rode alongside as they picked their way down Cat's Bield's grassy flank, towards a small farm nestled by a beck.

"From what Agnaar told me, this is the way to his Yewthwaite workings, but where are they?" Bear looked around, surprised that he couldn't see any activity. "Oh, hang on. What's that down there?" He pointed to where the steep slope of the fellside began to level out by the foot of a gill.

"Yes, that's the spot. "Gytha replied. "The men that should be working there are those you brought from Glynrhedyn. From what Leo said, they're still finishing the houses in the new vill. There's lead there, for certain, and if I can find a route, I think this will be the quickest way to get it to Butremere and on to Wirkynton. The best way down to them is to follow this track and then fork to the right at the bottom." Gytha knew that she was just one step ahead of her brother in understanding the lay of the land, and hoped she sounded more confident than she felt. "There is another spot that Agnaar wants to explore. It's just around to the left of this spur and about half a league up a little dale. He thinks that there are traces of silver in the rock."

Bear gave a low whistle. "We can but hope. From what you say, it's probably not on our route?"

"No, you'll have to leave it 'til another day. We need to cross the beck over a ford by the farm, just below where two becks come together. From what I remember, it's easier going on yon side of the valley, where we can follow a track along the flank of the fell."

"Is it up to being trampled by laden ponies?"

"Mayhap not. You'll be able to see for yourself, but I'm sure it can be built up over time. There'll be plenty of waste from the mines that can be dug into the softer ground."

"Aye, there will that." Bear cast an appraising eye over his sister, appreciating her grasp of what would be required to create a new jagger route. He changed the tack of the conversation.   "It'll be good see the old jarl again, it's been a while since I was last in that smoky hall of his. It was as well that you sent Rauði and Bjorn to warn of our coming. At least we now know that he's had problems with Black William somewhere beyond Lousewater."

"Aye," Gytha agreed tersely, before continuing, "I gather from what Rauði said when they got back that it was a stand-off. The Jarl's men outnumbered Black William's and forced an about face. At least they didn't get to Hlóratūn. That would have been a direct challenge to Walthoef."

"Mmm...," Bear agreed, "though I'm surprised he risked a direct incursion into any of our lord's land."

"He would though, if he was confident he had his brother's support and the King's authority. Sigulfson's the same, that's why he's been poking his nose into Wythburndalr. It's just that at the moment he's more interested in consolidating his interests in our old mines. This is just the start. I'm sure of that. Just as I'm sure Sigulfson will get a bloody nose when he pushes us too far." Gytha's resolve was obvious in her tone.

"I hope Buthar's of a similar resolve. We need to get him to agree to a Folkmoot. He's the one to call it. His voice carries more weight than mine in the central dales." Bear gave a deep sigh and laughed, "I'm sure you can charm him again, Gytha. He always falls for your Valkyrie look."

Gytha cast her brother a look that would freeze Valhalla itself, and then her face cracked with amusement. "We'll see."

They made their way up the dale. Gytha and Bear led whilst Raudi and Bjorn followed, enjoying relaxed time together. The hounds ran ahead, ranging over the fellside.

"I'm glad you had the foresight to cross the beck where we did, Gytha, we've made good time on this side...and just look at that!" Bear pointed across the narrowing valley to a torrent of creamy water pouring off a lip of black rock."

"Impressive, isn't it?" Gytha agreed, "Though there are even higher waterfalls yon side of Butremere. You'll be able to see across to them in a moment." As she spoke the faint track crested the top of the hause.

Bear gave a surprised whistle. "We're right above the Jarl's hall, I didn't realise we were that close. It's a pretty steep descent, mind."

"Mayhap, but not too steep for the jagger ponies. Some of the routes we've been using up until now have been every bit as steep. They cope fine with careful guiding. It's just that yours had it easy following those old stone roads past the fort." Bear heard the tease in Gytha's voice, and smiled back.

"Well, it'll certainly save us time."

"It will indeed. Hákon suggested that we should follow the track over yon hause into Mosedalr, and then along the shore of Lousewater. I think watering the ponies when they get to Butremere, before cracking on to a camp at Lousewater, should be achievable in a day. They could then get from there to Wirkynton and back in a day." Gytha was pleased that her plan seemed feasible.

"So, a three-day round trip from the new mines." Bear was equally satisfied. "Come on, let's get down to the hall. I could do with something off the Jarl's table."

*****

Bear's hunger was quickly assuaged. Jarl Buthar greeted him with a warmth and respect that Gytha felt exceeded the more teasing manner in which the Jarl welcomed her. Not that it upset her, she knew that she could always subtly gain his agreement to her ideas, which was what mattered. It was far more important for her brother to be treated with respect and his authority acknowledged. The need for a Folkmoot was quickly agreed. Gytha could tell that the Jarl welcomed it as a way of asserting his own authority over the central dales, and she was pleased when Hákon and Gille were ordered to leave for the dales to their south in the morning.

"Set the date for All Hallows' Eve. The last day of Winterfylleth will give time for all to gather, and is an appropriate date, don't you think?" Jarl Buthar slammed his ale cup onto the table as he drew the discussion to a close. Now! It's time for song and music. Young Bjorn, we've missed the magic of your harp. Borrow your fostri's and entertain us."

Bjorn glanced from Gytha to Haethcyn, both nodded. He rose and went to Haethcyn's hut, returning with a small harp a little over two feet tall. The men by the hearth cleared a space on their bench so that Bjorn could straddle it and balance the harp between his legs. Rauði watched intently, relieved that Bjorn had brought Haethcyn's oldest harp rather than his best one. He half closed his eyes, trying to blot out the sound of the hall, and gently plucked the strings as he twisted the knobs holding them taught. The warmth of the hall would constantly change their tension and as he worked he quickly decided upon two of his shorter songs, ones that would finish before the harp needed retuning.

Feeling a gentle touch on his shoulder, Bjorn blinked and looked up. Rauði was beside him. "I'll sing with you. It'll help show everyone here how close we are now. What have you chosen?"

"Butremere Hall, the first three verses, then I'll see how we go."

Rauði smiled encouragingly. "Good, it is simple and fitting." She abruptly nudged the knee of the man sitting in front of Bjorn. "Make way!" Before he could react, she stepped onto the bench and forced him to shuffle sideways.

Jarl Buthar, seeing that his foster-daughter was about to sing, stood and bellowed for silence.

Rauði gave him a swift smile of thanks, glanced around the hall and took a deep breath. As Bjorn plucked his first note, she began to sing

In Butremere stands a hall, more beautiful than
sunlight.
Thatched with ferns, the gift of the dale.
There bold men do dwell.
Jarl Buthar they serve and hail.

Men wear brown, the colour of the fell.
Bright shields they carry,
and spear, arrow and bow.
Foes, they chase and harry.

By the end of the second verse Rauði could see from the expressions around her, the smiles and the nodding heads, that they had all in the hall within their grasp. Bjorn played until he sensed the harp needed retuning, took a short break, and started again. Sometimes Rauði sang, but she also took breaks to let Bjorn take the credit for his music.

Gytha glanced around, enjoying the delight on the people's faces and then stopped, disturbed by the sight of two younger men scowling and muttering. She tugged Bear's hand, pulling him after her, and went to stand close by Rauði. It wasn't just that she wanted to hear more clearly, the men's behaviour and the direction of their looks worried her, and she sensed the need to show that Rauði and Bjorn were now sworn to her care.

Bjorn brought their seventh song to a close, stood with the harp raised above his head, and bowed towards the Jarl. "Lord, my repertoire is now as dry as Rauði's throat. May we take your leave and down some of your ale?"

The Jarl thumped the table in approval and raised his ale horn in a toast. "You may. Your music has been much missed, as has my daughter's voice."

Bjorn took a cup of ale from a serving woman and drank a long swig, before turning to Rauði. "I'll be back in a moment, nature calls."

Rauði turned to answer a question from Gytha, whilst watching Bjorn push his way through the throng in the hall. As he shouldered the hall's great door open she saw two other men detach themselves from the crowd and push after Bjorn. One turned to look back at the other; Rauði knew at once that Bjorn was in trouble. With a curt, "I'll be back shortly, my Lady. Bjorn needs me," Gytha pushed her way towards the door.

Bjorn grimaced and held his breath as he unlatched the gate to the hall's latrine. The guttering flame from a tallow candle threw an inadequate light within the fetid cubicle, but it was enough for his purpose. Relieved, he stepped back outside and took a deep breath of cleaner air, and halted, startled, as two men stepped from the shadows.

"You run off with the Jarl's daughter, then come back and flaunt yourselves in front of him. You're nothing but a low-born bastard with ideas above his place. Cnut, why don't we push him back where he belongs?" The taller of the two men jabbed Bjorn's chest with his forefinger as he spoke.

Bjorn stood firm, just as he did every time Erland Ormeson goaded him. They had fought many times. The causes for Erland's jealousy were many and varied, and had changed as the boys had grown up. Bjorn had long known that his ability as a harpist and storyteller were bitterly resented by Erland. He suspected that his closeness to Rauði was a more recent factor. Erland always kept close to Cnut, Hákon's son, and it was obvious to Bjorn that he tried to ingratiate himself with the slightly younger youth to gain favour with his father.

"Whatever it is that irks you, Erland, I don't have time for it." Bjorn leant his weight against Erland's finger. "Now step aside."

"Have you ploughed her yet? Or are you not man enough? Is that why you try and win her with sweet words instead?"

Ignoring the jibe, Bjorn stared into Erland's eyes as he spoke with slow deliberation. "Step aside now, or..."

"Or what?"

"This!" Bjorn hissed as he raised his right knee sharply into Erland's crotch.

Erland jerked forward. His initial scream turning into a guttural howl as Bjorn jerked his forehead down onto Erland's nose. He staggered blindly, one hand clutching at the burning pain in his groin and the other pressed against his dripping nose. He crashed against the side of the latrine and slumped down.

"This isn't your fight, Cnut." Bjorn stepped back as Cnut balled his fist.

"Oh, but it is. It's more mine than Erland's. Frytha was to be mine. My father had the Jarl's word. Even though she is only his fostri, she is still his daughter. A dowry and her status would come with her. I would be the equal of my father, or more."

Cnut swung his arm back ready to strike, and froze. "Argh! What?!" He knew by the pain in his neck that he couldn't risk moving.

"The only way you'll ever have me is in your dreams or my worst nightmares. My knife is at the back of your neck, Cnut. Relax your arm, unless you want to feel how sharp the blade really is. I can see only a little blood at the moment, but can happily bring forth more if you want?" Rauði's cold voice carried clearly in the night. "I heard your vile detestable words, and what you intended for Bjorn, and for me, so listen carefully. I may be the Jarl's fostri, but I am now sworn to serve Lady Gytha, as is Bjorn. We've been trained to ride and fight alongside her, so your fists and Erland's bullying are nothing to me now. And, I now know who my birth father was. Lord Æsc and Lady Gytha were his kin, so they are now mine, as is Lord Walthoef...and you know who he is, don't you?"

Cnut's look of glazed confusion cleared. "Uh huh," he croaked, afraid to move his head, or flex his neck by speaking.

"...And Rauði and I are hand-fasted in all but name." Bjorn interrupted, speaking slowly, letting Cnut infer his meaning. "Now, hand me your sword, hilt first."

Rauði lifted the tip of her blade from Cnut's neck. "If you try anything, I will cut you," she cautioned.

"Why do you want my sword?" Cnut hesitated, until prompted by a sharp jab at the back of his neck.

"I could throw it in that pit of cess, but instead you can look for it in the mill beck, along with Erland's when I've taken it from him, the cold will help sober you up. I'll leave it to you to make that piece of crap that passes for your friend understand that this was the last time he stands against me."

"And I expect both of you to ride out with Gille and your father in the morning. You can explain yourselves however you want, but I don't want to see you around whilst I'm here." Rauði's voice was icier than Bjorn had ever heard it. I shan't tell my father of this, but I will make sure my Lady knows. It will be for her to take it further if she sees fit." Rauði continued to hold Cnut at knife point whilst Bjorn disarmed Erland, and stood back to let Cnut assist the groaning youth.

*****

Water oused down the crag's rock faces, dripped constantly from branches, pooled in every hollow and turned the earth between the houses below it into a sticky brown mess. Gytha pulled the hood of her green cloak over her head and mused that at least the summer's accumulated dust would be washed away. She walked down to the foot of the crag and went directly to the stables, saddled her pony quickly and rode at a brisk canter to Bear's newly finished hall. He opened the door as she arrived, and held it whilst she tied the pony's reins to the porch post. With work on his stables still in progress, the porch was all the shelter she could find.

"Come in sister," Bear quipped. "At first I thought you were going to ride straight in! She'll be fine there. I doubt anyone's going out in this." He cast his eyes skyward whilst pulling the heavy door shut.

"I shan't stay long." Gytha said as she sat by the hearth fire. "I heard yesterday that Hákon has returned from the southern dales. The word is that the head men of all the communities will be there."

"I just hope they can get there. The becks will be over their banks if this keeps up, and I'm not sure we'd even get over the high tops. Those clouds are down below the level of the passes." Bear gave a burning log a frustrated poke, sending cascades of sparks across the hearth.

"We'll be alright. This is the wettest of the dales, so the others may be better. Anyhap, we don't have to go over the high tops. It's not much further to go over into the upper reaches of Wythburndale, and follow the reverse of the way you would have taken from Langdalr on your last jagger trip. I suggest we do that. It'll be a long day, but doable."

"Good. I've yet to get to know these fells, so I'm in your hands."

"I think we should take a section with us, Rauði and Bjorn too. We need to make a show of strength, without being overbearing. Have you thought about your choice of Huscarle?"

"I have, as it happens," Bear looked quite pleased, "I've appointed Ranald. I enjoy his humour and he's good with a sword. Osberht's in agreement too. It gives him a chance to make some other changes."

"He should stay behind when we go." Gytha spoke quickly, and then laughed at Bear's confusion.

"Sorry. Osberht, not Ranald. Of course, Ranald must be with you. But Osberht needs to take charge here." She apologised with a smile.

"Agreed. I think we should leave three days ahead of the Day of the Dead. We need to be in Langdalr in good time. Hopefully we can talk more with the Jarl and get to know others that come early. The more we can influence their thinking before the Folkmoot, the better.”

“That would be best.” Gytha agreed. “Hákon’s word was that Arne of Langdalr has room for us in his hall, whilst the men can use a dry barn. But he said it will be tight. The sooner we get there the better our chances of a decent bed space.”

*****

“Gytha. Blow the horn.” Jarl Buthar didn’t look at Gytha as a he spoke. Instead, he opened his arms wide in a gesture of welcome, and turned slowly from left to right, facing those standing on grass platforms cut into the side of the mound of the Ting Moot. He scrutinised his audience. Some stood in small groups, perhaps signifying that they were from larger vills or groups of settlements that had banded together, others stood alone. These men were generally the most shabbily clad. The quality of clothing tended to signify wealth and status, and Buthar was quickly aware that those who had grouped together were the men they would need to win over.

The long note of Gytha’s horn wasn’t needed to draw attention, but it did silence the exclusively male voices below her. The men’s eyes were already upon Gytha and her suit of armour. Its delicate interlinked rings of copper, brass and steel shimmered in the early morning sunlight, complementing the gold of her hair that Rauði had earlier that morning woven painstakingly into a single long braid.

“Men of the fells, I welcome you all. Few of you know me, but the fact that you are here, shows that you know my name and what I stand for. We are all proud people, proud and free. I have called you here to tell you that that our freedom is now under threat. The Normans who stole the flatlands surrounding these fells now want to steal the fells themselves from us. Though I called you here, it is those standing with me that will speak for me.” The Jarl’s voice boomed and his eyes gleamed under his burnished round helm. “Listen to them and mark the

150

warning they bring, for they already have long and bitter experience of fighting to save their lands. Hear them out, then we will discuss and agree what we will do next." Jarl Buthar made sure that his audience understood that he expected action to be taken.

Bear spoke next. He too wore mail; *Nadr*, his late father's sword, hung from his waist. "I am Lord Æsc of Ulueswater, but know me as Bear. This is my sister, Lady Gytha of Borgarárdalr, but known also as the Lady of the Lake. Our family is descended from Earl Gospatric and the great lords of the North; some of you will have heard of them. But it is of no matter if you haven't, for all are now dead and gone. Our family has fought the Normans for two generations, ever since William the Bastard's great harrying in which we lost our lands beyond the eastern fells. We fought them again when Red William came to Carleol, when we lost our lands in the Vale of the Eden and had to fight to protect our sanctuary at Ulueswater. Now there is a new king and he is intent upon enforcing his will upon us all, hunting down those of us who still live free and forcing us into bondage." Bear paused, studying the expressions of those looking up at him. He knew he had their attention, but would he gain their trust.

He continued. "The King has appointed a new strongman to do his bidding. His name is Ranulph Le Meschin and he has free rein to move his men wherever he desires. The Cumbric lords that still hold lands have been warned that if they oppose him they will be declared traitors and banished, so no matter how benign your overlord has been he will not be able to stop Le Meschin's men taking your grain and livestock in lieu of tax or forcing you into serfdom. It is no idle threat. All the fells east of Wythburndalr and Ameleseta are already so controlled, and my lands at Ulueswater have been taken too. Jarl Buthar and I hold the dales of Allerdalr, south of Kesewic. We have men and arms with which to defend our lands, and we will fight to keep them free...or die so doing. Our worry is that the dales that open into Kaupaland and Furness have no such protection. We can offer you sanctuary if you are forced to flee but we can't fight to protect your families. That you must do for yourselves, and it is why we bring you not just a warning, but an offer of help. We can teach your men how to fight and deny access to your dales. My sister, who leads my war band, will tell you how."

Gytha was startled by the sudden change in the expressions of the men looking up towards her. She saw, rather than heard, their collective sigh. "I can see some of you doubt I can do what my brother has offered. I can see too that some of you doubt that a woman could, or should, lead men in battle." She paused, knowing that she had to confront male prejudice head on and drew her sword so swiftly that the crowd gasped. It's beaten steel blade glistened. Her voice carried in the still morning air: the cold resolve of its tone matching the stern determination in her eyes. "This sword was held in battle by Aethelflaed, Queen of the Mercians, when she led her people against the Danes. This armour was hers too, and her blood flows in my veins, as it does in my brother's. The sword and the armour were passed to me by our moder, Lady Ealdgith. She wore them when she led our men alongside our fader in their life long struggle with the Normans. As Bear says, I now lead our men for him...I have never failed him, nor have I ever failed my people. I never shall."

Gytha let her words register, sheathed her sword and held her arms out as if to invite a response. "Tell me, when I say fight what do you see my men doing? Do you see us standing face to face, chest to chest with our foe in a shield wall?" She watched puzzled faces, patiently letting silence speak for itself.

"Aye Lady." One finally replied, and then another.

"How else would you fight?"

"I'd batter the bastards."

"But we can't batter Norman bastards."

Gytha laughed and held her hand up for silence. "You're wrong. You can batter Norman bastards. My men and I did so only two months back and we buried five of them in Wythburndalr. We let a sixth escape to give warning that our lands are to be avoided."

Several of the men exchanged questioning glances.

One spoke. "How?

Another laughed. "She's a Valkyrie, that's how."

Gytha was beginning to enjoy herself, she could sense she was beginning to win the men around and to build a rapport. She laughed, "You've been speaking to the Jarl. He would say the same about me. But no, I'm not a Valkyrie, nor am I just a shield-bearer; I'm flesh and blood, just like you. You don't fight Norman men-at-arms with brawn, you beat them with brains. None of us here could stand in a shield wall against trained men, that's not what we do. We use our skills and knowledge to give us the strength to defeat the Normans on ground they don't know and in a way they don't understand. All of us know the fells intimately, every fold in the ground, every crag, where ground is boggy, where woods give cover from view and shelter from the weather. The way we fight is in small groups of men, and some women, skilled in the use of the weapons we use day to day: hunting bows, slings, spears if needs be. We move on foot or fell pony, we track and we ambush, and we kill and depart unseen.
We are known as the green men...Behold!" Gytha gestured to her left as Ranald, followed by Rauði and Bjorn, led Kai's section onto the fellside to the side of the Ting Moot.

A rumble of appreciation spread through the men, those that had spears thumped the butt ends on the ground in approval.

Bear spoke again. "Men, you all represent your vills and farmsteads. Gytha has told you how you can defend your people if you choose to. We, or rather our men, can train yours how to fight as they do. Do you want that?"

A chorus of "Aye Lord" followed, though Gytha could see uncertainty remained on some faces. She shouted over the hubbub.

"Go and speak to my men, and then talk amongst yourselves. We will leave you for a while. When we return, we can discuss how, when and where we will start training.”

As they turned away Jarl Buthar stepped between Bear and Gytha and clasped them on their shoulders. “Good, that was well done, I think we have them. With trained men in the dales to our south, and an undertaking to send warning of any incursions, we can concentrate on our more immediate threats.”

“I spoke to Arne earlier. He’s agreed to accommodate the training here and to be the focus for sending warnings north and south.” Bear said, turning to Gytha.

“Good, I thought he would.” Gytha replied. “We’ll see how many men they think they can call upon, but I’ll plan on having Kai with two sections here from a week today until Yuletide. We can get a lot done in six weeks.”

Aere Yule 1101

Chapter 14

Bear stumbled and cursed as a gusting north wind caught the hall's door and thrust it from his hand as he turned the handle. A blast of icy air whipped into the hall. "By Hodr! It's bitter out there," he looked sheepishly at Gytha.

She stood up and gestured to a stool next to her. "Come, brother, and warm yourself by the hearth. But shouldn't you be thanking Ullr instead of cursing the blind god of the cold and dark? Remember what Fader taught us about the old gods. Ullr is charmed with good luck in hunting, and in sports on snow and ice. All of which we want just now."

"Ah! Happen you might be right little sister. Whilst there's no snow yet, I've just been told that the lake is beginning to freeze." Bear hugged his sister briefly and, as he sat, noticed to his surprise that a serving girl was the only other person in the hall.

"Rauði and Bryny are with Moder, making Yuletide garlands from holly and berries. Leo and Bjorn are away with some of the men to find a yule log; there's an oak that came down two winters past that they are going to take a bough off."

Bear lowered his voice. "How is she? Moder, I mean. Eir said that Moder had been with her and Adelind yesterday, and that she's taking a larger draught of poppy lotion to fight the pain."

Gytha nodded and took her brother's hand, surprised at the cold in his fingers. "She is. She's determined not to show her pain, but her breathing is getting harder, especially in this cold wind. I'm trying to keep her indoors, but you know what she's like. Time will tell," she said with a sigh as she released Bear's hand, "but that's not what we need to talk about."

Bear held his hands towards the hearth fire. "Now that winter has us in its grasp, should we not call our patrols in?"

Gytha gave a low laugh. "Hah! Osberht says we shouldn't, that the risk of a surprise is too great, Wealmaer says no one in their right mind would attack over the fells when there is so little daylight. I've told them to keep a section at Watendlath, with two men on Bleaberry Fell during the day. It's over a league north of the tarn, so some distance away, and they have a clear sight of Kesewic, and into Wythburndalr from there. They'll be able to tell by the glint from mail and spears if a body of armed men are on the move, and they can quickly pick up movement on the slopes just below them. I'll stand them down as and when the snow starts to lie thick."

"That's sensible. What about the lake?"

"Neven pulled the girls back this morning, before the shore freezes completely. She's going to have them riding the lakeshore track daily, just until the snow comes in."

Bear nodded his agreement. "And Kai?"

"He came back two days ago having finished training the last of the men that came forward. He was pleased with the turnout, and their ability. It seems that most took quickly to our way of fighting. The men of Langdalr, Dunnerdalr and Gríssdalr have all rallied, so I think that we can be sure that all of Konungrtūn and upper Furness will keep our backs safe should Black William look to come calling from the south. Arne is proving to be a good friend to have."

"He is that." Bear stopping turning his hands back and forth in front of the flames. "I'll ride over and tell Buthar tomorrow. It might be our last chance to speak with him for a while."

*****

"Ye gods! It's cold enough to freeze the...What the!" Ranald spun round his saddle to look across to Bear, riding alongside.

The wolf's sudden call was still echoing down the dale when Sköll answered with a long guttural yowl.

Bear laughed at his companion's startled expression, and then turned to look across the valley. "There. See it, no them. A mother and two cubs. Just above that central crag. They're dark against the snow." He turned back to Ranald. "A mother with cubs isn't a threat, though she may be calling to others in the pack. Hunger will be driving them down into the dale and, though they may fancy their chances against a pony and would certainly take our sheep, a clash with men and hounds isn't what they're after."

"Aye, Lord." Ranald sounded relieved, "Though I'll warn Leo to spread the word around the farmsteads. I'm just glad we saw them on the way back from Butremere."

Bear nodded agreement as he spurred Óðr into a quicker pace on the ice-hard ground. Although they were below the snow-line, Bear knew that the freezing weather would drive the animals that lived around the edges of man's habitat to take ever greater risks just to survive. Foxes were a constant, but controllable, pest. The wolves and boar that clung to a precarious life in the higher, craggier and wooded dales were more of a problem. He called Sköll to heel and shouted across to Ranald, "Agnaar's had reports of a boar in the thickets below the head of Lowthwaite, not far from the new lead workings. I want to see if we can find its spoor. A hunt and a boar's head for Yuletide would be good for the men, what do you think?"

Ranald grunted, daunted rather than thrilled by the prospect of a close tangle with a starving boar, but he forced a laugh of appreciation. "Aye, a good feast is what we all need."

As they made their way across the broad dale's boggy bottom, and up into the narrow confines of the steeper subsidiary dale below the Lowthwaite crags, Bear was sure that the reports were correct.

"Look yonder Lord, where the beck leaves the scrub. That looks to me like something big has been rooting over the ground." Ranald pointed to a patch of scarred bare earth a hundred paces away.

Bear dismounted, handed his reins to Ranald and took Sköll forward cautiously. As he got closer he could see that a long stretch of the beck's bank had been turned over until it exposed the underlying bedrock. All signs of vegetation had disappeared. Sköll growled as Bear bent down to poke at a large frozen scat. He looked up and saw that the hound stood frozen, his head pointing towards a dark tunnel that disappeared into the tall dead grey grasses bordering the scrub.

"Easy boy, come away." Bear spoke softly, urging Sköll to back away; the scrub was without doubt the lair of an adult boar. Whether it was male, female or even a family, he couldn't yet tell. Keeping Sköll close he moved methodically across the churned ground until he found the first of the cloven-hoofed tracks. He found more as he worked his way down to the beck. All were of a uniformly large size, it was a clear sign that a solitary adult had its den somewhere in the scrub.

Giving a low whistle, Bear waved for Ranald to join him with the ponies. He rode up, dismounted and examined the tracks.

"I agree, Lord. One big one I'd say, going by the size of the tracks and the skat. Thank the gods it's frozen."

Bear laughed, dropping the skat he had been examining. "I certainly wouldn't be handling it...and the smell!" He spat as the mere thought of it cloyed in his nostrils and the back of his throat, and added, "Come, mount up and we'll ride up onto the fellside and take a look down. If I'm right, the beck sweeps right into the bank on yon side of the scrub. They'll be no way the boar can escape if we come at it from the grass in front of the scrub."

*****

158

Bear stepped back from the model that he had built on the floor of Gytha's hall. "We'll leave at first light tomorrow. As best as I can tell, the weather looks set to be fair. Cold and dry will suit us. Anyhap, that's the plan, but before I take questions, I want to stress how important Gytha and Rauði's roles are in this." He could tell by her body language that his sister was far from happy, and he wanted to forestall an argument. "From their position on the fellside above and behind the beck and the scrub they should be able to see the boar's movement when it disturbs the bushes around it. Keep your eyes on Rauði. By positioning her pony in line with the boar we'll all know whereabouts in the scrub it is. Listen to Gytha's horn blasts. Remember, one blast means it is ten paces from our line, two means twenty, and so on. A long blast warns that it is charging. They really are our eyes and ears. Clear?" He glanced quickly at Gytha. She had unfolded her arms, and a hint of a smile told him that she was placated.

"Yes, Ulf?" Although Ulf wasn't joining the hunt he was keen to be involved.

"Are you just taking the two hounds?"

Bear chuckled. "Come on Ulf. You know Hati, she's my moder's hound and will do no-one else's bidding, whereas Loki is almost as loyal to Leo as he is to Gytha."

Catching sight of Osberht's frown, Bear forestalled the inevitable question. "Sorry, Osberht but I can't risk us all being away. I need your safe hands here, with Wealmaer and three sections in case you have to respond to either Neven's girls or the lads still up at Watendlath."

Osberht gave a wry smile, his frown fading. "So be it. The lads that stay behind will be disappointed. I know we can't take the risk, but I had to ask on their behalf."

Ulf cut in. "They won't be that put out. How about we work together testing the catapult's range and working out how to channel approach routes into killing grounds. That'll be the real work of the day."

Osberht gave his foster father a wink of appreciation. "Aye, Fader. Sounds good."

Bear broke up the meeting before it degenerated into a hub-bub of excitement. "That's it. Section commanders, run your lads through the tactics I've given you...and remember to lash crossbars onto your spear hafts. I've heard of a dying boar driving itself along the length of a spear to gore its attacker. You've been warned."

*****

The day was cold and grey. Featureless stratus cloud hovered just above the fell tops, blending into the white of the snow-clad ridge lines and blocking sight of the sun. Devoid of a vestige of warmth the ground remained frozen, earth and rock were equally unyielding.

Bear gathered the men opposite the thicket, where they were surrounded by the signs of the boar's rooting. "This is it lads. You can tell from the size of the hoof marks that we're up against a big beast, but just the one, I think." He gestured towards Gytha and Rauði mounted on their ponies on the steep slope above the dense thicket with the beck at its back. Rauði waved her arm up and down and then pointed straight ahead. She was about two thirds of the way across the two hundred paces wide frontage of the thicket.

"Do you all see where Rauði is? She's showing us the line that the boar is on." Five short sharp horn blasts followed. Bear concentrated on the image in his mind of how the thicket filled the wide U-shaped bend of the beck as it cut its way into the bank below the two women. "Five blasts, that's fifty paces. The boar must be almost directly below the women, by the bank." He hesitated, a sudden thought forming. "If the boar is over to our right we can cut down on the ground we have to clear. "Kai, Cerdik, yours are the left-hand sections. When we form a line across the front of the thicket I want you to take a line straight across to the bank ahead of us. Gufa's is the third from the left. Go straight in from his left-hand man. We'll

160

wait until you shout to say that you're in place, then we'll slowly move in and tighten the noose. Is that clear?"

A chorus of "Aye, Lord," confirmed understanding.

Bear waited for Kai's call and then ordered the men forward. He followed close behind the line, with Leofric and Bjorn either side of him. Doubt immediately started to nag. The thicket was denser and more entangled than he had appreciated. Thorns snagged at his clothes and he struggled to see more than three men in either direction. More worryingly, the scrubby bushes were higher than he had realised, and his ability to see Rauði was becoming constricted. A sense of panic seized him, and as he took a series of deep breaths Sköll look back questioningly, as if he sensed his master's emotion. He fought to clear his head, and thought quickly.

"Halt! Sections, hold it there a moment!" Bear's shout cut across the sound of rustles, heaving breathing and cursing from the men labouring through the undergrowth.

Bjorn!

"Lord? I'm just behind you."

"Can you see Rauði?"

"Aye, just. She's moved to her left a bit. Mayhap ten paces."

"That means the boar is moving away from us, across our front. I want you to move down the line to your right. Tell each commander to be prepared to fill across to his right when we move on. Tell Godfrid, his is the last section and that he is to pull out of the line and cross the beck. I want him to prevent the boar trying to break out across the water. Have you got that?"

Bjorn's "Will do" sounded a lot more confident than he felt. His only reference points in the half-light of the dense undergrowth were his partial view of Rauði on the fellside and the nondescript slopes of the valley side behind him. He struggled past two men, paused to brief Gufa, passed the last man in that section and looked around for the first in Arkil's section. He twisted about, looking left and right, and was about to call out when his foot snagged on a briar and he fell backwards. The ground seemed to drop behind him. He rolled over twice and struck his head before falling, dazed, into a shallow sump. Its icy sides would have oozed with water on a warmer day.

Bjorn pushed himself up with a grunt and took a deep breath before sitting still, trying to listen whilst his head cleared. He called out, but the voices that came back in reply were muffled, varied, and seemed to come from all around.

"Skita!" Bjorn cursed under his breath as he slipped on the icy bank. He bent forward and scrabbled with his hands, but still couldn't get enough purchase to make his way up the slope. Looking around he realised that the sump formed a natural bowl drained by a narrow gulley that seemed to provide a clearer way through the thicket from where it led into a clump of blackthorn bushes. Surmising that it would lead to the beck he gave one last shout for help. His call unanswered, he picked up his spear and made his way, crouching, along the gulley. He reasoned that when he reached the river he could find his bearings and communicate with Bear via Gytha. Fetid semi-frozen mud engulfed his feet. As the cold damp began to numb his toes he became distracted by the increasing discomfort. He was unsure how far along the gulley he had moved, but thought he could see a lightening of the gloom ahead.

Bjorn's dim, confined world changed in an instant. The horn's long blast caused his heart to jump just as the gulley's natural way under the scrub was suddenly blocked by a black, growling stinking mass, hurtling towards him. Two blood-shot yellow eyes glowed in the centre of the black. Bjorn reacted instinctively. Jabbing his spear butt into the mud, he braced it with his right foot and crouched over it, praying to the gods that his spear wouldn't snap and that the cross-brace behind the spear's tip would stop the boar sliding along its length. An immense weight crashed into him in a crescendo of noise and stench. As the spear tip jerked upwards, Bjorn felt a sudden thrust and rolled with it into a gap between the blackthorn trunks on his left. He felt his body being trampled, as if kicked by a dozen men, and the now-screaming mass swept past leaving a metallic smell of blood and fetid excrement in its wake. He lay momentarily stunned and then began to move, trying to flex his fingers and toes, followed by his hands and feet. His right hand seemed to be pinned behind his back and his fingers were numb. He strove to reach it with his left hand, but screamed with pain as he felt his fingers poke into his arm. "Help!" He gasped. Then he panicked and screamed again. "H...help!"

*****

Arkil felt his feet slipping under him and staggered, trying to keep his balance on the steep, icy bank. "Stay up there, Nudd. It's as slippery as hell here."

It was during the pause in their advance through the scrub that Arkil had realised that his left-hand man, Nudd, had lost touch with the right of Gufa's section. After some shouting back and forth he had realised that he needed to shift his men to the left, which meant pulling the section on his right across to the left too. He could sense from the increasingly exacerbated tone of the commands coming along the line that Bear was becoming frustrated, but at last they were in position, or so he thought. As the line recovered its advance the horn counted down their progress. Four blasts, and then three, implied that their prey must still be in its den whilst they moved forward.

Arkil glanced up and shouted to Nudd. "Hold on. Because there are no trees down here I can just see the lasses on the fellside. Ye gods...Rauði's pointing straight at us. We must be in line with the boar. There's a gulley that seems to run in that direction. Give Bear a shout to say that we are taking a look and then join me. I'll wait." He heard Nudd move away from the edge of the sump and start shouting to Bear, just as Gytha's horn blast warned of the boar's charge.

163

A sound of crashing and snapping undergrowth, then a long squeal of pain, exploded from the gulley entrance. Arkil felt the earth start to tremble and he stepped back quickly, away from the entrance. He had the heavy seax that he had brought instead of his sword drawn and poised, ready to stab down at the beast that must surely soon be upon him.

The boar's charge out of the tunnel was so swift that Arkil didn't have time to strike. He gagged as the stench of blood and gore caught in his throat and watched, shocked, as the squealing beast staggered halfway up the icy slope before its flailing front legs lost traction and it rolled backwards. A spear shaft embedded in its stomach appeared to have been ripped sideways, as a length of bleeding intestines spilled out of the deep gash. The boar lay on its side with its head raised and the black pupils of its yellow eyes fixed on Arkil. Its hind quarters were still and Arkil realised that it must have been paralysed by the spear embedded deep within its back. He approached cautiously, but stepped back quickly when the boar slashed its tusks sideways.

"Hold back, Arkil! I can finish it with a head shot from here." Arkil glanced up, almost surprised that Nudd was above him, kneeling on the bank with his crossbow braced.

"Good, finish him quickly, then get Bear here. That spear in its guts means that someone was already in the ditch. God knows who...and if they are alive? I'm going in." As he stepped back the boar's head jerked sharply then slumped down, with a bolt buried in its left eye.

Arkil crouched in the tunnel entrance and paused, the place still reeked from the boar's passage. He listened, and then crawled forward as quickly as he could. A feint, almost delirious call for help drew him on.

*****

Gytha felt increasingly concerned as she watched the drama unfold below her. Wondering why Bear had sent men forward to form a new line at a right-angle to his

164

main one, she quickly realised that he was intending to pen the boar into a corner, but was soon aware that the move was too complicated to work within the confines of the dense scrub. Whilst she could see where most of the men were by the movement of the vegetation she soon doubted that many could see her. That became more apparent when the advance halted amidst a confused reorganisation. She saw the line of sections start to fragment and a lone man stumble into a clearing. One of several small clearings in the scrub, it appeared to be joined to that of the boar's den by a line of blackthorn bushes. The man appeared confused by his situation as he disappeared from sight into the line of blackthorns.

"Was that Bjorn?" Rauði's concerned shout broke Gytha's concentration.

"Mayhap, it's hard to tell. Keep a close eye on the boar, and point if it moves into that line of blackthorns." Gytha suspected Rauði might be right, but there was little they could do.

The boar was becoming increasingly frantic at the sound of men crashing through the scrub. Running back and forth within its clearing, it suddenly bolted towards the line of thorns bushes. Rauði saw the branches tremble as it passed below, and moved her pony briskly sideways in line with the boar's position. She jumped, startled, as Gytha's long horn blast sounded, and watched aghast as the boar continued beyond the line of blackthorns into the clearing, leaving a red trail.

"Come! We're more use down there." Gytha's shout broke Rauði's trance. She wheeled her pony around and urged it into a cautious downhill trot, fearful of what she would find.

*****

Arkil didn't like the look of Bjorn's wound, but spoke calmly, "You'll be alright lad, it doesn't look as bad as it must feel." He helped Bjorn to sit on the edge of the ditch and moved Bjorn's right arm gently so that he could hold it with his left. Blood oused from a long gash in the forearm, but Arkil couldn't see bone and was reassured that an artery hadn't been severed. "I'm going to hack these lower branches off, then you'll be able to walk out. More help will be here soon." Arkil stooped to clasp the shoulder of Bjorn's good arm. "You'll be the hero of the day lad. Only the gods know how you came to be here, but you killed that bastard boar for us. Nudd's finished it off, but it was already dying."

As Arkil started to slash his seax's broad blade into the lower blackthorn branches he could hear others cutting their way towards him. He cursed as he strove to find space to wield his seax to cut through the branches above them. Sharp finger length thorns stabbed through his jerkin, ripping his hands and cheeks, but the urgent need to get Bjorn's arm cleaned and treated spurred him on. Able at last to stand hunched, he got Bjorn to his feet and led the way, hacking and slashing as he went.

Bjorn followed Arkil along the ditch, his jaw clamped firmly in an effort to control the throbbing pain in his arm. He felt dazed and oddly detached from what was happening. Although shocked at the sudden events, and still unsure as to quite how it had occurred, he was beginning to feel a pride in his ability to face mortal danger and survive. As he staggered out of the tunnel into a sea of grinning faces and a chorus of praise he couldn't help a shy smile of his own.

Bear gave Bjorn a warm partial embrace and guided him firmly towards the man standing behind. "Gufa and his men will see you safely back up the slope, they've broken up the ice. We've already hauled the boar to the top. Take a look at it. You and it will live in the sagas of my hall for evermore now."

Bjorn shook his head in disbelief, unable to speak through his clenched jaws. He felt almost carried up the slope, before pausing to stare at the dead boar. He was grateful that it was smaller than the black beast that dominated his memory of the past hour, but it was big enough. He gave a sigh and turned as Rauði's arms wrapped around his neck.

"Come, my love," she whispered into his cheek. "I refuse to shed tears in front of all these men. Let's get you to the beck where we can wash your wound, then Gytha and I will get you home and into Adelind's care."

Aefter Yule 1102

Chapter 15

Bjorn lay drenched in sweat, his mind in perpetual turmoil. He felt pain, a universal pain that racked his body and swept in waves through his constant haunting nightmares. He was panting, breathless from constant running, fleeing from the baleful yellow eyes of a lunging black beast. Occasionally, an angel came to him, at least he supposed she was an angel, or one of several. One had flaxen hair and a tender motherly face, another had piercing green eyes and braided fair hair. It was the third one that always seemed to break through into his world of turmoil. She was the one with crying grey eyes, hair the colour of autumn leaves and skin as pale as carved walrus bone. Once, he felt her stroke his brow and joined him in his delirium, running alongside as he fled. Somehow, they escaped from the hideous beast, bursting from the black forest into the waters of a dazzling lake, pursued now by jeering youths who tore the angel from him and held him down, forcing his head under the water. Bjorn felt his lungs fill, water suffocating him, and then he was free, gasping cool air, his head softly cushioned. Suddenly unafraid, he opened his eyes.

"My love, oh my love, you've come back to us." Bjorn recognised the voice, realised too that his head was cradled against the breast of the third angel as she washed his face with a wet cloth.

"Rauði!" He croaked, his throat uncomfortably dry. "W...water."

Rauði held Bjorn's shoulders with her arm and raised him up before reaching for an earthen cup. "Here, I'll wet your lips first, then take small sips." She watched him closely, and on seeing his eyelids start to droop, eased him down and kissed his forehead gently. "Rest my love. I think your fever has passed. Rest whilst I fetch Adelind."

Bjorn was sleeping when Rauði returned. She stood back whilst Adelind ran her fingers over his brow and used a fine sharp blade to cut away the thin linen dressing on the young man's forearm. Placing the bloodied dressing to one side, she felt carefully along the length of an angry-looking purple wheal, as her fingers probed tenderly to test the warmth and feel of the wound. She sniffed her fingers and then sniffed the wound. Looking closely at the scab of dried puss and blood she felt the peace of relief at how well her carefully placed sutures were holding the edges of the ripped flesh together. "Good," she sighed at last.

Rauði realised that she was holding her breath in trepidation, and sighed too.

"Mix another salve of honey and egg white, and bath the wound with it. We'll leave it open to the air for now." Adelind spoke quietly so as not to disturb her patient and, as she stood to leave, gave Rauði a gentle squeeze on her shoulder. "You're doing well, and learning quickly. Thank you."

"No. Thank you." Rauði turned to face Adelind. The latter paused, and with the back of her fingers wiped a tear from the younger woman's cheek.

"When he next wakes, feed him a little broth. He'll be weak for a long while yet, but thank God we have saved him."

The short day's light was fading when Bjorn next woke. His questioning disorientated voice roused Rauði, dosing on a stool by his bed. "I am here," she blurted, startled, but continued calmly, "Wait a moment whilst I light a candle."

Later, having helped Bjorn to his first food in many days, she placed the empty broth bowl to one side and took his left hand in hers whilst she looked at his injured right arm. "Can you feel your fingers?"

Bjorn nodded, flexing them a little. "When is Yuletide?" He asked. "Will I be well enough to watch the mummery? The hall will lack a harpist, that's for sure."

Rauði gasped, then gave a low laugh. "You've been abed with fever this past fortnight or more. Yuletide has been and gone." She hesitated, loathe to take Bjorn back to the turmoil of his nightmares. "What do you remember?"

Bjorn stared at her, wide eyed, and shook his head. "I...I remember a boar, then riding behind you, with Gytha by our side to hold me up." He frowned, then flinched. "Blackness and pain. That's all."

Rauði squeezed his hand and smiled into his eyes. "That's as well, my love, there's nothing more to remember. Save to say that you were the toast of the hall at Yuletide, and will be again when you return there. But that's for another day. All that matters now, is building your strength so that you can play the harp again."

"And lift a sword." Bjorn added grimly, with a determination that chilled Rauði.

*****

"Loose!" Eadwig's barked command resounded across the plateau at the top of the crag. Its echo from the far side of the valley was drowned by the sound of six men jumping from the plateau onto a broad ledge three feet below them, and by the squeak of greased wood turning in a wooden socket. Each man held a stout braided rope which he pulled sharply downwards as he jumped. The ropes, attached to a frame at the shorter end of the perrièr's long pole, jerked the pole into the vertical and the sling at its longer end released a dozen fist-sized rocks into a long high trajectory. They stood out as black specks against the white snow-clad fells and then blurred as their path dropped below the snowline.

"Mark their flight, lads." Cudel shouted from the centre of the plateau. "We have to be sure just how far across the valley they fall."

Ulf and Cudel had spent days trying to get the second and larger perrièr to sling rocks as far as the crags on the eastern side of the valley, but they had always fallen short, landing in the river. Almost out of desperation they had risked overstressing the pivot that held the perrièr's long pole, and added a sixth rope to the frame. The weight and extra momentum provided by the sixth man would, they hoped, provide just enough range. A raucous cheer confirmed that they had.

Ulf gave Cudel a friendly slap on his back and stomped over to the six men, winking at Eadwig as he went. "Well done, I knew Egbert's girth would come in handy." He teased the man who had been co-opted from the other perrièr team. "Where exactly did they land?"

Egbert grinned back at Ulf. Usually shy, the blacksmith's assistant was powerful yet soft-spoken and the butt of many a joke. He welcomed the old warrior's recognition. "They spread in flight and hit from the bottom of the crag to mayhap half a dozen man-heights up it." Egbert described the fall of the rocks in the best way he could.

"Good...good." Ulf nodded appreciatively. "And you've good eyesight, lad, I'd wager some of your mates couldn't track them. We need a good pair of eyes up here." He turned to Cudel and Eadwig, who were examining the pivot attaching the pole to its supporting trestle. "Problem?" he grunted.

"None that I can see, but I'll keep packing sheep fat around the pivot." Cudel replied positively. "We can work with two five-man teams most of the time. It's only if that far flank is threatened that we'll need Egbert's weight."

"Aye, but at least we've closed the last gap in our defence. Have the lads keep on as they are. I want to see how consistent that fall of rocks is. Once we're happy with the consistency of how they pull the perrièr they can recover as many of the rocks as they can, and have the ponies carry them back up. I want them practicing every seventh day. Between times we can work on building up a stockpile of rocks by each perrièr. Happy?" Ulf checked their understanding.

"Aye, Ulf. Consider it done. When we've finished here, can I walk the lines of boulder-traps with you? There're some changes I'd like to make." Cudel spoke confidently, sure that Ulf would agree.

"I'll come with you." They turned, surprised to see Neven sitting on the rock behind them.

"You've the stealth of a cat, that's for certain." Ulf chuckled, impressed. Neven smiled back, pleased with the compliment. "Yes, join us. It's best the green women know where I want to block Sigulfson's men should they come calling, where this young man of yours intends to shower them with rocks, and where you may well need to group your archers and slingers.

*****

Bjorn steadied himself, clutching at the edge of the hall's long table with his left hand. His legs were still unsteady from his time confined to bed. The fever had stolen weight from his body and his muscles felt wasted and powerless. "Again!" He spoke out loud, his voice resolute, masking the pain he felt. He was thankful that Ulf had taken Neven and Cudel to check whether the lakeshore ice was thin enough to take a svanmeyja out, and that Ealdgith and Brynhildr had gone for a walk down to the vill to see Adelind, leaving him alone in the main body of the hall as he forced himself to walk another round of its inside. He returned to the table, sat on the bench, took a small but weighty pig of lead in his left hand, and raised it slowly at arm's length as he counted to ten. Resisting the urge to drop his arm quickly, Bjorn lowered the weight slowly back to the bench and repeated the exercise.

Ulf had shown him what to do. Bjorn was very aware that, at least for the foreseeable future, he would be unable to use his right arm until the long tear from wrist to elbow had healed. Even then, he doubted that it would ever regain the strength it once had. Although he had previously been able to use one hand as well as the other, he realised that he must now focus on building up his left and was thankful that Dai had encouraged him to wield his sword with it. He was sure that a battle was coming, and he wanted to be ready and to be able to fight on his own terms. Bjorn had confronted his fear when he faced the boar, but it had been an unequal fight and one he had so nearly lost; he had to be stronger for the next one.

172

Early that morning Rauði had left with Gytha and Osberht to ride to the small outpost at Watendlath, and Bjorn was determined to have regained his balance before they returned. He stood as he heard someone coming quickly up the steps to the hall, and moved to open the door. Expecting to see Rauði's smiling face, he stepped back in surprise as the door was pushed open to reveal an exhausted stranger, sweaty and grimy from a hard ride. He stared, confused, before quickly realising that the stranger in the travel worn clothes was Arkil.

"I must see Gytha, or Osberht. Where are they?" Arkil was breathless after running up from the stables.

"Away, checking on Watendlath. But they should be back soon. I thought you'd be them. Why don't you sit by the hearth whilst I find someone to bring a mulled ale?" Bjorn pointed into the hall, pushed the door shut, and walked as steadily as he could in search of a servant. He returned moments later and eased himself down by Arkil. "It's on its way. What's up? Why are you dressed so?"

Arkil relaxed, ran a hand through his hair, yawned, and slumped forward with his elbows on his knees. "It's good to see you on the mend, Bjorn. Ye gods, but I thought we'd lost you when I saw you in that ditch." He gave a tired sideways smile, "How's the arm?" Then raised an eyebrow as Bjorn pulled the loose sleeve clear of his forearm. "Shsss...you were lucky." He said, sucking air though his teeth. "Does it throb?"

"More an ache. But it's weak. I'm working on my left one to compensate." Bjorn spoke almost dismissively, hoping to sound confident. He was gratified by the section leader's genuine interest, and was feeling increasingly that the incident with the boar had been seen by others as a rite of passage. He sensed that the men within the hall now saw him as one of them, rather than an outsider favoured by their mistress.

Arkil accepted the cup of warm ale from a young serving girl, grunted and sat upright, his mouth breaking into a grin under his matted brown beard. "You did well lad. There's not many who'd have stood their ground against that beast." He paused. "Anyhap, you asked what's up? The fight our Lady is planning for is coming. I'm sure of it now." He waved his hand along the length of his clothes. "This is what I wear when calling on Grimr at Ameleseta. That bastard Norman overlord, Le Meschin Lady Gytha calls him, is there. Or at least his men are. Grimr's place is full of them. A good score I'd say. I didn't dare go in, but hung around the well and caught his serving wench when she came out with a bucket. She then sought out Grimr and got him to speak to me. There're a couple of knights and their squires there who insist on speaking that French tongue of theirs, but some of their foot soldiers are English, from the south, like those who serve Sigulfson. The Normans speak to Grimr through them, and they're happy to brag about what they are doing. It seems that Le Meschin is waiting for Sigulfson to bring men over from Ulueswater, then they'll ride together once the snows clear from Dynfal's Raise and make a show of force to prove they control Wythburndalr and the fells east of Allerdalr, before probing into the central..."

The door burst open and a cold draft swept into the hall as Osberht entered, followed by Gytha. Rauði came last, carrying a sack which she passed to the servant girl as she asked for more ale to be brought.

"Ye gods! It's cold enough to...Arkil!" Osberht exclaimed.

Arkil stood quickly, as he placed his cup on the table. Bjorn raised himself slowly.

"Relax man. You look exhausted. Something tells me there's news from Grimr, and that it's not good." Gytha gestured for Arkil to sit, then smiled at Bjorn. "You're looking stronger, were you swapping tales of the boar?"

"I have news, my Lady, and it's not good. I was just telling Bjorn that Le Meschin's men are in Ameleseta."

Osberht offered Gytha a stool. She sat and listened whilst Arkil reported everything Grimr had told him.

"So, we have until the snows clear from Kirkstein, then we can expect a deliberate show of force in Wythburndalr followed by an attempt to cross over the tops to here." Gytha summarised Arkil's message.

"Aye, my Lady." Arkil nodded.

Gytha glanced at Osberht and back to Arkil. "Did Grimr speak of our lands at Ulueswater?"

"Aye, he did. He said to tell you that Lord William made a point of placing some of his men in the two halls at Glynrhedyn. It's to show that he can, and will, control the vills around the lake. But Sigulfson has taken over Ulf's hall at Grassthwaite Howe. They are overseeing the mining above Patrichesdale from there." Arkil gave Gytha a wry smile. "Grimr says it's not going well, given that nearly all the miners moved here."

Osberht interrupted with a chuckle, "And finding replacements will be like looking for hen's teeth. I heard that those in the Eden vale are being sucked into the King's silver mine at Aldeneby, on yon side of Cross Fell."

Gytha smiled briefly, "Thanks, Arkil. You've done well, very well. Did you get a chance to see how the snow's lying around Kirkstein?"

"No, my Lady, not on the pass itself. But it is generally thicker on the eastern slopes, and Helvellyn looks to have taken a pasting. I'd say it'll be gone from Dynfal's Raise before it is from Kirkstein."

"What do you say, Osberht?" Gytha looked across to her deputy.

"Arkil's right. The way from Wythburndalr to Gressemere will be clear before Sigulfson can get his men over Kirkstein. I need to take a close look at the road on both sides of the Raise and find the best ambush sites. Once the snow starts to thin I'll keep a section on watch near the top of the Raise. They can live in the round-houses that we repaired."

"Good." Osberht's plan mirrored Gytha's thoughts. "Bear and I need to warn Jarl Buthar. Rauði, ride now and tell Bear that we'll call for him in the morning as we head towards Roger Saetr. It'll be a snowy ride. And warn Kai that I want his section with us."

"Aye, Gytha." Rauði stood to take her leave. Her hand had barely touched the hall door when it burst open towards her. A cold blast caught her as Brynhildr stumbled past, panting for breath.

The girl paused, glanced around wide-eyed, and ran to Gytha. "Moder, quickly. It's Ealdmoder! She's fallen on the track. Ulf found us and sent me for help. Oh Moder, she's so cold and white." Brynhildr sobbed as Gytha pulled her close.

"Stay with her Gytha. Arkil, Rauði, with me!" Osberht shouted the order as he tore past Rauði and out of the hall."

Osberht cursed and forced himself to slow as his foot skidded on the half-frozen steps. He couldn't risk becoming a casualty himself. "There, fifty paces ahead. Arkil, don't stop. Run on and fetch Adelind." He called back over his shoulder as he saw Ulf stooped over, his one good arm around Ealdgith and struggling to lift her to her feet, whilst Hati hindered him, seemingly torn between nuzzling her mistress and barking to attract attention.

"Here, let us." Rauði pulled Hati firmly to one side and caressed her head reassuringly whilst Osberht bent down alongside Ulf and gently lifted Ealdgith to her feet.

"Slowly, Edie. I've got you." He said, as her felt Ealdgith trying to bare her own weight.

"I, I'm alright. It was the cold and the wind. They stole my breath, then my chest tightened." Ealdgith spoke faintly, her voice hesitant."

"Shush, Edie." Ulf spoke with a soft firmness. "Save your breath and breathe deeply through your nose." Catching Osberht's eye, he added in a tone that would stop any dissension, "Osberht is going to lift you and carry you back to the hall."

"And Arkil's on his way to fetch Adelind to you." Osberht added, as he placed his left arm under

Ealdgith's knees and straightened up, holding her close.

"Rauði lass, run back to the hall ahead of us. Have them prepare warm broth and a seat by the hearth. Once she's warmed through we'll get Edie to bed." Ulf smiled reassuringly as he spoke.

Ulf respected Ealdgith's insistence that she must walk into the hall. He took her arm as Osberht lowered her to her feet. Ealdgith coughed upon the door's opening as a wave of warm smoky air entered her lungs. "Oh for the sea's fresh air," she spoke huskily, talking to no-one in particular.

"Aye, Edie. For us both." Ulf replied quietly, recalling a memory of Bebbanburge's gull-clad cliffs and a bright-eyed young woman standing laughing in the bows of her uncle's snekke as it crashed through North Sea waves.

*****

Gytha rode with a heavy heart. Her mother's frailty had shocked her, and she cursed herself for having been blind to her continuing decline. She knew too that they had to warn the Jarl and prepare for the inevitable clash. Her mother had made it quite clear that this was where her children's duty lay, and Gytha had been grateful for Ulf's reassurance that Ealdgith was his priority now. He was confident that the crag-top perrièrs, and the teams of men he had trained to work them, could be left under Cudel's control. Bear shared in the worry of conflicting responsibilities, and the couple rode in silence, coming to terms with their thoughts and fears. Rauði and Ranald followed, talking quietly, as they made their way westward across thin snow, towards the high pass and steep descent into Butremere.

Rauði cast her eyes quickly across the faces in the Jarl's hall and was relieved to see no sign of Cnut or Erland, though Hákon's expression when their

177

eyes met inferred that Gytha must have spoken to him about his son's behaviour.

"Welcome Bear! Hákon, join us! You too Freja. Come and eat with your brother and sister." Jarl Buthar's effusive shout broke Rauði's distraction. She followed Gytha as they made their way towards the head of the hall's long table.

"Gille is away in the southlands." Freja told Bear and Gytha, kissing them before her greeting was interrupted by the Jarl's command that they sit either side of him.

"It's a bit late for Yuletide greetings, so I can only suppose your news is not of the best." Jarl Buthar frowned, looking questioningly from Bear to Gytha.

Bear nodded, encouraging Gytha to speak first. "No, it's not, Buthar. But at least we have forewarning of what is to come, and we have a plan to counter it."

The Jarl listened intently, his expression brightening as Gytha spoke. As she finished he clapped his hands to attract attention, shouted for ale and food, and good humouredly said, "It is as we thought it might be. Sigulfson or Le Meschin is bound to try to stake their claim to Wythburndalr, just as you are bound to bloody their noses when they do. Arne will hold Langdalr, Gille is there with him now. Once the thaw comes he will take his men over the high passes and see if there is any activity on the old stone road and in the valleys beyond. Hákon has men in Cletergh as we speak. Black William's men come and go, but they are just small numbers showing a presence. The lands to the north are free of them."

"And thank the gods for that." Bear interrupted. "We can't risk them chancing upon our jaggers taking lead to Wirkynton."

"They won't." Hákon interjected. "I'll have men to the south of the route whenever you send lead there. There will be enough of them to divert attention and send your jaggers a warning. Just give me enough notice to get my men in place."

"That's enough talking for now. Let's eat." Buthar commanded, raising a horn of ale to his mouth.

Chapter 16

Gytha shifted backwards, away from the lump in the mattress, enjoying the warmth of Leofric spooned around her, but less enamoured by his snoring in her ear. The dull grey light filtering through the part-closed shutters suggested to her that their crag-top hall was once again bound by low cloud or hill fog. As she roused, the sound of a rhythmic dripping broke through Leofric's snoring. Sitting up quickly, Gytha groped for her gown in the half-light, eased herself up from the low pallet, pushed the shutters further open, and grimaced as she looked out upon a wet, grey world outside. Moisture-laden fog, combined with sooty snowmelt from the hearth-vents in the roof, to present a very wet and unappealing start to the day. She snapped the shutters closed and turned to her husband as he stretched bleary eyed. "It's thawing Leo, and with a vengeance."

"Which means," Leofric sighed, "that you'll be taking the men for a very muddy sojourn in Wythburndalr."

*****

Osberht rubbed his palms across his tired eyes and squinted into the early morning gloom. As soon as the winter dawn's light was sufficient to ride by, he had left their forward camp in three refurbished round-houses that he had had the foresight to prepare before the Yuletide break. Tucked away on a rare piece of flat ground between The Nab's crags and the upper Wythburn beck, the round houses were hidden from anyone on the road over the raise. He tapped Kai on his shoulder, "I'm going forward to those trees, mayhap we'll see Gressemere vill more clearly from there. Follow once I'm in position." He moved off without waiting for an acknowledgement. Bent low and making use of a shallow fold in the profile of the field, Osberht's body was soon nothing more than a blur. Kai ran after him, determined not to lose sight of him in the dim light and patchy grey fog.

Kai squatted down next to Osberht under the shelter of a gnarled oak, shook heavy drips from the edge of his cowl and wiped his brow with the palm of his hand. "That's better, at least I can see without water in my eyes. But it's so muggy and surprisingly warm in this fog, I could well do without it."

"Tell me what you think?" Osberht asked, trying to refocus Kai's attention. They were looking down from a low ridge onto the roof tops and market place of the small lakeside vill."

Kai took a moment to take stock of the activity in front of them: indistinct shouts muffled by the fog, men passing heavy packages from one to another and loading them onto a cart, oxen eating from nose-bags. "Plenty of men-at-arms, Lord, but very few horses and just oxen with the carts. I'd say they are readying to march and that they are planning to take their time. Those look like tents of some sort that they are loading."

"I agree." Osberht replied, "What's more I can make out two sets of colours on those flags. Sigulfson's for certain. I'd wager that the others are Le Meschin's. From what Gytha said, I'm pretty sure that his are a red lion on a yellow background. How many of them do you think there are?"

Kai stared for a while, trying to make out what the murky figures at the far side of the market place were up to. "There're more than a score of them, but less than two, and unless they have horses elsewhere I'd say that the only ones that are mounted are two knights and their squires. I can see four horses tethered, but no sign of any more."

Osberht twitched a smile as he glanced over to his deputy. "I agree. I think they are going to make a show of force by marching through Wythburndalr to Trellekell, and have rightly concluded that their horses would be a liability on broken ground. Trellekell is more than a day's journey if they are tied to the pace of those ox-carts. My coin is on them over-nighting between the two lakes."

Kai grinned back, "So, as long as we keep off the stone road, we can ambush at our will, and ride off on trusted fell ponies without fear of pursuit."

"Aye, and there you have it." Osberht gave a low chuckle, "It looks like they'll be moving soon. We need to get back now. I want you and Arkil with your men in position this side of the top of the pass. I'm sure Gytha will want to have the third section mounted and up on the fellside, from where she can ride down and harry the flanks of any that pass by us."

*****

Their gallop through the mist to warn Gytha, and then the delay incurred whilst moving the men into an ambush position on the crags both sides of the narrow pass where it approached the top of the Raise, meant that Osberht's two sections were only just in place when the first of the marching men-at-arms appeared through the mist.

Osberht clenched a fist in frustration, his nails digging into his palm, as he tried to discern the Normans' order of march. The advance guard appeared to be just two men. He signalled to Kai's section, deployed either side of him, to let them pass whilst hoping that Arkil, in a position across the pass, would do likewise as he waited for the ambush to be sprung. The two men were moving quickly, having settled into a brisk pace, and appeared to be confident that the mist-clad fellside posed little threat.

"Psst! There're more, Lord." Kai, at the far end of the line of men, drew Osberht's attention to close-packed grey shapes now emerging from the clag.

Osberht frowned, concerned. He could make out the vague shapes of two mounted men, flanked by two on foot, and the same again maybe ten paces behind. He waited anxiously, straining to see the score or more of men that must make up the main body of the Norman force. As the lead riders began to pass across the section's front there was still no sign of the men that must be following, nor could he hear the ox carts that he was sure would be grinding their way up the road. "Skita!" Osberht cursed through clenched teeth. He couldn't risk letting a further eight men pass and risk having a large force holding the road on both sides of the two sections.

"Right hand man, wait 'til the front is level with you. We'll let loose upon your lead. Remember, the horses aren't a threat. Go for the men." Osberht was confident that the sound of his low voice would carry no further than his own men.

Osberht tracked one of the leading mounted men with his arrow tip, gradually increasing the tension in the bow-string. The poor visibility had forced him to deploy his men closer to the stone road than he would have liked, but at just fifteen paces he was sure that the arrows and quarrels would rip through mail and induce enough shock and carnage to give them time to loose three or four volleys apiece before those following behind could react. He took a deep breath, steadied his aim, and as the first arrow slashed through the mist he let his own fly. Osberht didn't enjoy killing, but he felt no qualms about killing Normans, and when he did he was cold and methodical.

The mounted men at the front were amongst the first to fall. But those at the back, given the briefest of warnings and time to react in the split-second between the leading arrow and the section's consequent volley, wheeled their horses and galloped back down the road.

Kai's carefully aimed crossbow quarrel glanced off the mailed shoulder of the knight who he had chosen as his mark. Without hesitating, he turned his attention to the killing ground off to his right. Men were falling whilst others were trampled as the horses, hampered by their dead or dying riders, reared up in fear. Arrows whipped in from both sides of the road, seemingly shot by ghosts within the mist. Osberht had been right, four volleys sufficed to leave no one standing. As he tuned to Kai's section and shouted an order to fall back to their ponies he saw more men-at-arms running down the road out of the mist and starting to clamber over the lower crags towards them.

"Go, Lord. I'll hold them. You cover me." Kai yelled above the sound of the echoing screams below them.

Osberht turned and led the section quickly along the line of the slope until they reached the tethered ponies. He turned to cover Kai's withdrawal, and froze. Kai lay on his back, writhing, a spear jutting from his thigh. Osberht gasped, shouted an order for the men to return to Gytha, and began to run, stumbling over the rough ground towards Kai. As he did so, two men emerged from the mist, seized Kai under his shoulders and dragged him down the fellside towards the carnage on the road. Osberht stopped, unsure how to force a rescue. Moments later the men threw Kai backwards over a low boulder, and as one held his arms down the other slowly twisted the spear sideways into Kai's wound. His scream pierced the mist and echoed across the valley.

Osberht gagged, fighting rising nausea. It was the coarse fenland English spoken by the man twisting the spear that broke his inertia. These weren't Normans, they were Sigulfson's men; turncoat English bent upon torturing Kai into betraying his own. The two were soon joined by the rest of the main party and the knight and his squire. Osberht knew without checking his quiver that he didn't have enough arrows to kill all Kai's captors. He barely hesitated before he notched an arrow to the bow string, took aim carefully at Kai's bare head, and spoke hoarsely as he let the arrow loose. "Go my friend. Join my fader, Hravn, Godric, Ada and all other true warriors." Osberht's second and third arrows slashed into Kai's captors. He turned without a backward glance, bile in his throat and tears in his eyes.

*****

Gytha waited with Wealmaer, Rauði and Paega's section on the slope of the hill above the crest of the pass

183

and Dynfal ab Owain's cairn. She could just discern the road on the far side of the huge pile of moss and lichen covered stones. Her mind flitted between images of the long-dead Cumbric king and his last battle in the pass, her strategy for their forthcoming clash with the Normans, and how the mist seemed to be burning off just above them. It was thinning visibly where patches of blue were appearing. She wasn't worried that her position might become exposed; they could always move and adapt. Kai and Arkil could not, and she fretted that they would be caught too close to the road or forced to abandon the ambush before it could be sprung.

"I think we have our answer. Look!" Wealmaer pointed down to their right, towards a group of ponies ridden by green-clad men.

"There are only three. Why?" Rauði asked. She understood as well as any of them that the men had been working in groups of four and five.

"We'll see." Gytha urged her pony forward, very aware that she couldn't see Osberht.

"Kai was taken by a spear, Lady. Osberht returned to help and ordered us to report to you." The first of the green men spoke breathlessly as Gytha halted beside him, concerned she might think they had deserted their captain. "We couldn't see what happened next, the fog was too thick," he continued quickly.

Gytha nodded in acknowledgement, aware of her soldier's concern. "What of the ambush?" She asked.

"We let two scouts pass on foot. Then we caught eight that followed. Four were mounted, but two of them seemed to get away. We left the others on the ground after four volleys, and were leaving with Kai covering us when he was hit. I think their main body heard what was happening and came from our flank. Osber..." He stopped as Osberht burst from the fog, galloping towards them.

"You've heard?" Osberht asked, as he reined his pony to a skittering halt. Although his face and hair were bedraggled from his fast ride through the mist, he still rubbed the back of his hand across his face to erase any sign of his earlier tears.

"Only that Kai was hit by a spear. I can tell by your face, and his absence, that the news is bad."

Osberht took a deep breath, and glanced at Kai's men before replying. "The two that caught him, dragged him down to the road and began to torture him. They were Sigulfson's bastard fenland traitors, I could hear them. Then a score or more burst out of the mist. I only had four arrows left." He paused as his breath caught in his throat. "I...I had to stop Kai's agony before they broke him and made him speak. I used my last arrows on the two who held him, and fled."

Gytha sidled her pony close to Osberht and held his forearm. "You could do no more. It is what Kai would have wanted. We all know the risks we face." As Gytha's words sank in, Rauði glanced at the men of Kai's section, wondering if they had really understood their fate if captured.

Gytha continued authoritatively, "We'll recover Kai and return him to Borgarárdalr with us when we can. First, we need to deal with Sigulfson's men. What do you think they will do next?" She looked from Osberht to Wealmaer.

Wealmaer nodded to Osberht, encouraging him to speak. "A knight and his squire survived. They will make sure their task is completed. I expect they will march to the lake and camp overnight. Whether they wait and load their dead onto the oxcart, I don't know, but any wounded they have will hamper them."

Gytha glanced up. Sensing that the sun was about to burst through and clear the mist from the top of the pass, she came to a decision. "This is going to clear. I want us back to our camp and then up onto The Nab. Rauði, wait for Arkil and his men and then lead them after us. From that spur, we can see exactly what Sigulfson's men do. If they move on and camp overnight we will harry them at first light. Though they may return to Gressemere, or even send a rider back for reinforcements. I want to know exactly what they are up to before we strike again."

Gytha led off at a canter, following the contours around the foot of the fell into the steep valley of the Wythburn beck, past their round houses and then across the beck and northward around the tip of the near vertical face of The Nab. She paused to let those following catch up and to give their ponies a breather. Looking back, she could see Rauði with Arkil's section several furlongs away. She noticed too that the cloying grey mist had disappeared.

Osberht removed his helm and wiped sweat from his brow, asking, "Is it me, or is it suddenly warmer?"

"It's not you." Wealmaer replied with a questioning look at the fell tops. "It's strange. The ground here is still frozen, unlike that under the fog. These past days, whilst we've been encased in the clag, it must have been still freezing up on the tops, in fact everywhere but in the fog. I've never seen anything like it."

"Nor I," Gytha agreed, as she tweaked her reins. "Let's get going. We need to get up onto the ridge and see what Sigulfson is up to. The others can follow." Gytha rode on, watching Loki and envying the way he romped up the fellside whilst she steered her pony on a more sedate but increasingly steep route. The higher they climbed the warmer it became, though here and there the surface of broad patches of snow began to glisten with water, whilst a stiffening breeze blew from the high ground on their right.

As they reached the crest of the ridge, upper Wythburndalr opened up before them. Gytha called over to Wealmaer, "Look down yonder! This side of the old king's cairn. They're on the move. All bunched up. Line the men up along the ridge. I want a show of force. If we can see them they can certainly see us with the sunlight glinting off our spear tips."

"Aye Gytha." Osberht agreed. "From what I can see, that's what's left of the men I saw in Gressemere. There're two on horseback, so no-one has returned for help, and they seem to be moving at the pace of the ox carts."

"Good. We'll wait for Arkil's men to join us and then I'll give a long blast of the horn to make sure they've seen us. The more intimidated they are, the better...what?...do you feel that?" Suddenly wide-eyed, Gytha turned to face the oncoming wind. The confidence in her voice turning to concern as the hitherto freshening breeze was whipped into a series of strong gusts. Loki whined, cowering against his mistress's legs.

All around her the men were reeling under the buffeting wind. Looking down the slope behind her she saw Rauði with Arkil's section drop from their ponies and force them to lie down as spray from the snow-melt lashed past them. Her own men began to do likewise.

"What's happening?" Gytha screamed at Wealmaer, desperately trying to conceal the sound of terror that she knew to be in her voice.

He ran over to her, crouching down to keep his balance. "I don't know for certain, but at a guess the warmer air in the valley bottom has been trapped in the fog and is now rising quickly and sucking down the frozen air from the fell tops."

"Ye gods! Look!" Osberht's shout drew their attention. He was staring down to the foot of the crags. Three mature rowan trees that had clung to the thin soil whilst wrapping their roots around the rocks below were now violently uprooted and hurled into the valley bottom. They watched aghast as the dead winter-grey grass was shaken and flattened by constant gusts tearing down the steep narrow valley with the sound of a hundred galloping horses.

"And across there! It's the vengeance of the gods, it must be." Gytha's eyes followed the line of Osberht's outstretched arm. Her mouth gaped in astonishment.

On the far side of Wythburndalr, the steep valleys incised into the sides of the high flank of

Helvellyn were a mass of agitated swirling air, spray, stones, and ripped and uprooted vegetation. On the road below, men and horses were lifted and thrown. An ox cart was flipped onto its side and pushed by the wind across the road and into the gorge. The oxen were pulled on to their backs, until their traces broke and they rolled free.

Suddenly it was quiet. The wind dropped to a breeze then slowly died away. Gytha rolled onto her back, took a deep breath and stared at the sky, her heart thumping and her mind numb.

Wealmaer recovered first. He stood shakily and turned to the green men who were watching, ashen faced. "It's over lads. It's over. God's will or not, we survived when the poor bastards down there didn't." He stooped, offered Gytha his hand and pulled her to her feet, saying quietly and less formally than normal, "Come, lass, the lads need your cool head more than ever now."

Gytha nodded her thanks with a weak smile. "Take the men and see how Rauði and Arkil faired. Osberht and I will watch from here to see what happens down there. Make your way down to the round-houses, we'll catch you up."

Gytha and Osberht stood emotionless, numbed by their experience whilst watching the pass below. A few men staggered and stumbled around those still lying prostrate, they helped several to gain their feet, and walked slowly towards the cairn and along the track to Gressemere.

"I don't know what just happened, but I hope it's enough to keep them at bay for a while. Come Osberht," Gytha said as she took his arm, "we've time to return and recover Kai's body. We'll rest tonight and return to the hall in the morn."

*****

Osberht, assisted by the three survivors of Kai's section, lifted Kai's body gently across the back of his still-

188

saddled pony and led it back up the road towards Gytha, where she and Rauði had checked the bodies of those left by the Normans, and found two who were conscious but immobile due to their leg wounds.

"Rauði, take the knight's cloak that's snagged on the wreckage of the cart and cut it into strips for me. We'll use it to splint this man's leg by binding against that broken spear shaft.

The man-at-arms, white-faced and with spittle dribbling down his chin watched Gytha and Rauði cautiously, keeping a constant eye upon the wolfhound that stared fixedly at him. He had screamed in pain when Gytha and Rauði had pulled his dislocated knee into place and dragged him backwards to sit upright against a boulder. Summoning the courage to speak, he asked in the heavy accent of the English fenland, "Who are you, women dressed as warriors? Why do you do this?"

Rauði glanced at Gytha, who carried on furbishing the splint before she replied without a hint of emotion. "We aren't dressed as warriors, we are warriors. These are my men and these are my lands. I know your turncoat English lord, and his grasping Norman overlord consider them theirs. Neither have any right to be here. My men would rather I had you tortured, as your men tortured my man earlier, or simply had you slain or left for the wolves tonight. But that is not my way. I saw that I could mayhap save your leg. If your men return for you tomorrow, you will have a life ahead. If not, then at least I have given you a chance."

"But why save me? If I can survive and walk, what is to stop me returning to fight?"

Gytha stopped splinting the man's leg and looked into his eyes. "There is nothing to stop you returning to the fight, if that is your lord's wish. But I hope that after this you would treat my people with respect. I want you to give Forne Sigulfson a message from me. If he intrudes onto my lands and harms my people I will respond with force. Last time he tried, my men burned his granaries and mills around Creistoc – do you not recall? Today again, I met his force with force, and you are one of many who have paid the price. My message is simple: stay away or pay dearly. Is that clear enough?"

The man nodded. Gytha sensed respect in the look he gave her, as he asked, "B...but, Lady, who are you?"

Gytha smiled enigmatically, "I'm Gytha, Hravn's-daughter, but some people call me the Lady of the Lake." She held his stare a moment longer and said, "That's all you need to know about me. Now, I must deal with your comrade as best I can, then we will leave you. You will each be left with a sword and my men will break the cart up for wood and leave you with a fire. Remember my message to your lord."

Lencten 1102

Chapter 17

"There you are, Bear. That's all of them laden. You can get on your way." Agnaar fastened the wicker panniers carried by the last of the dozen jagger ponies.

"Thanks, Agnaar. I appreciate the help. I've been so busy this past fortnight agreeing with the Jarl how his men are going to screen us from interference by Black William, arranging with Aidan's agent for him to be there when we get to Wirkynton, and riding the length of our route that I've had to leave the preparation of the load to you."

"Thank the gods that Wirkynton's on Walthoef's land and is a secure port without prying eyes. I'm just relieved to be able to shift this lot, and Leo'll be thankful for the coin you'll bring back." Agnaar spoke whilst walking across to Bear, who clasped him in a brief farewell embrace, swung himself up into Óðr's saddle and gestured for the line of ponies and the two sections of escorts to follow.

Agnaar stood and watched whilst the column wound its way towards the lake and disappeared into the grey early morning mist. They had a long hard day ahead he reflected as he mounted his own pony and urged it in the direction of Sefthveit and his latest venture.

He pushed his pony hard, keen to cover the three-leagues of rough track as quickly as possible. Although the days were lengthening there were still as many hours of darkness as of daylight. Pausing by the beck at the end of the narrow flat valley, that was home to the small mining community, he watered his pony before starting the tortuous ride up the fellside to where his men worked on the flatter ground high above the steep valley.

Agnaar had long grown used to the ever-increasing scene of desolation that greeted him when he crested the top of the valley. Several years of open-cast lead mining had left its toll. The little becks draining the fells above had been diverted repeatedly into dams that were then breached to create fast-flowing walls of water to scour away the top soil above the seams of lead. His miners called it 'hushing'. Rock full of lead ore was then hacked out of the resulting gouges in the ground, dragged away on sledges to be pounded and crushed before being washed in order to separate the ore from the rock. The ore was smelted in wind-vented charcoal furnaces on bale sites and the molten lead was channelled into moulds to form pigs to be taken down the fell slope and off to the port for sale to Aidan. It was a laborious hazardous process, and one that risked the lives of those working there whilst slowly devastating the land, stripping it of trees to provide fuel for the furnaces and leaving piles of sterile waste. The sight saddened Agnaar but it didn't distress him, it was the price of their freedom.

The seam of ore that his men had been exploiting had recently given way to soft grey flaky lumps that they were still trying to find uses for. It seemed that the hard ore they needed for smelting was in a lower seam under the ground. Agnaar had long debated whether they could safely hack their way along this particular seam but was worried that after more than a few paces the risk of the tunnel roof collapsing was too great. The miners from Patrichesdalr had laughed when told of the problem, saying, "Go down from above, it's what we do. If you know where the seam lies dig a shaft down and then follow along in all directions. Once the roof seems risky, or there's too little air, stop and drop another shaft a few paces away. It's hard work under the ground, but you'll get used to it, and it saves the hassle of hushing."

Having pondered the idea, Agnaar had agreed that working in a bell-shaped pit with access to the sky above was preferable to a long dark tunnel in which his men could be crushed by rockfall. They had started work once the snows had cleared and were now beginning to dig into the seam itself. He spotted his mining captain and dismounted to let his pony browse on the sparse vegetation, confident that it wouldn't wander off.

"How's progress, Ewen?" Agnaar limped across to the stocky miner and grasped his gnarled begrimed hand in greeting.

"Nay so bad." Ewen's gruff voice growled through his beard. "We had to sink a three-fathom shaft 'til we hit the load, but its wide enough, and we're still going down into it after nigh on another fathom."

Agnaar judged the depth of the shaft by the height of the circle of broken rock around its mouth. The shaft itself was no more than a couple of paces in width and it was topped by a windlass with two thick ropes from each of which hung a stout wicker basket. As one basket was lowered the other was raised, enabling men to be lowered one at a time, and ore-bearing rock to be brought to the surface. Two men worked the windlass and unloaded the basket whilst another worked at the bottom of the shaft. In the guttering light of a couple of tallow candles they dug out the ore-bearing rock as far as they could, and then dug down to its base.

"Its dropping the shaft as takes the time." Ewen continued in his deep growl. "Once we hit the seam the rock comes out well enough."

"What about flooding?" This had been another of Agnaar's worries.

"Aye, well, there is a fair bit seeping in. We fill buckets and bring them up in the basket. I've told the lads to dig deeper around the edge of seam, that way they stand on dry rock and can dip the buckets into the pools."

Agnaar nodded slowly. "When you drop the next shaft keep it close to this one. If we can link the two mayhap we could deepen the old one and turn it into a sump to drain the new ones as we go."

"Aye, 'appen it might work." Ewen was noncommittal. This way of mining was as new to him as it was to Agnaar. "It'll all depend on the lie of the lode and where its lowest point is. If it's dropping away into the fell, then we'd be as well to keep the pits separate. I'll see how we go." He added, appreciating Agnaar's contribution.

"Bear got the pigs away at first light. They should be on a boat for Mann this time tomorrow." Agnaar changed the subject.

The lines of Ewen's weather hardened face creased into a smile. "Good. He'll be able to keep paying for his green men. I guess they must be keeping them French bastards at bay. I heard what went on at The Raise a while back. Shows that God's on our side."

Agnaar smiled agreement. "It's been quiet since then. The men have been keeping a close eye on Wythburndale...and on the high passes to the south." He nodded in the direction of Langdalr.

"Ah, and to the north? 'Ow are them lasses doing on the lake? That was a canny idea our Lady had, keeping them altogether like that. I've never favoured them working with the men."

Agnaar gave a harsh laugh and cautioned Ewen with a frown. "Don't let Gytha hear that, nor Bear now that he's here. It's women being prepared to fight that keeps our freedom, and they fit in well with our way of fighting." Agnaar was irritated by Ewen's comment but didn't want to fall out with his mining captain. "The north's secure thanks to Neven, but my concern is what we can pull out of the ground here, Sefthtoller and over in Roger Saetr; and by the look of the bell pit we can keep mining Sefthveit for a good while yet."

"Aye, we can that." Ewen was thankful of the chance to regain Agnaar's favour, "There's good news from Yewthwaite too. I was there yesterday and there're definite traces of copper and silver in the load. It'll be harder to get out but mayhap we can earn more from there."

"So, it's as we thought. That'll please Bear when he gets back."

*****

Gytha rose early and went to see Neven. She paused outside the curtain screening her housecarl's sleeping space within the hall; sounds within suggested that Cudel may have stayed longer than was discrete. Gytha cleared her throat by way of a caution and went in search of Osberht instead. She found him in the kitchen, wrapping a cloth around some hard cheese and a loaf. "Good, I'm glad I caught you. I know you're taking a section from Watendlath over into Wythburndalr. I think we should make a show of our presence along the river through Saint John's in the Vale, to where it joins the Greta by Trellekell. Can you do that?"

Osberht set his parcel of food aside and looked up. "Aye, I could. But it would mean staying up in Watendlath tonight."

Gytha gave an appreciative smile. "Good, do that. I'll be there when you get back. I'll stay over and we can both ride into Kesewic tomorrow. It's market day and I'm due to meet Aric by the river."

The low sun was sinking, its light filtered by the mist above the western fells, when Osberht returned with Paega's section. Gytha left Wealmaer and the men of the other sections and, calling Loki to heel, walked away from the warming fire outside Watendlath's barn to greet Osberht as he dismounted. Paega tasked one of his men to attend to Osberht's pony and left the couple to talk.

"It went well in that I have literally nothing to report." Osberht explained, walking towards the fire. "We enquired at every farmstead and none had seen anything of Sigulfson's men since before Aere Yule. We then made sure our presence was known by riding into Trellekell, and the message was the same. I think that since the disaster on The Raise he's not willing to tempt Wyrd, at least not yet a while."

"I hope you're right." Gytha replied, "It's best you get a meal and some rest now. We've another long ride tomorrow."

Gytha didn't want to compromise Aric's anonymity and told Paega to take his men into the market whilst she and Osberht met Aric by the river. Gytha spotted him under the tree, gestured for him to join them in a small copse just downstream, and introduced him to Osberht.

"My master sends warning that William le Meschin is looking to assert his authority across Furness by Oestre."

"Which, given that we are already a couple of weeks into Lencten, means that he could begin any day now." Osberht interrupted.

"It does that." Gytha agreed. "What about further north?"

"If you mean around your cousin Walthoef's lands, then nothing. But don't infer that he hasn't got something in mind. I think it might be that he is not prepared to forewarn your cousin of anything his planning around Allerdalr." Gytha appreciated Aric's cautionary advice. "What does concern my master is that Forne Sigulfson was noticeably quiet last time he was in council. Mayhap he too is planning something?"

"Ah!" Gytha and Osberht chuckled together, as Gytha spoke. "I think we can explain that. I think he fears that he has incurred God's wrath."

*****

Gytha and Osberht were still feeling upbeat after their meeting with Aric when they left Paega at the head of the lake. He led his men up the beck-side track to Watendlath whilst they continued on towards the crag.

"Look yonder!" Osberht caught Gytha's attention by pointing across the lake's flood plain to a long line of ponies.

"Bear's back!" Gytha gave a whoop of joy and urged her pony to a canter as she called across to Osberht. "Come, we'll catch him where the tracks meet at the ford by his new vill."

Bear saw them and rode ahead to the ford. He reined to a halt and waited, stretching in his saddle until they joined him. "It was all good," he beamed, "An easy route, no trouble and good storage at the top of the beach. Aidan was there and I get on well with his agent. Well done choosing it. Oh, and I have a sealed letter for Moder

from Aidan's fader, the Jarl of the Sheading of Garth. I
wonder what that's about?"

Chapter 18

Oestre, with the end of Lencten fasting and lengthening days, was normally a time of celebration. Bear, seeing an opportunity to build upon the success of the Yuletide boar hunt by holding a festival that would bring the old and new communities together, summoned Leofric and Mungo to his hall.

"Let's enjoy the warmth of the Lencten sun out on the porch," he said, ushering them to seats. "Leo, Mungo was, as you know, Moder's reeve in our old lands. I want to reduce the burden on you by making him headman of this new vill, which we are going to name Grenewic. Is that..."

He stopped, hearing a frantic gallop. Moments later Rauði's pony appeared around the corner of the hall and skittered to a halt. She dismounted quickly and ran across, breathless from her ride. "Bear, Leo, sorry," she panted, "Gytha sent me, you both need to know. Fleeing families have just arrived. They fled from Konungrtūn to Langdalr, then Arne sent them on, over Stakes Pass down into Langstrath to Rosthwaite, and now they are at the crag. They say more are following."

Bear sat back, raised his eyes heavenward, and sighed. "This changes everything. I should have taken real head of Ligulf's warning and planned for this." With a quick glance at Leofric and Mungo, he said, "Rauði, head back to Gytha and tell her we're on our way." Turning to the two men, he added, "Leo, I assume you're content for Mungo to take Grenewic off your hands?" As Leofric nodded assent, he stood and walked briskly to the stables, whilst Leofric mounted his own pony and rode hastily after Rauði.

Gytha broke away from the dozen haggard men, women and children to whom she had been talking, and walked across to Bear whilst he dismounted. "What a disparate group," she sighed pitifully. "Most are from Konungrtūn, but there are a couple of lads from Furness who have been on the go for nigh on a fortnight. Black William's been pushing up the vales of Duddon and Konungrtūn with more force than the men we trained could cope with. Those who survived have fallen back to Langdalr where Arne is holding on. They say families that submit are taken into serfdom, but any that resist are hanged out of hand."

"It's a lesson to us all," Bear said, frowning heavily. He paused for a moment, deep in thought and conscious of their eyes upon him. "This is what we'll do. Gytha, I want you and Agnaar to speak to all as they come in. See what their skills are, as there might be some we can use. Of the others, choose the ones you think best for service with the green men or as miners. We need more of both. Women too if they are up to it."

Gytha nodded. "I agree. Osberht can look after patrolling whilst Dai takes over here. I'll have Arkil place two men in Rosthwaite all the time. They can direct people here as they come in."

"And I'll have Duwe stop spinning and turn her sheds into a place to receive and feed them. We still have stocks of grain, but we can't accommodate them all here." Leofric added.

"We won't." Bear was clear what he wanted. "Once Gytha and Agnaar have decided how to best employ them they will be directed to the most suitable vill. We'll have each vill build a temporary house now, and then more as needs be. It goes without saying that families will be kept together."

"I say that we shouldn't tell them about Kesewic." Gytha said firmly. "We need their labour and I don't want them heading further on. This is a big blow to them, but mayhap Wyrd is smiling upon us here. Anyhap, I doubt they'd be as well received in Kesewic."

Bear replied sternly, "I'm not so sure, Gytha. When you speak to them make sure they understand how women are treated here. That might be the biggest change some of the men have to accept. I suggest that any who dissent should be sent to Kesewic regardless."

*****

Osberht halted his pony on the crest of the long steep slope leading up from Watendlath to the heights of The Pewits. He turned in his saddle whilst his pony panted, and looked down onto the two sections following him and, beyond them, to the small farmstead hundreds of feet below. His spirits were the highest they had been for a while. The past fortnight's initial flood of refugees had turned into a trickle, and stopped; the clear blue sky heralded a fine day; and the cool easterly breeze was pleasantly refreshing. He was looking forward to leading two sections on patrol whilst Wealmaer supervised Osgar's men in the drudgery of domestic chores.

The distant cries of startled curlews drifted towards him. Intrigued, Osberht urged his pony beyond the crest so that he could look down towards Wythburndalr. He froze, cursed loudly, and held up his hand to stop those following behind. Reflected sunlight glinted on the helmets and mail of close on a dozen men-at-arms labouring up the track towards him. He wheeled about and forced his pony into a short gallop, stopping out of sight below the crest.

"Arkil! Cerdik! To me." Osberht shouted at the group of men emerging from the top of the track, and spoke quickly as the two section leaders joined him.

"We have uninvited guests, half a league away. Mayhap a dozen of them and I think two on horseback. They outnumber us and it's too open to engage them on these tops. Arkil, take your men back to Wealmaer. He is to fire the beacon and set an ambush in the farm yard. The people there are to go to safety in the woods yon side of the tarn. Cerdik and I will harass our guests. Snipe from the flanks, slow them and lead them into the ambush. If Wyrd is with us we will buy enough time for Wealmaer to set the ambush before they get onto this crest and can see down onto the farm. Cerdik, gather your men and I will explain how we are going to do this."

Osberht led the section at a canter down the track, closing quickly upon the Norman men-at-arms. He saw the two mounted men push to the front, and surmised them to be a knight and squire as at the Dynfal's Raise ambush. Waiting until the two men spurred their horses forward, he shouted to Cerdik and the section split into two. Cerdik and one man moved to the right, whilst Osberht led the remaining two off to the left. The knights choose to gallop off the track on course to intercept Osberht's larger group. Osberht steered his pony further to the left, drawing the two horsemen away from the track and onto rougher ground of soft peat and broken rock. Moments later both horses reared, neighing in distress. One stumbled as it came down, its foreleg buckling. Osberht winced, almost hearing the bones snap. The rider was pitched out of the saddle, clutching the reins to help break his fall. Staggering to his feet, he stumbled towards the men-at-arms now running towards him. The second rider moved his horse gradually backwards, guarding the retreat of his compatriot. Osberht dismounted next to the whimpering horse. He knew that the horse would never walk and should be released from its misery, and quickly.

"Urien. Give me your bow," he called to the nearest green man. "I can't get close enough to slit its throat without getting bitten. A shot through the eye should be instant."

The deed done, Osberht remounted and gestured to Cerdik to pull back and rejoin him on the track two furlongs away from the now-disorganised men-at-arms.

"What do you think? Will they come on?" Cerdik asked whilst watching his enemy.

"We'll know soon enough. The longer they delay, the more time we'll buy for Wealmaer and the lads." Osberht replied whilst considering his next move. "Yes, there's our answer, it looks like the knight is mounting and moving this way." He grinned mischievously, "They're nibbling at the bait. Give them a furlong, then go and snipe at their left flank. I'll then take their right. We'll play them for a while before we make a break for the far side of the crest and get some space between us and them. That knight is going nowhere fast trying to ride that horse on this ground.”

Osberht was conscious of the threat posed by the Norman crossbows. He kept his men just out of range, relying on the longer range of his men’s bows to force the Normans to walk with their shields raised, thereby tiring them further. Neither side took casualties, but the Normans’ progress was slowed.

“Osberht! The beacon’s been lit. There’s the smoke.” Cerdik’s shout drew Osberht’s attention.

“At last. That means Wealmaer’s got our warning and will have the men in place. Break away now and get over the crest. I’ll cover you. I want us well out of the added range that height will give their crossbows.”

Osberht waited with his two men. He gauged the Normans’ progress carefully and chose the last safe moment to start their descent, thankful that Cerdik was already well down the slope.

As they made their way down the fellside, crossbow bolts periodically struck the ground near them. They were shot inaccurately and Osberht considered the bolts to be a nuisance rather than an immediate threat. The ground steepened for the last couple of hundred feet of descent and they were forced to dismount and lead their ponies, thereby shortening the gap to their pursuers. Osberht was remounting on the flat ground at the foot of the slope when he heard a harsh cry behind him. He spun around, concerned. Urien lay spread-eagled on the ground with a bolt protruding from the small of his back.

“Rhun! Take the ponies. I’m going back for Urien.” Osberht yelled at the man in front, and clambered up the fellside as quickly as he could. A bolt struck the ground to his front and another glanced off a boulder by his shoulder. Upon reaching Urien, Osberht knew as soon as he turned him over that he was dead. The image of Kai’s tortured body flashed into his mind and he knew with a cold clarity that he could not leave Urien. Osberht hoisted Urien’s body across his shoulders and staggered back down the fellside, thinking as he went that at least his shoulders were protected from the bolts whistling past him. He regained the flat ground and, with lungs burning for breath, glanced up to see Rhun running to help. He pushed forward, gathered momentum, but pitched forward suddenly, his face and chest ground into the earth. Urien's body flew forward in a heap. Osberht's mind was numb. Blood pounded in his head. Then his left leg collapsed as he tried to regain his feet. Arms grasped him and pulled him up.

"Lord, I have you. A bolt has gone through your leg, though mayhap the pain hasn't hit you yet." Rhun's voice broke through the hammering pressure in Osberht's head and he placed his left arm instinctively over Rhun's shoulder. "We're moving now. There's nothing more we can do for Urien. We have to get out of range."

As the two men started forward, Cerdik ran towards them from the shelter of the farm. "In here, the farmyard is the killing ground." He helped Rhun take Osberht's weight and they almost ran in order to get clear of the falling bolts.

The farm door opened ahead of them, and as they staggered in other hands took Osberht and laid him on a trestle table.

"We're ready for them. I've just time to have a quick look at that leg." Wealmaer's grave expression broke into a brief grin, "When you said you'd lead them into the farm I didn't expect it to be like this. Leave the fight to us Lord. The barb has gone through your calf, but the fletches haven't gone in, which is a relief. I'm going to have to cut the barb off and then pull the bolt back out. That'd best wait 'til we've dealt with Sigulfson's men."

Osberht nodded agreement and lay back, thankful. His leg was beginning to throb.

Wealmaer signalled for the farm door to be secured and checked with the three section commanders that their men were in place. He was confident that only Cerdik's section had been seen, and that Sigulfson's men would assume that the few surviving green men were intending to escape through the farm buildings. He hoped that after the chase down the fellside their enemy's lust for blood would be enough to drive them headlong into the courtyard. If it did, they would be met by the arrows and bolts of eight of his men, whilst Arkil's section remained mounted at the back of the farm, ready to deal with anyone working their way around the outside. He was confident too that Gytha would send reinforcements, but when? Their firing of the beacon had been acknowledged by the beacon on the crag, however the climb up from the valley bottom was laborious and slow.

Wealmaer had chosen the killing ground well. The ambush was brutally effective, but not anywhere near as successful as he had intended. The Norman knight acted with understandable caution and sent five of his men into the courtyard, whilst remaining outside observing with his squire and the remaining five. Wealmaer's two sections, located in the barns either side of the farmyard, shot through the ventilation slits in the walls. Others, on top of the farm roof, shot from behind the cover of the roof ridge. The five men died where they fell, pierced multiple times by arrows released at very close range. The knight, momentarily stunned by the sudden massacre, reacted by leading his men around the side of the farm, only to see his way blocked by four mounted green men. Coming under attack from those on the farm roof, he wheeled about, galloped over the bridge across the beck flowing from the tarn, and ordered the men fleeing after him to form a shield wall at the top of its muddy bank.

Wealmaer ran to join Arkil, his men following once they had slid down from the farm roof and checked the dead.

The knight quickly appreciated that his short shield wall could be outflanked, and slowly repositioned it by having his men walk steadily backwards along the river bank towards a wood a furlong away.

Arkil was about to ride across the bridge in order to cut across the Normans' flank when he was stopped by Wealmaer. "Tell me what you see on the shoulder of Brund Fell," he asked, jerking his head towards the hill and its still-burning beacon.

Arkil glanced up, shielding his eyes with his hand. A row of bright lights twinkled where sunlight glinted off spear tips and helmets. He gave a relieved smile whilst Wealmaer ordered, "Stay this side of the beck and follow Sigulfson's bunch of bastards along it. Keep their attention and let them think they are going to escape. I'll send all the crossbow men to you. I want them to topple that knight, or at least take his horse down. He'll be Gytha's biggest threat when she takes them from behind." Wealmaer was beginning to enjoy their morning's work.

*****

Rauði twisted her wet green tunic in her hands to wring out the cold spring water, and slapped it sharply across a flat rock at the edge of the spring to remove creases. She was about to fold it when the sound of brisk footsteps and the laboured breathing of someone quickly mounting the crag's steps drew her attention. Turning her head, her heart lurched at the sight of Cnut disappearing towards the hall. "'t in Hel's name's he doing here?" She cursed under her breath and turned to follow at a more measured pace.

Rauði pushed the hall door open and stood still, surprised at the rigid formality with which Cnut stood in front of Gytha. His back was to her and she stood listening, still holding the door open.

"The Jarl sent me, my Lady. He...ah..." Cnut was gabbling, still trying to regain his breath, and Rauði could tell that he was ill at ease.

Gytha raised her hand to still him. "Take your time Cnut. I can see that his has nothing to do with Rauði, so take your time."

Cnut continued breathlessly, "We've been attacked, my Lady. Men-at-arms came to Hlóratūn two days ago, not to seize the land but to threaten the people and look for silvatici, whatever they are?"

"It's the Norman word for green men." Gytha was stern-faced. "Go on."

205

"They were William Le Meschin's men. They arrived late and forced the people to feed and bed them. The Jarl got word when someone from the vill escaped by boat. We rowed back down the lake that night, surrounded the vill, and attacked them as they were readying to leave. We killed them all, the bastards." Cnut had regained his composure and was sounding more confident, even boastful.

"Good." Gytha smiled coldly, "Those are Lord Walthoef's lands. I'll make sure he hears forthwith. Does the Jarl need my support?"

"Only that you tell our Lord." Cnut span around and Gytha looked across the hall, both were startled by Rauði's sudden gasp and cry.

"The beacon on Brund Fell's blazing!"

Gytha pushed past Cnut and Rauði and dashed out of the hall. A plume of increasingly dense blue wood smoke curled upward from the summit of the fell on the opposite side of the valley.

Gytha's decision was instant. "Cnut, ride with all haste. Tell the Jarl that we are under attack and to guard the passes between us. Rauði, find Bjorn and tell him what I want. He is to summon Dai. I want three sections mounted now, I will lead them, and you will come with me. Bjorn is then to warn Bear. Dai is to take charge here with the remaining four sections: two of which are to work with Neven and get in place on the lakeshore, two are to remain in reserve here."

*****

Gytha halted the three sections on the shoulder of Brund Fell where, with the sun beginning to fall behind them, she hoped they would be difficult to see. Men and ponies needed a rest after their furious climb up from the valley bottom.

She had arrived just in time to see three green men scramble down to the bottom of the fellside beyond the farm, and she regained her breath whilst watching the drama below.

"That's Osberht!" Rauði's concerned gasp confirmed Gytha's suspicions. "Should we not ride down now?"

"No." Gytha answered firmly, still focussing on the options open to her. "It's too late. Wealmaer will have a plan. Look, they've got Osberht away, though I fear we have lost a man."

Gytha glanced about her. Her men had already formed into their sections and were mounted in line, watching tensely. She spoke quietly to Rauði, whilst keeping her gaze fixed on the farmyard. "Can you see how the ambush will work? Wealmaer's got men on the roof, and no doubt in the buildings around the farm yard. That's where he wants them to go. He's got cut-offs too. Do you see them, behind the farm?"

Rauði nodded, awed by the spectacle.

Gytha came to a decision and summoned her section commanders. "Follow me by sections, quickly down into the dead ground behind the crags and along the spur to their left. We need to be in place to react immediately once Wealmaer calls that ambush."

Just as they started to canter down, short strangulated screams, followed by the raucous squawking of started wildfowl, confirmed that the ambush had been sprung.

As they emerged onto the low spur Gytha mused to herself that it was like watching a game of tafel unfold. The board-pieces had been reordered, but what was the game-play? Seven men-at-arms, one mounted, had formed a shield wall a couple of hundred paces to her front. They were faced by a miscellany of green men on the far bank of the Watendlath Beck. It was a moment before Gytha understood Wealmaer's intention. The Normans were edging away from the riverbank and moving slowly towards a wood off to her left. Wealmaer seemed to be deliberately encouraging them to escape the battlefield, and Gytha realised that as the gap between them and the beck increased she would be able to lead her men in a charge from their rear, and turn before their momentum carried them into the beck. She watched intently, hearing the staccato beat of metal biting into wood as a sudden volley of arrows raked the shield wall. She saw the men-at-arms duck behind their tall kite shaped shields moments before crossbow bolts whistled over their heads to strike the knight's horse. It staggered, whinnying in pain and collapsed, rolling its rider clumsily onto the ground. The knight pushed himself up, and without the protection of a shield stood squarely behind his men, ordering them to retreat slowly.

"Form line abreast. Saxi on my left, Paega on my right. We'll hit the shield wall at the charge. I want no battle cries as we go, surprise is our ally in this. Godfrid, follow in line abreast twenty paces behind and deal with any left standing. I want the man in the brown cloak taken prisoner. By his stature, I'd say he's a youth and therefore the knight's squire. I want him to take my message to Lord Walthoef. Kill the knight if you can. Rauði, take charge of Loki and join Godfrid's left flank. Use your bow and Loki to intercept any who try and flee to the woods. Any questions?" Gytha was clear in what she wanted and acknowledged the men's shaking heads with a smile. "Good. They're ours for the taking, let's go."

Gytha checked the line of men either side of her. It was a formation and tactic that they had rehearsed many time in the past six months, and she was confident it would work. "Remember, keep your spear held firmly under your right arm and release it as soon as it makes contact, then draw your sword and wheel back towards them." She lowered her spear and with a click of her tongue urged her pony into a walk and then a trot. The men kept pace, their knees almost touching in a very tight formation.

As their speed picked up the ground began to resonate with the hoof beats. The backs of the men-at-arms loomed closer. The knight turned. Shock, then panic, gripped his face and he yelled at his men to meet the charge. Most did, but lacked time to get behind the protection of their shields.

The knight was standing directly in front of Gytha and was still fumbling to draw his sword as she felt the impact of her spear on his mailed chest. He pitched backwards into the shield of the man behind. Gytha grasped her reins and with her knees pressed firmly against her pony's flanks urged it to leap forward, taking the next man-at-arms squarely in his midriff with it hooves. She felt the impact and then, through the shield wall, pulled her pony's head hard around whilst she drew her sword and came to a halt. Her men did likewise, forming into two sections.

They were confronted with chaos and trampled bodies. Three men-at-arms staggered to their feet and began to run, led by the brown-cloaked youth. Godfrid's men gave chase, bringing down the rear two. Gytha was about to react when she saw Rauði ride quickly to intercept. Rauði galloped past the running youth then wheeled to confront him. He stopped as she lowered her spear point to his chest. "Yield!" She commanded curtly.

The squire stared back then grasped the shaft of her spear with both hands, intending to push it aside. "Nay, vo iés un famme!"

Rauði didn't understand Norman French, but gathered the gist of the meaning.

"You will yield to a woman!" She urged her pony forward with her knees, striving to keep the butt of the spear wedged under her arm and pressing it hard against the squire's chest. As she moved she tried edging the spear tip up towards his throat.

The youth sounded as if he was choking. His eyes flickered from Rauði to Loki. Then the backward pressure was too much and he slipped, falling onto his back.

"Enough of your games. Get up, then kneel and yield!" Rauði looked up, startled by Gytha's voice and her use of Norman French. Gytha sat astride her pony watching with an expression of amusement. "Kneel!" She shouted again, her expression changing to one of irritation. "Else I'll leave you to my hound. Give your knife to my squire, and beg her forbearance." Then, she added for Rauði's benefit, "Moder insisted we learn our enemy's tongue. Dismount and take his knife, he's lost his sword and it is now his only weapon. He is your prisoner."

Rauði swung down from her pony and, with her sword in her right hand, held out her left to the squire as he passed her his knife hilt first. She tucked it through her belt. "Surely you speak some English? She said curtly.

The squire held her eyes briefly, then looked down. "I do." He acknowledged, churlishly.

"So, what is your name?"

"Jônas." The squire spoke quietly, sounding defeated.

Gytha took over. "Thank you, Jônas. I will see to it that you aren't harmed. After you have explained yourself to me I will have you taken to Lord Walthoef of Allerdalr. He is my lord and these are his lands. No doubt there will be further questions asked of you. Now, Rauði, take him to the farm and have Wealmaer secure him whilst I attend to Osberht. After that take Godfrid's section and return to the crag. Report to Bear, ask him to ready Eir and Adelind. I will return by the lakeshore track, it will be easier for Osberht on that track. Oh, and request that he takes Jônas to Walthoef tomorrow, and I want you to accompany him as his captor."

Chapter 19

Ealdgith rose early, as soon as the first light filtered through her shuttered windows. She had been unable to sleep, mindful of the words she wanted to submit to paper, and suffering with the constant discomfort she now felt. She shivered in the cool dawn air, pulled her gown over her shoulders and pushed open the shutters. With paper and a quill from a casket, she sat at her table and wrote.

Her words flowed quickly as her quill pen scratched them onto the paper. Her craving for the relief that she was sure sea air would bring to her aching chest, and the desire to be free from the constant threat of Norman violence drove her on. Now that her plans to join her cousin on the Isle of Mann were coming to fruition she knew that she must tell her family. Although she felt guilt at the prospect, she was sure it was right. It was right too, that Ulf intended to accompany her. Both knew their days to be numbered. Though she could never feel for Ulf as she had for Hravn, they shared a bond that stretched back to their childhood.

Ealdgith thanked Wyrd for Bear's decision to send their lead to the Isle in frequent small shipments. It enabled her to correspond regularly and develop the plan that had driven her once she was forced from Ulueswater. She would send the letter with the shipment that was due to leave as soon as the games were over, and then she would tell her children once Bear returned from Wirkynton.

Gytha shared her mother's insomnia, but for a different reason. She too rose early, leaving Leofric snoring contentedly, and slipped out of the hall. Loki followed obediently, sniffing at the early-morning aromas rising from the valley bottom. Gytha sat on the bank above the plateau and watched the first redness tinge the peaks around whilst lost in contemplation. Bear's plan to hold his long-delayed games in the next two days troubled her. She knew that she should accept Lord Walthoef's reassurance that the twin defeats of Le Meschin's and Sigulfson's incursions into his lands two months ago had resulted in an agreement to respect his borders, but this contradicted her perception of the men, particularly Sigulfson. This placed her at odds with Bear and Leofric, and she could not relax. Osberht shared her concern but, as yet unable to ride following his wound, she had relegated him to supervising training, and now relied increasingly upon Wealmaer and Dai as her deputies. The games would be an enjoyable culmination to their recent training, and she was looking forward to the dancing and music bringing the green men and women closer together. Yet she fretted that the games would be a distraction.

Gytha stood up and returned to the hall having come to a decision: she would keep patrols in place regardless of their impact on the morale of those denied the two days of relaxation.

*****

The first day's events started late, time having been allowed for those in the further-flung vills to make their way to the lakeshore on foot or by pony. The green men and women were the first to compete and crowds were amassing behind Gytha as she started the first event.

"Come on green women! Dig deep. You can do it!" Gytha stood by the edge of the lake, her voice quickly becoming hoarse from cheering. She was equally encouraging to each of the competing svanmeyja teams as they rowed their way around a course of wooden buoys, zig-zagging between the little floating hazards that would cost them a penalty of a count to ten if they missed or touched one. She glanced at Neven, sure that as umpire she was about to award a penalty to Tanuw's crew when it ploughed onto the gravel beach in a welter of spray and perspiration. The crew seemed to know it too, having rowed straight over the last buoy in their bid to maintain their lead over Gwenn's crew. She reflected that the penalty, when it came, would at least give the crew the benefit of a brief respite to catch their breath before running neck to neck with their rivals in the hundred paces sprint to their final task. Gwenn's boat grounded and the crew leapt out just as the penalty was complete, and Rauði joined Gytha in running alongside the two teams, still shouting encouragement, and urging them to quicken their pace to reach the final line. A rope across the grass marked the point at which they must complete their ultimate task: to topple a slender two-foot high column of carefully balanced fist-sized rocks fifty paces away by striking it with a slingshot or an arrow. The task was harder than it looked, requiring careful control after a lung and muscle challenging ten minutes. Gwenn's team won, their target collapsing only seconds ahead of Tanuw's. The young women hugged cheerfully and flung themselves onto the warm grass, enjoying the cheers from the crowd. It was a spectacle that none had seen before, and one that the women knew would raise their standing in the eyes of the onlookers.

Ulf joined them, his pony, an aging roan stallion, looking weary under his weight. "Ey up, lasses. Get yourselves over to the wicker targets. The lads are already halfway up the fell and will be finishing before you know it. Bear's already there."

Gytha glanced across to Shepherd's Crag and saw that Ulf was right. Green-clad figures were sprinting down from the shoulder of the fell. She knew that the six competing sections had already endured a lung-bursting dash to the summit, and once down they would compete in a spear throwing competition, run to cross the river at its deepest point, carry a colleague for a hundred paces, and finish with an archery competition with targets at one hundred and two hundred paces. It was a testing challenge, and one that each section seemed confident in winning. She called the green women to their feet and they jogged across to a low rise overlooking the targets and the river crossing. The determination and discipline of her men impressed and reassured her; she had been concerned that the recent rapid expansion in the number of sections might have eroded their capability, but her concerns were not justified. The men worked in pairs and as teams, as they helped each other up the steep river bank and arrived at the butts as compact cohorts, ready to complete their last task. The targets at one hundred paces quickly bristled with arrows. It was those at two hundred paces that decided the winners, with Godfrid's section closely beating that of Cerdik. Whilst the valley echoed to the sound of applause, Gytha walked down the rise to congratulate the winning sections, and presented their men and women with bone-handled knives that Bran had spent several weeks making.

With the martial activities complete, the afternoon followed a more pastoral theme: sheep herding, fell-running, wicker-weaving, slate splitting and wrestling. Done in north country-style, competitors stood chest-to-chest, each grasping the other with locked hands around the body, each opponent's chin on the other's right shoulder. The day drew to a close with communal feasting and copious quantities of ale being drunk, some of it less watered down than usual.

The second day brought families together in a miscellany of song and dance, and finished in the early afternoon with a spectacle that Leofric and Neven had taken time to prepare. It started with a holmganga, where Neven and Rauði sparred and showed off their moves and throws before challenging any of the men to try and floor them. Unsurprisingly, none were prepared to risk inevitable humiliation. At last, Cudel shrugged and stepped forward.

"Call yourselves men!" He waved disparagingly at the crowd, "I'd say mice, more like." With a cheeky wink at Neven, he pulled a wooden dagger from his belt and stepped swiftly over the boundary.

Neven frowned, uncertain of what Cudel was playing at.

"Now then, lass. Take me down if you can." Cudel spoke loudly, addressing the crowd of men rather than

Neven. He whipped the wooden blade through the air then lunged directly towards her breast.

Neven side-stepped quickly, grasped his hand holding the dagger and using her momentum against Cudel, forced it back against the top of his wrist, whilst pressing her finger tips into the spaces between his knuckles.

Cudel yelped in pain and surprise and dropped the dagger as Neven reversed her hold, swung his arm down and twisted it behind his back, whilst kicking him sharply behind his right knee.

Cudel collapsed to his knees, bemused but laughing. He had expected to be beaten, but not with such humiliating speed.

"Your knife, sir." Neven bent down, picked up the wooden dagger and flicked it to him. "No other takers, then?" She bowed to the cheering crowd and stepped out of the square, gesturing towards Cudel with a flourish of her hands: "I leave you with our captain of the catapults, but suggest you may do better if you follow me to where the music is about to begin."

As if on cue, a steady high-pitched drum beat resonated across the valley, the volume and pace of the beats increasing as they bounced back and forth in repeating echoes.

Neven joined her sister, Duwe, and added bass to the sound, picking up the beat on a larger drum.

The drumming drew men and women of the disparate vills into one crowd, all of whom focused upon the small group of musicians on a low mound at their centre. It was the coming-together that Bear wanted: the first time that the communities of Borgarárdalr and Ulueswater had truly joined as one in the year since their enforced union. Miners, shepherds, farmer, weavers and spinners were united in the enjoyment of a very rare festival.

Bear waited, judging his moment to speak, and raised his hand for silence. "Welcome all. I don't need to speak of the grave threat we all face and of the battles that must surely come, but those are for another day.

Yesterday and today we have relished the freedom to live our lives as we want, and to enjoy the company not just of our family and friends, but of the one great family to which we all belong. I want you all to remember that when we face the challenges ahead, no matter what the trials are that we must overcome, the strength of this family will always be here to support you. Now! I present to you Leofric, Bjorn and Rauði as you have never seen them before."

Bear waved to the threesome, seated on top of the mound, and stepped back as a crescendo of drum beats gave way to the clear, high notes of Bjorn's harp and Leofric's melodius lute. Sounds reminiscent of the curlew's haunting whistle, oystercatcher's piping call, the buzzard's mew and rising trill of the skylark floated across the meadow. It was a spectacle and sound that many there had never experienced. They listened in silence, and gave a low gasp of surprise when the notes of Rauði's clear high voice spoke to them of moments of love, bravery and joy in the places they called home.

Ealdgith, who had spent the day sitting with Ulf in the shade of an awning on the edge of the mound, felt tears trickle slowly down her cheeks.

Chapter 20

Gytha stood by the edge of the crag enjoying the early morning sun. It was her private time and an opportunity to think before the day's demands summoned her. She watched Bear lead the jagger ponies and a section of green men past Grenewic towards the track up the side of Cat's Bield, and then turned away, having decided to spend precious time with Ealdgith and Brynhildr.

A gong sounded to summon those in the hall to their midday meal. Gytha watched her mother and daughter make their way slowly to the long table, very aware that it was the chest pain and difficulty breathing that slowed Ealdgith's walk. The door opened just as they sat to eat.

"Father, what is it?" Gytha looked up, startled to see Father Oswin standing in the doorway, breathing deeply, red-faced and obviously exhausted. "Come, please sit and join us. Take a moment to gather yourself." She could see that the priest was as embarrassed by his condition as he was to be in the presence of three females.

"Thank you," he said, accepting the offer of a cup of spring water.

He sipped to wet his lips, and spoke quickly. "I must speak to your brother, where is he?"

"You must deal with me, Father. Bear is on his way to Wirkynton. He left this morn."

Father Oswin looked perturbed. "Then you must get word to him, now. I came as soon as they left the church, and almost ran half the way. Men-at-arms, a score at least, are on their way to Lousewater. They mean to attack the Jarl in his hall at Butremere."

"What? Gytha gasped. "But surely not just a score of them. Whose men were they? Sigulfson wouldn't dare challenge Lord Walthoef like this again, would he?"

"They said they came from Carleol, and came through Kesewic to avoid our lord's hall at Cokyrmoth.

They are to join with the younger Le Meschin's men. I was warned not to visit my flock in the next few days."

"Ranulph le Meschin's men, then." Gytha's face flushed red with anger. "We can be sure he's supporting his brother."

Gytha looked at Ealdgith and back to Oswin. "Thank you, Father. Eat with us, and then return to your church with best speed. I fear we may also face attack." Hearing Rauði and Bjorn behind her, she turned with orders: "Find Dai now and have him send a section after Bear and to warn the Jarl. They have to catch him before he gets to Lousewater. Then bring Dai to me, we have to prepare to defend ourselves."

*****

"The jaggers are back, Arkil caught up with Bear and Nudd just as they got to Butremere. That at least means that the Jarl is forewarned. Bear is staying there with Arkil and Nudd to help the Jarl, and to be in a position to warn us if Butremere falls. But it also means that we are two sections down. I'm going to assume that Le Meschin will attack the Jarl first in an attempt to draw us to his defence before attacking here and catching us out." Gytha glanced from face-to-face, as she spoke to those seated around the hall's long table.

"We won't be caught out," responded Osberht.

No, we won't," Gytha confirmed before continuing. "That is why I haven't yet sent word to Lord Walthoef. When I do, I want him to have a full picture. Rauði, Bjorn, be ready to ride to him at a moment's notice."

"What about Kesewic?" Osberht asked.

"I'm coming to that," Gytha said, slightly irritated by his interruptions. "Neven, warn the girls, double the watch on the island and then take a coracle and have a nosey at Kesewic from the bay. You might need to take a cautious trip ashore if you can't see anything from the bay. Just be careful. Dai, place a section on Cone Fell. They're to watch and be ready to ambush any move towards us.

218

Then go and warn Wealmaer. I rather doubt that Sigulfson will send men that way again, not after Jônas' tells him how exposed they were coming down the fellside. He's to reduce to two sections, send one back here and keep another on watch up on The Pewits from dawn to dusk. The beacon will be his signal if attacked. Likewise, our beacon will signal if we are under attack. A double beacon will mean that I want him to leave Watendlath and reinforce us here. Cudel, ready the perrièrs and the teams, and prepare a second beacon on the plateau. Leo, warn the vills and tell the people not to move away from them unless instructed. Mungo is to be prepared to evacuate Grenewic and fall back to here. Use the spinning sheds for any wounded and mayhap for shelter, and ready the women to cook for all. If we are attacked, we have to hold them in the rock-fields that Ulf laid, and pray that the perrièrs stop them out-flanking us. Dai, we'll have five sections here, though one's in reserve to ambush along the lake track. Osberht, you are to be with me. I want you to understand my plan at all times. If I'm stopped from leading the fight, you must take it on. Is that clear to all?"

Gytha wound-up the meeting after dealing with sundry minor concerns.

*****

Neven had risen early, shortly after first light, and was crouched at the lakeshore washing the sleep from her eyes when Aelf's shout drew her attention. "A boat...no, a coracle, it's just coming around the headland." The two women stood and watched its progress.

"My guess is that it's the headman's messenger." Neven spoke with a quiet resignation. "Ready the others, Aelf, and get a meal going. If I'm right then it may be quite a while 'til we can eat again."

Neven's foresight was justified. The man remained seated in his coracle, a few paces off the shore, as the small wicker and hide craft bounced gently on the low waves. "A score of men rode in last night, Lady. My

219

master spoke to them as he must, and was told to find them shelter and food, and to expect a couple more score on foot today. They too must be fed. My master objected, as was his right because these weren't our Lord's men, and was held at sword point until he relented. I'm sure he would have been slain if he had persisted."

"So, are they Sigulfson's men?" Neven asked.

"Some, for certain, but not all. A couple wore different colours. The same as the men who rode through a couple of days ago."

"Have they said what they intend?"

"No, Lady. But my master understood that those marching in will bring their own tents."

"Ah..." Neven acknowledged, drawing her own inference of the implications. "Thank you, I fear we have much to do...and thank your master. Advise him to keep the people quiet and out of the men-at-arms' way. My Lady will deal with the matter and will get word to Lord Walthoef." She waved him off and ran to their hut. "Fire the beacon! Aelf, once we've eaten we'll take a dug-out and report to Gytha. I expect Gwenn and Tanuw will be here within a couple of hours. No-one's is to leave the island 'til we get back."

*****

Neven and Aelf were barely halfway to the head of the lake when they saw the smoke from the crag's beacon pillar up in response to their own. Gytha was already at the lakeshore waiting for them when the dugout grounded on the shingle.

"It's as you expected." Neven said, after she had stepped ashore and embraced Gytha briefly. A score of mounted men arrived last night. Two score more follow-on foot today. Most would appear to be Sigulfson's with some of Le Meschin's added in."

"No doubt to oversee what they do. Sigulfson's taken a few beatings already."

Neven could see that Gytha was concentrating deeply, and remained silent, waiting.

220

Gytha spoke her thoughts aloud. "I think they'll come for us tomorrow, after first light, and they'll come down the lakeshore path. There aren't enough boats in Kesewic to move them. Though if they have mounted men here already, we can expect them to take a look at the track today. Depending upon when they march into Kesewic it is possible that they might even move men up overnight. Godfrid's men should have been in place on Cone Hill last night. By now, they will have seen what's developing. Their orders are to follow the plans we agreed with Dai. We can be sure they will disrupt any venture down the track today, and then return to the top of the hill, but if they are pursued they will have to fall back via Walla Crag. Godfrid will use his horn to warn you if any pass beyond the hill. That will give you time, just, to get onto the shore and in position in The Ings. So, get back to the island now and wait for Godfrid's signal this afternoon or tonight." Gytha pulled her friend and huscarle to her in another embrace. "Good luck, and may Wyrd be with you all."

*****

Rauði pulled on her pony's reins, stopping it in its tracks whilst she pointed across the lake to her right. "Look yonder! Left of Cone Fell, on the flat ground this side of Kesewic."

Bjorn's eyes followed the line of Rauði's arm. He was as impressed as ever by her sharp eyesight and he could just make out a series of white shapes. "Are those tents?" He sounded unsure.

"Not just tents. I can see the colour of flags and sunlight reflecting off mail. It's all the more urgent that we get to Walthoef." Rauði flicked her reins and urged her pony into a trot. Bjorn followed, leading the spare pony that he had insisted they bring in case one went lame.

The sum was at its zenith and its heat beat down upon their heads as they followed the track across the open fellside at the foot of Cat's Bield. Leaving Cat's Bield behind they entered mixed woodland at the foot of a lone fell and enjoyed the shade and cover it provided as they cut across the slope towards a river coming down from their left.

"Do you remember the ford we crossed when we rode to Kesewic from Hlóratūn? Was it over this river?" Bjorn asked Rauði riding alongside.

"Of course. Gytha said once we cross it we need to keep the second lake on the right and the fellside on the left. She said it's a poor track, but rideable."

"Stop! Rauði, get back under the trees." Bjorn shouted urgently, moments after Rauði led past him. "We can't cross the ford. It's under guard. Look!"

Rauði whirled her pony around, back into the cover of the edge of the wood. "Were we seen?"

"I doubt it, but we can't get past. How are we going to get word to Walthoef now?" Rauði sensed a hint of panic in Bjorn's voice.

She took a while to reply whilst she shielded her eyes, staring at the men by the ford. "We'll get to him, but mayhap not as quick as we thought. The two that are mounted have got coloured pennants on their spears. My guess is that they're Le Meschin's men. I think they are either guarding the ford because it's on the way between the two camps, or mayhap they've come from Hlóratūn, but don't know how to get to Sigulfson's camp."

"Or they could be waiting for a guide." Bjorn added, agreeing with Rauði's logic. "Look, we're safe here, we can't ride around them, not in daylight if they are waiting for someone from Sigulfson's camp, but we could get past once it's dark. We just need to watch and wait."

"You're right." Rauði agreed, relieved that they had a plan. She dismounted and sat with her back to a broad oak.

Bjorn lay down next to her, enjoying the feel of the warm grass under his back. "We might as well make ourselves comfortable whilst we watch," he said, relaxing with a sigh.

Bjorn was correct. Just as they were beginning to think that they were faced by a permanent guard, a lone rider galloped towards the ford form the direction of

Kesewic. It was obvious from the men's gesticulations that a brief argument ensued, after which the three horsemen rode off leaving half-a-dozen men-at-arms to follow on foot.

Bjorn laughed. "I don't envy them marching weighed down by mail in this heat. I hope they knacker themselves. At least we can get going at last."

"Not yet, we can't. Watch 'til they're out of sight. Then we should ride like Hel's behind us and get across that ford before anyone else turns up." Rauði mounted, readying herself.

They waited, fretting with impatience, whilst the marching men made their way across a ford over the adjacent River Derwent. It was only once the men had disappeared behind the low rise overlooked by Saint Kentigern's Church that they felt safe to move.

"They've gone. You lead. Let's go!" Bjorn urged Rauði forward and the couple burst from the tree-line, breaking quickly into a gallop as they sped down the grassy slope. The third pony followed behind Bjorn on a long rein. They splashed through the ford in a welter of spray and kept going across open fields for over a league until they reached woodland where the steep slope of Broom Fell touched the shore of Bassenthwaite Lake.

Bjorn turned to Rauði with an exhilarated grin as they let the ponies slow to a walk and regain their breath. "We should water them briefly at the next spring. That was fun though, wasn't it?

Rauði smiled back. "It was, but I think we should try and come back in the dark. We were very exposed. Anyway, this track is going to slow us down. It's so overgrown we may have to walk in places.

The track was better than Rauði had surmised. They rode through Cokyrmoth's narrow lanes just as the sun fell behind the hill of Walthoef's hall, to find the gate shut. Bjorn hammered upon it with his sword's pommel until it prompted a grumbling response.

"Open up!" Rauði shouted. "I'm Rauði, Maldred's daughter. We have urgent business with our Lord. His lands are under attack."

"What's that? Skita! Cardok, go and rouse our Lord. Be quick man!" An unseen voice cursed and barked a command whilst bolts grated harshly as they were pulled open.

As the gate swung back, the way in was blocked by a stout middle-aged man wearing a long leather jerkin. His face relaxed upon seeing the two riders. "I know you Lady. You were with Lord Bear when he brought in a prisoner a while back."

"And I you recall you too." Rauði smiled back, relieved at last that their mission was almost complete.

"Leave you ponies. I'll have Cardok water them when he returns. You know your way to the hall?" He nodded towards the porch across the yard just as the door opened and Cardok stepped out.

"Thank you, yes." Rauði replied, turning away and walking briskly towards the lamp-lit entrance. Walthoef greeted them as they stepped inside.

"Rauði, Bjorn, welcome. What's this of an attack?" Walthoef asked impatiently, before checking himself. "But first, sit, I'll have food brought whilst you talk."

Rauði looked at Bjorn. He nodded, encouraging her to take the lead, as was her right as Walthoef's relation.

Rauði cleared her throat nervously, having already thought through the quickest way to explain the situation.

Bjorn watched Walthoef as Rauði spoke. His face appeared frozen, expressionless, only the gradual deepening of a frown belied his increasing fury.

"Thank you, both of you, and for the risks you took to get to me. I had Ranulph le Meschin's assurance that my lands would not be violated so long as I held them securely for the King. This shows just what his word is worth. The time for treading carefully is over. From what you say it seems probable that your foster father will be able to hold Butremere as there is no lakeshore track from Lousewater to his hall. I suspect that Le Meschin's younger brother, being the arrogant excuse for a man that he is, will not know that his way is blocked, and that his men will come to grief trying to find a way through the fells. Our cousin's situation is different and I fear her fight will have already begun. It will take time to muster my men, but I should be able to ride by tomorrow evening. Return as soon as you have eaten and tell Gytha to hold for a day. I will come at Sigulfson from his rear. She should look for me at dawn the day after tomorrow. Once I have Kesewic, he will be trapped so long as she can hold him in Borgarárdalr."

Rauði felt relief, but also concern. "Will you not be seen as going against the King?"

Walthoef laughed scornfully. "The King be damned. These men have gone against me and mine. They will pay for that. My cousin has done nothing to incur the King's ire. She may have belittled Sigulfson by constantly defeating his incursions, but that was at my behest."

Bjorn and Rauði ate quickly, spooning warmed up pottage into their mouths whilst Walthoef summoned his master-at-arms and ordered that his men in the surrounding vills be stood to arms immediately.

"God's speed to you both." Walthoef said as he briefly embraced Rauði. "Follow the same route back. You should be safely past the track to Whinlatter before dawn."

*****

"What's going on down there? At the head of the Great Bay." Bjorn asked urgently, stopping his pony in its tracks.

"The svanmeyjas are ashore and...look beyond them...the green women are running towards the ford." Rauði answered hesitantly, unsure about the numbers of people she could see.

"Not all of them. There are two still at the lakeshore. They seem to be helping each other. I think..."

Rauði acted before Bjorn finished speaking. "They're hurt. We need to get down there. Now!"

"Rauði, stop! Look! The beacon has been lit. Is the crag already under attack?" Bjorn shouted, just as Rauði spurred her pony forward.

"No matter," she called back over her shoulder. "We can get the girls onto the spare pony and then decide what to do next."

As they dropped down from the side of Cat's Bield, Rauði could see the two green women were hobbling slowly towards Grenewic. Recognising them as Ankarat and Modron, she rode up with Bjorn and jumped down.

"What's happened?" Bjorn spoke first, as he rushed to help.

Ankarat spoke quickly, she was almost gabling, "It's Modron, a spear sliced her arm. Neven bound it, but she needs Eir to sew the gash closed."

Bjorn could see that the naturally pale Modron was ashen faced from pain and shock. "Come, let me take you." He placed his arm around Modron's waist, and as he took her weight Ankarat stumbled and fell, crying out as her left foot touched the ground.

"Sorry, I should have said. I went over on my ankle and Modron was holding me up. Just see to Modron, please."

"No, I have you." Rauði took Ankarat's hands and lifted her back up. "Put your arm around my neck and we'll get you both across to the spare pony."

"We'd best get you up first, Ankarat, then Modron can hold onto you from behind. I'll lead her, so you only need to keep your balance." Bjorn took charge. With both women mounted, Rauði rode alongside as Bjorn led them towards Grenewic.

Rauði could see that Modron was close to passing out and was ready to react if she slumped from the saddle. She listened with interest whilst Ankarat gabbled on, barely taking a breath between sentences.

"It was exciting and we did well. We had already crossed to the shore in anticipation, and it was dusk when the men on Cone Fell warned us when the Normans were moving our way, so we dashed quickly to our ambush position and took them from the flank. I saw a horse go down and a man stumble. It was enough to stop them and we shrieked and cackled like witches as we ran back to the boats. Our next spot was a couple of furlongs down the shore. We heard the men's next ambush and were well in position when the first Norman's came. They were all on foot by now and Neven made sure we let their front men go past before we attacked the main group. That seemed to catch them out and I'm sure we injured several, but there was so much shouting and screaming that it was too confusing to really tell. Our last ambush was where the track comes close to the lake at Strutta wood. We let them all go by and waited for those with the horses. It worked in that they lost control of the horses, but I think because the track was so close to the lake someone had looked back and seen our boats in the moon light. They came at us from the flank just as we were pushing off. That's when I went over on my ankle and Modron got hit by a spear that glanced off the gunwale and bounced across the boat." Ankarat finally paused for breath.

What is Neven doing next?" Rauði asked, her mind buzzing with the images that Modron's tale generated.

"The girls have been told to cover the ford. Cudel had his men make a couple of spiked barricades like ones they used at the castle he's from, and Gytha's blocked this side of the ford with them. Our task is to cover them with arrows and sling-shot. There's a section of men there already to deal with any who try to clamber up the river bank."

"Where do you think the Normans are now?" Rauði asked urgently. "We need to be able to get to the crag after we've got you two looked at."

"We would have heard the cry of battle if they had got to the ford. I know Gytha wants to draw them all the way to the crag and pin them down in those rock fields. At least, that's what Neven told us." Rauði could tell that, despite her injury, Ankarat was still buzzing from the night's excitement.

The slow-moving ponies had been spotted by the time they rode into Grenewic. Mungo dashed out from the vill to meet them, followed closely Leofric.

"Is Eir here?" Bjorn shouted ahead to them. "We've have two wounded, one needs urgent attention."

Leofric pointed towards the crag. "No, everyone with essential skills is at the crag, as well as some of the women and children. Mungo's keeping the men here in case we need to defend the river bank." He could see the disappointment in Bjorn's face. "Wait here a moment whilst Mungo fetches water for the two lasses." He glanced at Rauði. "I'll help Bjorn. Leave us lass, and report to Gytha as quickly as you can. She needs to hear what Walthoef said, and you can get the women ready for these two. You'll be safe enough, the Normans haven't reached the ford yet. Gytha's got a couple of sections in place to harry the Norman flank all the way to the rock-fields in front of the crag. The track is so close to the river along that stretch that our archers will have them in range all the way."

Leofric could see that Bjorn and Rauði each felt an overwhelming sense of relief at being back amongst friends. He clasped them reassuringly on their shoulders. "Well done, both of you."

Chapter 21

Gytha rode forward cautiously, leaving the ford behind as she moved north along the track, unsure when she would see the Norman men-at-arms she knew to be heading towards her. She rode a horse and wore her mother's armour. The five mail-clad men with her were similarly mounted. Wealmaer had spent the last two months training and equipping them to ride the six horses that they had acquired during their successive defeats of Forne Sigulfson's men. They provided the bodyguard that she was sure she would need in the coming battle.

"We should wait here, my Lady, and I'll send two men forward, we have no idea what's around that bend." Wulf advised as they approached the end of a narrow stretch where the steep-banked river, track and rising fellside came close together.

"I agree." Gytha nodded approval and halted. She was beginning to tire after a sleep-deprived night and recognised that her light-headedness meant she needed to eat.

The two men rode slowly into the bend, and then stopped and waived Gytha and Wulf forward. Wulf appreciated the situation immediately. "Look yonder, my Lady. They've stopped half a league away on the water meadows by the lake head. I'd say they're regrouping."

"That bears out the reports from Neven, Godfrid and Gunnar." Gytha frowned as she scrutinised the distant melee of men and horses. "If they've already lost a dozen or more men, killed or wounded, and had their horses scattered, it will take them a while to get the horses up and organise the men."

"Well, thank the gods for that." Wulf said with relief. "We need to sort ourselves out too, after Godfrid lost Bran and Cunoot whilst escaping from Cone Fell."

"I know," Gytha said sadly, "they were both good men. I'm going to move one man from Gunnar's section across to Godfrid's to give them three apiece." She wheeled her horse around. "Let's get back to the crag. We all need to eat. I'll shout to Neven as we pass the ford. Now that some of the green women are mounted, she can send a couple down the river to watch and then come and warn us when there is movement."

"Who's that?" Wulf asked, at the sight of a rider coming towards them.

"It looks like Rauði. But where's Bjorn?" Gytha replied, spurring her horse to a canter.

Rauði halted her pony and watched. She was impressed by the five mail-clad men looming above her on their horses, but she almost speechless at the sight of Gytha. It was only the second time she had seen Gytha in Queen Aethelflaed's armour. As the tri-coloured metal hoops caught the sunlight they shimmered in shades of copper, silver and gold that added an unnatural other-worldly fluidity to Gytha's movement.

Seeing Gytha's concern, Rauði pre-empted her question, saying, "Bjorn is with two green women who are injured. I've warned Eir and Revna, and they are preparing to receive them."

"Ah, good. Neven told me about them." Gytha replied, relieved. "What of Walthoef?"

"All good. He is mustering his men and promises to be here at dawn tomorrow. We must hold 'til then, when he will come up the lake track and take Sigulfson in the rear. He says that if Sigulfson threatens you with the King's wrath that you have nothing to fear. You are right to defend these lands in Walthoef's name. He will answer to the King, if needs be."

Walthoef's message refreshed Gytha almost as much as sleep and a meal. With the reassurance that he would be with her early the next day, and that he would accept responsibility for whatever destruction she inflicted upon Sigulfson's men, she felt certain that she could see the battle through.

"Thank you, you've done well. Ride back now, ahead of me and get a meal and some rest. Bjorn must eat and rest too. I'd say we have until noon 'til the fight is re-joined."

Gytha was roused from a brief deep sleep. She had been resting in one of the green men's huts at the foot of the crag, and went to meet Neven's messenger. "They are moving, my Lady. At least a score of horsemen and more than two score on foot. All wear mail and have shields. Neven thinks they have been reinforced. I left her making a show of force to deter any intentions they may have about forcing a crossing at the ford."

Having thanked the messenger, Gytha summoned her council. She sat on a ledge as they gathered to squat, sit or lounge on the sun-baked earth at her feet. "I have just had news that Sigulfson and his men are on the move again and that their numbers are still around three score, which can only mean that they have been reinforced. I've also had word that Lord Walthoef will be here about dawn tomorrow, so that is how long we must plan on holding. I want us to hit them hard as soon as they show face, stop them, hold them, and keep on holding them. All our fighting is going to be within the range of the perrièrs, so Cudel, you have to keep a very close eye as to where we are on the ground. Osberht, Dai, this is how we are going to do it. I want the green women mounted and kept by the ford. The river with its steep bank is their greatest asset and line of defence. Leo and Mungo are marshalling as many of the men from Grenewic as they can to back them up with pitch forks and scythes. So, as long as they hold the top of the river bank, that flank should be safe."

Gytha paused for effect and took a deep breath. "We are going to start killing them and maiming them as effectively as we can until Sigulfson calls them off. There has to be a limit as to how many men he is prepared to lose. I want an ambush, the biggest we have yet set, by the final bend in the river. You've got five sections, Dai. I want them all this side of the river, covering the track on the far side, from the bend all the way up to where Wulf and I will lure them. Wulf, you will be with me. We are going to be by the pool, just before where the river narrows. We'll have a clear view down the track for over a furlong. We're going to block the track on horseback, and wait. I want us to be seen, and my guess is that they will send knights forward to engage with us. Our surprise will be the caltrops. Cudel, I hope they are as harmful to horses as you claimed." Gytha referred to the four-pronged, metal spikes, the size of a child's fist, that once thrown onto the ground would pierce a hoof or foot.

Cudel gave a low laugh, "They will be."

Gytha gave him a knowing look and continued, "Wulf, choose a point on the track fifty paces from where we are going to be. Mark the track discretely, then scatter the caltrops for another fifty paces. Mark the end point and scatter dust or leaves on them. We can't risk riding onto them, and we'll need to clear them away once all this is over. Assuming they do send their horses against us, we will wait before making a mock charge that stops just short of the caltrops. That should be enough to draw them forward at a gallop, and straight to their doom."

Wulf, nodded, "Aye, Lady, if those caltrops do what Cudel claims, then they could be brutal to man and beast."

"Dai, the section of track with the caltrops on it will be your first killing ground. The horses should throw their riders as soon as they step on them. Pick off the men once they are on the ground. Don't bother with hitting the horses. Use two sections, then once they have finished have them fall back along the hidden ways in the rock field, and start to cover it from the home side. The remaining sections are to keep low until men-at-arms come forward on foot to see to the knights. Hit them once they start to bunch up, and then retreat through the rock field." Gytha gave Dai a questioning look. "Are you clear what I want? It's complicated."

"Oh Aye, Lady," Dai grinned reassuringly, "you couldn't be clearer, it's just what I want."

Gytha concluded, "Cudel, as soon as we're all back through the rock fields use the perrièrs to strike Sigulfson's men when they first try to push forward, a series of swift hard punches might just give him cause to stop. And finally, Osberht. I want you on the crag for the time being. You'll have a better view of the battle from there. Keep Bjorn with you and use him to warn me if you see anything awry." She clapped her hands sharply, "Right! Let's get to it. We've a lot to do, and very little time in which to do it."

*****

Rauði sat astride her pony with her mouth agape; shocked by the sudden carnage in front of her, yet awed by the prescience of Gytha's prediction and the success of her plan. She bit down on her lip, fighting a wave of nausea but determined not to show either fear or horror to the men around her.

Gytha also was awed, but not shocked. She had experienced enough brutal violence in the past to be able to accept its necessity. Close on a dozen of Sigulfson's knights were strewn across the track, some lay still, others writhed and moaned whilst maimed horses thrashed around, kicking and crushing them. She watched Dai's first two sections pull back through the rock field, gestured to Wulf to do likewise, and waited a little longer to see if the men-et-arms would come forward on foot. Her bait taken, Gytha wheeled her horse and guided it carefully back the way she had come. She didn't want to deter the Noman men-at-arms from venturing into the second killing area.

Gytha re-joined Rauði just as the second deluge of arrows and crossbow bolts scythed across the river and into the unfortunate Norman infantry. Noticing that Rauði's face was paler than usual she leant across from her saddle and said quietly, "Always bear in mind that it's only what they would do to all of us. It's better that we strike first, is it not?"

Rauði nodded, still biting her lip.

"Follow me." Gytha turned her horse away from the killing and shouted across to Wulf, "Take the men further back. Once the last three sections retreat through the rock field we can expect the perrièrs to start flinging

233

rocks overhead. I don't want to tempt Wyrd's sense of humour by remaining too close."

Almost on cue, the green men lining the river bank stood and ran in a wide loop, away from the river and out of spear range. "That's evened the odds," Gytha whispered out loud to herself as she counted over a score of bodies on the track. "Come on, take the bait again, just one more bite." She hoped that the threat Wulf's section posed from their position astride the track would entice Sigulfson to send his men across the shallower part of the river in pursuit of the green men.

Gytha held her breath as about twenty men ran from the cover of the trees. As she willed them on, half remained on the river bank with their spears poised, ready to cover their comrades as they ran splashing through the shallow water towards the far bank. They repeated the tactic, moving forward in two waves, fifty paces at a time, until the leading men stumbled and cursed, tripping on the myriad head-sized rocks strewn amidst the long grass. A sudden double thump followed by a soft swooshing sound drew her attention skyward. She shouted, pointing, "There! There! Watch the rocks as they fall."

Two clusters of rocks soared skyward above them, slowed gradually as they spread apart, appeared to pause momentarily before plummeting to smash onto and around the men caught at the edge of the rock field. The air surrounding the flailing men became instantly hazy with dust and flying chips of rock. Some fell, others staggered backwards and began to run towards the line behind them. Moments later another double thump resounded from the top of the crag and the second line of men was obscured by a haze of dust and splintered rock. The men fled leaving a further five bodies behind. The speed of their panic-driven flight was such that despite the burden of their mail they moved faster than Cudel could adjust the range of the perrièrs, and the third and final barrage fell into the river, throwing up a hail of spray just as the men clambered up the far bank and ran gasping into the cover of the wood. A loud cheer from the top of the crag echoed across Borgarárdalr. Its dying echoes were answered by a reply from the green men positioned along the rock field.

*****

Ulf stood alongside Cudel, to offer advice about sighting the perrièrs, which the young artilleryman tactfully ignored. He watched fascinated as the two machines' long arms were pulled sharply upright to fling a dozen rocks apiece high into the air and out across the valley. His excitement rose, and he could feel his heart pounding as he held his breath in anticipation, willing the increasingly small specks to fall onto their targets. When the men on the edge of the rock field disappeared in a haze of dust he turned to Cudel, punched the air with his good arm, and watched again as the second load of rocks was pitched skyward. This was just what he had hoped for. The catapults on the summit of the lofty dominating crag really were the fangs in the jaws of Borgarárdalr, snapping and biting any enemy that dared to try and enter the valley beyond. Ulf stamped his feet with glee and vindication when the second shower of rocks struck and, feeling suddenly light-headed, paused and gasped for breath. His chest felt as if a great stallion had kicked him before his ribs were bound by an iron band. Gasping for breath, his head pounding and his vision dimmed to a red blur, Ulf sank silently to his knees just as the third shower of rocks plunged into the river.

"Ulf! No!" Bjorn was the first to notice, his sharp cry attracting the attention of all on the crag.

"Cudel, keep the men in their places. Don't be distracted. I've got this. Bjorn, quickly!" Osberht reacted immediately. He sprinted across to where Ulf was lying on his face. "Help me Bjorn." He shouted, struggling to roll Ulf's heavy body onto his back.

"He's still breathing," Bjorn's voice trembled as he spoke, "and his eyes are flickering."

"Ulf, can you hear me?" Osberht asked calmly as Ulf's eyes opened slowly.

Ulf nodded imperceptibly and tried to move his lips to speak. His normally florid face was a disconcerting buttery shade of white. Osberht whispered quietly to Bjorn, "I fear it's his heart. The excitement was too much for it." Turning Ulf's head gently to make him focus upon him, Osberht spoke firmly, "Lie here until you're able to breathe again. We'll help you into the hall. Then I'll summon Adelind to care for you."

Osberht sent Bjorn to warn Ealdgith and ask her to ready a bed for Ulf. By the time he returned Ulf was already sitting up with a hint of pink returning to his face.

The two men raised Ulf slowly to his feet, each feeling the painful protest of their recent wounds as they did so. They guided Ulf carefully down the steps from the platform, into the hall and through to a bed behind a thick curtain where they laid him gently. They stepped back and let Ealdgith sit on the edge of the bed.

Taking Ulf's had in hers she lowered her face to his and spoke softly. "I fear that our fighting days are over for good. We must care for each other now."

Ulf nodded, still unable to speak.

Osberht laid his hand gently on Ealdgith's shoulder. "Bjorn will fetch Adelind and let Gytha and Leo know. I'll send Bryny to help you, and will be on the platform should you need me."

*****

Gytha returned to the crag top, checked upon Ulf who was now talking, and went to confer with Osberht.

"I think we may have stopped them, Gytha. For the time being at least. They'll have worked out that the rock field stops them moving fast enough to avoid the reach of the perrièrs."

"And that their range stops them trying to out-flank us." Gytha agreed. "But what about tonight? If I were Sigulfson, I'd try to infiltrate quietly in the dark."

"So would I, though it would still be a challenge with our archers covering the rock fields, and by now he must be wary of the unexpected. He must realising that conventional tactics don't count when it comes to fighting green men. But ..." Osberht paused with a deep sigh. "If they do get around a flank, the east vill and the houses at the base of the crag will be vulnerable."

"That's what I'm coming to think. It's the east vill that I'm most worried about. The base of the crag is still shielded by the rock fields." Gytha came to her decision. "If we act now, we've time to move the women and children from the east vill to the bottom of the crag. The men should remain, as in Grenewic, and be ready to fight with what they have. I'll place a section there to take charge. That'll leave four to cover the rock fields, Wulf in reserve, and the green women and Grenewic men by the ford. If everything goes awry, we all fall back to the top of the crag and hold it until Walthoef arrives."

Osberht gave a confident laugh, "It won't come to that. Don't forget that we must have halved their numbers already. Even if they sent for more men they won't be here in time."

*****

Gytha took a while to position her sections for the night's defence. She walked the inner perimeter of the rock fields with her commanders and decided upon placing Gufa's section in the exit from Broadslack Gill, it was a narrow defile that gave a very covered approach to the west of the crag. Cerdik's was placed by a broad shallow pool just down river from the east vill. It was the best crossing place for anyone trying to cut around their east flank. The remaining three were positioned within bow range of each other across the front of the rock fields.

The tedium of waiting began to take its toll. Gytha made sure that her sections took some rest, half at a time. She grabbed some sleep and made sure Rauði did the same. Both had a meal, and whilst the sun was still above the western ridge of fells she went up to the hall to check upon Ulf, Ealdgith and Bryny. Ulf was sitting up, feeling drained of energy and looking more than a little shame-faced. Gytha sat on the edge of his bed and gave an engaging smile.

"Well, you might be out of the fight, but that doesn't excuse you offering your advice. We've seen nothing of Sigulfson since we thrashed him, but I can't believe that he will have pulled his men back. What do you think?" Gytha could see that it was an effort for Ulf to gather his thoughts, and wondered if she should have asked him.

When Ulf did speak, it was slow and measured. "He's still there, be sure of that. Be prepared for him to come on a wide front through the rock fields, or to try and get around our right flank. As you know, it's right at the end of our range. "I'd have Cudel test the range and setting for both perrièrs before last light. If he chooses a fixed point you can still use them in the dark if you know where the rocks will strike, and then adjust from there." He lay back with a sigh and a tired smile. "That's your lot, Valkyrie. It's your battle, fight it the best you can."

Gytha squeezed Ulf's hand by way of thanks, and went up onto the platform. Osberht gestured to her to join him and pointed to the north.

"They're still there. Now that the light's fading, we can see the glimmer of their fires."

Gytha shielded her eyes from the glare of the setting sun. "There's movement too. I can see the low sun reflecting off someone's mail. I think they are this side of the river. Get Cudel's lads to stand by. Before the light goes I want him to set the left perrièr to hit the edge of the rock field in the gill, and also right at the centre of our front. Set the right perrièr so that it can hit the base of the crags on the right. If they try get around that way we might hear them, even if we can't see them."

"It's a pity you can't direct where you want the rocks to land." Osberht had anticipated Gytha's line of thought. "Fire arrows would destroy the night vision of those using them, and risk setting the undergrowth alight."

"Aye, agreed, and there's nothing we can do about the right flank. You'll all just have to listen out, but I can

238

give one horn blast for you to hit Broadslack Gill and two blasts to pound our centre. Even if Cudel misses, which he probably will, the sound of rocks crashing down in the dark could be enough." Gytha felt re-energised at the prospect of action. "I'll get back down and warn the lads that there'll be some targeting going on."

*****

Wulf sent a runner forward to where Gytha was watching from a small spur above the centre of their front. "Gufa's sent word that he can hear movement in front of him. He thinks they're coming up the gill."

"Tell him to engage when he can. I'll call for the perrièr now. It might stop them coming any closer." Gytha thanked the runner and placed her horn to her lips. Its single blast was answered a couple of minutes later by a loud thump above her and the swoosh of rocks overhead. She waited, listening, but could hear nothing other than the fall of the rocks. She blew her horn again. This time the crash of falling rocks was followed by a scream and a long painful moan. She blew the horn a third time, confident that this would be sufficient to stop the incursion up the gill. The fading sound of moaning, muttering voices and shuffling feet hinted that she was correct, and the front fell silent again.

The night felt dark and endless. Suddenly the scrubland falling away below her became visible again in the low light of the half-moon as it rose above the fells to her right. Gytha's relief at having something by which to measure the passage of time was short lived as she realised that the moonlight threw the whole of their right flank into shadow. The thump of a perrièr above her crystallised her worry that she was being outwitted. Anticipating the moon's rise, Sigulfson had waited until the bottom of the cliffs would be in shadow. She assumed that Osberht had heard movement there and that was why the right hand perrièr had been called to action.

"Rauði, run to Osberht now and see what is happening. I'm going to rejoin Wulf. Meet me there."

239

Rauði's mission was cut short. She met Bjorn just above the base of the crag's steps.

"We heard movement from the bottom of the crags. Osberht thinks they had passed before we used the perrièr. We've since heard more movement around to the right, nearer to the river."

Rauði turned at once and reached Wulf's section just as they were mounting.

"Osberht thinks our right flank has been turned and that they are heading towards the river." Rauði called out urgently before she got to Gytha.

"It's as I feared. We're going to the vill now. Follow close behind Wulf's men, then join me when we get there." Gytha urged her horse forward into a walk. She couldn't risk going faster on the shadowy woodland track.

The track widened as the wood gave way to scrub. Gytha was about to pick up the pace, just as the first sounds of fighting emanated from the edge of the vill. She reined to a halt and shouted back towards Rauði. "Get to Osberht now. He is to light both beacons. I want Wealmaer's men here, and have Dai prepare the base of the crag for attack." She waited briefly to see that Rauði had the message, and spurred forward into a canter. She rode with Wulf on her right and Loki running by her left. Acting as one, the green men drew their spears from their saddle holsters and prepared to fight in two groups of three. Gytha could see shadowy shapes running around the edges of the darkened houses. Her impression that an organised group of men was controlling the open area at the centre of the vill, whilst a disorganised group harrassed them from the houses, proved correct. A shield wall appeared suddenly in the centre of the clearing. It had barely gathered together when the phalanx of horsemen smashed through it and wheeled about with their swords drawn and spears left embedded in bodies or shields.

Gytha was thankful for the height and protection that her horse gave her. She was thankful too for the unknown green man who strove to keep his horse alongside her. Her slender frame and unique glimmering armour turned her into a mystical being and marked her as an obvious target. The man on her left repeatedly slashed down at men-at-arms trying to grab her reins and unhorse her. Loki, too, fought valiantly; avoiding her horse's flailing hooves whilst snapping at the legs of those around his mistress.

The confused maelstrom of bodies continued. Horsemen twisted and turned, constantly beating down upon what seemed like a mass of bodies pressing in around them. Gytha saw one of her men pulled from his horse into the crowd, but saw more of her enemy fall, many trampled under the forelegs of the trained war horses. Her body ached from the constant twisting, turning and slashing yet her arms didn't tire. The blade of her sword, forged centuries ago by a Carolingian smith, shimmered and flashed like a pale blue flame. It was so light and perfectly balanced that it seemed to lead its own path through her enemies as it sliced easily into their protective mail, and she began to see fear in the eyes of those who confronted it. She saw too the bright fires of the twin beacons, and that the top of the crag was side-lit by the first shafts of dawn.

"We have them, my Lady." Wulf's sudden shout in her left ear drew Gytha's attention and she turned to see that the centre of the vill was theirs. Sprawled, mutilated bodies littered the ground. Some lay still, others dragged themselves painfully away. Less than a dozen of the initial score or more of men-at-arms remained to confront them. They stood in a disciplined block between the houses either side of the track down to the river. Gytha starred at the begrimed faces wondering which if any held any rank and authority. A sudden shiver ran through her. The man in the centre, whom all others seemed to be shielding, had blue and white bars embossed on both sides of his helmet. They were Forne Sigulfson's colours. Gytha felt suddenly vulnerable.

"Cerdik, is your section here?" She called out, wanting to know just how many men she could muster.

"Cerdik is wounded, my Lady. I am Padrik, and Nudd is with me. There are only us two standing now." A voice spoke from the side of clearing.

"Do you have crossbows, Nudd?" Gytha asked, keeping her voice low and unemotional.

"Aye, and we already have them trained on the bastards." Gytha heard the humour in Nudd's voice.

"Good, make yourselves very visible. I want them to know that the first to move will be the first to fall."

"Are any more green men here?" Gytha asked more loudly, still keeping her eyes fixed upon Forne Sigulfson, and very aware that her men were still outnumbered despite their tactical advantage.

"I am, and Dai is coming down the track with two sections as we speak," Rauði's reassuring voice was just behind Gytha, "and Wealmaer is on his way down yon side of the fell."

Gytha relaxed and let a smile play on her lips. "Lord Sigulfson. I meet you at last. I am Gytha, though some people know me as the Lady of the Lake. I do not know why you have harried my lands for the past year, and why you tried to seize them. But it stops now. Have your men surrender their swords, yours too."

Sigulfson's reaction wasn't what Gytha expected. He laughed. "What? To a woman? An outlaw?"

Gytha was silent for a moment. "To a woman, yes. To an outlaw, no. You know full well who I am, for Jônas, whose life I spared, is standing next to you. I don't expect you to answer to me. You will answer to Lord Walthoef, my cousin. It is to him that I owe my fealty, and for whom I hold this land...and should you think that I have no authority to employ men-at-arms, you would be wrong. We are all in my cousin's employ, and he has the King's authority to employ us." Gytha didn't expect an answer, not yet. She beckoned Rauði forward with a flick of her hand. "I do however hold you answerable to Frytha, also my cousin, whom you orphaned when you took her father's lands at Hestrskeith. It is you that I consider to be an outlaw and a traitor." Gytha gave a mocking laugh. "If you turn around you will see that my men are behind you.

If any move, they will die instantly. So, I say again, lay down your swords."

Several of Sigulfson's men looked at him, but none moved. He continued to stare at Gytha, stony faced.

"Very well." Gytha spoke with an icy voice that carried clearly. "I will start with the man on the left of your line. You, there." Gytha pointed in order to avoid any uncertainty. "What is your name?"

The man hesitated, and Gytha repeated the question in Norman French.

"I'm Aelfsige. I'm not French."

"Ah! Progress at last. Aelfsige, if your sword isn't on the ground before I count to three my men here," she pointed to Nudd and Padrik, will kill you instantly...one..."

Aelfsige's sword fell to the ground before Gytha got to 'two'.

"You next!" Gytha pointed to the next in line. His sword dropped to the ground, as did all those until she reached Jônas.

Gytha could see that Wealmaer had positioned the strongest of his men directly behind Sigulfson and Jônas. "Master-at-Arms, bind the next two!" She commanded sharply.

Each man's shoulders was seized firmly, and a sharp kick behind the knees forced them to collapse, kneeling.

Gytha stared at the Lord in front of her, and spoke coldly. "Sigulfson, I shan't use your title, because in my eyes you aren't worthy to be considered a lord. Your arrogant disregard for the lives of your men, and the sanctity of my own Lord's lands, has brought you to this. I pity your people, I truly do. I will have you, and this worthless squire who betrayed my trust, secured in a sty until I can pass you both to my Lord. The rest of your men will be stripped of all weapons and armour and will then be free to go in whatever clothes they have left. Any of your wounded who have survived the night will, I am sure, already be under the care of my wise-women."

Gytha had been aware of movement behind her, and assumed that it was to do with the arrival of Dai and her other sections. She turned quickly, surprised by the voice that spoke from behind her shoulder.

"Very well said, cousin. You have the freedom to use better words than I could choose. However, I will relieve you of the burden of Lord Sigulfson and this worthless squire. Though perhaps you could secure them as you suggest whilst we talk together, share a meal and ensure that my men are fed. That may give these two time to reflect. I left my men at your vill by the crag after your deputy led us through those devilish rock fields." He urged his horse alongside and, leaning across from the saddle, said, "Given your very obvious prowess as a battle captain, mayhap you should become my master-at-arms."

Gytha blushed and smiled back, her tense body suddenly relaxing. "Hah! Thank you cousin, but I rather hope that the need for me to fight battles is now somewhat diminished. Come, I will take you to my hall. Mayhap there will be news from Bear."

Walthoef gave a reassuring smile, "He's there already, I felt it best that our friend here didn't connect him with you and your family's lost lands at Ulueswater. He brought news of another great victory. That Jarl of yours has wrought just as much destruction as you. Bear told me that the Jarl led Black William's men up a false track through the wild forest above the lake and into a dead-end valley. They was no escape and many were slaughtered there. I think we can be sure that these dales are secure for a long time to come. The Normans will never risk repeating such a devastating defeat, though I doubt that they will ever acknowledge what has befallen them."

Haerfest 1102

Chapter 22

The weeks after Sigulfson's defeat were not as trouble-free as Gytha had hoped. The families in the vills beyond the crag had known nothing of the desperate fight on their behalf until they received sudden news of dead sons, and in one case a dead husband because Cerdik had succumbed to his wounds. Gytha and Bear worked to console and help as far as possible. Then there were the funerals for the six men. Gytha felt some consolation from the fact that her green men and women had suffered fewer casualties than Jarl Buthar's men. Bear had already told her about the destruction of almost all the Norman force in the attack on Butremere after the Jarl's use of a false-road had led them into a catastrophic ambush in the steep side-valley of Rannerdalr. He had brought news, too, of the deaths of Gille, Erland and Cnut in a desperate stand to prevent a Norman breakout. Though saddened by the deaths of Erland and Cnut, their treatment of Rauði and Bjorn had never endeared them. Gille's death upset her badly. She had rushed to visit and console her widowed sister, and was very shaken to see how Freja had withdrawn into herself and away from the women in the Jarl's household. Freja had acquiesced immediately to Gytha's insistence that she return with her to live in Borgaradalr, with either her or Bear.

Dealing with the aftermath of the battle was difficult, but surmountable. The challenge that Gytha struggled with was Ealdgith and Ulf's announcement that they intended to move to the Isle of Mann to live out their days with Jarl Godred of Garth, Aedan's father-in-law and Ealdgith's and Walthoef's distant cousin. She was alone in understanding their decision, and worried that it set her against her siblings.

*****

"Listen to me Bear. I've already had this conversation with your sister. She accepts that what Ulf and I are doing is for the good of us all." Ealdgith's voice, though soft, was clear and firm.

"No Moder. You and Fader were always fascinated by the misty isle with its solitary high mountain, but it isn't the 'land of the undying' and it can't save you. I understand your desire for sea air, I've been enticed by its scent too. But why walk away from your families? That's what we don't understand." Bear tried to speak gently so as not to stress his mother, but instead sounded condescending, and then pleading.

Ealdgith's eyes flashed angrily. She was hurt by the accusation that she was deceived by the sagas of old. "Don't talk down to me. You haven't listened Bear, other than Gytha no one has. Sea air will do me good, that's true, but it is not the reason why. I've said it before, it is why I couldn't stay with Aebbe. Your fader and I were seen as rebels by the Normans, and rightly so for we refused to accept their rule. The new King wants all rebels hunted down and killed, and Le Meschin is his enforcer here. It's the excuse Sigulfson and Le Meschin's brother used to try and seize these lands. Yes, you defeated them, but Gytha and the Jarl did so in Walthoef's name. He is now answerable to the King for that. Sigulfson is sly and cunning. He won't risk his reputation by going against Walthoef like that again. Nor will William Le Meschin. But they will if they link me to you or to Walthoef. That would be a legitimate reason and just the excuse they would need to destroy all of you, Walthoef and his family too. Gytha understands that. It's why she was so careful to hide her true identity from Sigulfson and to keep you away from him when he was here as her prisoner. That's why I can't stay, so please...please don't make this any harder for me."

As Ealdgith held Bear's hand and starred meaningfully into his eyes, he could see their warmth and sincerity. He began to understand.

"Ulf is an identified rebel too, though mayhap not as well known. I've known him all my life and he has always been very dear to me. Although he is never as close to me in my heart as your fader was, he's been sworn to protect me since I was a girl. That is why he wants to come with me." Bear nodded slowly whilst Ealdgith continued to focus her eyes on his. "I must leave in order to protect you. Ulf must leave in order to protect me...and I will say this. It's is not out of duty that he does so now, it is out of love."

"I understand Moder, at last I do." Bear and Ealdgith looked up, startled by Eir's soft voice.

"I was listening. I just wish Fader had explained it like that. Mayhap it would have spared a lot of hurt and misunderstanding." Ealdgith could see the damp tears on her daughter-in-law's cheeks glistening in the candle light.

She reached out her hand. "Come my love, sit by us. It will hurt your fader and me greatly when we go, just as it hurt me when I said farewell to Aebbe. You of all people know just how limited our days are likely to be. But there is always a chance that sea air and a life without stress might be the miracle that saves us. It is but a day's ride to Wykrinton and the same again by sea to Mann, so mayhap you can visit in the days of peace ahead of us, all of you."

"Mayhap we will Moder, mayhap we will." Bear spoke gently. "Eir and I will go and speak to everyone. Tomorrow I will ride to Wirkynton, see Aedan, and give him your letter to Jarl Godred."

*****

Gytha rose early the next morning, Leofric having left at sunrise to join Agnaar in supervising the first harvest. She thought no one would be about and was surprised to see Neven and Cudel deep in conversation with Rauði and Bjorn. They were sitting on the parapet overlooking the valley. Gytha's greeting was met with an embarrassed smile from Neven. She got up, muttered something to the others and walked over to Gytha.

Neven spoke quickly in response to Gytha's questioning frown. She was blushing, with a secretive smile playing around her lips, "I... we, wanted you to be the first to know. I'm with child."

Gytha gasped and, trying desperately to hide her fleeting look of surprise, rushed forward to embrace her friend. "Oh Neven, you are a one...and after all your dire threats to the girls." Gytha felt a surge of genuine happiness, and held Neven close a moment longer before stepping back. "I am so pleased. I think we all knew that if there was anyone for you, it could only be Cudel."

Gytha waved to Cudel, smiling. "Come here, let me congratulate you too."

Cudel stepped forward with the broadest of smiles on his face. He spoke as he took Gytha's offered hand. "There's something else, my Lady. We want to be hand-fasted, as soon as possible."

"And so you should be, though Bear could speak to Father Oswin if you would prefer," Gytha suggested.

"Thank you, but no. Our promises to each other are enough, and it's always been that way in my family," Neven insisted.

"Well, if you want to hand-fast as soon as possible, let's wait 'til Bear returns. He should officiate, and I know Ulf will want to be here too, so it must be before he and Moder depart."

The couple looked at each and back at Gytha. Neven spoke for them. "No, Gytha, we want it to be you. You are our battle-captain and you have our oaths. We want you to hand-fast us." Neven glanced across to Rauði.

Rauði blushed as she cleared her throat. "Gytha, er...Bjorn and I want you to hand-fast us too...and, no, I'm not, before you ask." Rauði blurted quickly, suddenly afraid that Gytha would jump to a conclusion about a condition that she had striven to avoid.

Bjorn rushed to Rauði's aid, "I asked Rauði to be my bride, it's what we've always promised each other, and..."

Gytha stemmed their rising embarrassment. "Come here, both of you, let me hug you. This is not a surprise, I'm just pleased you waited 'til our fight was over. Of course I'll hand-fast you, all of you, and will be honoured to do so."

Cudel waited until Gytha released Rauði from her hug, and said, "Thank you, my Lady. Thank you from all of us, though I rather think it might be a triple hand-fasting. Aelf and Eadwig want me to ask you if..."

Gytha laughed loudly, all the tension from the past few weeks disappeared as quickly as a cloud passing from the sun. "Then they must come and ask me, but it shall be so. We'll wait 'til Moder and Ulf have made their arrangements, and choose a date. It will be a fitting way to celebrate their going and new beginnings."

*****

Walthoef sent a messenger four days after Bear's return from Wykrington. Bear had brought an offer from Aedan that he would host everyone travelling to see Ealdgith and Ulf off on their journey across the sea; and hoped his hall would be big enough to accommodate them all. The messenger also brought confirmation that Jarl Godred's boat would be at Cokyrmoth on the Tuesday after next. Walthoef also offered to look after everyone on the night before depature and to send a horse-litter the day before to save Ealdgith the challenge of riding to Cokyrmoth. The messenger, amused at the looks of puzzlement, had then explained that a horse-litter was akin to a bed suspended fore and aft by harnesses secured across a horse. It was, he assured them, safe and comfortable.

Bear had thanked him and agreed that the horse-litter should meet them at the landings at Kesewic. It sounded too cumbersome to navigate either of the lakeside tracks. Ealdgith would make the first part of her journey sailing by kára down the lake.

*****

Cudel stood on the platform between the two perrièrs and smiled whilst scanning the happy faces looking up at him and, judging his moment, raised his hands to attract attention. He waited until the burble of voices stilled, and called out in a clear authorative voice, "Thank you all. Thank you for coming to share this special day with us. I'll speak for all six of us, that way you'll be saved from hearing the same speech three times over. I'm honoured that Neven, my wife to be, has asked me to speak for us all. As Lady Gytha's huscarle, and leader of her green women, that privilege was rightly hers. It's an honour, too, to be able to call you our friends and be welcomed as your family. Five of us have each lost our families in different ways, mayhap that's why we've fought so hard to protect the precious freedoms that this family has given us, and why we now want to start new families of our own. Hand-fasting is our special way of doing that...a simple promise to each other in front of friends is all we need." Cudel paused, looking from face to face at those in Gytha and Bear's households. It was Gytha's cue to start the ceremony.

She stood behind a rudimentary table comprising a slab of slate on top of two up-ended pine logs, on top of which were three lengths of braided corn and three small cups of mead. She held her arms out in a welcoming gesture towards the three couples. They stepped forward to their pre-arranged places and held out clasped hands, left wrist touching right.

Gytha's voice carried clearly across the plateau, conveying the simple promise that each would make: "Neven, do you take Cudel as your husband until death do you part?" As each couple affirmed their intent, Gytha tied the braided corn around their wrists, saying, "You are now man and wife. Share from this, your common cup." At that she gave the couple the small cup of mead from which one and then the other, drank.

Finally, having married each couple in the same simple fashion, Gytha turned to all who were watching, and called out, "Neven and Cudel, Rauði and Bjorn, Aelf and Eadwig, are now man and wife within our family. Cherish them and support them in their journeys. Now come, return to the hall for the brýdeala."

*****

Ealdgith and Ulf sailed with their children along the twisting channel of the River Defena, making their way from the old Roman port at Cokrymoth down to Wykrington. The rest of the party rode as quickly as they could, leading the riderless ponies away from the river and across country, in a bid to arrive at Wykrington ahead of the Jarl's longship. He had sent a snekke, the sleekest and fastest in his fleet.

Bear was the last to leave the snekke. He clasped Ealdgith and then Ulf, in a long final embrace before stepping ashore, and urged Óðr up the track onto the headland. Here, overlooking Wykrington's shingle beach and small harbour, he joined his family group in a long line of people and ponies. He noticed Osberht paying close attention to Freja and wondered if their childhood romance might be rekindling, then he sidled Óðr into a gap between Eir's and Gytha's mounts and leant across to squeeze his sister's hand. Bear could see that she and Eir were struggling to contain their tears whilst Brynhildr, who was the closest of the grandchildren to Ealdgith, let hers flow freely. It had been a long and emotionally draining day, but now at last he started to relax, very aware that with farewells and final parting made, they must all look to their future. A future that was his duty to lead them towards. It was a challenge he wanted.

A ragged cheer erupted as the silver-grey longship rounded the tip of the headland below and began slowly to rise and sway as it turned across the low swell. They watched the snekke's sail fill and, as it picked up speed, it sliced through the wine-dark sea towards the setting sun. Bear knew that it would be a long night for the two figures holding hands, silhouetted at the stern.

<div align="center">~~~~~</div>

Hravn and Ealdgith's extended family throve for a generation or two in Borrowdale, but as control of their lands passed slowly and inevitably to others, their way of life merged with neighbouring communities. Their descendants live on. Today, they are the people of the Lake District.

Glossary

Aefter Yule. After Yule. January; the month after the Yuletide festival that became Christmas.

Aere Yule. Before Yule. December.

Blōtmonath. November. The month of blood sacrifices.

Breeks. Breeches. From Old English, brec. Northern dialect.

Brýdeala. Bride-ale or marriage-feast.

Burh. A Saxon fortified settlement. Typically a timber-faced bank and ditch with a palisade on top, enclosing a manor house and settlement.

Dale or dahl. Old English and Norse for a valley.

ð. ð is a voiced dental fricative. A consonant sound used in some spoken languages. Its symbol in the International Phonetic Alphabet is **eth**, and was taken from the Old English and Icelandic letter eth.

Ealdmoder. Grandmother.

Earl. An Earl is a member of the nobility. The title is Anglo-Saxon, akin to the Scandinavian form: Jarl.

Ēostre. Easter

Eostremonath. April. After, Eostre, goddess of spring and fertility.

Fader. Father.

Fell. Norse for a high hill, mountain or high moorland.

Freja. Norse. Goddess of love, fertility, and battle.

Furlong. Old English. An eighth of a mile or 200 metres.

Fyrd. The local militia of an Anglo-Saxon shire, in which all freemen had to serve.

Haerfest. Harvest. Autumn.

Hāligmonath. September. Holy month.

Hall. Old English: Heall, a large house.

Hefted. The instinctive ability of some breeds of sheep, including Cumbrian **herdwicks**, to know intimately the land on which they live.

Hel. Queen of Helheim, the Norse underworld.

Holmganga. Norse: "going to an island", a special place for a duel governed by rules of combat.

Hrēðmonath. March. Hreða, or Rheda's month. A Germanic fertility goddess.

Huscarle. Housecarl. A member of the bodyguard of a Norse or English king or noble.

Jagger. Northern English. Someone who controls a team of packhorses. A Jagger way = a packhorse trail.

Jarl. See earl.

Kára. The name of a Valkyrie in Norse mythology. Used to describe a fictional class of clinker built sailing boat resembling a knörr. Used to carry cargo or livestock, with a crew of three or four.

Knörr. The knörr was an Old Norse cargo ship; the hull was wider, deeper and shorter than a longship, and could take more cargo and be operated by smaller crews. They were built with a length of about 16 m (52 ft), a beam of 5 m (16 ft), and a hull capable of carrying up to 24 tons.

League. A league is a classical unit of length. The word originally meant the distance a person could walk in an hour. Its distance has been defined variously as between one and a half and three miles. I have used the Roman league which is 7,500 feet or one and half miles.

Lencten. Spring.

Liða. June and **July** were together known as Liða, an Old English word meaning "mild" or "gentle," which referred to the period of warm, seasonable weather either side of Midsummer. To differentiate between the two, June was sometimes known as Ærraliða, or "before-mild," and July was Æfteraliða, or "after-mild."

Logi. Norse god of fire.

Longhouse. A Viking equivalent of the English manor house, typically 5 to 7 metres wide and anywhere from 15 to 75 metres long, depending on the wealth and social position of the owner.

Mangonel. A torsion powered catapult using one long arm to launch objects when its tension is released.

Manor. An estate of land. The manor is often described as the basic feudal unit of tenure. A manor was akin to the modern firm or business. It was a productive unit, which required physical capital, in the form of land, buildings, equipment and draught animals such as ploughing oxen and labour for day-to-day management and a workforce. Its ownership could be transferred by the overlord. In many cases this was ultimately the King.

Moder. Mother.

Nadr. Norse. Viper or adder.

Neffa-tafel. The Viking board game hnefatafl (pronounced "neffa-tafel") was ubiquitous in Nordic settlements in the early Middle Ages.

Norns. Norse. The Norns were female beings who ruled upon the destiny of gods and men. They correspond roughly to other controllers of humans' destiny, the Fates, elsewhere in European mythology. (See Wyrd.)

Óðr. Old Norse. Pronounced Oh-der, Meaning: ecstasy, inspiration, fury, frenzy. Óðr is an obscure, seldom-mentioned god.

Perrièr. A type of trebuchet that uses the mechanical advantage of a lever to throw a projectile. Instead of counterbalance on the short end of the lever, the perrièr uses the strength and weight of a team of men. This made it lighter and simpler to construct, re-position and operate.

Rauði. From the old Norse word and byname, rauðr: meaning red. Pronounced Rauethi. 'ð' is the Old English and Icelandic letter 'eth'.

Reave. To plunder or rob. Reaver: a raider. From Old English: reafian.

Reeve. An administrative officer who generally ranked lower than the ealdorman or earl. Different types of reeves were attested, including high-reeve, town-reeve, port-reeve, shire-reeve (predecessor to the sheriff), reeve of the hundred, and the reeve of a manor.

Seax. A type of sword or dagger typical of the Germanic peoples of the Early Middle Ages, especially the Saxons. The smallest were knives, the longest had blades over 50 cm long.

Sergeant. Old French. The lowest military rank. A professional foot soldier, literally 'one who serves'.

Shire. Groups of hundreds were combined to form shires, with each shire under the control of an earl.

Silvatici. Norman term for the 'men of the woods' or the green men.

Sōlmōnath. February. The month of cakes, possibly referring to the cakes' sandy, gritty texture.

Skíta. Old Norse: shit.

Snekke. Or snekkja, meaning 'thin and projecting' was typically the smallest long ship used in warfare, with at least 20 rowing benches. Typically 17 m (56 feet) long and 2.5 m (8.2 feet) wide with a draught of only 0.5 m (1.6 feet). It would carry a crew of around 41 men (40 oarsmen and one coxswain).

Sumor. Summer.

Svanmeyja. Swan maiden or wish-bearer from Norse mythology. Used to describe a fictional class of boat that resembled a miniature Norse snekke, with graceful S-shaped bow and stern posts and designed to carry a self-crewing section of four plus a helmsman, if needed.

Thegn. A member of several Norse and Saxon aristocratic classes of men, ranking between earls and ordinary freemen, and granted lands by the king, or by lords, for military service. The minimum qualifying holding of land was five Hides.

Thrimilce. May. "The month of three milkings," when livestock were often so well fed on fresh spring grass that they could be milked three times a day.

Ting Moot. Old Norse. A terraced mound used as a meeting place for local government.

Ulueswater. Ullswater.

Vill. Medieval English term to describe a land unit which might otherwise be described as a parish, manor or tithing.

Warg. In Norse mythology, a warg is a wolf and in particular refers to the wolf Fenrir and his sons Sköll and Hati.

Weodmonath. August. Plant month.

Winterfylleth. October. The winter full moon. Bede taught that winter began on the first full moon in October.

Wyrd. Norse and Anglo-Saxon. Fate or personal destiny. Wyrd was one of the three most important Norns. The Norns were female and ruled upon the destiny of man.

Yule. The two months of the bleak midwinter. Aere Yule ('Ere Yule or Before Yule) is our December and Aefter Yule (After Yule) is our January.

Historical Note

Henry I's strongmen in Cumbria certainly controlled Cumbria's seaboard and the fertile Eden Valley. Whether they really controlled the dales within the central fells is an open question. Was this easily defendable mountain hinterland the last free-zone for the British, Norse and English who refused to submit? This is an intriguing thought.

The tantalizing possibility of resistance to Norman rule persisting in the Lake District has encouraged many to expand upon the idea. Local historian and publican Nicholas Size published a historical novel in 1930 called *The Secret Valley*, which tells the story of how this area resisted the Norman invaders in the 50 years after the 1066 Norman Conquest. According to Size, the Norman army was ambushed and defeated by native Britons and Norsemen at the Battle of Rannerdale.

The battle is thought to have taken place in Buttermere's side valley of Rannerdale, which runs east of the summit of Rannerdale Knotts, west of Whiteless Pike and south of Grasmoor. Bluebells grow in profusion in this valley in April and May. According to local folklore, the bluebells are said to have sprung from the spilt blood of the slain Norman warriors. In reality they are an indication that this area was forested. In Size's version, Ranulf Le Meschin escaped and lived in disgrace until he succeeded a relative as Earl of Chester in 1120. Little historical evidence is available to support Size's romanticised tale of the last stand of the native Britons against the invading force.

But the simple possibility of Cumbrian resistance is enough to inspire writers. Joyce Reason took up the mantle in 1946 with *The Secret Fortress* and Rosemary Sutcliff followed in 1956 with *The Shield Ring*.

As a Cumbrian, and with Earl Gospatric lurking in my family history, these stories provided very fertile ground for me to bring my Harrying of the North series to a natural conclusion. I have borrowed some of the characters from the stories about Buttermere and woven them into the lives of Ealdgith's extended family. I am sure that readers who are familiar with Borrowdale will agree that Castle Crag, an enigmatic feature that dominates all around, is the perfect place for those fleeing Norman oppression to make a secure home.

*****

Although evidence of an Iron Age fort and Roman artefacts have been found on Castle Crag, there is little evidence of early medieval activity in Borrowdale. The majority of the land was owned by the monks of Furness Abbey from the 13th century onwards. Much of the dale was purchased from Alice II de Rumelli of Allerdale in 1209, who had, in the closing years of the 12th century, sold parts of Borrowdale to the great Cistercian monastery of Fountains Abbey in Yorkshire. Granges (including the present-day village of Grange) were established and the area was used for agriculture and industrial activities such as mining, woodland management and iron working. During the 14th century, many farms and villages were abandoned because of Scottish raids in 1315, 1322, and 1345.

Whilst lead and other precious metals were mined in Borrowdale, it was the discovery of graphite (known variously as plumbago, back lead or wad) at Seathwaite in the early fifteenth century that really placed the valley on the world map: it was the most expensive substance ever mined in Cumbria. Shepherds had used it to mark sheep and the monks of Furness Abbey may have used it to draw lines to guide their scribes. Graphite became a vital national asset, however, when used in molds to cast iron cannon balls. Smoother, rounder cannon balls went further and straighter. It was also found to be essential for the safe manufacture of gunpowder. For a short period, graphite found favour as a medicine for easing the pain of colic, gallstones and strangury when ground and mixed with wine or ale. More recently, the early pencil makers of

259

Keswick used graphite to create the world's first industrial pencil-making centre.

*****

Following King William II's annexation of Cumbria in 1092, Carlisle and the lower Eden Valley were quickly brought under Norman control by the King's 'enforcer', Ivo de Taillebois.

Ivo's death in 1094 seems to have slowed Norman consolidation. Neither Cumberland nor Westmorland were granted Shire status until 1133, the jurisdiction of both being overseen from Northumberland. There is also an historical and demographic distinction between the King's borough of Carlisle, where the population was largely Norman or English, and the rest of Cumberland with its melting pot of British, Irish, English and Scandinavian names. This implies that the Norman's really only controlled the environs of Carlisle and the Eden Valley.

Ivo's widow, Lucy, was too valuable to leave unwed and she was quickly remarried by order of the King, first to Roger fitzGerold and, after his death in 1098, to Ranulf le Meschin.

Although most Anglo-Cumbric-Nose nobles were quickly dispossessed after 1092, at least two were not. Allerdale, to the west of Carlisle, remained under the control of Walthoef, Dolfin's younger brother and son of Earl Gospatric. This was possibly thanks to his family link to King Malcolm.

Greystoke, the area between Penrith and Carlisle, remained in the possession of Forne Sigulfson. Forne, who was of Scandinavian extraction, quickly came to an understanding with Ivo de Taillebois and retained his estates in Cumbria and Yorkshire. An indication of how quickly he switched allegiance is that his eldest son was named Ivo, in honour of his overlord. His status became such that he was the first Norman appointed lord of the Barony of Greystoke, and the 'Greystoke family', as it became known, continued to be lords of Greystoke in a direct male line until 1306. Forne's daughter, Edith, later

260

became a mistress to Henry I, bearing at least two children to him – a further indication of Forne's local influence and power.

Ranulf le Meschin was neither an earl nor a sheriff, though much later in 1121 he was made Earl of Chester by Henry I and required to give up his 'Cumbrian Honour' or group of estates. This may suggest that his rule in Cumbria was more an office-holding position than a feudal holding of lands, as otherwise he would have kept his Cumbrian lands intact for life.

A step-change occurred in the governance of Cumbria in 1100 with the succession of Henry I. Henry enjoyed good relations with both Alexander I of Scotland and Henry's nephew, the later David I of Scotland, and therefore he could concentrate on developing his northern lands without the threat of a Scottish invasion.

Henry strongly favoured Ranulf le Meschin, who was granted full power to rule Cumbria as he saw fit. Throughout more than twenty years as Cumbria's Norman ruler, Ranulf created new lordships for at least three Frenchmen, including his brother William who was given Copelend (or Kaupaland) after he returned from the first crusade.

The years of Henry I were transitional ones: from Carlisle and Appleby under the control of the strongman Ranulf le Meschin, to the partial introduction of a shire system by 1133. It is probably correct to say that the Normans had full control of Cumbria by 1133, but it was to be short-lived. With the death of Henry I in 1135, England fell into a civil war, known as The Anarchy. Stephen of Blois contested the English crown with Henry's daughter, Matilda.

David I of Scotland, who Henry I had appointed Prince of the Cumbrians in 1113, had been King of Scots since 1124. Having been brought up in the court of his mentor and uncle, as very much a Norman prince, he supported the claims of Matilda over those of her cousin, Stephen.

It is probable that, even at the beginning of his reign in 1124, David was thinking of the lands of Carlisle and Cumberland, believing that "Cumbria" in the form of Strathclyde/Cumbria covered by the diocese of Glasgow was under the over-lordship of the King of Scots and Prince of the Cumbrians.

Exploiting the advantage of turmoil in England, David took possession of Carlisle in 1136 and the first Treaty of Durham (1136) ceded Carlisle and Cumberland to him. David and his son, Earl Henry, seem to have ruled jointly and to have respected existing land rights and appointments north and south of the border. David may have been intending to enlarge his control of northern England when he fought at the Battle of the Standard near Northallerton in 1138, where some of the soldiers of David's force were Cumbrians from south of the Solway. Despite losing the battle, David kept his Cumbrian lands, and his son Henry was made Earl of Northumberland at the (second) Treaty of Durham (1139).

This arrangement lasted another twenty years, during which David minted his own coins using silver from the Alston mines, founded the abbey at Holm Cultram, kept the north largely out of the civil war of Stephen and Matilda and, by the "Carlisle settlement" of 1149, obtained a promise from Henry of Anjou that, upon becoming King of England, he would not challenge the King of Scots' rule over Carlisle and Cumberland. David died at Carlisle in 1153, a year after his son Henry.

The pattern of Anglo-Scottish relations trading upon the weakness of one side or the other continued when, in 1154, Henry of Anjou became King of England, as Henry II. King David of Scotland's death left an eleven-year-old boy, Malcolm IV, on the Scottish throne. Malcolm had inherited the earldoms of Cumbria (and Northumbria) as fiefs of the English crown, and did homage to Henry for them. However, at Chester, in July 1157, Henry demanded, and obtained, the return of control of Cumbria and Northumberland to England. The King of Scots was given the honours of Huntingdon and Tynedale in return, and relations between the two countries were amicable enough, for a while at least.